CHRONICLES OF TWO PENTECOSTS

Other Books by Mark Lee Golden

The Ring of Torrents: A Jewish Mary

The Drop: Secret Delivery

eBooks

Light • Medium • Dark

Chronicles of Two Pentecosts

Ancient People to Meet, Ancient Stories to Ponder

By Mark Lee Golden

Fancy Minds
Spokane, Washington

...those who ply the scribal quill.

Published by:

Fancy
Minds
Spokane, Washington

"It is written that when the Torah was given, the Israelites said *"Na'aseh v'nishma"* — 'We will do, then we will understand.'"

Special Thanks to

Rabbi Reuel Dillion
Tim Hegg at Torah Resource
Laurie Klein
Gloria Corn
Sandra Sinner-Young
Oscar and Ramelle Richardson
David Sams
Joanne Moody
John Sandford
James Leuschen
Bill Jenkins
That Writers Group I Attend

Contributing Editors
Paul Peterson
Brian Joyce
Ruth Danner
Mike Cantos

Table of Contents

BONUS SUMMARIES

A short biography of the author is in the back of the book. For those readers who have a deeper level of interest, the beginning, middle and rear of the book has several important sections which set the Biblical, cultural and historical foundation. These sections are challenging and explain much.

Time Line of Book

Book One

Moses and Aaron meet Pharaoh
Tenth Plague
Battle of Angels and Egyptian Spirits
Hebrews' Exodus
Mt. Sinai Encampment
God Arrives on Mt. Sinai
God Gives the Law
Golden Calf Rebellion

Book Two

Jesus Leaves Nazareth
Jesus Meets Cousin John at Jordan River
Upper Room Last Passover Seder
Jesus and Judas Die
Disciples Meet in Upper Room
Days Between Death and Resurrection
Resurrection Appearances
Pentecost Approaches
Jews Travel to Jerusalem
Ten Days before Pentecost Jesus Ascends to Heaven
Upper Room Meetings and Visitors
Pentecost Morning, Signs and Wonders in Upper Room
120 Disciples Move Down From Upper Room to Crowded Streets
Street Preaching
Night After Pentecost
Visitors on the Morning After Pentecost

Foreword

In the writing of this book, I carefully drew from Scripture. If a microscope and a magnifying glass could be used to see into Scripture more fully, I took that task in writing this book.

May these pages cause you to remark, "I never knew that!" and "I never thought of that!" and "They actually did that?" I have examined various teachings and theories concerning history, interpretation, and translation of the Holy Bible. As a result of this study, I found for myself the benefit and need to focus on certain persons and events in Scripture. I do this in hopes of bringing them to life in literature and situate the reader firmly in the Biblical world. As people and events fall into place the reader gets a clear idea of what occurred where and why. Every person in the Bible had a back story. I have considered what might've happened and presented lively Bible study in story format.

Much of the story content is educated speculation and not meant to be taken as actual holy fact. And so, the depth of certain (obscure) historical facts will cause some readers to scratch their heads wondering if it's the truth or merely the author's imagination.

In telling these two holiday stories, I emphasize certain incidents and elements more than other writers might choose. Such books on this episode of ancient Jewish history were written with varying truths because the centuries' old scholarship applied to the Bible is beyond calculation. The intense labors required to trace history, decide upon the contents, and assure faithful translations began ages ago

I am certain that the person, the Israelite Jesus, enjoyed being a Jew for all of the right reasons. Some Christians see Jesus as having submitted to wearing a costume, to playing a part in the Jewish lifestyle and religion, a part which his heart was *not* really into. They see him as having put up with Judaism and dodging the Jews just to get to the Cross for the world's salvation. However, I believe he embraced each day, living as a full-blooded Hebrew. I believe he sincerely honored and took joy in every holiday and in the many ways to please God by observing the hundreds of Torah commandments. He wasn't bound to His role—he volunteered.

In thirty-three years, Jesus attended over 1,500 synagogue Sabbath services. He participated in at least 33 annual cycles of 7 holidays, and well over 200 community events, such as circumcisions. Attendance at these ancient festivals proved lively, musical, and fun. Jesus enjoyed such activities. His mother, Mary, attended twice the number that her son did. These calendar events pleased and glorified God and drew Jesus closer to Him. He had a Jewish heart and lived it out better than anyone before or after him. His parents raised him to appreciate their forefathers and tribal lineage of Judah.

Wherever you are in the spectrum of Judaism, Christianity, Islam or whatever— you'll find profound, thought-provoking passages, revealing insights and certain

Biblical blind spots I've handled with practicality and common sense. A wise man told me that "Scripture raises more questions than it answers."

The Bible is not a history book. The pages contain history, but prophetic poetic sagas too-especially in the Old Testament. Also, the chronological timeline is not succinct. Curiously, Scripture also doesn't report on certain events or biographies because they have little bearing on the purpose of the dynamic narratives. We may think such facts would be helpful and make the Bible more credible. The "missing years" of Jesus' youth, are left out, just like Moses', Samuel's, Samson's or Joseph's and Mary's. Roughly 300 years after Jesus' birth, certain churches settled on the guessing game of his birthday. His birth date simply wasn't important.

Everyone has a backstory—even how and when angels or the other heavenly beings came into existence. It's not that such information must remain unknown or secretive. The question is at what point would the Bible be too large? At some 1,300 pages, there are more than enough interpretations, conflicts, translations, and ever-growing splintering religions. How many more pages or volumes would be necessary to satisfy all curiosity? The Bible is a collection of holy and unholy acts and what-ifs.

What's This Pentecost?

Does the word Pentecostal sound familiar? It should. Perhaps, like me, the word caused you to think of churches where kooky activities might take place. The modern Pentecostal movement began in the late 1800s and early part of the 20th Century after a rise in religious fervor generated by speculation over the return of Christ in 1900.

In 1976, as a new follower of Christianity, I'd heard some Pentecostal churches were often characterized by religious hype, excessive emotional displays, claims of spiritual superiority, a general lack of order, and overly demonstrative "holy rollers." I learned that so-called sensible, mainstream Christians avoided these unorthodox, Pentecostal style churches. I soon decided that most American church attendees wanted predictable services and little or no spontaneity. They expected respectable control from the elected and salaried leadership and no surprises by individuals and visitors. In contrast, certain Pentecostal fellowships wanted the Holy Spirit to come and direct the service by supernaturally influencing leaders and members. This meant the desirable Fruits of the Spirit, physical healings, and beneficial prophecy.

The popular Charismatic movement didn't grow out of the Pentecostal movement. It arose separately and originally within the mainline churches. Only later did Pentecostalism and the Charismatic renewal cross-pollinate.

I visited several Pentecostal churches. I found that as a movement, these Christians tried to revive the excitement of the First Century believers who had received the Holy Spirit's presence as a tangible and empowering experience. This experience is known by certain denominations as the Baptism in the Holy Spirit. For many Pentecostals' satisfaction, this baptism was primarily evidenced by speaking or praying in tongues and a fervent desire to tell others the Gospel. Above all, Christ must be accepted as Lord and Savior.

Pentecostals told me that during services, God did marvelous miracles of physical and emotional healing. Passionate congregants experienced angelic visions, gained scriptural insights, and used godly authority to bring liberation to those suffering demonic oppression. That sounded good to me.

So, I discussed miracles with other styles of Christians, and found that desirable spiritual doors did indeed open to Pentecostals who deeply sought the supernatural God. But to do this it seems they had to leave behind the comfort and safety of certain Christian traditions. Instead, they developed new and controversial traditions—some seeded from God, and others of man's own making.

Years later, I discovered that some characteristics of Pentecostalism morphed into the Charismatic Renewal movement of the 1960s. Including a carry-over of questionable behavior, as well as a mix of scripturally sound practices. A spectrum of Pentecostal and Charismatic churches and fellowships continue today worldwide.

The noticeable presence of the Holy Spirit and the dispensing of life-giving spiritual gifts can be common in such gatherings.

I also found that in varying degrees, God will indeed make Himself manifest whether members or visitors are uncomfortable or disagree with a churches' doctrines, worship styles, dress codes or traditions.

*   *   *

As a new believer, something else surprised me about differences with churches. Certain ones teach that signs and wonders ceased after the Apostles died. Others teach that this cessation occurred after the early church finalized the collection of the New Testament writings. Yet, other churches believe signs and wonders are still happening today, and that there is evidence of this around the world.

Most Christians know the dramatic New Testament story of Pentecost, in Acts, Chapter Two. This occurred fifty days after the Jewish Passover holiday. Most Bible believers, however, are unaware of the significant background behind that story. The church holiday known as Pentecost is not originally a Gentile church holiday at all; it is a much older Jewish festival that predates the emergence of Christ's disciples by 1,400 years—3,400 for us today. The Jewish and Christian holidays aren't the same, as you will learn.

In varying levels, the worldwide Christian church focuses on an ancient Jewish holiday, Shavuot in Hebrew, and Pentecost in Greek. That day, some twenty centuries ago in Jerusalem, the Holy Spirit (Ruach HaKodesh) came He filled 120 devoted disciples of Jesus—the first outpouring of an indwelling Holy Spirit. Signs and wonders came upon and through the gathering. A vast sound like a windstorm swirled, yet not a wisp of hair moved. Like miniature Burning Bushes, flames rested on each head—not a hair singed—and no smoke rising. Then, each person felt compelled to praise God in a loud passionate manner. But as they did, a language not of their choice or education moved through their worshipping lips.

*   *   *

Recorded in the five books of Moses (the Torah or Pentateuch), 3,400 years ago, God commanded Jewish men to make three pilgrimages a year (Shalosh Regalim), to observe His festivals: Passover (Pesach), Pentecost (Shavuot) and the Festival of Tabernacles (Sukkot). Adonai said He would choose a location once they settled in the Promised Land. He chose Jerusalem for His House, on the Good Mountain, Mt. Moriah. There, King Solomon built the First Temple, and the House of Israel brought sacrifices and offerings. Men, twenty years of age, who lived in Jerusalem or within a day or two were religiously bound to travel to the capital. Men from distant parts of the world tried to travel to the Holy City at least once. The festivals were a time to find happiness before Adonai, the Creator.

*   *   *

My guess is that average Christians today, whether church-goers or not, know little of Jesus, the most famous Jew, and his Jewish way of life and of Jews today. And so, many Christian's revere and worship a diluted, Jew-less Jesus. The gospels record brief accounts of his life. In America we read or hear of foreign lands, strange Middle-Eastern cultures and people who have been dead for centuries. No one in the Bible stories spoke English or knew about our lifestyles. For many centuries and in various countries, the Latin, "Iesus Christus" served as the name for Jesus Christ.

The Hebrew carpenter named Yeshua ben Yosef of Nazaret, of the Galil, was never called Jesus—that's an English translation. The letter "J" wasn't part of the English language until the early 1600s. Christ was not his last name. He didn't have one as we think of names today. The term "Christ" comes from a Greek substitute for the Hebrew word for "anointed." The Greek word Christ evolved to replace the Jewish designation of "Mashiach." Messiah is an Anglicized word. "Jesus the Christ" is more sensible as his title.

In Western countries, we modernize the Bible times due to lack of knowledge. Most medieval and renaissance painters portrayed Bible characters in the European clothes of their own day. Silly when you consider it. For instance, would we portray Neil Armstrong on the Moon in Levi jeans, cowboy boots and hat? No, wrong outfit. Is what Jesus wore or ate that important? In that religiously driven culture? Definitely. Should we live like ancient Jews or a modernized version? Debatable.

Many pastors, evangelists and teachers have never been to the Middle East. I get sad when I consider Jesus-loving Christians who have never set foot in a synagogue aside from perhaps a wedding or annual fund-raising kosher dinner. Yet, these common believers read of ancient Jews written by Jewish authors in the two-part Bible. Perhaps, as every century rolls further away from Bible times, church leaders teach a condensed and limited version of the Jew to whom they trust eternity. If so, is this done out of lack of interest, lack of knowledge, bias, or maybe not being able to see the "forest" of Jews, due to one large Messianic Jesus "tree"? The de-Judaizing process of one-third of the Trinity started many centuries ago, well before Santa and his elves joined the Christ-Mass season.

My hope and desire is that readers feel closer to the real person of Jesus. Also, that Scriptures which confuse some will be clarified. Lastly, the activity of the Holy Spirit will merge with your life—the effort is worth the benefits.

*　*　*

In certain contexts, the word "god" is used without a capital "G" for people who did not believe or understand that there is only One God. It's not meant to diminish God in the broad truth as the Supreme Being.

In referring to Jesus, a capital "H" is never used, only a lower case "h" such as "his" or "he" or "him."

Illustration courtesy of: Ramelle Richardson ©

BOOK ONE

Chronicle One

Chapter 1
Meeting Pharaoh

The two men dusted off their clothing. The elder, by three years, took out a wooden comb and a ceramic flask of perfumed oil from his robe. He straightened his brother's hair in a manner that showed affection, companionship, and respect. The oil helped, so Aaron combed Moses' bushy beard applying the liquid there. Moses' mind focused, caught up with the business at hand to consider grooming Aaron, his brother. Indeed, his thoughts captured his whole being.

They'd traveled from the territory of Goshen to Egypt's capital and royal city of Tanis in the lush Nile River delta.

Aaron put a firm grip on his brother's shoulder and said, "Are you ready to do this, O fellow ambassador? It is a mighty enterprise."

The words pulled Moses back from a place only he and God knew. Moses grunted, "Huh? Ahh, yes, yes I am." Sniffing the pleasant fragrance for the first time, he added, "Thank you, brother, for what you've done." Wrinkling his nose he said, "Let's see this grand man."

Two muscular guards crossed their spears barring the way into this outmost entry of the palace. Stern and fearless, one guard asked, "State your business, Hebrew."

Aaron answered, "We humbly request an audience with the Lord of Egypt. A short amount of his time is all we desire."

The guards looked the men over. One said, "Turn around. Arms up. Do you have weapons?" He patted down both strangers. His companion stood with his spear level and ready to attack. "Well?"

Aaron answered, "No weapons, of course. We respect mighty Pharaoh and mean him no harm. We have only our shepherds' staffs."

"Wait here." The guard struck a hanging cymbal. From the hallway into the palace a guard approached. By his uniform, Moses noted the obvious higher rank. Once informed of the situation, he turned and left. Within minutes he and the captain of the guard arrived with several other guards. "Remove your shoes if you want to see Great Pharaoh." They did so. The captain motioned for the two Hebrews to walk in formation surrounded by his men.

Aaron gawked at the beauty, nothing of which he'd imagined. But a palace was a palace. Tapestries, peculiar animal hides, statues, flowers and plants in vases and large pots. Artisans stood painting hieroglyphs. Some brushed zigzag lines depicting water and designs honoring Father Nile. The brothers looked down at their feet treading on polished marble tiles. Giddiness rose within the two as the grandeur enveloped them. Fancy dressed courtiers went in and out of rooms usually holding papyrus scrolls. Men and women both wore eye makeup. Turbans and high headdresses of magnificent fabrics and designs adorned people they saw. Heads down, servants broomed and mopped the fascinating stone floors.

Besides that, they saw high-officials and servants and visitors of different color skin and hair. One woman, with long braids displayed hair which looked yellow, like the sun. She also had bright blue sparkling eyes like sapphire. The eyes of some court workers were slanted upward, while others had eyes which were round like a circle—green like the ocean, blue gray, blue-green like coral, golden like a hawk, and some with light brown like hearty warm earth. A few men wore hair-pieces, short and narrow braided beards glued to the chin. Indeed, the empire drew citizens from the world at large. Egypt's seaport the Great Harbor, later named Alexandria, on the Mediterranean Sea shore, prided itself as a bustling destination known by kingdoms and merchants.

The entourage passed hallways and entered a spacious room with a high-domed ceiling. The architecture thrilled the two Hebrews. Here a man of some other special rank met them. With a quick brush of his hand, he dismissed the guards. Aaron gawked at this man's clothing. He nudged Moses, "It's unlike any I've ever seen." He wore shining metal wrist and bicep bands of intricate designs of turquoise. A sash of brilliant purple went from shoulder to waist and became a belt. Around his neck and down on his chest a necklace of precious stones Aaron had never seen before. The official's sparkling violet headdress rose well above his head and below his shoulders. Then Moses remembered his years in the princesses' palace as the adopted Hebrew, drawn by a princess out of the passive, yet deathly Nile. But for the last 40 years he'd lived as a shepherd in the wilderness.

Head cocked, the official stared at the Hebrews, studying their countenance. Silent and in no hurry, he considered their presence—where they did not belong. He strolled around them once, a hand fingering his chin. He spoke with restful confidence, "I see that you passed the brush workers painting the gods on the walls. Did you know that we worship over 40 great gods and goddesses?" By his expression, he desired no answer.

Aaron felt compelled to make a point in a matter of fact tone. "We Hebrews have one God and believe there is none but He."

Hand on chin, the official chuckled. "So, I've heard." He scoffed, "What power he must wield! One god, my, my. I can easily see what only that one has gotten you—generations of slavery—but, you are good slaves, I'll admit." Wicked humor played on his features.

Within that perfect room a fountain of water rippled. Small orange fish swam at the base of the stately tiered spring. Peacocks roamed. Parrots of startling colors squawked on their perches. The man drew the Hebrews to the water. He dipped his hands in, drank and splashed his face. Raising his hands to the domed ceiling he said in a booming voice, "All praise to our god the Nile!" Then he motioned for the two to do as he had done.

Moses and Aaron looked at the other, eyes-wide in alarm. What to do? Aaron cleared his throat. "This is awkward for us, master. Though the river is the source and indeed the life-blood of the land, we must disappoint you and restrain our devotion. Our strict allegiance and forms of worship belong elsewhere. And that is actually why we've come today." The brothers glanced at each other. Moses nodded. Graciously, Aaron offered, "May we pass?" He made a slight bow to the official.

The grimaced face said *how dare you*, but his gravelly voice said, "Follow me, fools." On the way he explained certain rules of court etiquette.

As they neared the throne room the magnificence increased. Broad windows and thin whitish curtains, like shear veils, let in much sunshine. Incense met their noses and music from flute and harps touched their ears. Servants with dazzling turbans had only one job: to hold huge fans made of ostrich feathers. On the throne an immense figure seemed to change shape from human to animal, to the next, and then to another. But as they neared, the light diminished. Gloom like swirling black smoke lay on the floor; the sunlight dimmed, and a musician struck an off chord.

Aaron later remarked that Moses appeared suddenly dazed and weary.

The feet of Aaron and his brother barely budged; the men suddenly bore heavy weights of unseen origin, their limbs drooped and last, their heads. Blurry-eyed, and chins sagging, they heard the official speak. He explained what little he knew of the visitors to a chief minister. That man nodded and went before Pharaoh. Kneeling at the steps up to the throne, he extended an arm and explained who the two men were. The gala pageantry stopped cold. A chained leopard near the throne looked at the Hebrews and growled.

A line of a dozen men in rich clothes held ornate staffs. At each top, a carved shape of an animal identified their priestly service. Large idols, gleaming with gold, silver, and precious stones representing eyes, seemed to turn and focus on the strangers. A pan of incense at the base of each idol at first smelled fragrant, but now in their Hebrew nostrils, in close range, an unbearable stink nearly suffocated them. No one in that room wanted the Hebrews there; Moses and Aaron were surrounded. Each sensed heaviness due to the evil spirits whose home they had intruded.

The Egyptian king's eyes squinted as if trying to pierce into the minds of the strangers, finally, he motioned them forward. "Worship me and I will hear you and your petty complaints, O fearless masters of the Hebrew ones. I am the representative on earth of the King and Father of gods, Ra. He is the Sun and maker of everything. Only he took chaos and created the universe from that. My wealth and power are beyond measure."

But their feet stayed unmovable. A further darkness, not seen with common eyes, started to fill the room, and Moses' and Aaron's minds suffered with confusion. They both felt short of spirit. The reason for entering the royal home of the most powerful man in the empire—maybe the world—vanished.

However, Moses felt his knees sag just slightly. But an object from outside one of the large open windows swiftly flew inside. As Moses' mind fought not to obey Pharaoh's ungodly command, he now felt his eyes grow larger and larger. The dim throne room had an otherworldly visitor.

A brilliant light expanded creating stark shadows everywhere. Moses shaded his eyes. Behind each of the large idols an ugly being sought shelter. The debris in Moses' composure blasted away; seeking his right mind. Weights dropped off his body, like waking out of a dream of terror and feeling rescued while in transit to endless life in a dungeon.

Laughter spilled from his belly and out his mouth. He turned to his brother and grinned. The light which had come took form. In humbled curiosity, Moses searched to take in the view. Pharaoh's royalty went to ash. On his mind rested in desert day, all alone, speaking to the Voice emanating from a peculiar fire. *A bush aflame, now what? More directions, another mission? No, this is why He sent me here. Now address the king!*

This light conformed to a man with muscular arms and mighty wings—wings that an ostrich would be envious of—no, a soaring eagle. This stranger appeared made of light, but he wore a kind of robe, and proudly armed. Here to fight, but fight whom? This soldier's face and sword frightened, and yet, encouraged Moses. The shining gold helmet covered a mane of silvery, whitish hair. Moses thought this thing has masculine features, but subtleness of feminine as well. The soldier stood taller than any man he'd seen. With authority written on his face, the warrior shouted something in a foreign tongue. The creatures hiding behind the idols shook and tried to plug their ears. Moses quivered wondering what he'd missed in the powerful outburst. The being wore sandals, but light shone down from under the robe, and Moses noticed that the feet hovered a handbreadth off the floor. Mouth agape, he dared to look again at the face: a handsome one, yet emotions blended through a variety of expressions. Through them all, Moses understood by the last one—a simple smile—*I'm safe and this someone is here to support me.*

The angel spoke to the uplifted Hebrew prophet. "You may not always see me as you do now, but I will be with you though I am hidden from your natural sight." Moses graciously nodded accented by a low bow. The welcomed stranger placed the tip of his glowing sword on the top of Moses' head. The hot blade sent a pulse of pure power through his body down to the soles of his feet.

Moses heard Pharaoh as if from a distance getting louder. Now with clarity, Moses made a minimal bow and apologized for being stymied by all of the grandeur of the Great Pharaoh.

*　　*　　*

During the meeting of this king and his slaves, Aaron did most of the speaking. Moses whispered instructions and answers to his brother who repeated those to Pharaoh. The leader of the empire didn't like this arrangement. He huffed, rolled his eyes, looked at his fingernails and threatened to have the two thrown out of the palace. Moses guessed the king could overhear his murmurings. If he himself spoke, would Pharaoh laugh at his slow, stuttering speech, assuming him to be dimwitted or even drunk?

A record keeper sat at a low table dutifully writing on papyrus. This scribe stopped to witness the court's unusual activity.

In the end, authority met authority head on. Pharoah refused the request of Moses to have the Hebrews freely go to worship their ancestral god for several days at a certain location in the desert. Pharaoh with sly ambition answered, "And who shall work those days? Are you free men, to leave work when you want to? Live like a slave or die as a slave—be gone! I am your Ruler, puny men. I rule over a multitude of puny men. You are nothing but trash. I accept no apologies or excuses for deliberate disloyalty in my court."

However, the rooms of this palace were homes of spirits who used spells and incantations to open doors of magic seeking to please the current royalty. The spirits came out in the open to better see this development. The darkness closed in, swirling toward the feet of the defeated Hebrews. As the royal throne room dimmed even further, more and more spirit creatures moved out from behind the idols. When this proclamation resounded down the halls, a strange thing happened. Emboldened, Moses surged in confidence.

Later, Aaron remarked that he didn't see the welcome warrior of light. However, he saw the change in his brother. His little brother had grown as a man, a man to stand up to Pharaoh.

The warrior had stood out of direct view, but the entire time Moses saw the shimmering out of the corner of his eye. This refreshed Moses' mind. *Now is the time to use the wooden staff as God had instructed me in the land of Midian, by Mount Sinai.*

Chapter 2
The Battle

Twelve Months and Nine Plagues Later

The angels' heightened morale in heaven was memorable.

The designated Angel of Death stood proud and bowed low before the throne and laid his sword across his knees. A hand reached down the steps to touch the tip of an ordinary sword of Heaven. When two fingers pinched the tip, the blade's color changed. The lower third turned a brilliant white.

The crowd of angels covered their eyes and turned away. When their eyes adjusted, mouths dropped open. The upper part of the precious sword now served three points. The end was actually three sharp tips, such as from a stem, each as strong as the original tip. It wasn't a trident, it was forked, and a new creation like, the capital letter Y. The middle tip stayed straight and its two companions curved out. The crowd smiled while "Oouing" and "Ahhing."

When the Lord changed the shape of the sword He also gifted His creature with discerning knowledge. Such a skill would make the journey over the millions of people below so much easier. In a moment, the Angel of Death descended to the earthly realm and hovered over a familiar landscape. Invigorated, he strained to spread his wings as far as his feathers could reach.

He had a powerful mission. His eyes searched for two commodities: those faithless and those faithful. His fast pace and mission of judgment were observed by a select number of angels, for the Lord had other related chores ahead for them.

Starting at the habitations of the Hebrews, he found the signs of blood and sought no entry. However, not all Hebrews had submitted to the life-giving divine power which had vied for months at Pharaoh's court.

Where there was doubt, lying spirits took up habitation. Moses and the miracles caused debates. Certain men chose to *ignore* the feats detoured by their own ingrown bitterness. Slavery for so long had caused anger and resentment for some that was a generational, cultivated, indictment of Abraham's God. Now this spiritual illness transferred to include the supposed appearance of a Redeemer. How many generations did it take to act? Defiling spirits goaded these naysayers and eventually took root in homes—for only man could open that door letting in enemies. Such men and women would wait to see what the next morning would bring. That was their downfall. They made no preparations. These rebellious humans had a problem beyond "just not sure what to believe." Their sinful response to the way God chose to move was stubbornness. Despising the prophecies of Moses and Aaron would have a terrible cost, death of the first born. Yet, the only plague, common to man which God cannot contend with is unbelief; men choose that, no matter their bloodline. Free will would always win—even if temporarily.

When the Angel of Death entered such a defiled Hebrew home, he grunted.

Weariness tugged at him and energy dipped. What had God told him about this night? "You will be knee deep in sorrow, for I have not decided on a fatal lesson on this level since Noah and the Flood."

These faithless ones were asleep, merely expecting another day of slave labor come sun up. A chuckling "Hee, hee, hee!" caught the Angel's senses. But the Angel wasn't given orders to be aggressive with Israel's unseen enemy—unless necessary. He extended his sword, and with a sweeping motion life left the firstborn of that home, man and beast. Then the angel pointed at the small, defiling dark creature perched in a corner. It yelped and disappeared.

The Chosen People were not perfect, and the imperfect, who lacked faith, even like that of a child, were punished—mercy had ended in the land of Egypt.

During the nine plagues, the wicked spirits, masquerading as deities acted in a double-minded fashion. They thoroughly enjoyed the various methods of suffering with which Adonai afflicted the Egyptians. Humans in pain was their favorite entertainment. However, with the destruction wrought by the feats through Moses came lack of belief in the gods. They didn't want to lose their detestable centuries of secure footing. Fools, layering foolishness upon heaps of utter foolhardiness. Pharaoh, indeed, sat as the supreme fool, indicted by nine horrendous acts.

*   *   *

News in the spiritual realm traveled fast. The doings of the Angel of Death at midnight moved swiftly. Signal fires of an otherworldly color were lit on the hilltops. These caused other signals which led to warn the spirits who lived at the capital. The demons in charge of this warning system saw a winged being of light, a warrior, pass overhead and zigzag into the distance. In the capital, there was enough time to rally the already half-beaten spirits bearing the names of the gods and goddesses.

Indeed, the Angel of Death found deep sorrow as he traversed the devastated empire, the land of slavery. Though he flew at a remarkable pace, Egypt was a sizable country. The death he left behind his flapping wings was God's specific will. Nine and more warnings, evidenced by the plagues, made room for the Egyptians to seek out the Hebrews for guidance. Some did. These found open doors to the Hebrew homes on the night of this tenth plague. They stared at the doorways, believing that the animal blood streaked on the doorposts would somehow save their lives. But that amounted to faith.

Meanwhile, the capital's temples, built for the multitude of deities, rumbled. The walls and floors cracked. Besides the single Angel of Death, God was sending one of His armies to do other deeds—each one a volunteer, fitted for battle. Each pagan temple housed priests, priestesses, and various servants. The structures were breeding grounds of falsehood, and sacrifices which went nowhere. The signal fire worried the demons. When word reached the religious demonic forces, they decided to seek the most powerful among them, the god Ra. Leaving their temples, more than 40 gods and goddesses huddled around Ra to hear instructions from him. The stronghold of Egypt was about to be attacked.

Ra took his stand at the bottom of the steps leading into the royal palace. Barefoot, he stood 30 feet tall, the muscular body of a man, with the head of a fierce looking falcon. His menacing beak could snap a log like a twig. His massive hands could break and crush anything. Ra feared nothing. Simple but regal clothing covered his frame, a kilt, a breast plate of shining gold, jewelry on his wrists and biceps. A blue and gold headdress covered and flowed to the fleshy shoulders. Of that same design he wore as sash around his waist. Around him, increasing every moment, gathered the array of gods and goddesses and a mass of their smaller, look-alike copies.

The army of angels floated down to face their enemy. They strode into a square formation with helmets and breastplates on, swords drawn and shields in place. Each angel's shield was golden and was embossed with a different scene of the Kingdom of Heaven. God's throne, like a logo, could be seen near the top of each large craft of armor.

Their captain left the ranks and approached the monster and tilted his head back to see Ra's detestable face.

Holding a metal scepter, Ra spread his arms as he made an appeal to the invading soldiers. Bird eyes roamed over the enemies. In his squawking, authoritative voice he said, "You warriors from above, we here, were such as you are. Come join us and be worshipped and held in honor—instead of serving, and serving…endlessly." He boasted, "Be served! Leave that God behind, become your own. He has plenty more than your small band to please Him. Come, be a god!" Ra looked down at the brave little captain, and shook his feathered head. A booming laugh followed. "Let us make peace shall we?"

This holy, battle-ready commander wasn't affected by the speech. He looked to either side of the abominable beast, and beheld the shocking, sickening pantheon of the land's living idols. Worthless and evil, gods and lesser gods; their eyes knew no joy, no solace, not one wit of selflessness. Death glazed over the variety of eyes, creating an ill, unquenchable stare. The captain was told by Adonai before he left for battle, "There are an incredible number of gods and goddesses in Egypt. There's at least one for almost every situation and place. The Egyptians are a superstitious people. They believe that each animal has special gifts or powers."

Now the captain saw these opponents:

- the god Khnum, a man with a ram's head with sharpened horns;
- Khepri, a man with the head of a large black scarab beetle, who bore into torture souls;
- Apep, the lord of Chaos, holding a wild serpent, who turned himself into a gigantic serpent the length of a palm tree;
- Anubis, god of the underworld, in the appearance of a man-sized jackal snapped his jaws and bared his teeth;
- Hapi, goddess of the Nile River, the source of life and fertility, she stood in a perpetual puddle of water;

- Shu, the god of the atmosphere and Father of the Sky, blew wind from its jowls;
- Tefnut, a lion-headed goddess of Moisture and Wetness, growled and roared ;
- the god Hunefer and his wife, adored by their seven chattering baboons;
- the goddess Heket, a woman with the face of a frog, an ugly sight;
- the earth god Seb, with a goose which laid eggs, nesting on his head, when he laughed this caused earthquakes;
- Apis, a bull, chief god of the city of Memphis, stamped his hoofs, ready for anything;
- the god Typhon, aide of magicians, an illusive shape-shifter;
- Serapis, defender of the land against locusts, revenge on its face for the plague of locusts which trimmed his power to a grain of sand;
- Sopdu, god of war, only he bore a sword, spear, shield and a chariot pulled by unknown creatures;
- Nekhbet, the vulture goddess and winged serpent, the unnerving caws had no affect on God's soldiers, but the viper snapped wanting to kill;
- Osiris, god of the underworld and afterlife, he lived in a dim shroud;
- Bes, the bringer of happiness, her face beckoned with a full, yet hideous smile;
- Qebui, god of the North wind, his body spun while his head stayed in place;
- Qetesh, goddess of fertility, sex organs and fetuses were embroidered on her robe;
- Sekhmet, goddess of lions and the destructive power of the sun, she held a mirror to reflect light which blinded any who haplessly looked her way;
- Set, god of chaos, storms, evil and death with a beast's muzzle and square ears;
- Sobek, god of crocodiles, a man with the head of a crocodile, jaws snapping;
- Selket, the scorpion goddess, who guarded one of the four gates of the underworld;
- Tawaret, a huge female hippopotamus standing upright with large human breasts, the legs of a lioness, and the tail of a crocodile which swished in the sand;
- Wadjet, goddess of protection, a coiled cobra, flicked her forked tongued;
- Isis, goddess of love and magic, she casts spells drawing strangers together to lust with no thought of consequences;
- Hathor, a woman with the head of a cow, a sexy feminine figure, had full

breasts and eyes which entranced men;

▲ the goddess Tuat, of the land of the dead, black smoke swirled like a ribbon around her;

▲ Mayet, the goddess of truth and justice, judging of the souls of the deceased in the Hall of Judgment in the underworld;

▲ Sehkment, god of fire, flames burst out of his mouth;

▲ Min, god of rain and crops, in the form of a white bull, impatiently stomped his hooves;

▲ Nephthys the goddess of death with outstretched wings, her eyes black, no white;

▲ Maahes, lion-headed god of war, roared and shook its mane;

▲ Bastet, cat goddess, a cat as tall as a woman sat on her haunches, patiently waiting;

▲ Geb, the maker of snakes, wore a white crown with several cobras winding themselves around his body;

▲ Bast, the goddess of music and dance, had the head of a fierce cat, but also long blonde hair and bright blue eyes with angry cats at her feet;

▲ Plus, departed spirits of Nefertiti, Akhenaten, Aten, Smenkhkare, Amenhotep, Tutankhaten and Karnak and more, with defiant expressions. Gods and goddesses of dolphins, dogs, fish, geese, hawks, herons, lynx, rabbits, pigs, swallows, wolves, and the ibis.

Tension filled the air. Evil upon evil. This concoction had a hierarchy of ranks. The vast duplicates of gods and goddesses who were smallest would attack first.

The captain eyed the spirits' tactic of slowly surrounding his army of angels. The briefing which they had before their deployment did not prepare them to combat this hideous array of beings. Lying, oppressive, unclean, foul, afflicting, seducing, divination, sickness, fears and defiling spirits were ready to do their worst to the intruders.

The repulsive horde spread to either side of their monstrous hero. His fighters managed proud and yet pulsating and contorted expressions. Snarling and twisted howling came from each foe. Most angels remained unafraid. Some shuffled their feet or dug toes in the sand.

Ra remarked, "As you can see, we've created our own lives here. Foolish humans believe we are essential for their existence. Egypt is mine, my dominion, and under my authority. I am its lord, and I can use fresh helpers such as your fine troops. Why fight: you are here—*stay!*" His words worked a spell. Ra was most cunning in the binders of spells.

The multitude of ferocious spirits had no swords, spears, or shields. But their true, even larger, unseen evil master—the prince of darkness—provided them with other means for defense. The spirits' most strategic weapon was the oldest—

deception. As Ra made his speech, with every angel listening curiously, the gods' look-alikes had surrounded the entire angelic host.

God's commander moved nearer to his opponent Ra, the closest he'd ever been to such malice. Certain of his troops, though ready for this fight, questioned the wisdom of making oneself so vulnerable. The soldiers tightened their grips on their armaments. They made quick sideways glances to check the countenances of their comrades. Some warriors experienced a shortness of Spirit, their nobility wavered. Combat would change that.

When the captain had heard enough and stood dangerously close to Ra, he gripped his double-edged sword with both hands and ran toward his huge adversary. With all of his might he swung one long arc slicing through one of the giant's ankles, and then spun and sliced the other through. The captain yelled, "For the innocent children sacrificed to you!" Bewildered, Ra started to plunge face forward toward the packed troops, angels quickly fluttered away from the enormous falling being. But his heavy, slender scepter dropped out of his hand, this crushed two angels who didn't move fast enough. It struck hard on their shields, and the scepter broke and turned into acrid dark smoke—the smell of wickedness. If the angels had stomachs, they would've been nauseous and doubled-over.

Ra's body dissolved into a pillar of black smoke, except for his feet, which remained in place. Then two wisps of dark smoke momentarily rose out of them, and the feet vanished. The gods howled and made stout gestures of vengeance. Their menacing wrath grew voluminously. Those on either side of Ra moved in to stand side by side and protect the palace entry.

A blast from the captain's shofar announced the battle for Egypt. The goal? To destroy every false god and goddess, overrun the palace, and secure entry for the Angel of Death. This pagan stronghold must lie in ruins and every worthless idol revealed as such. The core goal demanded death in the palace.

This last terrible plague, death of the first-born, would directly affect Pharaoh's family. "Measure for measure," Adonai had spoken to Moses. "Israel is My son, My first-born, and you, Pharaoh, are guilty of murder. You have refused to let My son go to worship and serve Me. Your desire is that He serve you and not Me. Therefore, justice is demanded. Your son, your first-born, I shall slay, including all first-born within your land, man, and animal."

The angels moved forward with shields up and swords at the ready. The first wave of the enemy moved in. In hot anger at the loss of Ra, his smallest servants who were the height of the warriors' kneecaps, raced. They dove in like a pack of monkeys but worked in sly cooperation. When they spit, bit, or grasp an angelic body, God's soldier dissolved, and his armor fell to the ground. So, they targeted any exposed skin. A fragrant white wisp of smoke occurred and then faded to nothing. However, the released aroma of Heaven caused the frantic foes to reel over in jags of coughing. That's when the nearby soldiers cut the heads off. That caused wisps of black smoke. A revolting odor hung in the air for a moment and then dissipated.

Wild sounds came from across the battleground. Now face to face, angels were aghast at the hideous foes. Spirits with talons jumped on the backs of the warriors to rip throats and bellies. They also sought exposed ankles and hands. Several would jump and pile on a warrior and take it down. The aroma of holiness suffocated them. But the spirits had vice-grip hands and searched for armor to cling to and then spit, slime, grab or strangle. The spirits would move on and gang up on another. Swords, helmets, and shields lay on the battlefield. One spirit grasped a fallen sword. Immediately, a shriek from burning pain came forth as the holy blade dropped to the ground.

Bastet, the cat goddess, sent out her dozens of duplicates. With claws extended and teeth bared, these sprung at the warriors' faces or leaped on their back seeking to dig or rip necks. A crowd of small Khnums, the ram-headed god of the Nile, and Maahes, the lion-headed god of war, sent their forces into the mayhem. Together, these sought to bash into kneecaps and knock warriors over and then trampled the fallen soldier. Small versions of Ra pecked at eyes and tore skin open.

The captain's second in command used a shofar to command movements of the troops. He sorrowed when he heard grunts of pain, watching his soldiers go down and white smoke rise.

With anguish in his heart, the conflicted commander planted his feet, raised his eyes and glowing sword to the heavens. In a loud voice, heard by many battling he sang a verse from a song of glory, which only the angels knew. As the voice permeated the air, a slender beam of light slowly rose up from the tip of his blade. Within moments, in response, a much bolder beam, and one of mixed hues, raced down from the heavens and landed, slamming into the violent scene. Like a ray of sunlight streaking through an opening in dense clouds, this event surprised both sides. The impact caused every enemy to lose footing and fall on the ground. The angels had instinctively flexed their wings and fluttered to miss the forceful horizontal shockwave. They quickly took advantage of this godly maneuver. Much evil ended.

However, after the first wave of spirits, the angels faced stronger, but equally disorienting, enemies. These included the bodies of men and women, but with heads of frogs, rams, lions, vultures, serpents, beetles and falcons. Fighting grew fierce. No angels had witnessed or fought in such a face-to-face battle. Though the trained soldiers were made of embodied light and their mass a brightly lit force, their numbers diminished. The signal fires, set by wicked hands, were seen from far across the land. The exiled, defeated, and dethroned spirits of the plagues returned for any vengeance they could inflict. From each direction, horror sought this fight.

The captain shouted orders and eternal truths. "Pay attention, O Israel, for you are my servant. I, the Lord, made you, and I will not forget to help you!" and "Sing, O heavens, for the Lord has done wondrous things. Shout, O earth! Break forth into song, O mountains and forests and every tree! For the Lord has redeemed Jacob and is glorified by Israel." and "The Lord and Creator says, 'I am Adonai, who made all things. I alone stretched out the heavens. By Myself, I made earth and everything in it. I am the one who exposes the false prophets as liars by causing events to happen that are contrary to their predictions!'" These life giving words enhanced the color of his troops, clearing their minds. More clever, swifter and unafraid, they moved closer to the palace to take it out.

Then in a final strategic wave the dark enemies moved with fury. In full life-size form, jackals, bulls, hippopotamuses, crocodiles, and baboons sought out their angelic prey. This left the entrance to the palace vulnerable. Improvising reigned on both sides. Striking here and there, plumes of light and blackened smoke rose in the fray. The spirits of the dead seemed to be coming from all sides, some from the distant horizons. Nefertiti, Akhenaten, Aten, Smenkhkare, Amenhotep, Tutankhaten, Karnak and pharaohs long dead raced across the sand dunes toward the war. The swell concerned the holy warriors.

The captain saw how these spirits used confusing thoughts to distract his soldiers. Then in coordinated attacks the gods would close in on a weakened angel. The fast paced crocodile, Sobek, approached a warrior and snapped its life-taking jaws while its massive tail whirled around thrusting the angel off its feet. Anubis the jackal, leaped in the air, its bone-breaking teeth ready. It came down on an angel whose back was turned. Apis, the bull, bellowed as an angel drove his sword into the beast. Nekhbet, the vulture goddess, flew above and then dove into angels busy defending fellow soldiers. Seeing this, the captain flew with sword pointing, and with a swish, slashed off its head. Duels in the air cast hideous shadows.

On the ground, the goddess Tawaret, a hippopotamus, sat on a panting soldier, eyes bulging. This wicked creature rested on the angel's flattened, golden shield. Unfortunately, his sword was flung out of reach. Barely alive, with little time left the spirits passing by pointed and laughed at the sight. With a smile, she squashed him more.

Golden horned bulls trotted looking for targets, and then lowered their heads, and charged. When they hit a soldier they tossed him in the air and moved on.

As the battlefield grew dim, the captain thought, *The battle could be lost when more of the spirits of the dead arrive.* Yet, he never considered requesting reinforcements. While still in flight, he called out to Adonai, "How long, O Lord, before your Angel of Death comes to end these gods forever?"

At that moment, a spearhead of brilliant light broke through the darkness of the horizon. The being's growing presence could be felt by both sides. God's wrath propelled the deeds of this new phenomenon. They watched in curiosity, and all slackened their movements. In that pause, the captain yelled, "To the steps! Keep them clear! Victory is assured." But by the time the angels understood, the mighty Angel of Death flashed by and entered. Snarling spirits standing in his way became wicked wisps of smoke. Within moments a blast of light exited the palace and zigzagged across the landscape. The angelic radiance soon disappeared on its way to further destruction.

The palace walls and floors showed cracks and stone columns buckled as if an earthquake struck. Shelves emptied their goods. Sleep left all.

Outside, silence flattened the battlefield until the captain blew his shofar and led the charge into the palace searching for the Prince of Egypt.

Chapter 3
The Hebrews Flee

The moonless night helped set a darkened mood. Even the stars seemed to have gone elsewhere. At midnight, outside Pharaoh's bedchamber two guards made a commotion. A wooden spear with its metal tip clanked on the marble floor, followed by a thud. The other guard knelt over his companion, he stared at the unmoving body and then shook him. He'd landed face down and arms outstretched. When flipped over by his struggling partner, clearly the man lived no more.

Pharaoh asked why the disruption, but he received no immediate answer. Putting on his robe by himself, he went to investigate. Once out of bed, and through the curtained entry, he stood over the dead man. Dismayed, the other guard spread his hands open wide and looked at the king. At that moment, Pharaoh heard screams of anguish from other ends of his palace. He went to investigate. In the first hall, he almost tripped over a peacock, which lay still on its side.

A servant carrying a torch moved toward him from a far corridor. At night, wall sconces, olive oil lamps, and candles here and there, lit the darkened palace. Within moments, the captain of the guard met Pharaoh, sorrow filled his eyes. After a briefing, Pharaoh knew that in all quarters dead were found. In the queen's chamber two maidservants breathed no more. Elsewhere, a cook, a musician, three counselors and two magicians lay dead. Before the guard could finish his report, the king pushed him away because, like a rock falling from the sky smacking his head, he remembered his child. Pharaoh ran to his son's bedchamber. While racing through the corridors he hopped over a servant sprawled on the polished floor. Pharaoh heard wailing as he drew close. His belly soured. Bile rose in his throat as his head hung. "No, no!" His entire body rapidly produced sweat, some splashed to his feet making his steps unsure.

He wailed, "The prince, the prince, my young son, my only son." Three women and the queen wept. The king hesitated at the doorway, his feet not wanting to move. But he brushed aside the curtain and found himself lifting the lifeless body off the bed. Without shame, tears ran down his face. But as blinding anger rose in him, he handed off the boy to the queen and stomped out into the corridor.

The captain of the palace guards awaited orders. The man glanced at a cat on the floor; death took what came first.

Throughout the differing tensions and pain of each Hebrew plague, none compared to this scrambling of falling emotions. A hot firebrand like a sword, had its way and struck the deepest it could into the remnants of the battered empire. Darkness swallowed the life of these people. Using stealth, an unknown visitor, which neither sword nor shield could thwart, had come and gone.

The Angel of Death bore in mind the relentless years of tens of thousands of infant Hebrew boys thrown into the ever uncaring, unforgiving Nile. That chosen accomplice had failed only once in its dutiful acceptance: Moses. He'd floated in a tiny ark and made landfall, met by royalty.

In less than an hour the holy assassin sped through or over more than one million homes. After his visit in the palace he flew invigorated. As the creature explored each dwelling, a song of joy and praise came from its lips. Other angels had desired to do this deed and act as the strong hand of the Lord, ending more than three centuries of slavery.

Meanwhile, pounding his fists into his palms, Pharaoh stomped with every step. Another dead parrot, one of his favorites because the bird talked, lay still. Grunting, he kicked the bird with all his might. The lifeless bundles of beautiful feathers tumbled down the hall. The king's style and poise—gone. "I've mocked, and now I'm mocked. For this I will be remembered. When did reason fly from me." Yet, Pharaoh had no remorse.

In his white-knuckled hand, he grasp a useless jewel-encrusted dagger, he couldn't have held it tighter. In haste he looked and wished for an exposed killer. But captive of a racing pulse, sweating he knew no one—loneliness set in tight. No one tried to comfort him. No one could. Responsibility for his son's death lay heavy crushing his battered, meager soul.

This magnificent palace turned into a battleground. Pharaoh, his family, and servants exerted a tremendous defense against frogs, locust, fleas, and flies. They'd sat in darkness for three days, scratched at countless boils, and yearned for fresh, clear water to drink. A strong roof had protected them from storms of deadly hailstones. He'd watched from that safe place the hailstones pelting those running in the streets seeking shelter. He wasn't aware of the story of Sodom and Gomorrah—they'd been warned too.

Now, pacing into the throne room, he noticed three baboons. One gently touched and nudged a much smaller one, trying to awaken the creature. A larger baboon made high-pitched flaying noises in a language known only to its species. With erratic waving of his hands, he waddled in close circles around the lifeless child and mother. The king stared. He connected with the grief of another parent, though an animal. He shook his head as if trying to shoo away a buzzing fly. Then the king stared at the floor and throne before him. One thought smacked him over and over, *Am I no more than a wealthy baboon, who has lost everything?*

Pharaoh instructed the captain to send military messengers and officials to locate and summon the two Hebrew prophets. The communication waiting on Pharaoh's tongue? "Go now! Leave my land! Every one of you, young and old; take your cattle, flocks, and herds. Leave nothing behind." The heat shone in his red-face and sweat-soaked skin. Dismay pulled the stubborn leader down. "Truly, I'm only a heap of trash on the palace floor." Grief racked his body and then the proud king lay prostrate, the mighty humbled. A man of royalty who didn't know what to do in this compelling state. All of the failures he played into felt like nine mighty punches deep into his gut. Each one rushed back, filling his mind. He had no one to blame.

In one long moment, the unseen commanding servant of a higher God stood tall and pressed a foot on Pharaoh's neck, stifling life-giving air. The monarch's eyes closed, squeezing out tears, his hand slowly opened and lay flat. In exhaustion, Pharaoh exhaled a weak "Enough."

The sound of flapping wings drifted as its owner returned to Heaven.

*   *   *

The Hebrews lived in the large storage city of Rameses, which they were forced to build. The messengers found the same peculiar sight within each of the Hebrew households they stopped at. A sticky red substance of two vertical and one horizontal splotches marked the doorways. Families were fully awake, dressed for travel, bags packed, wearing sandals, belts tightened, and the husband always held a walking stick—all family members appeared to be waiting for important news. The anticipated message motivated the Hebrew families to be ready to leave their lives of slavery. Bags and crates were packed with essentials, sentimental possessions, and food. In faith, they carried out the warnings and instructions from their leader, Moses. They trusted God's word through him. The dumbfounded messengers said, "It's your time!" and in a matter of minutes, droves of villagers walked out, away from their homes and the country of their forefathers forever. Their "time," their adventure, had started. Then in the early light of dawn an exodus of huge proportions strode on, morale boosted as high as the clouds.

Adonai reserved this night to bring His people out from Egypt, so this same night now belonged to Him. He told Moses that it must be celebrated every year, from generation to generation, to remember the Lord's mighty deliverance. As a shepherd watches over his flocks at night, Adonai observed the proceedings on earth below.

Pharaoh slumped on the steps leading to his throne. The pressure building in his chest created short breaths and the rise and fall of his upper body. He shook and went down on one knee. He now understood with a clarity of mind of which only death can bring, that, worshipping the various gods of Egypt proved foolish and unnecessary. "I am no son of Ra. There is no Ra. The sun rises as on any other day. Where was Ra during those three days of utter darkness which no flame could penetrate? He provides no redemption from the dastardly slaves. What benefit is there in our religion? A lifetime of splendid ceremonies, prayers, offerings, dancing and kissing the feet of idols—for what?"

This man of rebellious majesty stooped consumed by sullenness with no bottom. He mumbled, "Who is Adonai that I should obey him? Humpf. Were those really my words?"

Shortly after midnight, the Egyptian king put both hands to his head and pressed in hard. He moaned a bellowing moan like he'd heard only from oxen straining in their brutal labors. "Why? Why?" In his mind he imagined his kingdom, a land of misery, built upon yet newer and newer miseries otherwise unimaginable and unfound in the history of man. Pharaoh reached for a goblet of water and he poured it over his head. An "Ahh." came. He mumbled, "Living came to me, but dying has taken it with him."

Egyptians of a less stubborn nature had made such decisions months ago when the seemingly endless routine of plagues distorted their lives. Whether priest or mere peasant, the revelation remained obvious: Egypt now paid the price for sustaining a slave race. No one thought a god with any challenging resources would claim the Hebrews—only the lowest would choose worship by slaves. Apparently, not.

Sensible or senseless, divine help had sought out the redemption of these people.

*   *   *

The two brothers took their wooden staffs and bid their Shaloms to family and faithful supporters. With an armed escort they hurried for the final, awful, showdown. When they entered the palace the two had lightness in their steps. The downtrodden man awaited them. The conversation, if it qualified as one, took a few moments. His hardened heart blurred the truth he had created. Yet, Pharaoh finally spoke the right words. "Leave us! Go!" Then he said something which Moses wondered about until the day he died. "And bless me too." Had the truths which were beyond reach now something he desired?

The guards at the entrance stood straighter at the sight of Moses and Aaron exiting. They saluted the brothers. "We, that is, we Egyptians, know you've been sent by God, the One True God." They bowed. With tears in his eyes Moses placed firm hands on their shoulders and said, "Then you are friends of God, now." Moses and his brother smiled a broad and very satisfying grin as they skipped down those steps for the last time.

As the two famed Hebrews walked home, every Egyptian who recognized them did something unexpected. They bowed low, cheered them with favor, offered valuable items as gifts, and esteemed their God, the King of the universe. One gave them an empty wagon with two stout donkeys and hitched them. Once that happened, people ran into their homes and placed jewelry, fine robes, gold and silver utensils, and many thoughtful items. A heap formed. Another wagon arrived and the owner tossed out his belongings. They pleaded, "Send your fellowmen and their wives back to us. We will fill all the wagons we can with the best of our possessions. Do make them come, will you? Don't disappoint us!" Other voices said, "Let's use oxen and horses for carts and anything with wheels so they will bear heavier weight! Find crates and large containers. Get wine and water skins! They'll need weapons wherever they are going. Send men to the garrison and palace armory; get swords, spears and whatever else is used in battle. Tell their commander it's for the Hebrews. They'll want musical instruments wherever they're traveling to and celebrate their grand departure from lives of slavery!" Moses and Aaron cried and grinned and cried more. They affirmed the requests and fast work. "Yes, yes, we will do as you please." When the two brothers moved on, they confided, "We'll leave rich." Many donkeys were laden with cargo on their backs. And so the Hebrews left the land of slavery with great wealth.

The two brothers knew they were free. The centuries and decades, one after another, were closing like sand filing in a hole never to be seen again. Without guards escorting them, the jubilant men returned to the ready mass of Hebrews. As a sandstorm knows its direction, the storm of Hebrews began theirs.

*   *   *

As the day wore on, the towns and hamlets with mixed neighborhoods where the Hebrews lived proved vacant. A warm breeze passed through these silent, deserted towns. Curious neighbors and those nearby traveled to see this sudden disappearance. Far in the distance a long dust cloud marked the path the Hebrews took. Later, there were only bare landscape and blue sky. The mass movement traveled on the well-used southeast route toward the peninsula of Sinai. If they had traveled north on the popular road along the Great Sea, an organized garrison force might've ended their progress. The destination? The land of Canaan, several days straight across the desert—but their route, God's route, would take them elsewhere first.

While investigating the multitude of empty homes, they found something strange at the doorway to many homes, something strange. Streaks of dried blood marked parts of the two doorposts and the crosspiece above; brushed on overnight. The red had splattered and dripped; life-giving markings signaled to the invisible Angel of Death: pass over, keep going.

Inside the homes at the fire pit, again, a similar oddity met their curiosity. Charred lamb or goat remains lay in the ashes. The skull, empty of brains, and every bone of such animals were piled in the cold remains of the cookfire. The hide, and every organ usually not eaten, were burned as well. The spit to roast meat lay bare.

*   *   *

Until that day, every morning at sunrise, priests and priestesses performed rituals. The lifeless idols were rinsed with water and respectfully dried. The cast idols or those with hammered gold and silver which overlaid idols of wood or stone would shine anew. The solid gold statues, such as for Ra, were also enshrined in a small temple in Pharaoh's palace, for the convenience of royalty. Incense lit, a pleasing aroma to the gods? Only imagined. The clergy knelt and lay prostrate before making sacrifices, offerings, petitions, and prayers. But this morning all was forgotten. Duty confused, the variety of Egyptian priesthoods lay faithless, each temple vacant of spirits. Incantations, momentum, and hearts of dedication—gone.

Chapter 4
Forty-Seven Days Later: Heaven Meets Earth

Mt. Sinai Encampment

Maddening. The pressure pushed them on.

Yelling, stumbling, and shoving adults chased their scampering excited children. Over the bustling encampment dust clung like fog. This and other activities played out in the enormous mass of humanity.

Their leader, the man, Moses. His leather sandals supported an intense man whom God loved. They had a relationship born in controversy, one from which Moses, early on, ardently tried to excuse himself—but failed.

Now in an exodus from what generations of Hebrews called home, they needed food and water. Hearing the demand for water, Moses requested the Creator to produce a solution. A miracle burst forth with horrendous noise, white water surged out of a rock formation. The thundering birth smashed anything in its way. A hardy river which forked into three branches issued forth from the base of Mount Sinai, a mountain of stone. These streams blessed the arid land with refreshing cool water, a new feature to the landscape. Now, over a million travelers depended on that water.

Pulled and goaded by their masters, tens of thousands of goats, donkeys, camels, and oxen plodded through the crowd for a drink. Hundreds of thousands of mothers chased their small children. Once caught, they huddled near their mothers, who then herded them toward the flowing water. Mothers with children up to age twelve or before puberty, had them remove their clothing. The chaotic scene—soaping, scrubbing, rinsing of clothes and bodies—bordered on a game for the children, and annoyance for the mothers. However, some families pleasantly accomplished the duties and left to make room for those waiting for a spot. Before leaving the banks, they filled buckets and skins with water.

The tribal leaders met and settled on a system for water usage. One stream, on the outside, serviced the men; the middle one, women; and the last for general use by everyone. The men drank and cleansed their bodies first. Women drank, bathed, washed after their menstrual cycle, and did laundry in the middle. In the third, women washed clothing and cookware, animals drank, children played, and anyone could drink or collect water for cooking.

After much conferring, the seventy tribal leaders agreed to construct a temporary head-height stone wall downstream for privacy. Youngsters past puberty and adults were required to bath in the nude. The elders posted guards at the structure, which stretched across the three streams and into the desert on either side, like a fence. Men used this private area until noon, women afterwards. Hand-picked by the elders, trusted older members of each sex took turns policing this.

Perhaps, if a bird flew low, gliding upstream toward the mountain, it would have heard a repeated, brief explanation given by the multitude of mothers to their curious children; "You, your father and I, plus all of the tribes and foreigners with us, are preparing to meet God. He's coming to that mountain." Perhaps a bird would miss the goals and spiritual side of those washing below. But many birds and similar creatures benefitted from the god currently spoken about by these busy travelers. Recently, in the midst of an Egyptian palace some miles to the west, decisions caused the rerouting and accelerated creation of edible insects: lice, flies, locusts. The birds didn't know whom to thank. They feasted again and again as the months passed. Not since the plague-of-water in Noah's day and the following institution of the rainbow, had a widespread miracle occurred. But once again birds would be the recipients of Adonai's hand in a few short hours. Not food, not this time, but an awesome sight and better than the land-bound humans were limited to—indeed, a bird's eye view of God, in person, looming at the top of Mt. Sinai, the island of stone.

Along each of the banks the travelers had duties and reasons to ready themselves, for today was different; an appointed day which held prominence and had requirements. A vibrancy from another world rippled at this single place on earth. Here, a mystery, beyond belief, and of the greatest kind, hovered, ready to descend on Mount Sinai.

Moses murmured to himself, "That burning bush, so many months ago. God promised me as a sign that I would return and worship at this mountain—this mountain. That palace of grandeur in the capital…who would sit on Pharaoh's empty throne now? The blighted landscape of Egypt. The dead…hundreds of thousands. The disbelieving Hebrews, bloodless doors, and lintels…the Angel of Death stopped at their homes and didn't pass over…every firstborn died. The leftovers of Egyptian military, and their animals, had gone to the bottom of the sea. A trap, God's trap. Marvel after marvel…would men speak of these mighty deeds until the end of time? Now free food—manna—from the sky. Water from rock. What next? He paused in his thinking. This God knows how to kill. I must keep these people safe."

*   *   *

Children questioned their parents about this "meeting" with their God. "Isn't He a mean god? He killed a lot of people—even babies and animals. But He's really smart, right? I'm afraid to meet Him. Do we have to? I'm glad He tricked the Egyptian army, and drowned them. I'll never forget walking through the sea; water stood like beautiful walls—I even saw fish swimming. I had never even seen the sea before until then. He also filled the land with frogs. I liked His idea of the tall tree of fire at night—it's pretty—and protects us too. Some people call it a pillar. What's a pillar?"

Parents had mixed answers and much on their own minds. They had their own questions and concerns about this God and their future.

Chapter 5
Moses and Joshua Walk at Night

Moses and his aide, Joshua, walked through the encampment in the evening. They sought the elders of the tribe of Naphtali to discuss a matter. Twilight settled in. A half-moon rose over the nearby mountains. Stars glittered. They followed the empty boundary of sand dividing the regiments of the twelve tribal camps. The noise of laughter, quiet discussions, stimulating debates, and squabbling siblings filled the air. Mothers sang lullabies to sleepy children.

Moses overheard talk from a nearby campfire—someone spoke his name in conversation. Curious, he slowed his pace. The two men moved through the shadows to just outside the flickering light. Moses winked at Joshua and motioned with a finger to his lips that he didn't want anyone to notice him.

Older men spoke plainly to a compact group of families about Moses, their leader, the servant of the Lord. A man with a long graying beard named Rehum, said confidently to his son, "Abdi, understand, Pharaoh was obsessed with himself and his royal position. Two Hebrew shepherds entering his court intruded upon the Ruler's business. He didn't seek out Aaron and Moses. These unheard of new leaders of the slaves would be a bother to Pharaoh. He wasn't receptive and a confrontation followed. Moses and his older brother Aaron—who did the talking—warned Pharaoh to comply with a request from their god, Adonai, or he'd regret his mocking decision. 'Let My people go to worship, feast and sacrifice to Me in the countryside for a few days. After that, routine work will return to normal.'"

A woman pointed out, "Aaron did the talking to Pharaoh, but his brother spoke the truth from his heart. Adonai spoke to Moses who then repeated the messages and warnings to Aaron."

Rehum said, "Yes, good point. And what did Moses and his brother do to show the Ruler to agree meant the cooperation between the two peoples would remain open?"

Another man, Jamlech, replied, "You know the wooden staff Aaron carries around with him—"

A boy shouted, "His magic staff!"

Jamlech corrected. "That piece of wood isn't magical, it's the rod of God. Adonai uses it for holy purposes. He can use your sandal if He wants. However, each tribal leader's staff is an item of no little honor." Jamlech leaned back and stretched his shoulders; clearly, he considered his next explanation. "What happened? Aaron tossed his staff on the tiled floor and it clanked and rolled a little. But then the wood changed to flesh. A living snake, a fierce cobra, took shape, coiled, and arched defiantly. Everyone except Moses and Aaron stepped back. Safe on his raised throne, the Ruler looked to his court sorcerers, sages, and magicians. He laid open his palm and outstretched fingers—meaning, do something about this. Those finely dressed, well-paid men scratched their beards and heads. After a short time of conferring with each other, they spoke incantations and tossed their wooden staffs to the floor."

A different boy blurted out, "And they all clanked too!" Nods followed. Then the boy sheepishly asked, "What's a clank?" Chuckles came next.

Jamlech's eyes scanned his audience. He said, "Yes, yes, son, but now back to what happened next. The new serpents, all cobras, coiled, faced the challenger, and rose to strike. Pharaoh grinned at the odds. However, due to the frightening untamed power before him, he scrunched back in his throne. Then he smirked at these leaders of the Hebrews, fresh from the fields. His gods outnumbered their one god. Pharaoh waved his hand in a quick shooing motion for Aaron and Moses, these fools, to get out of his palace. But our God had dominion over Pharaoh's sorcerers. Only God can do the impossible; after all He invented it. More correctly, He created the possible and stepping off from there always lies the impossible."

The nighttime audience leaned in and held their breaths, their faces reflecting yellow and orange flames. An older man named Bazlith added in his gravelly voice, dramatically swaying one arm wide from left to right, "God holds the power of life and death. A dead staff became a living being. God is unmatched by any authority. The powers of the otherworld lay for all to see—eight snakes against one. The competition quickly ended … or did it? Was this contest truly a bad plan?"

A voice from the shadows interjected, "I heard Pharaoh had a dozen snakes, not eight."

Unseen in the shadows, Moses shuffled his feet; anticipation written on his features. Several times he eyed Joshua, raised an open hand, lips moved about to interject or object. But, he let those men tell the tale their way.

The fire crackled and sparks flew to the sky. Bazlith said, "One or a hundred, serpents are no match for our God. Listen! What could never occur in nature— wood into snakes—took another turn. An impossible turn! Our snake sprang at its enemies. Adonai crushed the head of the house of the wicked."

Moses elbowed Joshua and grinned.

Bazlith continued, "This tangle of writing serpents captured the court's eyes. With such odds, it seemed a brief battle awaited—and so it did. But in the dramatic struggle, fewer and fewer serpents tussled and twisted before Pharaoh's throne. One by one our snake …" He paused obviously judging that comment. "Yes, *our* snake struck, managing quick, deadly bites. Then after each kill, it opened its jaws wide enough to swallow every lifeless opponent … and yet the conquering snake showed no gain in the belly!"

Listeners gasped. Others laughed. A few sneered in triumph. Someone said, "Superior God, superior snake!" Heads nodded.

A little girl at the campsite passionately questioned, "What happened to Aaron's pet snake?"

Rehum, the man with the long gray beard, answered, "God had Moses, His servant, do something—again in nature which should never take place—because it is dangerous. Moses reached out and grabbed the tail of this mightiest snake. As he did so, the flesh of the reptile returned to solid wood as if nothing had happened."

Some murmured, "Yes, what a handy pet to have." People spoke in hushed voices, "Adonai has no equal. The display showed that only He held the power of life and death. Yet, He's involved in daily, petty human affairs, as well as in immense occurrences."

Abdi, one of the first to speak, said, "Pharaoh's royal court and nearby palace guards stared in disbelief. Most pointed to the empty tile. Jaws dropped. Pharaoh leaned forward, eyes wide. He pointed to our two leaders and shouted, 'Trickery!' Aaron shrugged, 'We can do it again if you wish!' In a slow, sly tone he added, 'Of course your magicians will need to get new sticks.'"

At the fire, people laughed loud, long, and hard. Moses kicked at the sand and tried to stifled a belly laugh. Bazlith waited for the noise to quiet. In a serious tone he said, "Indeed those sorcerers also accessed the power of their lesser gods, when the plagues started. For a time, they duplicated Adonai's choices of destruction: the water to blood, multiplying frogs throughout the land. Until dust turned to lice, they couldn't copy Him—not to make a lifeless substance into a living horde. These sorcerers could not reverse or end the plagues. Hah, they could only copy, which made life in the palace worse. Only when Adonai caused that blanketing swarm of lice did those men grudgingly tell Pharaoh this powerful act pointed to a God beyond Egypt's many gods. Indeed, after the early plagues, Adonai placed boundaries to limit the destruction and keep us—His people—noticeably free and healthy. After such a fact, my, how dearly those learned, magician must've wished they could secretly get away from their stubborn Ruler and join us."

Moses' eyes shone with tears. He wiped at them and nudged Joshua to go on. They walked in silence, clearly deep in thought.

Chapter 6
Walking On

The two soon passed by the tribe of Asher's encampment. Again, in time, Moses heard his name spoken in a story. Joshua stopped. Using a slight pushing gesture, Moses motioned to move closer to view the unseen spokesman. Moses held out a hand and gestured. Joshua understood and grinned. The two remained in hearing distance within the nearest shadows.

A loud man stood by this campfire. He held a long, thin palm branch which dragged on the ground when he walked around their fire. "Like a storm approaching, Pharaoh faced his adversary. The two brothers never feared the Ruler of that land. And the Ruler never acted sensibly long enough to submit to our God and let things be."

Anyone peering at Moses in the flickering light would have seen he liked this man.

"After the swarm of lice covered every man and beast, the magicians with their secret arts had something important to tell Pharaoh. They concluded a more powerful god made the rules. Only His 'finger' moved to set forth these horrible events—merely His finger." The man stopped and looked down at a wide-eyed boy gazing up at him. "This vital news spread. Pharaoh, a fool, tried to take a swing at a much larger, stout opponent. He lost every time." The man pointed his stick at the boy. "News, rumors, gossip and educated guesses by worried court servants, staff and military guards exited the palace. Pharaoh, who a god to the Egyptians...well, you might say he stepped both feet into a heap of warm camel dung."

Chuckles wafted, joining the flying sparks into the dark sky.

In the crowd, a man named Eber said, "It'd be hard to exaggerate that man's stubborn folly. He led the nation into ruin with each rotten decision." He pointed at the man dragging the stick. "Pharaoh wouldn't submit to whatever signs and wonders Adonai did. Nature bows to God's will as a mere servant, for He is almighty. However, Pharaoh convinced himself that our Moses functioned as a superior magician and no more, so the whole country, step by step, needlessly suffered. Apparently, a king or god can act stupidly, just like one of us. As the mighty plagues added up, Pharaoh's sorcerers were ashamed to be in the same room as Moses and Aaron." For a time, Egyptian sorcerers could copy, but couldn't stop or reverse the plagues.

People smiled. A few children cocked their heads and questioned, "Stupid?" Parents answered, "Apparently so. Now hush."

Eber started up again. "None of the royal staff or the Ruler knew how long this destruction would continue. I don't think our servant of Adonai knew either. However, the whole population, including the thousands of people passing through the land on business or as emigrants, saw more trouble ahead. Tension filled the land.

Imagine what the palace staff told their spouses after work, "Our Pharaoh is acting absurd. We're scared. Wisdom has left him. Not a god, a fool!" Even captives from other lands managed to disappear. Ambassadors left in the night. Many wanted to leave—and leave quickly. As you know, thousands did join us in secret. We absorbed them into our community. They proclaimed, "'I will revere this god of yours!'"

A man said, "And we welcomed them all, each who defected. Smart choice. Though slaves, we were—are—favored by a mighty God. We are redeemed only because of His mercy and intervention. Without the sacrifice on the last night, there would've been no Exodus."

Eber spread his arms wide, stick in hand. He made a fine sight in the firelight. "As destruction followed destruction, one by one the royal officials didn't show up for work. Soldiers deserted. They and many of the other people I mentioned quit Egypt or sought out us Hebrews. Those on the run asked for refuge, begging to live in safety. They wanted to learn of our powerful god. Though Pharaoh picked a fight, this adversary ravaged his empire and in the end killed his firstborn son and then him last of all!"

Moses' grin grew into a broad, lasting smile. He gestured with his staff for Joshua to follow. The two walked away with minds deep in thought, good thoughts. Moses recalled how after each plague he sought solitude with the Lord. He'd ask for the plague to stop—to satisfy Pharaoh. His relationship would recharge, refresh, and strengthen. A pleasant joy and peacefulness covered him like a needed warm blanket. He looked forward to such times.

Joshua overheard Moses quietly talking to himself, "I always wondered what creative miracle, what plague, Adonai would bring next. Not even I knew the extent of His ways and His mercy. I pitied the stubborn fool on the throne made by men's hands."

Standing in Pharaoh's court took a disciplined relationship with Adonai. Standing in Pharaoh's presence wasn't something he wished to do. Moses stepped into the enemy's camp, as a target. Stepping back outside of the palace returned sunshine and freedom to him.

Chapter 7
Moses Goes Up the Mountain

At that time, this area of planet Earth consumed Adonai's interests, and angels went on errands no one knew about. The plan? God wanted men to hear His voice, His heart.

Four days earlier God had privately communicated to Moses a list of desires for this people. He called Moses to join Him by hiking up Mount Sinai.

Now he climbed the small, solitary mountain in the desert, one in whose shadow he had shepherded a flock a lifetime ago. He passed by the Burning Bush, now just another piece of foliage, not one twig singed. God had thoroughly explained the meaning of His desire to be God to the Hebrews as a husband is to his wife. Such righteous ideas ministered to Moses' heart. Glory wafted over his heart as he heard the words of God spoken to him—only him. He understood the Creator better. They both cared for the multitude below. Yes, Adonai had done miraculous deeds on their behalf in their House of Bondage. But, what made His heart tick besides ability to destroy and punish evil was a heart beating for a people who righteously sought Him.

Moses came down from Mount Sinai and repeated the conversation to the tribal elders. These 70 influential men agreed that God's good plans required their obedience. Then these elders left the confidential meeting and set about repeating what Moses taught them to their own tribes. The next day the population of Hebrews, and minor population of non-Hebrews, agreed to Adonai's desires and His commandments.

Those of the exodus had sworn an oath of promised living to their Deliverer. Adonai told Moses to make the people prepare for His appearing in three days. They were to stay pure. To ready themselves for this momentous day, they bathed, washed their clothes, and had foregone marital sexual relations for three days. The Hebrews prepared their hearts with wholesome fear and thanks for Him who would come to nearby Mount Sinai.

God had laws which Moses communicated. These were not merely commandments, but statements of facts. Adonai knew that the Hebrews must first accept His sovereignty; only then would they agree to His laws. Requirements weren't new to these people, for they remembered their former task masters. They knew those faces too well. But the face of this heavenly Master they could not imagine.

Confiding in Moses, Adonai explained that He wanted to break the silence of Mankind's wondering of who and what He, the Creator, was like. He would speak in His own voice from the mountaintop the multitude would listen. What did the Creator want of them?

Chapter 8
Pentecost: GOD Speaks

The fiftieth day since the Passover Seder—the last dinner the Hebrews ate in their Egyptian homes, God gave the Law (Torah). On this day the people rose in the morning, gathered manna as usual. Unknown numbers contemplated what they had put in their mouths, this otherworldly tasty food. When breakfast and clean-up chores ended, the ground trembled.

Then God stepped on the mountain in a dense cloud.

A nightmarish crescendo of natural and supernatural elements slowly covered Sinai's heights. In the midst of this growing holy tempest, the Hebrews surrounded Mount Sinai, which raged with thunder, lightning flashes, clouds of thick darkness, strong winds, and quaking. Smoke rose in a furious pillar high into the heavens. Adonai descended upon the mountain in fire. Visibly, by fresh and intense fire, the Creator moved from His home in the heavens and settled on the mountain top. The dazzling flames shone hues of which no one had seen before: beautiful, unearthly, and delightful. No one, not even Moses knew how long this triumphal entry would last.

Everyone had witnessed thunder and lightning storms moving in the sky and passing across the landscape. However, what the Hebrews now beheld an unmistakably an isolated stationary storm. Some mused, "It's not drifting."

The concentration of this powerful display on Mount Sinai made everyone feel small and cautious. They did not feel wanted, they felt caught, and many backed away. If anyone spoke, they had little to say. Awe was defined that day.

In addition to these sights, out of the sky came a trumpeting ram's horn shofar to further catch everyone's attention. The fanfare heralded the arrival of the Almighty. All the people were to draw close to the mountain. However, the sound increased louder than one could have imagined. Children stuck fingers in their ears during the long blast; some cried. Fearing for their lives, the people cringed to think of such a powerful God calling them "special" and "His treasure" and "His Firstborn." They knew what He did to those He called "enemies." However, in His benevolence and limitless power He'd also caused certain alienation in His chosen people. They had on their minds the recent destruction of Pharaoh and the Egyptians. Adonai was still a stranger.

While the blast of the horn permeated the surrounding area, Moses cupped his hands around his mouth and yelled toward the Mount. Out of all the noise, God heard this one, particular voice and the loud horn ceased abruptly on a high note. Moses shouted his praise and tried his best to magnify God's glory.

Meanwhile, also on the desert floor, a mix of personalities strained with curiosity—tempted to hike and see inside that smoking blaze above them. Sneaky scoundrels, who lacked sense and had no fear of God, huddled to discuss where to start upward. These show-off adventurers sought praise from the squeamish and compliant crowd upon their return. Yet, as a prank and a dare, groups of teenagers discussed plans to rush through the crowded perimeter. Some of the men of rank thought they deserved to see His face and be recognized and accepted for their tribal leadership responsibilities. Certain men simply enjoyed the ferocity of a terrifying storm and wanted to move closer into the danger. Other credible types honestly wondered what such a God looked like? They considered getting close enough to gaze at this marvel Maker—a glimpse of where this glory emanates. Ecstatic others wanted to more tangibly thank and praise the God who had done so much on their behalf. Like a moth fascinated by the devouring flame, these worshipping souls begged in vain, for personal relationship. They were ready to give their lives to achieve such a goal, the true essence of intense holiness.

Knowing their thoughts and motivations, God gave a severe warning to Moses. "Whoever crosses the boundary line you've marked at the base of the mountain and touches or travels up the slopes shall be put to death!" So, Moses made this announcement and the admonishment spread. He also set armed guards around the perimeter.

Pharaoh had struck out at Moses and Aaron while in his elegant royal palace and power, "Who is Adonai, that I should obey Him?" Early on at that first meeting of confrontation, all gods existed in designated celestial positions. Due to human stylization and mythology, man and priest perfected each one represented. But a One God and Only God required a wide use of vocabulary in order to be described. From then on, no one could fully portray God. Adonai easily proved His superiority by the experiment with the snakes. Now, by means of the horrendous activity on the mountain, His superiority and eternality laid claim to mankind yet again in a broad sense. But within the hidden heart of hearts of certain Hebrews and non-Hebrews, they protected their own free will. They reserved personal decision making with a "We'll see about this god" attitude.

Chapter 9

Ten

The crowd's bustling excitement stopped with the first syllable of God's audible message. For miles around the booming voice flattened the air waves. Animals perked up their ears and stood still; no creature made a sound. Stillness swept over the scenery. Everything stopped. Babies quieted. No one thought about food, water, or their bladders. All eyes were on the mountain. Ears grew to take in the words made of spirit and life. Moses wasn't the only person who thought the sea didn't roll or the entire vast universe went silent and mute, and no angel flew. Oddly, the voice and words appeared to some like burning torches descending like sparks away from the mountaintop and beyond the desert.

An understandable voice overwhelmed the entire region. "One. I am the Lord your God Who brought you out of the land of Egypt, out of the house of bondage.

"Two. You shall have no other gods before Me. You shall not make for yourself a carved image—any likeness of anything that is in heaven above, or that is in the earth beneath, or that is in the water under the earth, you shall not bow down to them or serve them. For I, the Lord your God, am a jealous, an impassioned God, visiting the iniquity of the fathers upon the children to the third and fourth generations of those who reject and hate Me, but showing kindness and mercy to the thousandth generation of those who love Me and keep My commandments.

"Three. You shall not swear falsely by the name of the Lord your God; for the Lord will not hold him guiltless or clear one who swears falsely or takes My name in vain.

"Four. Remember the Sabbath Day, to keep it holy. Six days you shall labor and do all your work, but the seventh day is the Sabbath of the Lord your God. In it you shall do no work: not you, not your son or daughter, nor your male or female servant, nor your cattle, nor your stranger who is within your gates or settlements. For in six days the Lord made the heavens and the earth, the sea, and all that is in them, and rested the seventh day. Therefore, the Lord blessed the Sabbath day and made it holy. Dwell on me.

"Five. Honor your father and your mother, that your days may be long upon the land which the Lord your God is giving you.

"Six. You shall not murder.

"Seven. You shall not commit adultery.

"Eight. You shall not steal.

"Nine. You shall not bear false witness against your neighbor.

"Ten. You shall not covet your neighbor's house; you shall not covet your neighbor's wife; his man servant, his maid servant, his ox, his donkey, nor anything that is your neighbor's."

Thus, the ten words or ten utterances stopped. These words from God's heart and mind rolled over the immense crowd. They sank in. Fertile soil of the heart received seeds of learning. Yet, hard or shallow soil didn't get it—they were they, and He *enough*. Some decided they could figure life out on their own, one day at a time. The freedom from slavery had awakened a certain unknown freedom, for good and not good.

Each person sensed a nudge or an indictment as the awareness of God revealed His ideas and stern expectations and felt vulnerable, exposed. Minds mystically connected to another Being's say-so. No one stood protected. This education served students on a first day of class that would never end. Some loved the wisdom, more grumbled, or even hated the restrictions, and a few felt precious, as if folded into God's heart like a beloved pet, held close and cherished.

How much time it took for Him to deliver His message couldn't be measured. When Adonai finished His list, the majority of activity on the mountain disappeared. The people recoiled in fear—because they were unworthy of such a relationship. They scurried away from Sinai's doorstep. As they did, a rumor spread through the congregation that anyone who had approached with any ailments, now left the mountain's base totally cured. Soon they discovered that any sick or diseased livestock enjoyed vigorous health. No one knew that in the years ahead sickness would not encamp with their moving multitude. Neither did they suspect the odd future in which their clothing, sandals and accessories would not show wear and need replacing.

Word reached Moses from the tribal leaders who spoke for the fearful multitude. They pleaded, "You must talk with God, you be the only one and tell us His doings, but we must not, we cannot, do this sort of meeting again, we are awed and… overwhelmed, terrorized by His presence! Do this for us."

This rejection caused Moses to wonder how many thieves had listened? How many adulterers; parent haters; plotting murderers; veteran liars; and those absorbed in jealousy and unhealthy cravings? *But*, he thought, *such doings, make us human. What number were saying No! in their hearts while listening?*

Moses recalled that since the manna started to fall, more than one scoundrel tried selling the free God-given food. Not only selling, but promising that theirs would last longer than the one-day limitation; because stored overnight, manna consistently spoiled, bred worms and stank. Moses hadn't known that during the mass audience around the Mountain, a few people were busy elsewhere. Though the voice of God filled their ears, thieves rummaged through vacated tents, huts and various shelters taking what they pleased. Also, scampering and laughing, infatuated young lovers, and lustful adulterers furthered their secret affairs taking advantage of the deserted camp.

The meeting with Adonai ended; He hadn't held back. The whole mountain roared during the violent earthquake. But now, the Hebrews trembled in emotional aftershocks. In the end, the majority of Hebrews feared this god and wanted to keep Him at a distance. They wanted Moses, who had lost such fear, to go, listen and report back the messages of this god. Moses failed to convince the congregation that

Adonai did fearful acts to convince them not to disobey and sin. In his heart Moses moaned, *Don't run my people. Don't fear, our God. Rest in His care.*

But the leaders told Adonai's servant, "We are your pupils, Moses, and from your waters we will drink."

He slumped upon hearing this. Moses knew he had the most difficult, stressful, and unimaginable job in the world. Moses, the name on every tongue. On one hand, over a million souls pushed him into God's private camp, away from them. On the other hand … well, who could explain God? Yet, between the two, Moses knew what tiny meant—a messenger. His job to do things on God's behalf took a more important stature and with it came isolation. He would go up the mountain a total of eleven times and then deliver truths to the elders. Only Joshua, Aaron and Miriam (Moses' older sister) could see the stress this tough job bore. The young aide said little. His role defined the need for a someone—perhaps more like a wife—to be there when Moses simply had to express himself and didn't want any advice or anything other than consolation or unspoken companionship. Joshua's servant heart served Moses well. To confidently share one's burden requires an honorable person, no matter what age.

After he accepted the elders' request, prayers of thanksgiving rippled through the crowd. However undone, Moses once again stepped into his burdensome role. He broke down, crying for his calling, his role to shepherd so many who'd witnessed so much and whose needs were so great. The riptide of grumpy rebellion sucked at too many souls. So, Moses prayed for their loyalty to increase.

"Do not fear." Moses told them. He assured them that God didn't want to harm the listeners. Rather, God had made them participants in these monumental miracles in order to elevate them in His awesomeness. Now that they'd seen His greatness, they would resist the normal human temptation to sin. Only God can demand that people sanctify their hearts and attitudes to the point where they purge themselves of such natural tendencies.

Chapter 10
Seventy-Five Up the Mountain

(Exodus 24:9)

In the early morning the mountain made no sound. Quiet and immense. God peered down.

However, He wanted a bonus meeting with the leaders below. They had to come to Him. This exclusive invitation attracted the multitude's attention. Yet, certain requirements for clearance insured the chosen men's safety. In fact, where this mountain met the ground and the mountain's roots disappeared into the soil, there, a simple manmade boundary marked safety or death. A tiny number from this multitude, seventy-five, could pass into this frightening uphill sanctuary—crossing the perimeter line marked in the dirt the day before. This consecrated path, they were to climb, meant private property in the most extreme terms. An emphatic warning of a quick death accompanied by specific instructions scared the hearts of this recently formed mobile nation.

Before the chosen men left the flat desert, each participated in a final ritual which qualified them to pursue their, unseen, host. Their Deliverer invited the 75 and assured His hospitality, yet He wasn't one to deliberately disappoint.

As directed by Adonai to Moses, young men guided a dozen oxen, chosen for sacrifice, to the base of the mountain. Moses, with the help of these younger men, set up a stone slab as an altar. Moses' sun burnt brown skin reminded them of tough lizard hide. They used large stones kept as they found them, no chiseling or shaping. The twelve tribal crews hefted flat, rectangular rocks in a row six on each side of a fresh altar. These rested on boulders below waist height; each slab wide enough to strap down an ox.

After prayers and the sacrifice, men carefully collected the gallons of ox blood. As burnt offerings and peace offerings were performed, bowls of the warm blood passed to Moses, which he sprinkled on the altar and then sprinkled on the seventy-five leaders chosen to venture up the mountain. As the quantities of ox blood lasted, Moses sprinkled the steady lines of the quiet, worshipful tribes who obediently passed by the altars. After that the masses further encircled the small mountain before them.

At the end of this lengthy ceremony, the seventy-five men crossed the scratched line and departed. They said sincere, yet worrisome Shaloms to wives and children. As the sandaled feet wound around the barren terrain, the men thought of the implications of the blood covenant they just committed to. The population had accepted the terms unanimously. Yet, who on earth, who in all history, knew enough about the One who sought them out, to call Him God?

Bringing up the rear, Moses approached the line in the sand. Before he crossed, he turned and saw a woman holding a female baby. The baby's beautiful face caused

34

him to stop, though he didn't know why. Their eyes met, hers fixed on his face. Then an innocent smile spread her tiny lips. As he stared, her face brightened. The baby's smile stretched wide, as did her acceptance of Moses. He felt laid bare and almost faltered in his next step. He grinned at the child and her young mother and proceeded.

Seventy-five men snaked their way from the desert floor toward the troubled sky. Silence prevailed on the mountainous trail. As the trek ascended, refreshing, cooler air met the men. This single file of long-bearded, middle-aged and older men wore robes, turbans, sandals and held wooden staffs. Before this day, only two of the men had ventured to this lofty unknown peak. On that first hike, the broad shouldered, white wavy-haired, Moses spoke little to Joshua.

The seventy tribal elders, Moses the leader, and Joshua, plus the leader's older brother Aaron and two of his sons—a small team of future priests, kept all thoughts to themselves. While their emotions smiled at the newness of scenery, contemplation of the godly destination mingled with fresh passions. Yet, with every step this task led them toward possible danger.

Few bushes, trees or animals added to the stone mountain. No comfort. None of the men had ever hiked up a mountain before. Flat farmlands of Egypt were all they'd known. The geography of their people for generations hadn't changed. Here the climbers dodged cracks and stone rubble wondering what awaited them. Each man peered into dark crevasses. Their searching eyes saw nothing but overbearing, unfriendly rock.

Gaining elevation presented changing panoramic views. Altitude affected each man the same; the same as all men down through history who have ever sensed what expanse means—comparable to viewing the seemingly endless ocean for the first time. The mountain's overwhelming view of unknown earthly distance made the men feel an independence achieved by their own strong legs—different than a voyage on an ocean, achieved by manmade wooden vessels with wind filling the sails.

Fellow mountains, reddish rock outcroppings, and mountain ranges stretched through the vast arid distance. After a certain height, the people in their huge fan-shaped encampment appeared to the men as mere ants, and camels as grasshoppers. The twelve camps showed clear rectangular divisions. Each tribe had their insignia illustrated on colorful flags or carved standards on poles: Reuben, Simeon, Levi, Judah, Dan, Naphtali, Gad, Asher, Issachar, Zebulun, Joseph, Benjamin and Joseph's sons, Manasseh, Ephraim. Next to them a separate and less compact camp housed some of those who, though not of Hebrew blood, joined their departure from Egypt. When the Hebrews fled the land of Egypt, escaping lives of slavery, a number of smart, awestruck Egyptians and God-fearing foreigners living or doing commerce in Egypt joined the spontaneous Exodus. Only fools stayed in that country. They'd seen vast destruction. Many chose to follow the God of amazing success—it just made sense. But follow to where, they didn't know.

The hikers never imagined seeing such a sight. Thrill filled each one, yet intense shockwaves of fright occasionally pushed through the captivating vistas. Most thought, God, our Maker, our powerful Deliverer, wants to see me?

Chapter 11
Seventy-Five Meet God

The servant of Adonai led the seventy-four men around a minor rise, and then he stopped. Brightness not far ahead made him place a hand to shade his eyes. Moses lifted his fist high while grasping his staff. The men understood. Moses turned back to look at the tight group of men behind him. He wanted to say the right words. But, what were those right words? He knew God better than any of them and more than any man alive. How do you introduce men to God, especially when He's done miracles on your behalf?

He pondered much in the next moments. His legs seemed heavy, like solid gold, but useless. Moses studied the sky and the height of the bright sun moving across the heavens. A different kind of brilliance radiated in front of him. He stood in that pose, arm rigid, a bold, yet hesitant man.

Moses trusted God's benevolence, and so said nothing. His legs returned to movable flesh. Waving his arm, he motioned them to proceed. As each man turned that corner they too shaded their eyes.

In a saddle of the mountain, unseen from the desert floor, a flat area pleased the men. They smiled, seeing a small meadow of vibrant grass and a spring-fed stream with green moss at the banks. Tiny purple and lavender flowers lay embedded in the soft compact growth. They grinned at the welcome sight and considered the vast unsown desert below.

At the end of the lush meadow, the bright glow remained as a stationary cloud. Men stared and yet tried not to stare. All moved closer as those in the back nudged those in front. Eyes soon adjusted to the otherworldly light. Golden sparks glittered. Fine streaks of shining silver swirled in pleasant orbits. White, whiter than imaginable, made up the mass of this soft light.

Then from within the light, a Voice addressed the stupefied congregation. "Do not be afraid. Have no fear. You are welcome."

Without a signal, each man knelt and then lay prostrate. Eyes squeezed closed. No one knew how much time passed. But next, they found themselves sitting or standing facing the engaging light. Aromas of food and fragrances wafted in the air and found welcoming noses. All felt expected and grinned at the leisure banquet before them.

Later, during the hike down, each man said that when God spoke, it seemed as if they were the only one present. They liked this. "He made me feel like I'm His favorite!" Whether thought or spoken, each agreed.

The Voice explained that He provided for all of the men to eat and drink their fill. They were His guests. No one remained nervous or awkward after that compliment. Moses had a smile on his face that wouldn't budge. On the grass, giddy men settled in. A comfortable breeze kept the meadow delightful.

In a mystic awareness, they sensed that they'd returned home, to a special home, but couldn't remember anything about it.

When God spoke, streaking balls of fire, some likened to flaming torches, flew out of the cloud and over the heads of the 75 men and far above the encampment below. Some of these fire-like birds seemed to soar, sent in all directions on life-giving errands.

On the grass the men found a collection befitting a king: golden bowls, silver decanters with matching cups, and large metallic platters of a beautiful color no one had seen before. Each of the utensils held intricate designs which no man could recognize.

The Voice explained that all of the feast items included only the produce from the land He would lead them to, a Promised Land. The men enjoyed wheat bread, barley cakes, grapes, figs, pomegranates, olives, olive oil and dates. They drank wine, all sampled and grinned. Words could not properly describe the drink and so none tried after beginning broken sentences. Men did manage, "What a wonderfully sweet spring." Time passed like days of loveliness.

God said, "The Promised Land is good in that its climate is pleasant, the country is filled with desirable features, and it is spacious with adequate landscape for living. A land with such advantages will produce healthy livestock that will give abundant milk, and fruits that will be rich and sweet as honey."

Later, on the hike down, each man remember God's instructions. What each man told the others held to the core of the instructions, but with an added unique facet. No words conflicted with another's, only a broader understanding of the teachings.

No one asked God questions. A peace consumed their analytical drives. The sunny day on a mountain, in a luxurious stretch of land, made them feel like they were in a pocket of heavenly wonder. They ate the best food one could hope for, and safety comforted them like a blanket. No one wanted for more. They described their god as one of plenty, not of need and starvation. Their faces exuded a proud countenance anyone would delight to see and want to possess.

At times, during that afternoon, still stranger things happened. Certain men broke into laughter for no reason; joy had overtaken them. Their host gifted them with this uplifting silliness. Other men cried healthy tears of warm comfort as if embracing someone they dearly loved. A few men, who had drunk only a little wine, appeared to wobble when they walked and shone fun and happy expressions. Each man who saw another which had succumbed to this influence had a lovely envy. Some wondered if this behavior, "Is this due to something in the heavenly food?" Some said it felt like a pleasant wave overcoming them. No criticism, just rest in the heart. Men lay on their backs and closed their eyes or stared into the sky, thinking how blessed they were.

Hours later, on the hike down, the men behaved jovial and solemn—their souls—emotional see-saws. They discussed how best to describe Him to the curious waiting below. Strangely, they agreed upon very little. They spoke of a sky blue, sapphire-colored, raised stone platform or dais, of grand design. On this airy flat surface, they saw two feet—on that they all agreed. At that point, their minds went blank. No description of Him came to their imaginations. And they were content about this. Soon they realized that this was for the best and better to remain a mystery. They also exuberantly agreed, "We had an excellent time!"

Toward the end of the meal and visiting, the Voice said, "Moses, come further up the mountain—alone." In an unspoken communication, Moses knew that Joshua would trail behind him and be welcomed.

Seventy-five went and seventy-three returned.

Chapter 12
Trouble

No one knew Moses wouldn't return to the encampment for over a month—46 days. So many days passed that unity among the Hebrews fell apart on the desert floor. During his days with God, specific plans and means expanded and filled Moses' memory and imagination. He viewed the beauty and marvels God intended for a new vein of worship and fellowship for humans with their Creator. To call it a religion only cheapened the immense, full-scale, heart-driven love Adonai held in His open hand.

Moses busily wrote the terms of the Covenant on parchment—a record for the current and future generations. Also, the working out of living life in its varied ways amongst a large community and soon, a country of their own—not too many days to the east. Unique, new information lay etched: fantastic survival skills for civilization, written by the One who knew man best.

In those days, if indeed they could be titled days and nights, the two—one Creator, one creature—mingled in ways heretofore unknown in such intimacy and details. In this fellowship with the Creator, neither Moses nor Joshua, (slightly below in a nook) required sleep, food or drink. The Presence of Adonai fed them fully.

Weeks passed like this. But then, an angel flew in, landed, and interrupted the private meeting. He bore dramatic news. The creature's majesty dimmed with the heart-wrenching observations. Apparently, much of Adonai's stabilizing efforts to create a nation on foot, had failed. God turned and saw this rebellious behavior below. After much consideration, He desired to destroy the twelve tribes. But, Moses consoled Adonai and mercy prevailed. God decided Moses must hurry down to the encampment and regain control—then proper judgment would follow.

Before his departure, with hope in His heart, He gave Moses two rectangular objects. In the man's muscular arms, he clutched two signs made of thin, stout stone. On the four surfaces, front and back, the finger of God had engraved the Ten Commandments. He used small letters, creating room for hundreds of letters. These two durable documents would be preserved as the start of Adonai's desire to "Live among the people of Israel and be their God." He wanted to begin now. However His people already rejected Him and replaced their Deliverer?

With God's lethal words filling his mind, and the furious angel at Moses' heels, he sprinted down the mountain. He heard Adonai grumble, "My stiff-necked people."

When Moses came upon Joshua he sped up. Joshua made a gesture to relieve his master of the cumbersome cargo. But one sharp expression and a downward shake of his wooly head registered a definite No.

During the days and weeks of their leader's absence, the Hebrews felt increasingly alone in the desert—leaderless and godless. The multitude's unanimous and quick acceptance of the Covenant proved worthy of suspicion. Too true of many of the Exodus, their hearts leaned one way and their mouths another. The disappearance of their mighty leader up the storming mountain whittled away at what trust had recently sprouted; their pledge faded. They needed a tangible presence to take Moses' place.

The idea settled in that Moses was gone on another adventure or even dead. Did the ominous mountain top of Sinai swallow him up? Worry merged with insecurity and spawned bitterness. These emotions produced a strong three-banded cord. Headstrong men, spat and voiced, "Moses left us here weeks ago. Not even his servant has traveled down once for provisions—no food, no water. No one can live that long. Neither is leading now. How will we survive? Where do we go?" This aroused impatience, the temptation to panic, and yet, the desire to somehow reconnect and get divine attention.

These discussions made sense. All knew that a powerful god ruled through Moses. Now their go-between, their mediator, appeared lost. They needed a tangible replacement to provide them comfort, brought on by their lack of control, lack of comprehension, and lack of some "thing" representing an actual miraculous Deliverer.

Within the multitude, a divide happened. Factions formed.

Such disorientation confused the evidence of Adonai's amazing acts. Impatience ate away at faith, the body consumed, until only bones remained. Yet the skeleton lay sturdy, and so a carry-over of pagan Egypt layed upon their Deliverer's altar. This pained and angered God after everything He'd done and still planned to do on their behalf. The spiritual pollution of Egypt had seeped out and found fertile soil. A spiritual downfall manifested in the worst possible way—an idol.

An age-old uncertainty re-emerged, due to unbelief borne by the forked-tongued serpent's venomous words to the first two humans. Now, the lie not to trust Adonai spread, gaining speed. The escaped slaves needed something else to prefer, to claim an allegiance to, and acknowledge as superior. A minority of Hebrews chose the popular and deeply loved cow-headed goddess, Hathor. She acted as the Mother of mothers, pharaoh's mother, goddess of female fertility, love, and laughter. More Egyptian children were named after Hathor than any other so-called god or goddess; the mother and the daughter of the Egypt's sun god Ra.

It all started when one man mentioned to another man, and he to another, that a "golden calf" would solve their problem. "That's a god we could worship—will worship!" Certain Hebrews celebrated the wisdom to re-label the statue "Adonai." And to work they went on a solid gold cast idol.

3,000 core worshippers were put to the sword for this sin.

They remained camped in the region of Mt. Sinai for 11 months.

Born in controversy for long years Moses' relationship to God rooted deep.

*　　*　　*

The giving of the Ten Commandments and other decrees marked the first Pentecost—fifty days from the commemorative "passing over" by the Angel of Death in Egypt and start of the Exodus. Once settled in the Promised Land, the Hebrews remembered the Laws for life and annually made sacrificial offerings to Adonai from the produce of the land. After the festive yet somber Passover Seders, Hebrews looked toward the honoring of God during the early harvest and need to live by God-given laws.

Aside from Creation, and later, the Plagues, the miraculous activity at Mount Sinai became the pivot point as the supernatural establishment of a nation. The accounts accented the following centuries as the paramount proof of One, and only One God. No other gods, though worshipped, ever existed. The revelation at Mt. Sinai caused the people to believe in Moses and in later prophets as well, for they would see and hear that God speaks to man. Every member of the new nation experienced prophecy during that unmatched and unprecedented event. They would have trouble doubting that prophecy is a reality and not formulated speech crafted by man.

The final aggressive act, the ambush, drowned the remaining army of the land where the enduring pyramids stood disinterested.

Boasting filled the revelry of Adonai's total success over many Egyptian gods. He shamed the slaves' masters' beliefs into folly. Protection by Egypt's gods failed miserably. Pharaoh's stubbornness drove the country into ruin. Such a powerful victory caused endless jesting, jokes, and parodies among the freed Hebrews. They jested, "Have you heard the latest? The one about Pharaoh…?" Or, "What did Moses say to Pharaoh after…?" When wine flowed, the praise and allegiance rose even more so to God as their surprising champion. The Hebrews' unseen, benevolent, all powerful God was the source of children playing in mock battles of Moses and Aaron fighting against Egypt's manmade gods. Makeshift idols met destruction by wooden swords, fire and sling-shot. Adonai always won.

Epilogue

Beyond the shadow of Mt. Sinai, the light of God dimmed. Amongst the huge populace of the homeless Hebrews, restlessness brewed. In the mix of disruptions, even Moses was to fail. Instead of peaceful tranquility, the sons of the House of Jacob rested with ragged hope. In the mix, they even pricked the heart God, and He bled. His patience suffered tests multiple times. Love and kindness chewed away and found hard bone. The muscle built up by the benevolence of Abraham's God, lessened. A series of squabbles swirled through each generation. The last thought on God's mind—he never expected—to destroy the Chosen.

Unlimited mercy, unlimited grace, found rock hard hearts. The following centuries marked families at war with each other, and wars that never were meant to come from other nations. Failure nestled into the foundation of the Chosen People. A perfect civilization wasn't expected; but one that turned its back, discarding their Maker, made horrible history.

A fresh and faithful husband, brimming with hope, repeatedly found an adulteress in His bed. Ultimatums, threats, gifts, and great loss, cost her dearly, but she continued. Highlights of unification did occur. Reunions made for wonderful times. Yet, even the wisest man who ever walked the earth, Solomon, left God in loneliness, while he housed and slept with 1,000 women instead. Their various gods failed him, and he failed the one God of his fathers.

Prophets come and go, but false gods prefer to stay. By the end of the first devastation, one astonished Jewish Temple crashed down. Sacredness diminished to a trickle. The twelve tribes became aggressive and divided the Promised Land into two lands. The family of Hebrews warred against each other for centuries. A series of good and bad kings ruled. A nightmare had happened. God used the vicious Assyrians and Babylonians as His tools of judgment.

Dispersion from the Promised Land; Exile shamed the Jews. The way back to God, and His many good promises, always remained open—few took it.

The great and wonderful plans of a Heavenly Father were switched to a wrathful, displeased, and vengeful Overseer. There would be a magnificent second Temple lasting for a time, the priesthood corrupt, God stepped aside. Until, He let the Roman Empire, tired of the Jews, destroy it and its sacred beauty.

Certain of the Laws delivered by Moses were meant to remind men to stop thoughts of wrongdoing before carrying out such sins. In time, men interpreted the words of God into intricate, laborious, and distorted products. Volumes grew. Faith mixed-up with ever evolving traditions; belief, devotion and loyalty, suffered.

In the following centuries, Jews migrated around the globe. The land of Israel barely had a descendant of Abraham, Isaac and Jacob, until modern times. The Jews are back. They have a lot of catching-up to do.

END BOOK ONE

Bridge 1
Over the Centuries

Observations of Moses, Pharaoh, Gods and Life in Egypt

Only God can do the impossible; after all He invented it. The Hebrews knew Adonai came from another world and stood as God of their ancestors: Abraham, Isaac and Jacob. Plus, Joseph—second only to Pharaoh in authority. The faith of the ancient Hebrew men intrigued certain descendants. Though slaves, most adopted reverence and honor to Adonai. Other Hebrews, not ignited by tales of their forefathers, let faith fade to a fable and rumor, at best. Still others sought to please the gods of their slave masters, discarding their own people's so-called history.

Centuries passed.

The Egyptian task masters pressed more and more burdens upon the Hebrews. Their suffering fueled many to cry out in prayer to an invisible god. In time, Adonai moved to respond. More powerful meant more dangerous, more creative in strategy. Being a people chosen by the only God made the Hebrews distinct from every other people group or nation. That One God had unthinkable, unbelievable plans of His own. Ten steps to freedom, by plagues. Agony, stupidity, disaster and countless deaths would lie in the aftermath.

Religious Egyptians worshipped a variety of gods and goddesses, whose existence pivoted around Egypt. Of course, compared to Adonai, they were smaller, less powerful and localized. As in every nation, different gods had different purposes—obviously—how else would the world work? Royalty and citizens presumed that as they did required worship and sacrifices, no invading army could win in battle. Though Egypt had lived as a powerful empire, its gods were truly weak compared to the Hebrew's one god. He alone is entitled to the veneration of human beings.

This unusual Hebrew god didn't want representation by an idol, a statue, or carved images of any creatures He'd fashioned. Nor stylized fanciful abominations by the mixture of two animals, or a human and animal combination. By identifying Himself to the Hebrews as "your God," the Almighty announced that He was the Hebrews' own deity.

During some 300 years of Egyptian slavery an ingrown slave mindset entered each new generation. God showed His care for this race of people. He fired up a strategy: supernatural, horrible plagues, this in part, to undo the negative psychological inheritance. Once free of the confined lifestyle in Egypt, the Hebrews knew God sought their allegiance. He enticed them with their very own Promised Land with Him as their Almighty benefactor.

Pharaoh didn't expect that a god had infiltrated his land unnoticed. The Creation Maker, Himself—had arrived. This supernatural force hadn't attacked from the borders seeking to invade. No. That is, unless you consider a lone shepherd wandering in from the desert with his older brother, men of no standing. The god's human mediators, Moses and Aaron, were all wrong—a team of shepherds, not generals of a trained military force at Egypt's borders threatening invasion. The two men explained the requests, and then demands, and then pronounced supernatural attacks.

The Hebrew's god could do and undo Creation. At first, the supernatural workers in wonders of Pharaoh's court, paid wizards, met challenge to challenge. Then they realized the truth of their limitations. Undressed as nakedness does, their court stature diminished to mere employees.

The royal power couldn't comprehend an extremely strong god within his borders who took a forceful grudge on the side of a slave race— Pharaoh's slaves. This ruler had more than one god to call on and together, more fierce—he presumed. That is, until he became so stubborn and felt his constant companion, pride, diminishing. Such embarrassment kept him from admitting defeat after defeat after defeat. In the splitting of the Red Sea (Sea of Reeds in Hebrew), Pharaoh drowned, weighted by his incredible foolish anger and failures. In the overwhelming rushing waves of the Red Sea, royalty could only issue gurgles in his final breathes. The refreshed seabed welcomed another body to its increasing collection. Egypt disappeared as a world power.

These brotherly ambassadors, Moses and Aaron, knew of a god which Pharaoh thought should instead be on his side. Pharaoh himself should have already known of this meddler. He'd gladly add the new god to head up the others he and his population served. "My right, my privilege. The mighty rule the weak. This new god should have approached the royal court and given him the opportunity—through proper emissaries."

Lack of information about this deity infuriated Pharaoh. It was all backwards. He figured this god of the Hebrews should be impressed by what made him ruler of an empire. However, Pharaoh might have believed that his stubbornness to this strange god would eventually be rewarded by this god changing to his side—finally being sensible.

But the Ruler of Egypt would not ask, bow, or seek to please this new god while his own unwise choices continually proved inappropriate. Pharaoh said, "Who is this Adonai, god of the Hebrews...I do not know of him! One all powerful god—none others—ridiculous!" Miracles alone do not transform beliefs; those who refuse to recognize the hand of God will always interpret events to suit their own purposes.

Moses' god represented the twelve tribes and desired worship and sacrifices. This god maneuvered and strategized. The early efforts of Moses requesting to institute a new god's three-day worship festival far out in the countryside failed to get approval from Pharaoh. "The power struggle brought on by an ambassador—this meager representative to a world leader? Truly unheard of!" Pharaoh believed he had more than equal gods who were more dependable. But that pathway led to his death. His humiliation compounded so broadly, he couldn't admit defeat.

Pharaoh probably thought, *If this god had approached me differently, in a way that made more sense, perhaps I'd agree to the special request for worship by my property, the slaves. Slaves do not ask—they do. Slaves deserve no privileges, and if they did, that would be my choice. The god who chose these slaves as his obviously had an off-kilter soft spot in his heart. That failure in divine character used against me could make me, Pharaoh, appear as a stubborn tyrant and as a victim. But I think this god can be broken and give in and give up. Surely his indiscretion could be reversed and exploited to bolster the Egyptian Empire. What fame, pride or glory is there in generations of slaves praying to him instead of the masters of those lesser people? He will give in, and without my begging. He will see that such benevolence to slaves is shameful and not virtuous. Even a man can see that.*

Bridge 2
Jews

Two Pentecosts of the greatest significance occurred centuries apart. The direct descendants of the first Pentecost celebrated the holiday and adjacent Sabbath after settling into the Promised Land. The giving of God's laws and the thanksgiving for a (potential) good harvest entwined through the years. If God had a hobby after Creation, it was the Jews. We might think He could've made a better choice—and such, is a topic of debate.

At Mt. Sinai, the Hebrews' future lay ahead. God desired the very best for His People. Peculiar to us is the idea of an unseen God literally loving and wanting to shepherd two million people. That means many more millions of people throughout the Jews' existence.

After some 1,400 annual Pentecosts, Judaism changed. A new sect, begun by an ex- carpenter, turned the holiday in an unexpected, additional direction. A change anchored the commandments and teachings into necessities with otherworldly personal aid. The Holy Spirit entered humanity to guide followers toward a consistent holy lifestyle. Certain of the Laws implemented on the first Pentecost required such assistance, but not an indwelling, empowering help. We cannot serve God without failure. We are Law breakers and sinners. In our humanness, we strive to please God by obeying His teachings via the prophets, apostles, rabbis, teachers and their writings, but we are born vulnerable, tempted to break laws both small and great.

The two themes of Pentecost met in Jerusalem one spring day. Compared to the first, the second one was miniature in signs, wonders, and audience size. Jesus, the 'prophet like Moses,' himself served only a few brief years. Jesus didn't even live long enough to match Moses' 40 years as a shepherd or then as Adonai's redeemer.

Every day around the world, God is busy. What location you are in, can determine a Holy Spirit encounter of varying impact resulting in a relationship or deeper one with God. This will happen whether in prayer alone or in a group meeting. Will there be a tornado, flames of fire and new languages again? Maybe. The true common denominator is a sincere love for God and for others to know Him too.

Bear in mind, the Early Church was a strictly Jewish production. Years went by before God convinced Peter that a Gentile, such as Cornelius, merited the same interest to God as Peter's own people (Acts 10). Also, that when Acts or the Epistles mention a church, this implies a Messianic Community, lead by Jews and converts. But don't image a small steeple church. No, the meetings took place in people's homes. So, the church in Corinth might've meant twelve home groups.

Bridge 3
Passover to Pentecost

Moses knew God better than any other man in history, except perhaps the first man, called Adam, in his pristine state. That first man lost that kinship and favor. However, Moses' duties made him the most important person, with the most responsibilities on Earth—since Adam. With this came a change in his humanness. God improved Moses' memory, understanding and dignity. Also, he received a unique view into God's heart to represent Him to others.

Therefore, he wrote down much of what God dictated. Yet, his mediator role of overseeing a million Hebrews required an expanded use of his brain and his heart. The detail for any of God's moral, spiritual and legal laws, His many good promises, followed by plans for worship, sacrifices and a priesthood—filled scroll after scroll. The Oral Torah or Oral Law represents those laws, statutes, and legal interpretations that were not recorded in the Five Books of Moses, the "Written Torah," according to rabbinical tradition.

Moses had trouble expressing himself in spoken words, but he could write. The elders soon memorized and or copied these scrolls and taught the tribes. Teachers and students spent intimate days in education. In time, most Jews learned these intricate laws by heart from an early age and could recite them by memory. Yet, Moses could specifically recall and recite his conversations with God. Such private visits placed Moses in an otherworldly existence. His protégé, Joshua, most likely experienced the same miraculous changes during his days waiting for Moses to return.

Over forty-five days had passed since the Hebrews fled the land of Egypt, escaping lives of generational slavery. They'd seen vast destruction by ten unforgettable plagues. The world would never forget their God's pervasive catastrophic choices. Doing as He pleased, God left the condition of a powerful empire in accelerated decay. The horrific last plague left over a million firstborn humans and animals dead in one night—babies to old men. Adonai said that He'd done these acts for His people's benefit. God also recalled promises to His "friend" Abraham from ancient times, and to his son Isaac and grandson Jacob. He planned a means to release the captive descendants and for them to glorify Him.

Before the Exodus, Egypt prospered as a crossroads of power and trade via the Nile River, the Mediterranean Sea, and overland routes of criss-crossing caravans and nomads of the Sinai Peninsula. Thousands of people from other lands, other cultures and religions, emigrated to the prosperous land of the pyramids. Now, these various people were unaware as to how their plans would entwine into an empire set for devastation. Soon, serious decisions lay before them as each day passed and the land grew dim from the stubborn heart of Pharaoh on his stately—yet ultimately, worthless throne. For intense months, those who woke up in Egypt found their lives changed. Hundreds of merchants, ambassadors, high ranking civil servants, superintendents, and royal attachés went about their assigned business while two unobtrusive Hebrew shepherds asked for an audience with the ruler of the land. These two men entered wearing their work clothes—no finery—for they owned no wardrobe.

God put idol worship to shame for the sake of His name. Adonai chose the downtrodden Hebrew slaves as His love object and hoped the Hebrews would become His.

After accepting this new life of total freedom, the seventy tribal elders discussed the permanent destination of where God wanted to lead them.

Organization, logistics and squabbles occupied their days. Men who approached with big questions met responses of open hands and shrugging shoulders. Even Moses only knew so much. Superstitions of the astounding sights and sounds started. Rumors spread.

Moses reflected to himself, "Adonai has sounded forth a trumpet that shall never call retreat!"

Pentecost came next.

Bridge 4

Temple Times

Innumerable streams of pilgrims made their way to Jerusalem from towns and villages all over the Land, in large bands and individually. Many families traveled by foot, with the little children in tow; some rode atop camels and donkeys; some even rode in wagons and chariots. As men, women and children trekked through bountiful golden and green fields of harvest, the entire land teemed with excitement and anticipation as the great throngs of festival worshippers took over every road and path. They crisscrossed the countryside from every direction and approach, converging together as they traveled towards the city of each vicinity's local Assembly Head, who responsibly officiated for the pilgrims.

From there, the entire multitude continued their procession to Jerusalem in a large entourage. As they make their way, they sang out "I rejoiced with those who said to me, 'Let us go to the House of the Lord!' (Psalms 122:1) "And you shall rejoice for all the goodness which the Lord your God has given to you and your household." (Deut. 26:11)

At the head of these grand processions might be an ox with an olive crown on its head or wreath of flowers on its head and neck. Villagers gilded the horns of the beast with gold. Later the sacrificial animal died by the holy hands of the priests at the Temple. People brought baskets of the choicest fruits and vegetables. The rich brought their Firstfruits offerings in baskets of gold, or of silver; the poor brought their offerings in baskets of peeled willow-shoots, or straw. The baskets contained wheat, barley, grapes, pomegranates, olives, and dates, (Deuteronomy 8:8) and loaded onto an ox.

They awoke at dawn, as the first rays of sunlight begin to illuminate the sky, by the overseer who cries out: "Get up, and let us go up to Zion, to the House of the Lord our God!"

Once in Jerusalem, most Jews entered the Temple Mount from the south by walking up the Monumental Steps and by the five Hulda Gates (small entry ways). The experience of bringing the first fruits served to unite the entire nation. All stood together, side by side, rich and poor alike, and participated in this humbling and gratifying experience in the holy courtyards of the Temple.

For Pentecost, worshippers brought two home-baked loaves of bread to the Temple, or they purchased them in Jerusalem just prior to the holiday. Bread and the other sacrifices could also be purchased in the Temple courtyards—but not on a Sabbath. Long lines formed; over a 1,000,000 Jews waited their turn. For each family representative, a priest looked to heaven, spoke a blessing, and waved the loaves before Adonai as a thank offering. The streets held multitudes of men clutching two loaves of the sacred bread, wine, baskets of fruit and a lamb or goat. The lines to the Temple increased by the hour.

A commandment for this day called for the blowing of trumpets: "And on the days of your joy and on your festivals...you shall sound off with trumpets." (Numbers 10:10)

In Jerusalem, Pilgrims carried Firstfruits baskets upon their heads. Those who lived near Jerusalem would bring figs and grapes (because they would not be spoiled on a short journey); those who came from afar would bring dried figs and raisins.

At the conclusion of the Temple ceremonies, the wealthy brought their baskets home with them, and the poor gave theirs to the priests.

Local men brought, or if from a distance, bought, a one-year-old lamb purchased in the city prior to Pentecost, or at the Temple courtyards. A drink offering meant a quart of wine. Also, four pounds of fine flour mixed with olive oil—these are the four pounds of grain, set aside shortly after Passover, seven weeks previous. The Levitical priests would lift these up in dedication to Adonai.

At the Temple courtyards, the giver of the basket said to the priest, "I told God that I came into the land that He swore to our forefathers to give us." (Deuteronomy 26:3). And, "The priest shall take the basket from your hands and set it down in front of the altar of the LORD. You must then make this formal statement to affirm and declare in the presence of God, 'My ancestor Jacob was a wandering Aramean who went to live as a foreigner in Egypt. His family arrived few in number, but they became a great and mighty nation." Deuteronomy 26:4 & 5. Then facing the Temple, the priest waved the basket before the Lord.

By this statement, the bearer affirmed that God had kept His promises to the forefathers, that their children would be brought to the Promised Land. Pilgrims would express their thanks to God—the source of all blessing, a gesture of profound gratitude to the Holy One for all the abundance with which he has blessed His people—material, as well as spiritual.

The priestly tribe of Levites came to Jerusalem from their 48 towns spread over the land. Though only a small number were needed for the daily routine shifts throughout the year, besides the musicians and 300 man choir. Jews gave the sacrificial food to the tens of thousands of Levites flooding the city. Required to attend the holidays, the tribe Levites (men over 30 years of age) were extremely busy serving at the Temple.

Shofar, goblet of wine, pomegranate, fabric covering for loaf of challah.
Illustration courtesy of: Ramelle Richardson ©

BOOK TWO

In this section, jump ahead 1,400 years to the First Century. This period is 2,000 years ago for us. Bear in mind that the annual holidays of Passover, Pentecost, and Tabernacles had already been celebrated over 1,400 times. The telling of this part of ancient history starts when, at age thirty, Jesus, son of Joseph and Mary, starts his ministry to the people of Israel—the descendants—some 70 generations.

Simcha Torah event at a Messianic synagogue. At the end of a one or three year reading cycle of Torah, in some synagogues the scroll might be unrolled for all to hold and see—needing plenty of clean hands. 24"x 148' (max.) apprx. 25 pounds. Certain synagogues never handle the sacred Torah in such a way.

Chronicle One
Life, Death, Life

Chapter 1
Jesus Leaves Nazareth to Meet John

Jesus walked into his family carpentry workshop for the last time, where, he had had taken on the supervision of his brothers, being the oldest and longest apprenticed by their father. He entered the stall built next to his family's house. Not all four of the brothers had continued working in the trade.

One married into a farming family south of Nazareth near Megiddo. Another's father-in-law traded and traveled, occasionally taking the young man with him; they lived to the west in Acco. Years of hard and precise work had made each brother a capable craftsman. After their father's death, Jesus climbed a step up in his manhood. Fresh responsibility beckoned.

Built next to the house, the 15x20 foot stall, the work shop, held over 20 years of good memories. Without thought, Jesus' gripped one large hammer. He loosely spun the tool a few times on the thick wooden countertop. The heavy iron head made a thumping noise on each rotation. He set it aside and surveyed the other tools. Seeing the irregular line of various chisels caused Jesus a slight groan. He spoke his thoughts, "Judah, how many times did I instruct you to organize and stay organized? Tidiness is a virtue which that young man never learned." The veteran carpenter now laid the chisel heads side by side, slowly adjusting their alignment from small to large.

Now at 30 years of age, Jesus faced a different responsibility. He'd been away from the shop ever since news of the unusual teacher who immersed the repentant at the lake or along the outflowing Jordan River. Today, before Jesus made that defining walk to where John preached repentance and holiness, nostalgia visited him. This last look at the workshop closed a meaningful door as he sought the new one God pointed him toward.

He stepped back through the door and closed the shop. Next, he wanted to visit his mother.

Mary sat on a wooden stool in a corner. One grown daughter, named Dinah, visited. She instructed her own daughter, Michal, on how to knead dough and bake bread. Mary eyed her granddaughter's habits. She'd taught her daughter well.

When the eldest son walked in, they stopped and hugged him in greeting.

Little Michal hopped from foot to foot and spoke quickly, tilting her head to see him better. "We are baking bread. Just the way Momma does. Stay and eat with us!" Jesus' sister Dinah smiled at him. He smiled back at both of the bakers.

He went to his seated mother and knelt. A beautiful set of wrinkles from the highs and lows of a satisfied life stretched across her face. He sensed her old feelings and beginnings of sagging strength. Little of her dark brown strands remained. Gray streaked her hair, winning the race of aging. After an embrace, he said with firm finality, "It is time for me to leave."

His niece groaned. "But, my bread."

"Michal another day, bring me bread. A day when I need it, and to also see your beautiful smiling face."

"Okay, Uncle!"

Mary rose, standing shorter than her prize son. She had many strong thoughts about him and words to say. Somehow, he saw them all, and somehow, she knew he did. Nothing but 'Shaloms' marked his departure.

Jesus walked east all day to reach the encampments of the desert prophet by the river. The next day, as he'd done on other days, Jesus listened and watched the behavior of the forceful teacher. He studied John from a little upstream, staying in the willows. He enjoyed the success and continual fresh faces. Though fierce, he remained popular. Jesus found it interesting that this spokesman for Adonai never sought converts in towns or cities. Instead, they sought him out.

Chapter 2

Jesus' Immersion in the Jordan River

Indeed, John took his duty with the utmost seriousness. He and his disciples immersed only those who humbly feared an all-seeing, sinless God. For different reasons, men, women, and even children lived in anticipation of a continuation of the prophetic momentum stirred up by the forerunner's proclamations of, "the One who is to come after me!"

That "one" to John's timid surprise, looked an awful lot like family. A pleasing surprise; he shook his head and grinned when they stood face to face. No doubt amused; God had playfully kept His ardent servant out of the loop of this part of the divine plan. The one to come? He'd known, but not seen for many years.

John spoke as he hugged his kinsman, "As the saying goes, 'The fig does not fall far from the tree!'"

"Yes, John, we share a bloodline and are both called to redeem our people. But you, the son of a priest! Do these people even know that? Talk about, 'not falling far,' Cousin, you are doing the work of a priest out here in the wilderness, not in a synagogue or temple made by man's hands! I know your parents would be—are proud of you!"

John shook his wooly head. "Thank you. But I could never be as good as either of those two."

Overlapping each other's words, they said, "Baruch Haba BaShem Adonai!" (Blessed is he who comes in the name of the Lord!) With earnest smiles, their faces beamed.

The crowds watched and respectfully turned off their curiosity when the Immerser interviewed each repentant. They saw two men mirthfully chatting, grasping each other's arms and gazing intently with unusual warmth. A bystander commented, "It's as if the fact that they're visiting while standing waist deep in the river, with us waiting here, hasn't crossed their minds."

Indeed, the tiny family reunion raised the usual questions of relatives. "Jesus, it has been so long. How are your parents? How many brothers and sisters did you finally have? Are they all here, or any of them?" John looked past Jesus and scanned the banks. "You look well! What have you been doing? We should talk tonight!"

Smiling, Jesus raised a hand to slow his cousin's enthusiasm. "I can't visit with you tonight though my heart yearns to…after this ritual I will be alone for days, in the wilderness. However, I tell you, so much is racing through my mind. I remember playing with you in Hebron. Now we are both men, strong in Adonai's ways and blessed!" He stroked his beard. "My mother is well. She talks of you and your parents occasionally. We know they went to the next life shortly after you entered manhood. News arrived from Hebron, of course. After that, we lost track of you. My father spoke of you coming to live with us, but no one could locate you!" Solemn, Jesus looked at the eucalyptus leaves and bark floating by.

John grasped Jesus' shoulders and in a serious tone said, "Your parents went through so much for you."

In turn, Jesus tilted his head and with deep sympathy replied, "Yes, and your parents went through much for you." Silence followed as each looked away.

After a moment, John broke the solemn mood. "My parents told me tales of when our mothers were both pregnant with us. They enjoyed a wild time with Adonai!"

Jesus emphasized, "Yes! Your father couldn't talk for nine months until you were born. I've heard all the stories." Subdued, Jesus added, "My father died just before I turned twenty. I do not know why Adonai took such a good man—a real family man—a great father. You might not remember him. I think you met him only once for Pentecost at your home when we were kids. But listen, we had a good family. I do miss him. But no, none of my brothers or sisters are here. I'm alone. We didn't know that the fearsome desert preacher was our cousin. I suppose they could've all come and repented as a family." Light chuckles came from both men.

John stroked his beard. "Yes, yes. I only have good memories of your family—I only wish I had more. Living with you… where did I go… that's a long tale. I'd like to tell you someday."

Jesus smiled and said, "Me too. But, now, Cousin, we have business to tend to… and I'm so glad it's you!"

John grinned back, "And I am so glad it's you!" He paused and looked thoughtful. In sincerity he asked, "But shouldn't you be the one supervising my immersion?"

"Yes, I could do that—I'd be honored. However, tell me, what is this talk about you not being worthy to untie my sandals?" Jesus poked John in the ribs. "Cousin, you can untie them anytime you like!" He chuckled and spoke in seriousness. "But no sandals for now. My time has come. As of today, I am no longer a carpenter. That career is over. My brothers have taken over the business. I'll serve Adonai in a public manner, traveling throughout the land of our fathers." With the conversation at a close, Jesus followed custom. He faced upstream and knelt, submerged in the waist-deep water.

John made sure that every hair on Jesus' head went under. He grinned and slapped his cousin's back as he rose. "You are now ordained, Rabbi, 30 years of age!"

As Jesus turned to leave the river, he whispered to John, "Pray for me, will you? I enter into a battle now. We may never see each other again in this life."

Chapter 3
The Last Passover Seder

Three and a Half Years Later

Mary, and her dear young friend Mary Magdalene had traveled to Jerusalem for the Passover. Mary stayed with her longtime "Jerusalem friends" Yoel, his sister Shirel, and their families. They prepared a large Passover Seder and of course the Marys would attend.

Decades ago, on one of the pilgrimages, Joseph's grandfather made friends with a family in the city. After taking him in they invited him back. This went on annually, sometimes three trips a year. After Joseph had grown big enough for the journey with his father, he stayed with these kind people, too. They expected the Nazarenes each holiday and prepared a room. The children whom Joseph played with as a child were now married and had children of their own. These adults were Yoel and his sister Shirel, and their spouses. She and her husband lived in an addition to the original house. After the death of their parents, Yoel remained in the house. Then they welcomed Joseph's and Mary's children and the new, fourth generation as it grew.

The two groups of children had fallen in together, running about the neighborhood, playing games and telling stories. The parents happily watched them as they remembered their own youth in the holy city. But on this trip, years later, a lifetime later, Mary, mother of the Messiah, stayed in touch with the local disciples.

Jesus chose to celebrate the Seder in Jerusalem with only the Twelve, a day early, on Thursday night. They met at a large home, owned by Jashen, a disciple and successful financier. He made ready a large open upstairs room. He rented this out for parties and as an inn, especially for the holidays. The situation of the Temple authorities seeking Jesus' arrest had grown to its limit. So, Jesus had sent a trusted messenger to confirm his plan to have their Seder at Jashen's. In attempts to keep his whereabouts safe, Jesus sent Peter and John into the city on a mission. Jashen had one of his personal servants stationed at a certain intersection at noon, the sixth hour, with a jug of water on his shoulder. Women carried water—not men. This odd signal worked. The humiliated servant walked the men to his master's home. Then Peter and John shopped for food and wine necessary for the meal. They also went to the Temple to procure the sacrificed male lamb.

*   *   *

Part of the Passover Seder is the drinking of four ceremonial cups of wine and eating of the flat cracker-like, unleavened bread, called matzah. During the retelling of the Exodus, Jesus added a personal request to his men. Holding the Cup of Redemption, the third cup, he compared the death of the Passover lamb with his own soon coming death. This would inaugurate a new covenant, an extension of the current one, and sealed by his blood. The Twelve didn't know what he meant

Chapter 4
Judas' and Jesus' Deaths

Judas had contrived that he must give destiny a shove in the right direction by arranging the easy nighttime arrest of Jesus. That strategy failed. Misery pounded on his soul while self-condemnation ruled without restraint. He'd glimpsed the soldiers' mocking brutality. Nauseated, he feared the imminent crucifixion of the righteous rabbi, and cried.

Judas decided to kill himself. He sought the refuge which only a noose could provide.

In a nervous hurry, with evil snapping at his heels, Judas went to a lonely spot far outside the city's south walls. He'd cut a strand of rope from a cargo shed at a nearby stable. With one activity on his mind, he sought out a tree. If someone, a hidden bandit perhaps, had murdered him on the way, he would have greatly appreciated the heartless act. Having the mind of a thief, he squinted this way and that; misguided hope searched for a surprise attack. He admired deception never more than now.

The betrayer huffed, "A kiss...I embraced him. What for? What gain now? He'll die—that good man—because of me. Fool!" Dread, along with the desire to expel guilt, flooded him. He muttered, "A kiss. A kiss." and spat.

Judas' motivations spun in his mind. For three years he'd followed Jesus, hoping to benefit by acting at the core of this rabbi's sure-to-come reign of political power. Messiah or not, he knew Jesus had what it took to rule the land. "Fool, I led the enemy right to him. Fool! His mission failed. Jesus' mission failed—whatever that was!" Resentment surged through every breath the trotting man took.

Fueled by conceit, again he huffed in a mad rant, "This is all Jesus' fault. Why does a wise man make foolish choices? He could've had it all." Judas' sweat increased, running down his forehead, stinging his eyes—he didn't even try to wipe the nasty liquid away. Envy rose up and rushed from every pore. He shook his head in disgust. "Kingdom not of this world...what good is that with a Roman sword at your throat and nails through your hands!" He grunted, "The teachers say the Messiah will not die! Others teach he will die in a battle and someday a second Messiah will come and avenge his death. Bah to it all!"

The ex-disciple sped up his pace when he noticed an old tree. The limb he decided on probably wouldn't hold his weight, but his mind had suffered the loss of much common sense in recent hours. He could not work the noose and the knots fast enough. Fiery rope-burns bloodied his hands while the tree stood ready to oblige this stranger. Below the weather-worn tree lay broken, pointed, branches and sharp-edged rocks.

With labored breathing and the noose around his neck, Judas crawled out on to the limb to snug the rope tight. Focused on his knot, he mumbled, "How can someone who walks on water—" He lost his grip and fell from the limb. When the short length of rope played out, Judas' body jerked, snapping his neck. The corpse swung wildly. Passive, deathly silence started its work. The man's rapid heart stopped. Blood pulsed its last—the circulating journey within the vessels slowly succumbed to gravity.

Minutes passed. With a loud crack, the tree limb snapped and broke off. On the sharp heap below, his torso ripped open, intestines spewing. Eyes bulging in pain and shock remained unblinking.

Within hours a passerby noticed the vultures.

Chapter 5
Marketplace

Three Days Later on Monday

Giddel reached the shuk, the outdoor marketplace, just when he had planned to, before the rush of shoppers crammed the narrow streets. For once he could take his time and browse, casually sample food, make his purchases, get out, and arrive home well ahead of sundown.

Work on the Temple Mount (Mount Moriah) left a day's worth of stone dust accenting his beard, clothes, and feet. Dripping sweat stung his eyes, blurring Giddel's vision. Passing a fountain, he stopped abruptly when a surprised flurry of water doused his face and chest. This felt good but? He looked down at the pool and noticed a dripping hand. A smiling face met his.

The splasher's hair, face and beard glistened with moisture, which trickled onto his clothes. Lips parted and lively words came. "Giddel! Giddel, you dog. You should see how startled and silly you look. Come sit here and clean up for the Sabbath." The voice, so familiar and welcome, came from his neighbor and co-worker Amos. They'd known each other all their lives. Banter and pranks from this friend, were inseparable.

Giddel sat next to him and put his dry, dirty hands deep into the cool water. He rubbed off the day's labor. Then as he raised his cupped hands for a drink, he threw the puddle into Amos' unsuspecting face. Open-mouthed, Amos looked shocked. As he stared at his friend's sly grin, both men took advantage of the moment. Each slipped a hand back into the water and splashed the other. On realizing the refreshing commotion, the men increased the furious splashing. Laughter propelled the spontaneity and added to the end of the workweek.

More than a few old men, women, and mothers with little children stopped to enjoy the young men at their game. A stooped old woman stood still, took in the scene, clucked her tongue, and with a shake of her head looked skywards and shuffled off.

"Whoa, whoa! All right, enough already!" Giddel put up open hands to block any more water. Amos gave in and started wiping his face while Giddel cautiously did the same. He kept both eyes on his friend's hands knowing the trickster inside of Amos. In years past, parents from their neighborhood in Bethany, came to know that childhood trouble, though usually good-hearted, seemed to be rooted in time spent with Amos.

After catching their breath, Amos spoke in a voice dancing with humor, "Shalom, my good friend! Now tell me, don't you feel better?" He gave a wink and held a grin waiting for a response.

Giddel relaxed and nodded. "Yes, yes. Thank you. Only next time, could you first turn yourself into a beautiful maiden with an appealing smile and eyes only for me? Then you may splash all you like."

"Consider it done, my friend. In fact, I'll get to work on that right away!" Amos stood, pushed back dangling wet locks of hair and added, "I must be off to Bethany. Shalom Aleichem for now."

"Aleichem Shalom!" Giddel waved and felt the weariness of the day settle back on him. Standing up, he stretched, relieving the tension in his shoulders, neck and back. The labor of stone cutting made men strong, and yet drained life from them too. He cocked his head and held the position, enjoying the sensation. Suddenly, strong hands grasped his shoulders; his body spun, and his arms reached out for balance.

This new surprise? Not Amos.

Chapter 6

Intruders

When the unpleasant wobbling stopped, he looked into the eyes of two vaguely familiar men. Their hands steadied him but didn't loosen. Each face held Giddel's eyes with stern disapproving scowls.

"What do you want? Let me go!" He pushed the hands away. Straightening his clothes, he awaited for an answer. Frustrated he barked, "Well, speak up!"

The two men let their gazes veer. One looked off while the other stared at his own sandals. Seconds passed, and then one spoke while staring into Giddel's waiting eyes. "This is hard, we know. It is awkward...especially for me. When we saw you here and...sorry, we must've startled you without a greeting. We've wandered around Jerusalem hoping to find you. We can all guess what you're going through. And don't think we haven't had the same thoughts ourselves. Now, all we ask is for you to listen and give us—give him—your attention." The other man thoughtfully squinted at Giddel.

Giddel looked to the silent one expecting something to happen, but the man said nothing. Giddel said, "Huh? Wait! You wha—"

"Please listen to us, It is true!" one of them asserted. "You might think we're all confused...this has—is really happening. Consider the claims, the evidence... would we be lying about such a thing—and to you?" They gazed into Giddel's eyes and waited.

He considered how to answer these strangers. Whoever they are, each seems quite sincere, but sincere about what? "Look, I'm sure—"

The same man interrupted him again. "Just come with us. We've no doubts you'll reconsider—as so many others have already. Why not spend the Sabbath with the other close disciples? We've all missed you and been worried!"

The disciples? Missed me! What? Giddel broke in, "Excuse me, wait, wait. Hold on! You two look a little familiar but...." He thought through their request and searched for clues, trying to make sense of their interest in him.

The silent man smiled and rested a hand on Giddel's shoulder, while the man who did the talking pleaded in a slow earnest manner, "Thomas."

Understanding came to Giddel's mind, and his words came out like a groan. "Ohh, Thomas! Ohh. Now...now I see." He shrugged, and a grin grew up one side of his face. "Thomas is my brother. You know him—not me. That's who you want, I'm Giddel."

Awkward silence enveloped the three men as noisy people passed by, merchants shouted, and animal sounds added to the growing cacophony around them. The shuk shoppers crowded the small huddle and pushed on by. In every direction the marketplace teemed with frantic people trying foods, bargaining, paying, and trying to get home before sundown. Amos and now these strangers ruined Giddel's plans. He would join the throng soon enough and head home.

The quiet man named Matthew turned to his friend and finally spoke. "Peter, I remember Thomas saying his family, and twin brother, lived in Bethany. This must be him. But, how would we know the difference…how would anyone? They look identical."

Slightly annoyed, Giddel took a stance as if he were explaining something to the unlearned, "How? I'll tell you how. Our parents know us because of our different personalities, what clothes we wear and," with a chuckle he added, "by my good looks!"

The two men cocked their heads with odd expressions. The talkative one stepped in. "Your good looks? Thomas…I mean Giddel, but you are exactly the same." A confused expression remained on his face. "Thomas, come now! Tell me it's you, stop joking!"

Matthew placed a hand on his companion's arm and looked him full in the face. In a sober tone he said, "Peter, I can tell it's not Thomas."

"Oh you can, can you? Then tell me how?"

"Because Thomas never jokes about anything, that's how." Exchanging glances, all three went silent.

Chapter 7

News

Giddel murmured, "I see you've spent time with my brother." He recollected pieces from the last time he had spoken with Thomas and ventured, "So, you must be the fisherman from Galilee. Some call you Cephas or Simon Peter, right? You're the biggest of the lot. Thomas said you are the most talkative, too." A nod acknowledged his correct guess. "But Matthew I'm not sure about. Are you from the same region of Lake Kinneret?"

"Yes, I'm from Cana. And with Peter and Jesus around, it's easy to say nothing and be quiet, and therefore not noticed. That's probably why you've never heard of me."

Peter looked at the ground. Quiet in thought and with chin in hand, he said, "Yes, we have indeed mistaken you for our friend Thomas. We apologize."

Matthew spoke up, "See what I mean? He speaks for both of us—I ask you, who has need of a tongue with him around?"

Giddel responded, "Oh, thanks for the apology, but I'm used to it or, should I say, Thomas and I have been mistaken for each other all our lives. So, you may use Greek if you prefer and call me or my brother Didymus since we truly are twins." The tone in his voice changed from light-hearted to serious. "But tell me now, why the stern countenance and your hurry to find him? Is he missing, and if so, for how long? Is he in trouble?" His eyes went back and forth looking for an answer.

Peter's expression changed to one of befuddlement and then into a hard stare. He wiped tears off the small of his cheeks before each fell onto his large bushy beard. Turning red, he made attempts at an explanation, but they failed to come together into full sentences. He squatted on the edge of the pool and then clutched the leg of his companion and gave in to full weeping. He reached a hand up to Giddel motioning for him to indulge him this time of emotion.

In this awkward moment, Giddel noticed the increase of shoppers and the rising noise of haggling. He pondered what to do. Whatever is driving these men I need to find out. No doubt their news is of some trouble and will be of interest to me and my family. Perhaps spending the Sabbath here in Jerusalem would be the best means to find out about Thomas. I've spent hours daydreaming of my brother's life following this mysterious rabbi who travels where the wind moves him.

He ventured, "Men, you offered for Thomas to spend the Sabbath with you and the other disciples and of course your rabbi. Ahh…could I take my brother's place? Who knows, maybe he'll even show up! If not, you could tell me of his life and journeys pursuing this rabbi from Galilee. How about it?"

Silence met Giddel's frank proposal.

Both men looked at each other and then away. Peter rubbed his chin trying to clear his beard of remaining tears. Matthew looked to the ground, squatted and drew aimlessly with a finger.

Giddel studied their withdrawn postures. Grunting the words, he pointedly said, "Oh, I get it. Since I'm not an insider, it is rude to ask! No bother. I need to get back ho—"

Peter held up a hand. The poised wrist and fingers wobbled, seeming to struggle against an invisible force. Strained words came from Matthew, "No, no! Giddel, it's not that at all. You are indeed wanted. As Thomas' brother, please come. Your company would be an honor. Welcome in the Sabbath with us and, of course, have dinner, only...."

Angry and perplexed, Giddel said, "Only what?"

Matthew looked at Peter for some sort of permission, but no expression met his. He then went to the waiting piercing eyes—eyes so familiar yet seated in a stranger, with a different name. "Thomas...I mean Giddel. Sorry! We hold the most important news. You indeed are not your brother...and well, Thomas didn't believe our news. Maybe you will. Our Master, the teacher, Rabbi Jesus...he, ahh...died. But, no! Well, I mean, put to death by the Roman governor several days ago." He paused and with an odd expression placed both hands on his listener's shoulders adding, "Three days after the rabbi's crucifixion—."

Giddel took a step back and Matthew's hands dropped. Giddel shrieked, "Crucifixion! What? Just whom have you—has my brother—been following? What offense did Jesus do to be killed?" Sweat shone on Giddel's face. His legs buckled, and his body sagged to one side. He reached out for something, anything to steady himself.

Peter spoke up, "That will take time to explain, Giddel...and we will. But our news to you, to all of Jerusalem, is amazing. Unbelievable though it sounds, our teacher lives; he came back from death and has visited us."

"He did what? When? Then where is he? Where is my brother? Tell me! Tell me now!" With each demand for an answer, his voice rose louder and tightening fists readied themselves for whatever came next.

"Since the crucifixion, Jesus visited many of us. Some saw angels, and even saw him at his tomb, which is empty! The rest met him at the same upper room where we had eaten our Passover Seder and continue to have meetings—all except your brother. We ten closest disciples and others, after being startled, welcomed him back from the dead. Thomas returned to the meeting place, but the teacher had already left...disappeared, really."

"Left! Left where to? Where, and how, and why? Wait! You said the 'ten closest' and my brother. I thought the rabbi always traveled with twelve men. Didn't this other man miss seeing these ghost appearances, too?" Giddel's mind whirled with the strange and fascinating news. What if it were true? What could it mean?

Peter choked out a few words, "Ju–Ju–Judas, you mean?" He put a hand to his chest and bent over. Sobs came. Giddel looked to Peter with wide-open arms as if waiting to catch an answer. Peter spoke in halting phrases, "Dead. He killed himself. Hanged...himself."

Giddel took another step away. His eyes went wide straining in shock. Fear raced throughout his soul. *What has my brother gotten himself into? What folly and insanity does this Jesus breed?* Aghast, he shouted, "Killed himself?"

Shoppers passing close by, with minds intent on purchases, glanced at the three men and faltered in their footing when Giddel lunged and grabbed Peter with both hands and shouted into his face, "Is Thomas safe? Is that why you're looking for him? Will he do the same as this Judas did—will you? What lunacy! You are disciples of death!"

Chapter 8
Scene of Death

Disciples told Mary of her son's dire trouble with the chief priests and the secret night time arrest in Gethsemane. Mark had barely escaped arrest. He went and told certain key followers. He knew the people where Mary and Joseph used to stay and found her there. She roused certain of the other followers. Mark cautiously sought the whereabouts of Jesus' body.

Joseph of Arimathea, a prominent member of the Sanhedrin Council, went boldly to Pilate and asked for Jesus' body. Joseph returned with a sufficient roll of linen cloth. Using a cart, Nicodemus brought a 100-pound mixture of myrrh and aloes.

In contrast, several of those who loved Jesus came to his cross of death, waiting and wishing to be of some comfort. Nicodemus and Joseph bit their lips as they watched the nails pulled out of the fresh corpse. Their hatred of the Romans intensified. One of the lovers tearfully but carefully tugged at the despicable crown of thorns. Many sharp ends had to be pried out of the scalp or snapped off first. The long stiff thorns jabbed the helpers and Jesus' blood merged with theirs. Disgusted looks crossed the sympathetic faces. These small injuries meant nothing, and yet, meant so much more than they knew.

The empathetic overseeing centurion, who had perceived that this prisoner held a supernatural birth and persona, commanded his men to gently lower the spiked crosspiece of timber and lay the man down with respect. "Not a criminal. Not he."

Mary; her sister Salome; the young Apostle John; Mary Magdalene; Mary the wife of Cleopas, the mother of James and John; Joanna; and, Mary the mother of the Apostle James and Judas all stood a distance from the ghastly scene.

The two older men and their servants placed the body on the cart and rolled it to a tomb cut out of rock. Then they placed the body in linen wrappings with the herbs in the folds and tied ceremonial knots. Last, a covering veil settled over Jesus' face. The quantity of the herbs exceeded all normal proportions, fit for a royal burial.

The women followed to see the body's resting place and left; they could not see the burial activities into the dim tomb. Like a crushing blow mowing down faithful hearts, news of the crucifixion roared across parts of Israel. Some said, "Stronger than every evil. How could he die so suddenly and leave us alone?" Others said, "Who was he? Why didn't he come down off that awful criminal's cross while they taunted him? Adonai made him the most essential person in Israel—the most important man since Moses, David, or Solomon." An elderly woman shrugged, "Such a short life, only thirty-three years!"

Hebrews commemorated Passover on Friday at sundown. Now, on Friday, after the trial, beating, crucifixion, with sundown closing in, the burial rituals sped up.

After seeing where two kind men of the Sanhedrin laid her son, she made straight for Yoel and Shirel's. Participating in a Seder never entered her mind. Grief struck her down, she walked hard and stilted. Her heart suffered a sword run through her to the hilt. When she arrived, Mary stumbled and felled by grim despair.

Chapter 9
Two to Emmaus and Back

Early on, after the Resurrection, disciples told and retold this one peculiar story. In the town of Emmaus, seven miles from Jerusalem, lived two disciples whom Jesus favored: Cleopas and his wife. They experienced a private and unique, post-Resurrection visit. Jesus demonstrated affection to them, but he also included his dissatisfaction of the two.

A delightful atmosphere saturated the Upper Room. At different times of the day each disciple came and went to the Temple Mount to join the liturgical prayers. This coming and going created little and big stirs. In the evening those who lived in Jerusalem, or who stayed at another open house, or camped in the hills, eventually visited the Upper Room. The buzz of who said what, or did what, circulated among the disciples. The telling of previously unknown or known sayings and doings of the Messiah never stopped. The Upper Room remained saturated with God's spirit. Some sensed this presence in ways others didn't.

The story started with Jesus' death. Devastation had rocked every disciple. Nails driven into the hands which had healed, blessed, and raised the dead meant an end to the heavenly momentum of the Kingdom of God coming to earth. The Galilean prophet? Stopped in his mission—this was clear. He'd done much in three and a half years but apparently failed to meet his goal. God didn't stop the hand which held a Roman hammer. However, God did have an angel stop the hand of Abraham which clutched a knife ready to kill his son Isaac. *Why not now?*

The ideas of freedom from Rome and the reinstatement of a powerful Jewish kingdom had shattered like a clay pot on a stone floor. Disillusionment spread.

No one had a good answer.

On the third day after the brutal death, before dawn, an angel rolled away the heavy disc-shaped stone blocking the tomb's entrance; the Messiah left. Joined by a second angel, the two waited for the first mourners.

Soon, Jesus started making appearances.

At first light Sunday, the half-dozen faithful women visited the tomb to perform the corpse burial rituals with spices. They hadn't seen the preparation Nicodemus and Joseph had already done. To their utter astonishment, only the grave shroud and herbs remained in the tomb. An empty tomb? *An empty tomb?* And so, they quickly returned to the city, telling stories of the empty tomb and talkative angels. More *doubt* than faith met their shocking tale.

On that same afternoon while visiting Jerusalem, the husband and wife from Emmaus heard the hard to believe stories. Perplexed, the two left for home, leaving behind eleven skeptical apostles, the colorful women, newcomers, and others.

Then Jesus appeared to Peter, who told his account to the other apostles and convinced them. But Thomas disbelieved; he needed more than the melodrama driven and too often, impulsive words of Peter.

The two from Emmaus left and were unaware of this empowering update of another sighting. Yet, it was true, Jesus could somehow alive and able to travel great distances invisibly.

They walked the dusty road home, the slowest pace of their lives. The husband and wife, like Thomas, had missed the supposed appearance of the ghost-man, Jesus. Although they didn't know it, these two found themselves in the same psychological mire in which the Apostle Thomas trudged: believe or not believe. The two didn't hold as rigorous a refusal as Thomas had, which demanded absolute proof of life.

The sad and gloomy couple knew their way home but had lost their way spiritually.

That is … until a stranger joined them on the road, walking in the same direction. Jesus. YES. However, he chose to utilize a mystical shroud of disguise, and at this point back-from-death, he really did play dead for a brief time. Jesus appeared full of curiosity as to the travelers' sorrowful mood and talk. Cleopas stared at him and saw an unknown face. Strong emotions stirred when he stated, "Are you the only one around Jerusalem who doesn't know what's been going on?"

Jesus, acting the stranger, holding himself back, replied with innocence, "What's that?"

He patiently listened to their story of himself: from water immersion to death … and then that day's remarkable news by the early morning women. He understood the disorienting report of a possible return from the dead. As he stroked his beard, he responded, "True, if he'd done such a miracle for others, couldn't he do so for himself… even though he died? One would think so."

After a few miles of explanations while dodging the occasional pile of camel and donkey dung, the couple finished all they needed to say. Jesus gathered his thoughts and began his strategy. He decided on a private, lengthy lesson to encourage and settle their burdened hearts. With kind boldness, he called them, "Foolish students" and "stubborn and slow to understand." For the last miles to Emmaus, he gave them an astute Bible education about himself, yet referring to "the Messiah." In his victorious state over sin, brutality, and the grave, he vigorously played his hand from the beginning to the end: explaining everything written in the Scriptures about him, starting with the Genesis, the Law of Moses, books of the Prophets, Psalms and Writings.

The familiar trip to Emmaus now seemed endless in a slow, wonderful way. The two eager and enriched students barely noted the sun moving lower in the sky. Dusk held twilight firm within its reins. Splashes of bright orange and turquoise presented themselves where fluffy white clouds had dominated moments earlier.

When the couple needed to turn off the road for their home, the stranger stopped, motioning that he had elsewhere to go. They pleaded with him to eat dinner and stay the night with them since darkness approached. Using any reasoning at hand, they didn't want to lose this learned man.

After acting as if it were a tough decision, he gave in. So, the teacher entered their house to stay with them. He relaxed as his hosts busied themselves making dinner. He remarked more than once, "Smells good!"

His intensive lessons from Scripture had their minds soaring. They even giggled as their faith grew. He'd changed the couple's entire understanding and expectations. Hope rose high over all of their earlier dismay. Thankful for the coincidence of meeting this unknown disciple, they now knew more of Scripture than they ever imagined possible.

Cleopas whispered to his wife, "How little we understood *until now*. This man must be a Torah Teacher or by his accent, a rabbi from Galilee. Strange, we never saw him before today of all days."

She smiled broadly while kneading the dough. "He's a special man; kind and firm. Is it only me or do you feel drawn to him in an odd, yet familiar way?" She didn't need an answer. Each looked forward to further listening and asking more questions.

They lit olive oil lamps in their dimming home. When settled for dinner they honored their guest by asking him to recite the common blessing over the meal.

He accepted the hot loaf of bread, lifted it, and said, "Blessed are You, Lord, our God, King of the Universe who brings forth bread from the earth. Amen." He broke the bread, gave them pieces, and smiled.

Pleasant memories zinged through the couple's minds. As caught in a sudden and brief shower of cold rain on a windy day, all of their enthusiasm whipped up. Jesus had always been the one who broke bread at meals and said the blessing. That thought struck home—in their house now. They glimpsed a man whom they knew. But an instant after his eyes met theirs his seat held only air, for he vanished.

Cleopas gasped. "Jesus. That was Jesus! The whole time!" His jaw dropped. "But, but, how?"

His wife screamed, "Ah hah!" and slammed her hands down flat on the table top, causing the food to bounce. She said "The whole time? You're right! Did he— did Jesus—just trick us somehow? That explains his strange—I mean—his mastery of Scriptures. He knew everything—*more than everything*."

Cleopas stared at his wife. "But isn't this out of character for him to do something like this? I don't know, did you ever hear of any people becoming invisible in Scripture stories? Or… was that he—him—a ghost, a spirit?"

They'd trusted this stranger's words and inspiring influence. Now they knew that the man wasn't a man at all. For that instant of seeing a dead person's face compounded the alarming shock of his surprise disappearance.

In a sweat, Cleopas said, "He'll be back, any moment… sitting and eating with us. He still has to eat food, *doesn't he* or does he?" His voice didn't sound convinced. They looked in all directions expecting to see Jesus standing, red-faced in his alarming fun.

His wife said, "I'll go look outside in front, maybe he's there. You go look in the back." She reentered and muttered, "Nothing." She made a grimace. *"Why did he leave like that?"*

They both spoke and even yelled as they wandered inside and out, "Jesus, we know you can hear us. We're sorry we didn't believe in you better. Please come back. Eat with us. We'd really like you to come back now."

As minutes rolled by, they finally decided that the Risen Jesus had done his business with them and had moved on. Downtrodden, perplexed and lightheartedness ran through their emotions.

Cleopas exclaimed, "Well that was some joke! I didn't know he had it in him. Kind of embarrassing for us though."

She said, "How did he do that?" With added emphasis, "Why did he do that?" A curious expression filled her face. "I wonder what pranks he's played on those close friends of his, Lazarus and the two sisters."

The couple drew close in awe, feeling little in comparison to God's abilities. Now watery eyes shined as they embraced. Then the tears flowed. Soon the crying turned into tears of laughter. What had happened was good. They'd never forget the unusual love they sensed coursing through their souls. "Jesus is alive and chose to visit our home. He likes us. He really does."

Cleopas let out a deep sigh." The Messiah is probably visiting other disciples he loves right now—perhaps miles from here."

They discussed what to do if anything. Both spoke rapidly. They had news—important news—the most important news. The couple agreed they must tell others immediately.

They quickly packed dinner into a basket and a skin of drink, for a meal on the road. They headed out into the night toward Jerusalem and those in the Upper Room. Their feet barely touched the ground for seven miles. What a story they had on their tongues.

Later that night in the Upper Room, behind locked doors eleven apostles, others, and the tale-bearing two from Emmaus reunited with the mighty Man they thought they'd lost forever. He walked through a wall—two-stories from the ground. After their fears died and appropriate laughter took its turn, they talked. Later, Jesus left, by disappearing through a wall. So many in the room shouted, "How does he do that?" Others replied, "How did he do *anything?*" They also wondered, "Will he be back another day?" No one knew where he would appear next.

In the Upper Room, Cleopas told their Jesus story nearly every day, and his wife interjected comments with enthusiasm. Of all the accounts and reports of the Messiah's otherworldly powers and ministry activities, no adventure included the ingredient of deliberate, humorous humiliation. This private reprimand was now public knowledge. However, such a personalized scenario benefited others, creating faith and hope.

Side Note: Thirty Days After the Crucifixion

The Torah has a list of causes of physical defilement and remedies. The most serious or highest grade of defiling came from handling a corpse or preparing it for burial. Defilement also occurred from being in the same room as a corpse and other connected activities. Handling, preparing, and burying a dead person was, of course, normal, necessary, and considered a blessing. But the highest degree of ritual impurity. Numbers 19:1-22 tells how such voluntarily or accidentally unclean persons became clean again. Personal cleansing after corpse defilement called for water purification—not once, but three times. On the third and seventh days after the last defiling activity, the persons were sprinkled using a hyssop branch dipped in a container filled from fresh running water. Added to the water were ashes from a sacrificed, rare, red heifer. Travelers to Jerusalem's Temple transported small amounts of these important ashes from Jerusalem to synagogues in distant communities and lands. Then the unclean persons were to immerse themselves on the seventh day (never for medicinal or hygienic purposes). The water could be in a common, manmade ritual mikveh bath, a lake, river, or ocean.

Such a temporarily unclean person could not ascend the Temple Mount, attend synagogue services, nor participate in congregational holiday festivities. If the defilement occurred on the holiday of Passover, an unclean person had to wait one month to enjoy a substitute, trimmed-down version of the traditional Seder dinner. When the Romans removed Jesus' body from the cross, Joseph of Arimathea and Nicodemus and unnamed others helped to tend to the body for burial. Thus, they voluntarily chose uncleanness and to miss celebrating that evening's national holiday. Instead, they choose to have a belated Passover Seder thirty days later, called the Pesach Sheni. This took place at Nicodemus' home.

God commanded that there be no leaven or leavened bread in homes. The servants had seen to that by noon and burned what they found in a fire. They had carefully cleaned the entire house, moving furniture and pillows in hopes to find crumbs or scraps of bread and food leavened by fermentation from the last 12 months. Then, the father, or in this case, Nicodemus, following ritual, inspected the household in a symbolic serious demeanor. If he didn't discover anything, the Seder could take place. Jesus grew up with his siblings carefully searching their small home. When they said "Done." Joseph patiently checked to make sure.

Chronicle Two
The Gathering Begins

Chapter 10
Mary Leaves Nazareth for Jerusalem

Eventually, Mary, Jesus' mother, went home to Nazareth after the crucifixion and Jesus' Resurrection from the dead. Though she knew her son had forgiven her, she still felt shame and self-criticism. The past three years held mixed-up highs and lows. She had shamed herself along with his siblings, by addressing Jesus as "mad" and "out of his mind." He'd been a grown man and didn't need his mother chasing after him, trying to protect him or control his behavior.

For her unbelief, her son had publicly batted back an envious compliment of his mother, "How blessed is the womb that gave birth to you and the breasts that nursed you!" But Jesus replied, "On the contrary, blessed are those who hear the word of God and observe it." Oh, how that pained her memory as a prick of a sword blade piercing skin above her heart.

Before Jesus' birth, thirty-four years ago she envisioned her errors as the mother of Adonai's child: accusing him of lying, avoiding chores, making him play better with his siblings, or favoring him too much. She and Joseph had juggled and wrestled with do's and do not's. But her time, and Joseph's time in his life were over.

She pondered, "Is it even right to call Jesus her son? She never dreamed, what parent would ever dream of wrongful death by crucifixion, and then a miraculous, robust return to life?

Now, in Nazareth, forty days after Passover and his Resurrection, Mary received the news of her glorified son's final instructions—stay in Jerusalem until a special heavenly event occurred. She immediately made plans to go back to the capital.

But on this trip, years later, a lifetime later, Mary, mother of the Messiah, would join the core disciples at Jashen's Upper Room and enjoy his hospitality instead of staying with her dear old family friends, Yoel and Shirel.

In Nazareth, as Joseph's widow, and the mother of four other sons and two daughters, she enjoyed grandmothering to fourteen. Joseph had seen the birth of many of his grandchildren. All but the youngest grandchildren had known and loved their Uncle Jesus. All loved their grandmother. They came to visit her for a meal, or stayed with her overnight, or even longer. The older ones, ages ten and eleven, helped her with chores. James, her and Joseph's first child together, had the oldest grandchildren. She never daydreamed of marrying again.

Now, Grandma Mary wanted to take James' two oldest daughters with her to Jerusalem for Adonai's next bestowing to Israel. She wondered what God would do next since Jesus' ministry ended. However, her sons, James, Joseph, Judas, and

Simon, had already planned for the journey—the holiday pilgrimage of Pentecost, the two girls Mary had in mind would be making the trip too. Some brought their wives and a child or two. Mary would be 'Grandma Mary' in Jerusalem to her own grandchildren, and to many not of her blood or tribe. Mary understood her continued duty to Adonai meant service to others.

Chapter 11
Passover Seder at Nicodemus' Home

Thirty Days After Passover

Nicodemus and Joseph from Arimathea were not the only ones from the Sanhedrin who attended. Though for years, the two of them sat in the council chambers of 70 judges, they'd been more strangers than friends. Since Joseph of Arimathea lived 25 miles northwest of the capital, Nicodemus and his wife decided to open their doors for Joseph and his wife to stay. Both men were wealthy and had servants. Both men were unclean due to their joint efforts for preparation and burial of Jesus. Because of this, both men and the selected servants performed the water cleansing rituals at Nicodemus' home. On the seventh day after the burial they went to a nearby enclosed mikveh bath, for the final holy cleansing.

The two men decided to hold the make-up Passover Seder at Nicodemus' home. Of course, the servants who were involved at the cross and tomb were to join in. Nicodemus purchased a one-year-old male lamb without blemish. His servants roasted the skinned carcass on a traditional pomegranate wood spit in his spacious courtyard. The palm trees and other green foliage, stone benches, lit torches, and a warm night created a most pleasant environment. Before eating the lamb, Joseph pronounced this blessing: "Blessed are You, the Eternal, our God, the King of the world, who has sanctified us by Your commands, and has ordained that we should eat the Passover."

When seated, Joseph handled a ritual announcement, "Today is thirty days, which is four weeks and two days of the Omer." All present recited the blessing, pronounced every evening for forty-nine nights until the evening when Pentecost started. "Blessed are You, God, King of the Universe, Who made us holy with His commandments, and commanded us to count the Omer."

This Seder profoundly different than any Seder in all of the previous fourteen centuries—1,400 Passovers—the recent, *last* Seder of Jesus. He'd died a horrible death—those present had buried him. Then three days afterwards, word came of angels and his escape from the tomb. He'd shown himself alive, proving to the apostles and other perplexed disciples that he lived.

Meanwhile, the activity of wine in their bloodstreams only beckoned more joy about the Messianic future. Not only had they chosen a difficult and unpopular confession of support for Jesus when alive—now their heart investment had paid off. Beyond the miracles of Jesus, nothing greater and grander than this could have been hoped for—his Resurrection. They'd chosen well.

"The new Jesus has made almost a dozen appearances." Joseph said with mirth born out of his heart. "Up in Galilee he spontaneously spoke to a crowd of over 500 people. That's only counting the men." While resting on his elbow, Joseph thoughtfully swirled his goblet of wine. "Maybe he'll show up here—*tonight*."

Short chuckles followed, and then expressions turned serious; they looked about.

One of the wives said, "I've heard one thing from more than a few of those privileged to have recently seen and heard him." This aroused the attention of all. "Well, he's not so serious, so heavy now. He used to be all business. He's actually joyous. Jesus is lighter, more chatty. Probably because if you know you are going to be beaten, tortured and crucified by evil men for nothing wrong you did—how could happiness much survive?" Her statement sounded like a question which needed no solution in reply.

The two men and guest servants turned thoughtful. A servant said, "Yes, he had a lot on his mind—all of the time. And now he's a complete success. Jesus is untouchable. He did what he came to do. Right? The worst is over. Now on to what God has next!"

Joseph's wife added, "He's still got that serious, personality; it's just not as prominent as before. Joseph, you said 'the new Jesus' I think you're right. He's more refreshing. He always had his spikes of laughter. I heard he enjoyed helping parents teach their children how to swim at the lake—little did they know that he could simply get up and walk on the water—better yet, teach kids to walk on water—no drowning there." Chuckles. "Ten or so, drown at that lake every year. Swimming relaxed Jesus probably got his mind off things. He enjoyed doing good deeds, that rabbi did!"

Joseph added, "I heard that in Galilee some time ago, he sent out his twelve core men—even including that greedy traitor Judas—to represent him in the villages. Meaning, he empowered them to teach, cure illnesses, make demons leave and raise the dead. So, when they returned to him some weeks later, Jesus was the happiest any of them ever saw. His plan worked."

For the meal, Nicodemus wore a favorite turban, one of sky blue and palm green stripes. Joseph's particular turban, a gift from his wife, displayed an orange hue and stripes of red. The two wives had grown close during these days. They spent time in the hostess' wardrobe and finally settled on what she wore last year, a robe of pure yellow with sparkling pink on the hems. They also helped each other put on cosmetics from Alexandria, Egypt.

The home also enjoyed the playing of instruments while singing the holiday collection of Psalms 113 to 118, called the Hallel, and other songs of deliverance.

The serving servants brought out extra pillows and sleeping pads for the traditional meal eaten while lying on one's side, propped up by an elbow. The eating arrangement took on a U-shape. This way the servants could easily serve the group. They filled wine cups, and pitchers of wine were aplenty. The particular servants, now ritually clean, lay close, while the other servants served the dishes of food. Each participant received a plate of flat, unleavened matzo bread. Then the traditional oral liturgy started, which all Jews, even by six-year-olds, knew by heart. Retelling of Moses, stubborn Pharaoh, and the ten plagues. During the meal, at the naming of each plague, each person dipped one fingertip into their wine goblet and then flicked the drop away.

Chapter 12
Matthias Replaces Judas

Forty Days After Passover, Ascension Day

The eleven and all followers had wept for their Master and his terrible end. After his betrayal resulted in Jesus' arrest and death, Judas' suicide sounded just. Peter pointed it out as a need, a requirement to continue to have a twelfth apostle. The ten others agreed to keep the Messiah's number of twelve. But how to choose? They decided that candidates needed to have been among the Galilean disciples from the beginning of Jesus' ministry, starting with the immersing by John at the Jordan River. In addition, they should have been among the 70 men whom Jesus had sent out to the villages. And one final requirement: they must have witnessed the resurrected Jesus. Names and reasons narrowed down to two good, faithful men—Barsabas and Matthias. The eleven hadn't wanted to put it to a vote. Instead, they'd cast lots to let God decide. At the Temple, in one method used, a priest would put stones of different colors into a basket with a hole in its lid and the vessel would be shaken until one stone fell out; and they took the needed position or performed a deed. In situations involving more men, the names of the candidates would be written or initialed on stones. Since the decision of Judas' replacement settled on only two men, the process went quickly. They used a method of one black and one white pebble: rejection or acceptance.

The lot called Matthias to take the place of the betrayer. This man, so blessed, replaced Judas. He'd known Judas well. Yet, he also now knew awkwardness as his substitute. After the lot, Matthias found Barsabas acting reserved and short in conversation. It is hard to accept that you weren't picked for something. But harder when you know God Almighty said 'No' to you—publicly.

The chosen man, the honored one wept. In his sorrow, he considered the sandals he'd fill. Not wanting to entertain superstition, Matthias knew if Judas could become ruthless—couldn't he? Couldn't Peter? Hadn't Peter publicly denied that he knew Jesus of Nazareth? On that night of betrayal and arrest, the other 10 ran away to save themselves. Matthias and Barsabas, though close to Jesus, were not included in the final Seder or the quality time which followed on the Mount of Olives. Yet, they were present when Jesus rose into heaven.

In the days ahead, Matthias pondered what Jesus—what Adonai—would want of him.

In trying to patch things up with Barsabas, Matthias sat next to him. He said, "My uncle, who worked for years on the Temple Mount, once told me how the priests cast lots. As you know, there's a variety of duties inside and outside of the Temple, but too many eager priests. He told me there are four lots cast each day, four shifts. They meet each time in that chamber called the Hall of Hewn Stones."

Barsabas mumbled that of course he had heard of it.

78

Matthias assumed so. But he continued, "The priests stand in a circle around the leader. He removes the turban off one of them to indicate he'd begin counting at him. Then all hold up one, two, or more fingers—since it is not lawful in Israel to count persons—due to King David's sin in counting his army."

Barsabas nodded dully.

"When the leader names a number, such as 25 or 67, he walks by the priests and counts and until he's reached the named number. This marked that the lot fell on that priest. Interesting?"

Politely, Barsabas narrowed his lips and let air out. He said, "I think I knew that. But, I forgot the part of King David's faith in numbers instead of Adonai's strength. Tragedy followed from Adonai's anger; thousands died by His plague."

A confident older voice stated, "Due to the census, seventy thousand."

The two men turned to see Nicodemus, who had apparently overheard the conversation.

Barsabas and Matthias nodded and spoke no more.

Regrettably, from that time on, the word "traitor" entered into almost every conversation Matthias had with anyone. Memories of their camaraderie remained. The images from the report of those who kindly prepared his ragged corpse for burial, stuck in Matthais' mind. Judas had been a mixed disciple. He had witnessed hundreds of miracles. Then he ended his privileged position and damned his own life and afterlife. On occasion, thoughts of that unbelievable decision caused Matthias to weep.

Side Note: Destination Jerusalem

The Torah commanded Jewish men to make three pilgrimages a year, to observe the festivals. Adonai said He would choose a location once they settled in the Promised Land. He chose Jerusalem (Yerushalayim) for His House. There, the Children of Israel brought what they offered and sacrificed.

During the holiday of Pentecost, Jerusalem, a densely populated city with a maze of winding streets and narrow passageways, swelled to several times its normal population. Every home took in new strangers, or previous travelers, now considered friends.

Whether from past exiles, trade, family or adventure, these visitors to Jerusalem came one, two or three times a year representing the Jewish populations in foreign lands. At great expense and time in transit, Jews sought to worship in the holy city if only once in their life. For those of the farthest distances who weren't wealthy, such a trip meant the highlight of their life. Pilgrims inspired others to make the sacrifice and go. Veins trailing thousands of miles in all directions surged life-blood back to the beating heart of their homeland.

Well over 4,000,000 Jews filled the Mediterranean world—over two million lived in Israel. One million lived in Alexandria, Egypt—called Little Jerusalem—Yerushalayim Hak'tanah. On a spring day, as the Pentecost celebration approached, traffic of people and animals overwhelmed the city. No quiet place could be found. Every home took in relatives or strangers. Hospitality came with a home in Jerusalem. Bidding welcome to the poor, sick, or travelers meant great merit, a special mitzvah—good deed. Everywhere, flat roofs lay covered with eager gazers who either feasted their eyes on the holy city for the first time, or once more enjoyed the sights. A custom of hanging a curtain on the front door of a house signaled to weary travelers room for guests. In this welcoming, a home stood to receive a blessing. The men of Israel and of other lands came to worship, make offerings and present sacrifices. Jerusalem's 400 synagogues filled with worshippers.

Thousands of pitched white tents dotted the outskirts of the city. Those camping on the Mount of Olives had the best view looking down into the Temple courts of Mount Moriah. Smoke rising from the outdoor altar of burnt-offering made a daily pillar before their faces on its way to Heaven's nostrils. Inside the Temple's Holy Place, from the Altar of Incense, slender pillars of smoke rose out of the ten windows. They joined into one dense pillar above the Temple.

Obedient Jews respected the requirements of their race's covenants and the Creator who placed each of them in His Chosen People. The annual inconveniences of leaving home, family and work laid the foundation for their religious way of life. The synagogues were for reading, instruction and expounding of the Law; the Temple a House of Prayer.

Chapter 13
Ancestral Home

Pentecost approached. Those who made friends or had relatives in the capital stayed with them. Elsewhere in the holy city many disciples slept and ate in the spacious Upper Room where the 12 and the Master had eaten his last Passover Seder. The owner, Jashen, took it upon himself to make sure his guests were as comfortable as possible. He provided extra cushions and rolled sleeping mats. Some stayed in Jashen's open courtyard or on the flat roof. His wife and daughter served food and refreshments.

As daily responsibilities allowed, these pilgrims returned to Jashen's safe house. The vehemence of the high-level Temple officials had subsided. Those who succeeded in having Jesus executed set priests and spies to listen in on the daily meetings in the Temple courtyards. What they heard disturbed the authorities. However, if the misguided followers of the crucified, would-be Messiah kept to themselves, there would be no trouble. The rulers would wait and see how foolish these false Messiah's followers were. No one had tried to take the Galilean's place. If or when someone would, that man would find himself against formidable enemies.

Forty days later, the core group of disciples banded together in one accord, gathering at Jashen's during the next ten days. Mind and spirits mingled under the hope of the coming Promise. They prayed at the Temple every day.

Months before, Jashen, an indebted follower, brought his leprous daughter to Jesus, who healed her and restored the damaged fingers and toes. In gratefulness he had begged Jesus to have the Seder at his home, fully provided for. Then, after the Resurrection, by hope and holy intuition, he knew to keep his doors open and be at peace with the coming exciting future.

The upstairs proved a wise investment by his grandfather many years ago; an attractive room, made from quality stone and wood with plenty of windows. On a third level an open courtyard allowed guests to enjoy the stars and weather. Jashen rented the space for meetings, weddings, parties, and pilgrims to the three annual festivals serving as an inn.

Jashen proved to be an extra-accommodating host. At the outdoor marketplace he had his servants purchase generous amounts of figs, grapes, raisins, dates and date syrup, olive oil, wheat and barley. Jashen made these available to his houseful at no cost. This included freshwater dried fish from Lake Kinneret, and saltwater dried fish from the Great Sea to the west. He raised goats and chickens in a rear courtyard.

Commenting on compliments of his generosity, smiling he would say, "Jesus would want me to do so, besides it's a mitzvah!" Indeed, Adonai smiled down on his good deeds.

Nicodemus, Jashen and Joseph of Arimathea owned papyrus scrolls of all the Scriptures and loaned them to the upstairs guests. The three men set up baskets to

hold the scrolls in, and tables, like a bimah in a synagogue, for reading. All members of the Sanhedrin had private libraries containing all 24 scrolls of the Torah, Prophets, Psalms and the Writings. Collectors could buy scrolls separately, but more income meant a larger library of the sacred writings and other Jewish literature; some written in Hebrew or Greek.

Families came; generations huddled together. A dozen or so graying women wore their long hair in braids. Their conversations braided the women in friendship. Gray-bearded men, some balding, found rest at Jashen's; they told tales of when their heads had much hair.

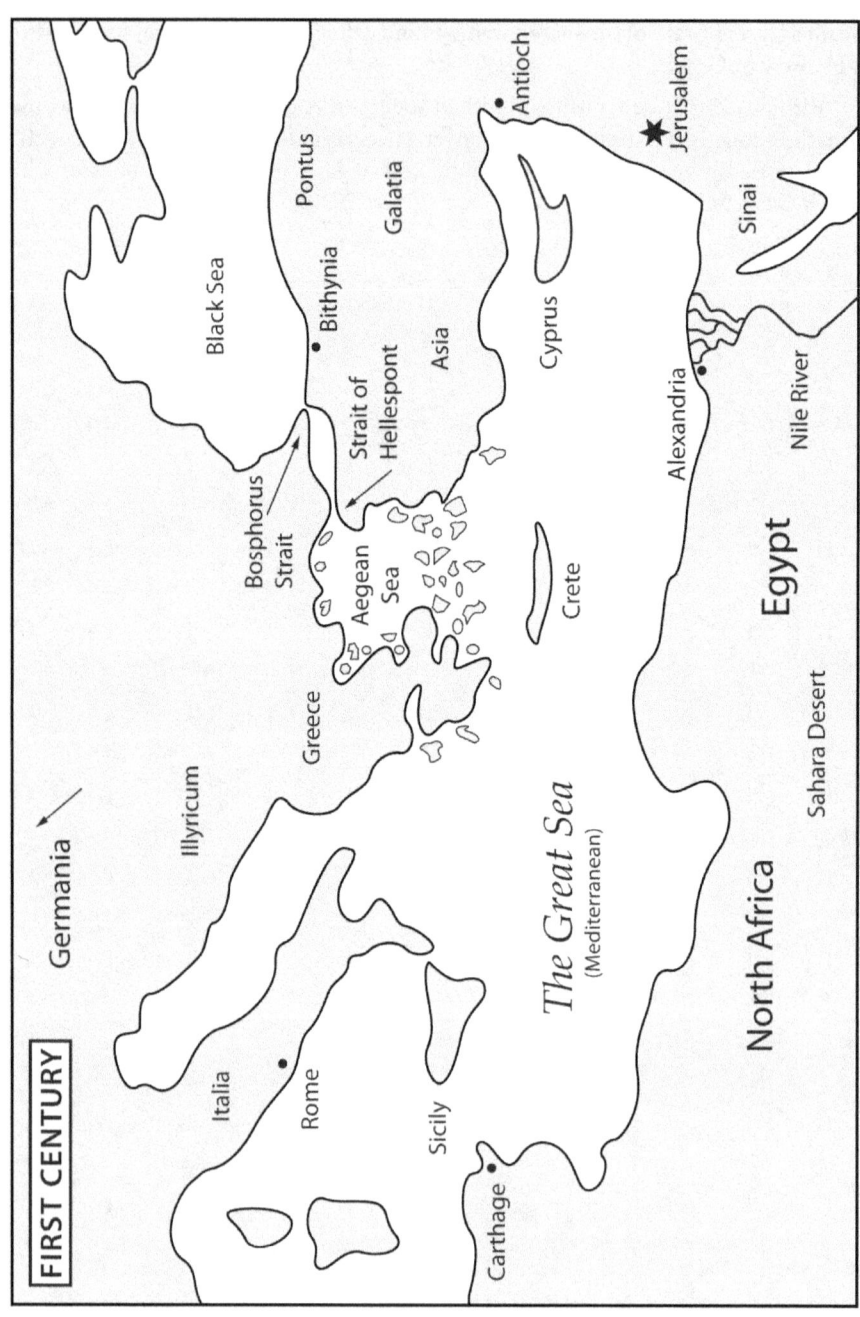

FIRST CENTURY

Germania

Italia

Rome

Sicily

Carthage

Illyricum

Greece

The Great Sea
(Mediterranean)

North Africa

Sahara Desert

Black Sea

Bosphorus
Strait

Aegean
Sea

Crete

Bithynia

Strait of
Hellespont

Asia

Cyprus

Alexandria

Egypt

Nile River

Pontus

Galatia

Antioch

Jerusalem

Sinai

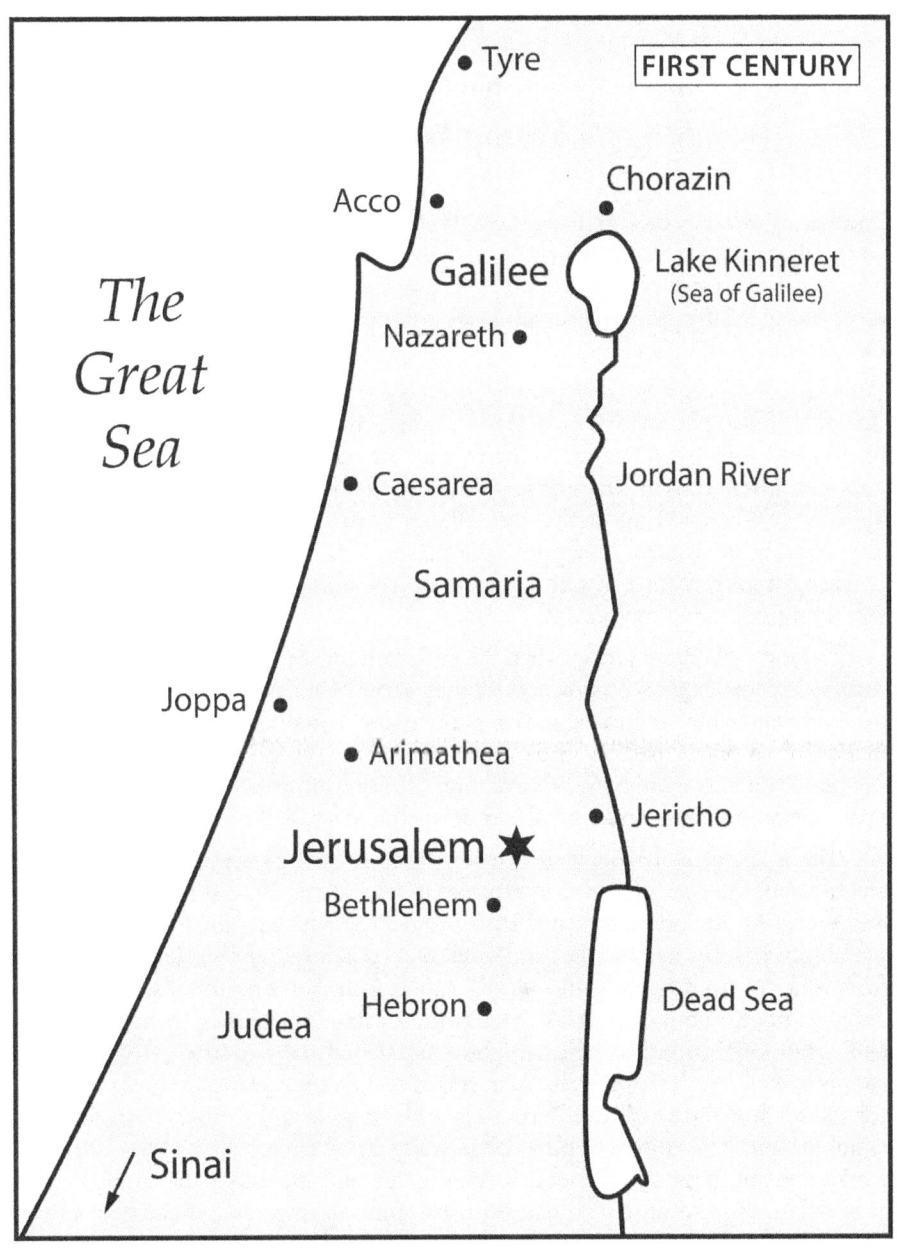

Chronicle Three
Six for Pentecost in Jerusalem

Chapter 14
Young Women

The young women crowded together. They couldn't believe how fortunate they were. The big adventure, which they'd wanted all their lives, had finally been planned. This wasn't a rumor. Giggling, jesting and lightness of foot proved how the news energized the group. "Jerusalem! We are going to Jerusalem—our families too. Goodbye, city of Antioch!"

Outside their synagogue near the Orontes River and the Daphne Gate in Syrian Antioch, the gaggle of five girls made a noisy, lively homespun knot. Brothers, uncles, and aunts who had made the trek before watched, amused. Delighted, the girls anticipated the camaraderie and future remembrances of the 300 mile stretch between Antioch and the capital by walking, occasional donkey, or wagon riding, and sleeping in strange, uncomfortable places. Yet, such would weary everyone. Even so, far away from home and in sight of Jerusalem, joy would fill the travelers with traditional songs of journey.

I a long 300. Three years earlier, the fathers of these five teenage girls had made the trip to Jerusalem for Passover, traversing 15 to 20 miles a day. The men joined a local caravan, which increased in size as the mass neared the holy city. They stayed in inns on common roads or trade routes. Some inns, already ancient by centuries, provided the bare minimum of structures, safety from robbers, a fire pit, certain provisions for humans and animals, fresh water and a roof if desired.

The girls dreamed of being princesses. Three of the five were betrothed. The girls chatted about the wonderful marketplaces in Jerusalem, and this topic went round and round in the following days. They begged their parents for freedom to shop for fabrics, jewelry, hair brushes and ornaments to adorn their heads. They pleaded for cosmetics from Egypt—the world's expert in fragrant ointments, scented oils and perfumes. The fathers tried to calm their excited daughters by making small and conditional promises which slightly dampened the enthusiasm. So the girls simply stoked their feminine charm in response. Over the years, as money allowed, the fathers had returned from Jerusalem with trinkets and various items for their children. But, explaining the math concerning travel expenses and time lost from work rarely made the sensible conclusions the parents intended. The families could accumulate only so much to load on pack animals, wagons and carts for return cargo. During the days close to departure, in the five households, each father made the same speech, "I am not made out of shekels!"

From an early age, parents raised children hoping to instill the value and necessity of hard work. Days held fun, play, and social activities, but the undercurrent of labor prevailed. The idea of an excursion to the capital met with curious looks— none of the girls could picture the immensity of the city and its teeming population. They knew stories of the spectacular Temple Mount, a jeweled crown shining in the sunlight, which stunned first, second and further viewers.

Mothers explained in more depth, the coming major holiday of Pentecost. This education of the young ladies fostered pride for their heritage. This blended with the girlish drive for new, exotic sights and possessions. Each grew up praying the ancient liturgical prayers; doing the monthly ritual female washings; lighting candles on the eve of the Sabbath (when given the privilege), butchering, cooking, reading Hebrew, speaking Aramaic, Greek and some Latin. They knew Holy Scripture, and of the One God and Creator, and that He lived where they were going.

The God of Abraham, Isaac and Jacob designed a lifestyle and a calendar for His people. The rituals of presentation, sacrifices and blessings varied much from male to female babies. This dedication to God's commandments in the Torah, given through Moses, depended upon the parents' finances and distance to the holy city.

One mother, the wife of Medan, explained to her daughter, Prisca, "Oh, listen! Your father and I did this on a pilgrimage to Jerusalem before you were born. Did you know that when Jews travel to or from the country of Israel, and then return, there's something we do at the borders?" She had her audience's attention and waited silently.

"First you shake out all of your clothes. Then you take off your shoes and shake them or even better wash your feet. You do not want to defile and pollute Israel's soil with the dirt—even the—dust—of pagan lands. It is considered so unclean, as if it came from a grave. Even little children shake their clothes."

Prisca asked, "What of travel to Israel by ship, then what do Jews do?"

Her mother answered, "Before your sandals touch the sand, you dangle your feet in the water, stand and shake off your clothes, too."

The girl's mother raised a finger with confidence and said, "Oh, here's another interesting custom. I traveled to Alexandria with my parents at your age. My father said that there, as in other lands, when a Jew dies, the family might sprinkle dirt from Israel on the face of the dead person. Sometimes they also put this dirt in a small linen bag and place it under the crook of the neck when the body is inside the cloth shroud or coffin. It's a mitzvah, a holy act to bless the person who died, because he or she wouldn't be buried in the Holy Land. Isn't that something? Well, we went to two or three funerals in Alexandria, and this happened. Understand that travelers put Israel's soil or sand into a bottle and bring this to foreign lands and donate it to the synagogues to keep for funerals."

The five traveled to Jerusalem once, when taken to the Temple as infants by their parents for newborn rituals. Everyone spoke of the historic capital, but none of the girls remembered visiting.

Medan, father to Prisca, explained about her trip to Jerusalem fourteen years ago as an infant. "After the day of your birth, your mother, like all Jewish mothers, entered an unclean period. No physical intimacy for at least 14 days, and impure for an additional 66 days, 80 in all. The math of the appointed times for your brothers—boy babies—is different, it's half the time."

Prisca grunted. She chewed on a fingernail. "And what about a boy's...."

Medan said, "Circumcision is performed in Jerusalem or elsewhere on the eighth day. That's when his name is given. At the Temple we made animal sacrifices of thanksgiving according to rules in the Torah: a one-year-old lamb, two pigeons or two turtledoves. Forty days after birth, the mother comes to the Temple for purification. Mothers are required to immerse in a sanctified mikveh pool, or the ocean, lake, or a river. After birthing a child, eventually a woman's monthly cycle starts again. Seven days after her bleeding ceases, she immerses in a mikveh pool—"

Prisca interjected, "For spiritual cleansing like we do on the shores of the Orontes River for other immersion rituals?"

Medan replied, "Yes. Except in the city, the new mother uses an enclosed 'women's only' mikveh pool and undresses completely. But here, the first Sabbath after your birth, I and your mother, friends, and family celebrated. Also, in our synagogue the leader called me to the front, and I had the honor to read from the Torah scrolls. Afterwards, the leader held you up, pronounced a blessing over little you, and then announced the name Mother and I had chosen for you."

"And I was very cute!"

"And you were very cute."

They both laughed.

Chapter 15
Papa Gamul

Simmering in the back of his mind stood the magnificent gleaming white and gold Holy Temple. He'd seen it as a boy, decades ago. The vision of Jerusalem's Mount Moriah remained in the minds of all who'd lived or traveled there. Gamul stood with an arm resting on a stout branch of an apple tree in his large orchard. At his side a dark-skinned boy tugged on the old man's white tunic. Rising out of his daydream, Gamul looked down at Hanan, one of his grandsons. A smile broadened as the picture of Jerusalem faded.

"What is it, child?"

"Papa Gamul, the meal is ready. Aunt Marsena sent me to find you. Did you not hear the bell?" The boy stared at the man who loved him: dark lines of wrinkles, graying beard, thick moustache, and ochre colored turban. "Why did you not come, Papa?"

Gamul lowered his head toward Hanan. The familiar map of wrinkles formed a wink. "Me? I found myself in the Holy City, peering at God's home. I forgot where I was. Yet now I'm back."

Cheerfully, Hanan said, "It's on a hill, a big flat-topped hill. Priests blow silver trumpets there and ram's horns, too. Thousands and thousands of our people sing, dance, and pray. In the bright sunlight, walls of shiny white marble and gold shout that God is here. During the holidays it is as though each generation has sent a family representative for celebration. There is no place like it in the entire world. Isn't that so, Papa?"

The old man's pride caused him to stare in bewilderment. "You have listened well, and well have you spoken." He rested his hand on the boy's shoulder as they walked to the house.

Before settling at the large outdoor wooden table and benches, Hanan squeezed Gamul's hand. Looking up with tears in his eyes, full of sincerity, he said, "I'll miss you. I want to come with you, but my Abba says my time will come—as did his." On the young cheeks two narrow rivers gleamed in the sunlight.

The last meal before Gamul's trip drew all the nearby relatives, nearly two dozen of his descendants. They did not openly speak of the questionable undertaking: more than a thousand miles south, crossing rivers and through mountainous Germania and Illyricum on land, by horse, wagon, camel; then the southern voyage along the Adriatic Sea's eastern coast and into the Great Sea. Next would be the island maze of Greece, past Cyprus, to the seaports of Israel, ending with transportation by animal and on foot to Jerusalem.

Gamul's children feared for the old man's safety and health. Each male relative and old friend had had an awkward and yet respectful talk with this patriarch about bandits, shipwrecks, storms, hunger, wild animals, and foreign food not suited to his stomach. The women prayed through their fears, knowing not to double up on the men's advice.

Gamul's wife had died four years earlier. Since her death, he had set aside a small amount of money on every business transaction. Two years passed before the idea of traveling to Jerusalem for Pentecost took hold. With this as his goal, he increased the incremental savings by charging his fruit customers a bit more. Then he disclosed to his children his secret ambition of traveling to Jerusalem six months before the planned departure date.

At this meal, Gamul, with his signature wry grin, ordered the wine to flow, songs and instruments and happy faces. "Let the little ones chase the chickens and bother the young goats!" He bellowed, "No scolding, no harsh words, and no stern looks at this festive time." Gamul looked at the precious, familiar faces. In a solemn tone he added, "And to you, dear ones, who worry for me, I say that looking for what's reasonable can do away with what's wonderful."

Most believed they'd never see their beloved Gamul again. If he didn't die on the journey to Jerusalem, he would die there, or on the hard odyssey back. Yet, they had made enough effort for peace to settle in their hearts, knowing that such an end of his life would've been on well spent, final journey. "The goal is a good one." He explained. However, Gamul's sons had insisted that one stout 20-year-old nephew join him as his steward, protector, and traveling companion. The idea had grown on old Gamul. He decided that the young man, though not his favorite nephew, would do. "Better two than one, indeed." Each relative contributed to cover the nephew's traveling expenses.

In the morning, the men saddled two horses. A third bore their cargo in bulky saddle bags. Gamul's waiting family were more than he expected for his departure. Cheerfully, he called out, "Shalom Aleichem!" Peace be to you!

They replied as one, "Aleichem Shalom!"

Smiling, he tugged on the bridle, the horse turned, and after a kick, they rode south.

Chapter 16
Father and Son

In the southeastern desert region of Israel, Judea, near the Dead Sea, lived the highly religious and ascetic Essenes. These Jews had withdrawn from society into small, private villages. Across the Dead Sea, in the mountains of Moab, were the large pink sandstone hills and cliff faces of the thriving city of Petra. In the hot Judean hills, merciless heat drove farmers, traders, and workers. They coaxed shade as a protective possession, priceless as water; shadows meandered through the day. Kerioth, located amid rugged, desert canyons and mountains in the southern Judean region, close to the border of Edom, the town's name translated into Greek: Iscariot.

In the obscure village lived a man named Simon and his wife Jehoaddan. Their children grew up learning that the hard, stony soil, if worked properly with tedious effort, could produce meager crops and feed farm animals. In one day's walking distance lay the great salt sea—great, but dead. This long body of cursed water provided only shimmering mirages of drinkable liquid. No boats ever traversed the open grave of blue water. On the sandy shores camels trod without interest, mindful of the toxic liquid their thirsting owners raised a fist to.

Simon's sons and daughters grew up with bent backs and rounded shoulders. However, one son wanted out—demanded out. Not only did he want to change his life, but also the life of his people. Roman control filled his nostrils with disdain. Though few foreign forces passed through their family's scrap of land near Kerioth, memories and stories lingered. Fresh news ground into his raw heart. When the son and his father made journeys to the cities to barter and buy supplies, the Roman taxes stung like bees—too many bees for the young man. His strong will pivoted on the destruction of the Roman infrastructure. He had ears of stone for any talk of acceptance and conciliation. The young man daydreamed of patriotic confrontations like the Maccabees rebellion 200 years ago.

A nearby town housed rebels, plotters, and assassins called the Sicarii, meaning violent men or dagger-bearers, from the name for the Roman dagger Sica. This son left home and joined with those set against Rome's oppression. They assassinated and murdered prominent Jews considered collaborators, who preferred Rome over revolt. Israel had no army—only discreet street fighters, and Sicarii, who struck unlucky Romans or Greeks while in a tight crowd, alone in a narrow winding street, or on an empty road or such.

While in his mid-20s, this eldest son moved with the group to a secret base closer to the capital. His parents rarely saw him after that. He lost respect and love for his younger brothers, who didn't follow his daring lifestyle. He chose not to marry and only to devote himself to national freedom.

A network of Zealots operated as a political movement and occasionally caused open, violent confrontations. A revolt led by a captivating leader occurred 20 years before. Many Jews died in the failed effort. Zealots sought to incite Jews to rebel with or without force. They were determined to protect Judaism from the imposition of Roman rituals and Greek influence, and to end pagan rule over the Jewish people. The Sicarii killers left the Hebrew God and His Torah to other Jews.

Simon and each of his other sons made the four-day journey to Jerusalem three times a year for the annual festivals. There he tried to locate his eldest son. If he did, Simon, with paternal care, gave money and food to him and expressed his and his wife's steadfast affection. Simon suppressed voicing their worry. He and Jehoaddan's emotions jostled as to whether pride or dread apprehension should prevail. The parents experienced sadness with one missing from their meal time.

The ruthless men of the secret Sicarii assigned this emboldened young man to follow a new, people's rabbi and teacher who lived north in Galilee. They wanted to know more of his politics and whether he might be turned into an asset. The chosen member promised that he would try to sway this popular figure. Rumors of Messiahship made him rub his hands together and chuckle, "That's awfully convenient, now isn't it? An actor shall I be, and a faithful follower, too."

Judas stayed with the Galilean teacher for over three years, much longer than he'd expected. He even earned the privilege of discipleship. Then he joined the inner circle of 12—the only one not from the Galil. Even more surprising, though, the rabbi trusted him as steward of the donations to his ministry. Judas secretly passed coins along to his dark, zealous accomplices. Tempted, he also set aside a private treasury of his own. Greed suited him. He wanted to be on the inside of political power when this Rabbi Jesus made his revolt. When the people shouted for the rabbi to be their king, Judas shouted the loudest of the twelve to join in. He longed to stir political grievances and point to Jesus as the obvious solution. Jesus, the miracle rabbi, could stir up the population into an army. Jesus could heal the wounded and raise to life those who'd die in battle.

Judas' hidden agendas worked well. The fire in him found outlets. The desert man's young heart had become conflicted. Righteousness to him meant overthrow by violent revolution. Power: kingship. Money: other's earnings in his own purse. Hero: faithful and zealous, even to death by martyrdom. Sacrificing: others' lives as deemed necessary for the cause. Prayer: unnecessary. Temple: pointless. Forgiveness: never. God: unavailable.

This wasn't sound, but he didn't know it. Months moved on and his heart hardened while severe ambitions and conceit rose.

*   *   *

Simon heard stories of the man his son followed. Good works, special powers, demons gone, engaging Scripture teachings and criticism of the pagan government superintending God's people. Simon didn't know what else to believe—the Son of God? No. Kingdom of God? Hopefully. Son of David? Good. However he understood well enough that his son followed one who would not bow to Roman or corrupt Temple authorities, and that made sense—dangerous sense. *Our ancestral ways and religion, could these survive once more? Are the Zealots leading our countrymen to ruin? Mere protests are over.*

This year, due to illness, Simon didn't travel to Jerusalem for Passover. His sons made the trek. They returned with disturbing news: A riot in Jerusalem. The chief priests had the Romans arrest their brother's messianic rabbi.

In guarded speech the sons explained, "The man shouted outspoken condemnation of the priesthood on the very Temple grounds. This included violence amongst the merchants and money-changers, whipping them in fierce anger. He flung the transaction tables, scattering tax money and ill profit, calling them hucksters and thieves. Jesus accused the priesthood of corruption. People liked him. His popularity has grown." The brothers said they didn't know more than that.

A chill went down Simon's spine. He stiffened and spoke, "No surprise to me. I knew that a revolt or arrest would only be a matter of time. But, what has my son chosen…are they succeeding or losing this fight?" As he pondered these deep possibilities, the sirocco wind blew in from the Sahara in North Africa. Heat and dust, stronger by the minute, made Simon take shelter indoors. While he and his wife covered their meager windows, his thoughts blew in all directions.

*　　*　　*

After the weather cleared, Simon planned to go to Jerusalem forty-five days after Passover for Pentecost. He wanted to locate his son in the mass of festive Jews. "If I can find this Rabbi Jesus, then I can find my son," he said, chuckling to himself, "Whom they've designated 'Judas of Iscariot!' True, Judas has a common name, but, 'Judas of Iscariot!' It is as if he represented the whole town. Hah!"

The day before Pentecost, Simon arrived in Jerusalem. He asked for news of Jesus, his disciples, and of the man from Iscariot in particular. He traced the trail. He found his beloved son at a silent, lonely place. Fresh graves of unmarked strangers lay close by. Simon mused, "Only fifty days have passed. Death, you are always hard at work!"

Simon knelt and wept.

He didn't know the full story, but a father doesn't need to, in order to grieve.

Chapter 17
Dinah of Alexandria

Bilshan, his wife, Dinah, and three of their grandchildren sat in a boat ferrying passengers and cargo from Alexandria in the broad Nile River delta. A series of such boats networked between the irregular strips of fertile land. The couple and grandchildren traveled north to the Great Sea and boarded an ocean-worthy vessel. A final voyage took them to Israel's southwestern seaport of Joppa. Then they traveled east by land and sought lodging in Jerusalem.

Bilshan had ventured to yet another of the three annual festivals in Jerusalem. But on this trip he invited his wife. An excited Dinah wanted to include the grandchildren, and Bilshan raised his eyebrows and dutifully agreed.

Thirty-two years earlier, shortly after their marriage, Bilshan had taken a promising position in the shipping trade. Family connections helped to secure this opportunity. Bilshan and Dinah moved far to the west, 1,200 miles across the Great Sea to the massive northern African port city of Carthage, on the Tunisian Peninsula. This ancient Phoenician stronghold lay southwest of the large island of Sicily.

Dinah cried every day for the first three months away from home. However, they raised their five children there and lived an affluent life. Then her husband's business partners moved him back to Alexandria to take a different post. Gladness filled Dinah—an answer to old prayers. Her husband, a good man, they had prospered, she dearly missed her family and childhood friends. Alexandria, her home, contained the largest population of Jews—at least one out of five—outside of Israel. No wonder people called it Yerushalayim Hak'tanah—Little Jerusalem.

At age 17, she had spent one year during her betrothal in service to an elderly, retired priest and his wife in the Israeli town of Hebron, in Judea. During her time as the servant girl to Zechariah and Elizabeth, the elderly woman became pregnant with their only child. This surprising development compounded Dinah's role in strenuous and yet wonderful ways. She smiled at Adonai's faithfulness while performing her duties.

Unexpectedly, a young cousin of theirs, named Mary, from the small Galilean village of Nazareth, stayed for three months. The girls were the same age, height, and build. Soon they were close friends. After the baby, named John, arrived, Mary traveled back home to the hills of Nazareth. She herself in the early stage of pregnancy, but that topic remained private and shadowed with mystery. Thirty-three years ago; like Dinah, Mary would be fifty now. She had always wondered what life Mary had led.

Dinah knew on this trip she couldn't press her husband to travel 80 miles north to seek out her old friend in Nazareth—especially with the grandchildren. Had they booked a ship to the northern port of Acco, such a side trip might've worked. But, her husband made other plans.

"Another time," he said. However, Bilshan had agreed to his wife's pleading to revisit Hebron, 25 miles southwest of Jerusalem, into the stony hills of Judah, after their holiday obligations of Pentecost. Dinah wanted to locate the tombs of her deceased masters and place small stones by their chiseled names. This custom meant much, for it showed remembrance by the living. A memorial of stones marked people of respect and benevolence—now living in the next world. The old couple's kindness and role modeling helped shape her adult character and a lifetime of spiritual commitment.

Dinah beamed at her husband. "They were so special! Everyone in Hebron spoke well of them. They lived the most perfect lives imaginable. Townspeople envied my twelve-month intimacy with Zechariah and Elizabeth—even Mary did—the cousin I spoke about."

Bilshan rolled his eyes, "You! Speaking of Hebron. Nah! You?" He grinned. But when he saw tears flowing, he hugged Dinah. "I think I'm just jealous. What a good year you had! I would thank them for their influence on my bride. But remember, you left me behind in Alexandria. Every day while working at the docks I pictured you sailing home from Israel."

Part of Pentecost meant celebrating God's giving the Torah. These written words, chiseled on stone over 1,400 years ago at Mount Sinai, and later penned, described the behavior for the Children of Israel. As good grandparents, Bilshan and Dinah instructed the holy ways of life at home and to the grandchildren on this extraordinary journey. She recalled the twelve months of constant rich mentoring by Elizabeth of their unique Jewish religious culture.

When these Alexandrians arrived at the burial site in Hebron, Dinah teared up at the two tombs, especially when she saw two sizable piles of small stones. Obviously by those who lived there. Yes, Zechariah and Elizabeth impacted the town. Dinah's heartfelt assessment proved true.

Chapter 18
Bithynia and Gone

Murky saltwater lapped higher and higher on the shore. Ikkesh looked to the ship's crew and muttered, "Pirates, for sure." Though Ikkesh knew the harbor and nearby coastline, he'd not heard of this ship, the *Tanaerum*. "Pagans." He spat. The old man grunted, "Idol worshippers! Rats below and rats on deck."

Ikkesh's eldest son, Enan, had done what he could to plan this expensive expedition. His father's critical remarks shamed Enan. Much of the following weeks' transportation lay unforeseen. Yet the ship proved a fine one and would take them, weather permitting, to their first port and beyond.

Enan enjoyed the whole idea of visiting their ancient homeland. He welcomed this long journey as an adventure. Their goals were to arrive in Jerusalem in time for Rosh Chodesh, the new moon festival of the month of Iyar, and stay through the following month of Sivan until Pentecost. With 25 to 35 days of travel, Enan thought of new scenery, foreign cities, strange customs, different dialects, interesting food, and exotic beautiful women.

Though not elderly, Ikkesh bore a divided heart and burdensome mind. He had done such an extended voyage and land travel twice before: Passover 40 years ago as a boy with his father, and 18 years ago with two old friends for Chanukkah. Of his synagogue friends and local relatives, Ikkesh remained the only man to seek this religious pilgrimage three times. What with the days lost from home, relatives, and work, to risk the unknown—one trip remained truly remarkable. The poor simply didn't go. He had met many men who made a once-in-a-lifetime journey to Jerusalem, typically for the most crowded of holidays, Passover—when the city swelled to six times its normal size. Every home opened its door for travelers, while others had to camp in tents wherever they could.

The older man's growing fears and petty complaints pecked at Enan's enthusiasm—and the ship hadn't even sailed yet. He knew that his mother, Taphath, though worried for both of them, enjoyed the break from her increasingly annoying husband. As their marriage aged, she herself had remained upbeat. However, Ikkesh's frame of mind had taken significant downward steps for no reason other than age. Yet, Enan noticed increasing frailty since the death of his father's own elderly parents two years ago. Ikkesh seemed lost since then, a piece missing. Now, 'grumpy and disoriented' described him more accurately. The children and grandchildren were doing well. The aging couple saw them often. Ikkesh's business in fragrant oils, which he inherited from his father-in-law, brought in a hardy sum of money and bartered goods. But, aside from his gaining foibles, a journey, a last trip to Jerusalem apparently tugged at him as a must.

Ikkesh's embarrassing side remarks caused his son to wonder why his father chose such a distant, difficult destination. Enan kicked at the sand in frustration.

Several Jews waited on shore for the departure at high tide. However, from the talk Enan overheard, none shared the far-away goal of Jerusalem. Besides captain and crew, the venture's passengers included a few merchants, husbands and wives, fathers with sons or daughters, slaves with masters.

This journey from upper Bithynia on the southern coast of the Black Sea passed the strategic city of Byzantium via the Turkish Strait of Bosphorus—a twenty-mile long and two-mile wide waterway with city on both shores. Another ship would take them through the Marmara Sea and the dangerous, narrow channel of the Strait of Hellespont, where they'd pass ancient Troy. There they'd board a third ship and sail to several ports in the Aegean Sea. The crew would take on fresh supplies and new passengers. They'd sail to the isle of Crete and later the island of Cyprus. The destination ports of Israel, due east, were one to two days from there if the weather held. Donkeys, camels and carts finished the month-long trip to Jerusalem.

And so, set sail they did. As the ship gained leagues by the billowing linen sailcloth, the fresh salt air breathed life back into Ikkesh. The adventure faithfully revived his old, worrisome heart into a wholesome one. Cheerfully, he spoke to the crew and other passengers. Others approached and they swapped travel tales. Also, his appetite improved, and he put on needed weight.

Enan easily noticed the difference. Relieved, he stated, "A wonderful start to our journey, Father." After moments of silence, the son carefully asked, "Tell me again, why you are returning to Israel? Why now? Tell me more."

At the wooden railing, Ikkesh opened his hands. "I'll tell you." As he continued to speak, his arms spread wide. "Where we live is not our home. The soil on which we tread is not our own—not God-given. Where we live—and no doubt will die— is a land not promised to us. Adonai blesses our friends and family there because He's in the business of blessing. Our ancestors traveled to Egypt, left Egypt, went to our homeland, lost our homeland, then traveled to exile in foreign countries due to our disobedience. When Babylon became a comfortable nest, which we appreciated, many of our people chose to remain there even when the gateway of freedom rose for returning. Our forefathers chose to be elsewhere than return." The old man turned to face his son. "Was our God hurt by these choices? I say yes. Does He want us all to return? Again, I say yes."

Enan's forehead wrinkled. Ikkesh said, "To make aliyah and move back to our ancient homeland…." He sucked in his lips. His eyes swept the wide sea. "Hmm… that time has passed. As is our tradition and blessing, not many days from now, before we board the ship for our return voyage we will fill a bottle with the holy soil of Israel—"

Enan interjected, "and when you die we'll sprinkle some of the dirt on your face and place a small sack of the earth under your neck." Enan looked at seagulls circling the ship and asked, "But, is that enough to please Adonai?"

Ikkesh gripped the railing harder. "Please God? I'd say He is pleased right now."

Chapter 19

Beggars

Bruised knees bled. Chaffed skin on the man's elbows stung. Calloused fingers gripped the stony ground. His ragged clothing did little to protect him. Bleary senses carried the message *move on, keep moving,* to his boggled mind. Beside him trudged a stooped woman. Ragged shoulder-length gray hair made the two beggars a pair.

Puss reappeared, due to the latest butt end of a Roman spear had sliced open an unhealed wound. The man, Gishpa, groaned at the memory of that spiteful jab. The powerful soldier had walked away mimicking the pained voice, followed by a chuckle.

The crowded streets promised many shekels for such beggars. This holiday, as with Passover and Tabernacles, brought a multitude of travelers into the holy city. However, the presence of foreign invaders dimmed the term "holy." Trampled-upon Jews, whether wealthy or poor, nursed physical and spiritual sores. Even so, not everyone thought Rome should withdraw from Israel's Promised Land.

The elderly couple found shade and stopped their crawl on the paved road. Helah, the wife, arranged the sack of skin, muscle and bones that was her husband. She pushed to seat him against a stone wall. Then Helah drew in his feeble legs so cart wheels, feet, and animal hoofs would not damage him more.

After Helah settled next to Gishpa, the filthy and disfigured couple leaned shoulders into each other. He sighed, "I can barely breathe. No calling out from me today. No one would hear me in this tumult anyway; such noise." They heard Hebrew, Aramaic, Latin, Greek—and a significant mix of voices from foreign lands, along with the complaining sounds of pack animals.

Helah patted Gishpa in a gentle petting way. "I will do the calling out. You do some praying. Surely Adonai sees us and must remember our trail of sorrow." She brushed his matted hair away from a wrinkled, sweaty face and fevered body. Her expression showed pity—and honor.

He nodded through a hacking cough, and then let his shoulders droop. His eyes stared straight ahead at nothing.

Gishpa vaguely remembered a time when they had lived in a house and he worked with leather. Helah assisted him and also made the meals. They went to synagogue, paid their taxes, worshipped at the Temple and fasted. Sadly, no children blessed their home. Now, he couldn't piece together what had happened, what went wrong—he just knew that the streets of Jerusalem were their home.

In spite of his troubles inside him, unexpected peace rose. In his mind's eye he saw a captivating, glowing smile. Light shone around the golden lips. The inviting picture grew. He heaved a sigh and let out a slow breath.

Suddenly, a jovial man stood still on their side of the passing parade of citizens and travelers. With his dark skin, bright turban, oiled beard, and swaying robe, he stared, as if considering their plight. Then he bent down. In a strong but not boisterous voice, he said, "Shalom! I'm Maaziah from Cyprus, a merchant. I do quite well, bless Adonai! In praise to Him, I decided I would bless someone once I got to Jerusalem for Pentecost—that is, if I made it safely." He paused and looked for their responses. Only the old woman raised a dirty, gnarled open hand.

He continued, "However, I will be blessing two, it seems. Now I wonder how many shekels it would take to provide the two of you with enough food, clothing and shelter until Pentecost next year. Oh, and get you off the street and this cursed beggar's life."

The woman's eyes went wide and tears welled up. Frightened at the friendly intruder, she scrunched her back against the wall. Her husband didn't move.

Maaziah drew out a leather pouch from a fold in his robe. He hefted it while suspiciously looking both ways at the stream of strangers. He gently pulled on Helah's wrist and put a firm calloused palm under her frail bony hand. There he placed the sack of coins. She quickly covered the heavy bag with her other hand. Maaziah rested his other palm over hers and gave a reassuring squeeze. When he let go, her arm sagged under the weight.

Maaziah smiled. "Baruch HaShem! Blessed is His name!" He turned, and his robust gait was lost from her sight in the bustling momentum of the multitude.

Helah shook her husband. Through her brightened face she said, "Gishpa, why didn't you say something, bless him or nod in thanks at least?" She looked fully into his face. He stared straight ahead, eyes open, unblinking. The slight edges of a grin remained due to the smile only he had seen. His poverty in this world had ended moments before the rich man appeared. Wincing, Helah closed his eyelids and grasped his hand.

She pressed her back against the wall and rested. It had been years.

Chronicle Four
Forty Days after the Resurrection

Chapter 20
Ascension Cloud

Those in the Upper Room overheard Peter and the other core disciples discussing unusual stories about the Messiah. True, all their stories were extraordinary. To hear better, people moved closer, hoping to be included in the conversation. Mary and other familiar faces did the same.

Acknowledging the growing audience, Peter spoke more loudly. "Several weeks ago, Jesus led us, the Eleven, to the Mount of Olives. Gazing at the massive city below, we questioned him about his plans. We, as all of you, assumed the Messianic kingdom was about to start. To our disappointment, it sounded like his resurrection visits were finished. However, he said we needed to stay in Jerusalem and wait for another wonderful event."

Indeed, his final instructions to them remained open-ended. "Stay in Jerusalem until I send the Promise from my Father and you receive power from heaven. For John immersed with water, but you will be immersed with the Holy Spirit and fire— not many days from now." When the closest disciples heard this and then watched him float away in the sky, they knew Jesus meant something unusual beyond the miracles and glory they'd already been privy to.

Now, James looked into eager faces shining with anticipation. He asked Peter, "Do you remember people asking us 'What can your rabbi do that we haven't seen before?' More than once they asked if he could fly like a bird. Well, on the day Peter is speaking of, something like that did happen. When Jesus finished talking, he looked to the sky. Without noise or wind, his feet lifted off the ground. Watching him rise higher, our mouths opened in astonishment as he silently left. Then a brilliant white cloud, glinting with golden sparkles, about the size of a house, came into view. This glowing heavenly cloud came lower as he rose to meet it. The cloud surrounded him, then quickly moved out of sight high into the sky. Dumbfounded, we simply stared.

"Suddenly, two tall men in shining robes with radiant silvery hair and glowing skin stood nearby. They had our attention. These two angels—for angels they were—said Jesus would one day return in the same way we'd just seen him leave. After that, they vanished, like a mirage in the desert. It's true, Jesus will return with clouds."

John chuckled, his eyes sparkling. "'Can your rabbi fly?' Yes, he can. Higher than a bird. Jesus traveled to heaven by cloud." The listeners grinned, and children flapped their arms like gliding birds.

Mary spoke to herself, fusing mirth with regret, "So many wonders. I missed so much, too much."

Matthew said, "Isaiah the prophet of old, wrote, 'They who wait for the Lord shall renew their strength." Heads nodded.

John added, "Though not our expectations of God's kingdom of timetable, we were full of joy on our walk back to Jerusalem."

Chapter 21
Clouds

Aron, one of the Torah teachers, and a friend of the few believers in the Sanhedrin, spoke up. "A cloud, you say? But not just any cloud. Not birthed in this world, and not the first seen in Jerusalem." He tugged at his beard. "Recall with me the otherworldly clouds in Scripture, will you?"

Heads nodded. Listeners smiled, eagerly motioning him to go on. They sat in a semi-circle on the plank wood floor. Aron sat in front of the willing souls and prayed silently.

After prayerful thought his eyes opened. "Yes. Yes. This descending or sudden presence of the shekinah glory in the form of clouds started in ancient times. In effect, it is God dwelling among men—whether for brief or long periods. Of course, in the Wilderness Wanderings a protective, fiery pillar of cloud stood between our forefathers' camp and the vengeful camp of Pharaoh. The mighty pillar led our people for years. Scripture revealed, an angel took that form. Also, when Adonai presented the holy commandments to Moses, a dense cloud covered the top of Mount Sinai. Moses entered the cloud for 40 days." Aron turned to the Eleven. "You witnessed a thick cloud, no doubt."

They agreed.

"Remember when our ancestors traveled and set up camp, they rebuilt the Tabernacle and the Tent of Meeting. The first time they constructed the holy site and finished it for use, Adonai appeared in such radiance, filling the entire walled-off pavilion of sacrificial holy ground. A glorious, gleaming cloud rested above the Tent, and His glory filled the area where the Ark of the Covenant rested. Fire swirled in the cloud at night. Whenever it lifted, our people broke camp and set out behind the mystical leader. This supernatural sight remained on the Tent of Meeting throughout all of their journeying."

Aron rocked a little, stroking his long beard. "Let's see. Where else? Ah yes, a wonderful story—the opening day of King Solomon's Temple, nine centuries ago; all of Israel sought out Jerusalem, this after years of construction, creating silver and gold utensils, sacrificial equipment, immense tapestries, hundreds of gold tiles a cubit in size, musical instruments, and priestly robes and turbans.

"Hundreds of thousands of our forefathers from all tribes came to celebrate. The lifeblood of tens of thousands of sheep, goats and oxen spilt that day. From Bethlehem, priests carried the Ark of the Covenant, by then several hundreds of years old, on long poles, and they entered the inner sanctuary of the Temple. When the priests, chosen by lot, set the priceless Ark down in the Holy of Holies, a dense cloud filled the rooms. The intense glory, the presence of Adonai, grew so powerful, the priests ran out through the huge double doors. Everyone saw the dazzling sight." Aron raised a fist in triumph. "And what a sight to see!"

A child spoke, "Teacher, where is our Ark now? It's not in the Temple, is it?" The child's parents shushed him, and his father said in a loud whisper, "Son, that's a rude question to ask."

Aron raised his eyebrows and wrinkled his forehead. He sighed, tapping his lips with fingertips. "Ahh..." He hunched and exhaled heavily before continuing. Just above a whisper, he moaned, "That, child—well, we do not know where the holy Ark rests... no." He eyed the three core disciples and extended a hand to them. "Back to recent times. Did I hear a tale of Jesus and a cloud on a mountaintop in Galilee?"

Peter, James and John looked at one another. James volunteered, "Yes. However, this is awkward for us. Yet, right now this room has become a place of learning. What I'll say took place less than a year ago. Yes, Aron, we traveled around Galilee and camped at the base of one of the mountains. What happened? Well...it is a difficult story to accept." He stared hard at a now grumpy Peter, and then looked to the audience. "Jesus wanted to hike to the top and pray. He asked us to go with him. He told the other close disciples and followers to stay below. Once we settled at the top, instead of prayer, sleep overcame the three of us. After a time, we woke to see Jesus as a living flame against the night sky. His face, skin and clothing had turned to a gleaming, glowing white—as bright as the sun. We recognized true royalty and heavenly might which none of us will forget. As our eyes squinted and soon adjusted, we noticed two strangers had arrived. They held a serious conversation with Jesus. Do not ask me how we knew—we just knew—our eyes beheld Moses and Elijah."

A shudder ran through many of the listeners. One woman fainted. A low chatter engulfed the room. Debates started. Fingers pointed toward the apostles.

Two young girls, Michal and Hannah, granddaughters of Mary, sat together. They turned to face each other and started up a rhyme. While clapping their hands in criss-cross action they sang, "Un-cle Je-sus, know-sus Eli-jah and Mo-sus! Un-cle Je-sus, know-sus Eli-jah and Mo-sus!" Mary couldn't help but chuckle. After several rhymes, she finally put a finger to her lips. The girls whined but stopped.

Peter stretched out his arms and waved for quiet. "I know the story sounds outrageous. To have seen Moses, what can I say—awe-inspiring. You wonder, where did they come from and how did they get there? I don't know. You don't have to believe us. There's so much you've already seen for yourselves and accepted as truth. Now, back to the mountain top. These prophets of old also glowed—but less than Jesus. We were not involved in their discussion but did overhear the topic—Jesus' coming death in Jerusalem and his departure beyond the grave."

Glancing again at Peter, James continued, "I think Peter spoke while still half-awake at this unbelievable sight. Just when the two prophets seemed finished and started drifting away, Peter shouted that he had a great idea: we were handy men and could get to work right away building huts or small shelters for Jesus, Moses, and Elijah. He said, 'You don't have to leave so soon.'" James smiled, "I know, do not try to understand everything Peter says—that's one of our secret rules."

Peter rolled his eyes at another retelling of his foibles. Then, using a shooing gesture, by flicking his hands, he motioned to James to continue.

"As Peter babbled, a dense cloud, emitting light, suddenly appeared and enveloped us. Moses and Elijah disappeared into—" here he looked at Aron—"the cloud shimmering with gold." Then turning back to the other listeners, James continued, "Inside the cloud, as fright overtook us, a bold, confident voice spoke, interrupting Peter. The thunderous voice rang in our ears, filling our bodies. The hairs on our arms and necks stood straight, our skin tingled. We heard, 'This is My beloved Son, whom I have chosen. Listen to him!' When the voice stopped, the cloud vanished. Jesus looked normal—or should I say human—again."

The same boy who'd spoken earlier glanced at his parents for approval, then asked another question. "Peter, sir, why did you think the prophets and Jesus needed a temporary place in which to live?" The boy's father made a motion with his hand meaning no more questions.

Still seated, Peter stuck his tongue into his cheek. He crossed his arms and spoke. "I believed that Jesus in his glorious state and with such powerful men by his side—gone for centuries…well, I believed this was it! Jesus came to rule Israel. This must be the start, the beginning of his reign. Talk about excited. His radiant, kingly state made me expect him to stay like a candle, a flame ever burning, amazing everyone—Jews and pagans. Perhaps the three of them would start to make plans— many plans—and pray. Consider this: the Messiah will be extremely busy in his reign. Remember, when Moses met Adonai on Mount Sinai, he stayed there alone for 40 long days more than once. I thought it would be the same. Do you understand?"

While others nodded, the boy eyed his father and proudly whispered, "See?"

Thomas spoke up in Peter's defense. "Peter's heart was pure in this. A gesture of hospitality. I recall him saying, 'Rabbi, it is good for us to be here!' Often in our travels, evening would catch us on the road. We were accustomed to gather branches from trees or bushes, anything available and made temporary shelters. But surely, Moses and Elijah didn't need someplace to lay their heads."

James added, "As Jesus commanded, we didn't tell anyone what we'd seen and heard. After something like that, or when Jesus chose to walk across Lake Kinneret instead of sailing in a boat. He walked as if strolling on any street, as if he couldn't sink. When he entered our boat in the middle of the lake we couldn't say anything, anything at all—except for Peter."

Mumbling and chatter, heads waddled, and shrugs followed the bizarre tale and explanation. A shudder ran through Mary. She voiced to herself in recollection, "My son, my boy. I remember when his feet were so tiny…and his first steps." She clutched at her heart. "Joseph and I were really his parents, the Messiah's." A tear ran down her cheek. "I rarely saw my son these last few years and visited so little. Tell me, what mother goes through this?"

Mary's sister, Salome, commented, "One who was asked to by Almighty God."

Chapter 22
Mary to Share

These important disciples met daily at the Temple Mount either in the large Court of the Gentiles, the Women's Court, or one of the many rooms around the porticoes available for meetings. They returned to Jashen's for dinner, relaxation, chatter and sleep.

As the city swelled with worshippers for Pentecost, those headquartered in the Upper Room enjoyed daily visitors who stayed and slept elsewhere. One morning, Mary woke before anyone else and looked at the dedicated gathering. She had a secret, one of great value. She decided that the time had come to tell. Once the morning sun and the roosters woke her companions, she sought out Peter, James and John. It seemed right to ask their permission first, and then they would announce a meeting. Glad, she wanted to explain her marriage to Joseph, followed by mysteries of her pregnancy with Jesus. Such highly packed secret facts only Joseph, their deceased parents, her siblings, and her deceased cousins Zechariah, Elizabeth and their son John had known.

Mary's desire to make a speech impressed the three men.

Peter eagerly told everyone, "My friends, listen up. Tomorrow, at night we will have a special meeting. Invite those close to you and those who have visited here."

James added, "We have only so much room, so it'll be snug." Nods followed.

As a lifestyle, when meeting someone, Mary's politeness had an overwhelming effect. She'd learned humility in her teen years. Her passion moved hearts, broadening their awareness of Adonai. As mother of a miraculous prophet, many had envied her role in Israel's evolving history. Every day she considered how to bless those who sought her out. In addition, she sought solitude each day to recharge herself and her special role. Women tried to knit themselves to her. Some made or gave gifts. A few named babies 'Mary' because of her obedient honor. This attention caught the inner core of Mary. Awkwardly, she wanted some recognition, "Yes. That's my son. I'm so proud of him, of course." However, any exaltation from others felt like grains of sand she needed to rinse and spit out of her mouth.

Humbled yet again, to host this marvelous one-of-a-kind gathering, Jashen turned away to shed tears. Inspired by the importance of tomorrow night's special meeting; in his quarters on the first floor; Jashen prayed from Scripture and worshipped. "Knower of thoughts. King of worlds. You have dressed Yourself with majesty, grandeur, and splendor. You enwrap Yourself with light as with a garment. You spread the Heavens as a curtain. You stretched forth the Heavens and established the earth, the abode of whose majesty, the seat of whose glory is in the Heavens above, the loftiest heights. Adonai who forms light and creates darkness and all things; You have made all with wisdom. The earth is full of Your possessions. I put my trust, my hope in You."

Sleep pursued him and his bed awaited. Before so, he readied himself to solemnly recite the affirming Shema proclamation. The first prayer all children learned. Jews recited it when their lives were full of hope and when all hope lie distant, in moments of joy or despair, in thankfulness or quitting.

Jashen considered how Jews confidently spoke it at their time of death—before leaving this world for the next. Many Jews, martyred for being defiantly Jewish, affectionately said the Shema as their final confession.

The ancient words left his mouth and soared above the earth, dodging the stars, aiming to pierce the limitless void to an unseen throne. "Hear, O Israel, Adonai is our God, Adonai is One. And you shall love Adonai your God, with all your heart, with all your soul, and with all your might. And these words shall be upon my heart. Blessed is the Name of His glorious kingdom for all eternity...."

He considered how the dozens of souls on the floor above, no doubt, spoke the Shema at their bedtime. In the deepening dark, this beginning of a new day, thousands around him in Jerusalem had recited the prominent Jewish declaration... and then slept.

His thoughts scanned over hundreds of thousands of tiny flickering oil lamps in Jerusalem and the dimmed land of Israel. His imagination saw where Jews lived and flecks of light struggled against the dark. Even in Galilee to the north, this more than 1,400 year-old ritual leapt off young and old lips, ascending to the same throne.

Jashen considered the northern rim of the Mediterranean, its seaports, coastland villages, hill towns and cities set on mountainsides in countries which he knew little of. In all directions, the lands whose names lay unknown to his limited geography where further daubs of light representing millions of scattered Jews dwelling far from their ancient homeland. Though they knew many languages, they kept Hebrew by their heart. As light faded, and blackness progressed across familiar islands and rolling landscapes, God heard the repetition of His servants at slumber and awakening, the last words and the first words. In the dark of each night, and again in the ever-coming dawn, spoken in Lashon HaKodesh—the holy tongue, Hebrew: The Shema.

Chapter 23
Mary Tells All

The next evening after the usual communal dinner, the Upper Room filled beyond the average of 80 or so. A flock of men wore their fringed, black-striped prayer shawls; all had head-coverings, some wore turbans. The crowd sat on the floor. Jashen laid extra carpets and rugs and supplied cups and pitchers of water and wine. Loaves of bread lie on two tables. Many shared skins of liquid they'd brought. Interested others, and late comers, sat on the stairs leading down to the street level door—which Jashen closed and eventually locked.

Burning torches and candles, secured on the walls, illuminated the room. The attendees near windows enjoyed seeing a twilight-silhouetted Jerusalem. The first stars took their places in the heavens. Mary sat on a wooden chair with a soft tapestry seat and arm rests. She smiled and listened to the whispers flowing through the room. She adjusted her shawl around her head, shimmering green fabric with gold stripes along the edges. An admirer had given this as a gift imported from a city in Asia. Against her resistance, the person had insisted Mary take it, and now she looked happy in the headdress.

In her hands she clutched one of her most precious possessions, a prayer shawl—tallit—she'd made on the loom at Zechariah and Elizabeth's home. Her aged cousin had encouraged Mary to spend some of her time making a wedding gift for Joseph. A prayer shawl and an ornate bag to hold it with a design or name were a common gift. Of course, his parents had already presented Joseph one when he entered manhood. Many years later, when Joseph died, Mary considered passing the dear possession on to the firstborn—Jesus. However,, years ago he'd already become a man. Since they never owned a loom, Joseph purchased a prayer shawl for their first son in the busy Mediterranean port city of Acco.

*   *   *

More than three decades ago, Mary spent time on her cousin's loom. Back then, she feared Joseph's rejection of her on her return to Nazareth—pregnant. She cherished her handiwork for the unique man Adonai chose for her to marry and help raise the Messiah. Years later, Mary considered giving the tallit at the birth of her first grandson, but when that child arrived, she changed her mind. Mary wanted to keep it as a reminder of her loving, sacred, and God chosen husband of so many years. They lovingly named the boy Joseph, after his deceased grandfather.

While waiting for the crowd to enter, sit and settle, Mary reminisced in her heart.

Day after day, I devoted hours to weaving, pondering Joseph's appreciation of my craftwork. Using crimson yarn, I made good progress on the tallit bag. One time, while I sat on the cushion on the floor in front of the tall, oak, vertical loom, Elizabeth checked on me.

She asked, "What's your special choice for decorating the bag?'

"You look and guess!"

Designs of brown and silver nestled on the crimson background. Elizabeth hesitated, looked at it from different angles and ventured, "A tree with silver leaves?"

I giggled. "Is it that bad? No, this is going to be a hammer. To remind him of Judah HaMaccabee, you know, called 'The Hammer.'"

Elizabeth remarked, "Yes, son of Mattityahu, a priest. Judah is one of our most famous warriors against foreign oppressors…the Syrians…about two hundred years ago. So mighty, a merciless hammer, striking in short, effective blows."

I replied, "Yes. True. But because Joseph uses hammers in his trade, there are two meanings for him. Understand now?"

Elizabeth smiled and left me to my craftwork. "Looks good, Mary. Making gifts and giving gifts have power. I'm proud of you."

When I completed my wedding gift, I was so proud of myself. Elizabeth's wisdom proved true again. Working on the loom helped me pass the time, giving me seclusion to meditate and pray and let feelings which only a bride can feel well up.

Then I, the young weaver, called Zechariah, Elizabeth and Dinah, the servant girl, to the loom room. I confidently showed off my skills. The crimson carry-bag measured 10 inches by 14 inches. One side displayed the glimmering hammer and on the other in bold black Hebrew letters, "Joseph." After pulling out the bone clasp on the bag's flap, I took out the tallit—taller than myself. It measured 40 inches by 70 inches. The rows of fringes and knots added two inches on each end. From the four corners, four long white tassels with a blue thread each, reached down ten inches. In Hebrew letters, I'd stitched on the long, wide, sturdy collar, From Out of Zion Comes the Torah.

*   *   *

Peter stood and silence took hold. The smile on Mary remained as her daydream ended. "Many of you know of Jesus' mother but have never seen or met her. Stories, gossip, rumors, and praise follow her. However, here, only praise is welcome. Yet, this woman looks for none, but patiently and graciously accepts. She is one of us, however her tale will reveal how her son was not quite one of us—as we now know. What she has to say will stir and educate us, and that we will share with others.

"Remember, this is a rare room. This is where Jesus visited with us after his death and Resurrection. And I think Adonai claims Mary as the rarest of women alive." He took a deep breath. "I'll tell you a story about her—" But, Peter's wife tugged at his tunic and gave him a look he'd seen many times in their marriage. He tilted his head in understanding. "Another time." He threw his hands up, grinned at the older woman and sat down.

Mary slowly looked at the faces eager to hear. She had never been in such a situation. She pondered how men did this, and how, for years, her own son spoke to much larger crowds. Mary's heart swelled at the thought. She admired her special child even more.

Raising her hand, all went quiet. A lively mood unexpectedly filled her. Happily, Mary shouted the common greeting, "Shalom Aleichem." Peace be unto you.

The crowd roared back the respectful, "Aleichem Shalom!" Unto you be peace.

Chapter 24

Her Story

Affectionately, she started. "I will tell you a story—one that has two parts—and yes, they meet in the middle where I once stood. Zechariah was an elderly cousin of our family, and a priest. One morning, in the Temple, while serving a once-in-a-lifetime honorable duty and the last priest in that shift to exit that holiest of buildings. While alone in that magnificent Holy Place—in which only a few have ever been—he lit the fresh incense at the Altar of Incense, a short distance from the Holy of Holies. There, an angel named Gabriel visited him."

People in the Upper Room gasped. Hands gestured surprise and alarm, while others stiffened with shock. Fingers pointed toward her as discussions erupted.

After a few minutes, silence returned. She continued, "Imagine his fright, and how you would be too—thinking you were alone in the grandest building ever—except for Adonai … and now this amazing stranger.

"Understand, Zechariah and his wife were childless. Gabriel announced that Zechariah's wife, Elizabeth, though aged, would bear a child. They were to name him John. Their child is known to many of you as the prophet who in recent years taught as a voice crying in the wilderness. Remember, his execution, for his righteous words." She paused, eyeing her restless fingers.

"Both of our sons were executed." She swallowed.

"John chose not to be a priest like his forefathers, and his privilege. Or, should I say that Adonai chose different for him. John prepared the way for Jesus, our Messiah. John taught the prophesied forerunner—like an Elijah. He supervised immersing the sincerely repentant, and those with other required or desired symbolic cleansings. John oversaw the immersion of my son, his cousin—but not for sin. As you know, a teacher, a rabbi or priest begins his service at age 30, as Jesus started his service to Israel. Of course, immersion is part of the ordination."

Chatter erupted in the room. People spoke of John, one to the other, recalling his teachings by the river or at the lake where thousands went in the water. He challenged all hearts, however authorities from Jerusalem wished him trouble.

Mary caught the attention of the congregation again and spoke up. "Our Messiah needing cleansing from sin? No." She paused to let that profound idea rest in her audience. "Of course, only Adonai knows each of our sins—not even our own hearts do. However, I believe Jesus lived righteously and in such a way that sin gained no grasp, no foothold, not even a sliver." Heads nodded. "And the only reason why he could live the life he did."

Murmuring swelled again. She placed a finger to her lips. The room quieted. "Back to the beginning of my story. Six months after Zechariah's visitation, Elizabeth, though quite old, no doubt lived happily being quite pregnant. But I only knew that to be true because of who told me. They lived faraway in Hebron, and I in Galilee." Mary stood; confidence roared out of her. "The same angel, Gabriel, appeared to me—" The crowd erupted again. She spoke over the tumult, "a common, young country girl, alone in her parents' home." She paused, again motioning for silence, and she gained some. "And he also spoke an important message to me."

Mary, now the 50-year-old widow, closed her eyes to remember 34 years ago.

*   *   *

"I will tell you what happened." Silence prevailed once more. "Something similar to sunrise burst inside our house—a fast, speeded-up, stunning sunrise, brilliant and beautiful. No, the walls hadn't fallen away to expose the daylight…not that. Neither had our roof vanished. I had no idea what was going on. I likened it to a dream, but different from every dream I've ever had. Fright and curiosity filled me and kept filling me. I embraced both.

"A hot day, I wiped the sweat off my face. My hands held a bucket; I'd been sifting grain. Now in the kitchen area, to my shock it fell to the floor. All alone, yes… all alone. Everyone else…outside…doing chores. My eyes adjusted to the bright glow of light. Shimmers flecked out toward me and illuminated their source—a person. Then I saw what had entered our home. I knew I stood in danger.

"First, the appearance of a warrior startled me. Taller than any man I've ever seen, strong, massive, and serious, he looked heroic. I caught my breath and held it. Weakness overtook me. Where's my family to rescue me, to explain to me this sight, the reason for his appearance? Had they forgotten about me? I backed away.

"This angel called me…Mary. My name, how does a stranger know my name? I decided this was not a dream!"

The Upper Room buzzed with talk. Some had stood or leaned toward others and held discussions, others raised hands in worship and others looked down in prayer. With encouragement from his wife, Peter stood and whistled using two fingers (as he did to signal others on the lake when fishing).

Chapter 25
Talk

The audience quieted, and Mary continued, "I wanted to yell for my father so badly. Before this, I'd seen only Roman soldiers and Temple guards. But this warrior didn't resemble them, and he had a conquering might and thrilling power. Below his glimmering golden helmet I discerned a handsome broadening smile. My legs lost their bones as my eyes grew huge. Flexing on his back were immense folded wings with beautiful feathers. These shimmered, blending colors moved and changed, resembling shifting clouds at dawn. The tips of his wings hung close to the floor as the massive tops rose well above his human-looking face and full head of brilliant white hair. Once again, this amazing bird-man's lips spoke my name. I recognized kindness and care in his eyes and the pleasant spread of his mouth—I then knew I was safe—just stunned. I noticed a beautiful, jeweled sword hilt, which surely crowned a prized blade hidden within the elegant sheath. This had intricate designs in rainbow colors. A shiny golden breastplate covered his chest. And, he wore a bright dazzling white robe, fringed in purple with a sparkling silver sash.

"I don't remember anything about his feet other than a glow emanated from the bottom of his robe. Oh yes! He floated above the floor by about two handbreadths." Mary stood and swept a hand up to emphasize height. She then went to the ground and swept at nothing to show how his feet floated. Both arms stretched out from her sides to draw attention to the wings.

"I wondered why a soldier of any sort had entered our home. Who'd sent him? Would there be more? Was I to serve him or them—and how? My mind whirled. Had I done something wrong—really wrong? I hoped I wasn't in trouble. I had no idea what he wanted. Surely, I thought, he's not here to talk with me, but perhaps my older brother.

"When our eyes met, I knew he came while on duty and obeying orders. He must have been an officer of high rank—but of what army?"

The Upper Room went still. Mary clasped her hands; she lost her concentration. Lifting her head she gazed about, slowly, and carefully, at the many faces she'd never seen. Everyone's eyes longed for more; she sensed the hunger and keen interest in the listeners. She started to pace back and forth.

"Before this, I had no idea how quickly I could feel so small. I wanted a mouse hole to scurry into. Why was he here? Whatever he wanted, I'd have to ask my parents first. He knew that ... well, of course he must know—unless he came here by mistake. However, he looked too smart for that.

"When he spoke, I could tell he'd been prepared for meeting me. Me! He knew his arrival startled and interrupted me. I cringed and thought: 'He really should talk to my father or Joseph first, which is right and proper—polite too.' Then I thought:

'I'm too young to be approached and spoken to this way—he should've known.' I remained cautious.

"He stood a few arm lengths away. I wanted to back up even more, but my feet stayed in place. How did he make it into our house? Where had he come from? I stood in front of, and closest to, obviously the most important person I'd ever seen. I knew he could accomplish anything. Fear drained away as I understood, I had some sort of chore to do.

"Our strong walls and roof meant little to him—but I did. The authority in his voice quieted my worries; he knew exactly what he wanted to discuss. Aside from the scare, he honored me. I began to listen, really listen. I was important? No, not me! What angel ever talked to a girl? I couldn't recall a story from the Scriptures.

"He spoke to me about me. Meaning, this messenger described me in Adonai's eyes. Me 'favored'—I never knew. 'Highly favored' He said. After that, he described wondrous attributes of the child I would have one day—even his name, Jesus. Yes. He'd be great and called Son of the Most High, and he'd sit on the lost throne of my forefather King David. I thought, 'Joseph is going to be so excited!' Our son will reign over the House of Jacob forever. How proud a father Joseph is going to be when I tell him the news. Parents of the Messiah!

"Oh, how I wished one of my family would've walked in and helped me with this powerful stranger. It is one thing to be astonished, and another to be astonished with others.

"Gabriel also said that six months ago he'd visited our elderly cousin Zechariah, while on duty inside the Temple. God had wanted two baby boys from our families.

"I felt a sudden awe and reverence for Adonai, plus a feeling of wonder. I felt the dirt and grime on my hands and reached for a nearby rag. But then I realized that my outward appearance didn't matter to him.

"When the warrior spoke again, calm overtook me. I became so aware of myself. I know how strange it sounds. Authority rang in every word. He came to speak to me—only to me—not anyone else in my family or probably in the whole village."

Then Mary sat. Her words flowed fast. "I listened. Each word shaved off a strip of me…as I've seen a carpenter, such as Joseph and my sons, do with a tool, in order to shape wood. Less of me, but more fashioned into a person I hadn't been before. The angel knew it too. I could discern his pleasure in the workmanship his message had on me. This angel liked me. Me! And he knew I liked him—was in awe of him. There pulled in me a desire to owe him some form of worship…but I didn't—right or not? I didn't know." She looked at her audience; in their gleaming eyes she found no answer. "I delighted in this evidence, this glorious opening to a world I'd heard about since my childhood and wanted to believe in. Here I stood, chosen to gaze at one who flew in Heaven as a bird, a mixture of more-than-a-man, plus an honorable, majestic bird—so powerful, I almost fell off my feet." A bright, inspiring smile spread into Mary's cheeks.

"He looked down at me; I looked up into his face. Confidence rode on every feature. For all of his sternness, I saw a gentle side too. His beauty reminded me of a dangerous animal trotting about in the wild, perhaps a lion or leopard. But one which decided to set aside its attribute of winning force to approach one of us in order to be stroked like an appreciative pet. Then the creature would return to its realm and do as it pleased."

When Mary expressed how Gabriel liked her, Mary's children and grandchildren beamed, and many tears shone. Solemnly, her other sons' heads nodded.

"Like an evening flash of lightning exposes much of the dimmed countryside, I saw the style of messenger I stood before. His kind—for I knew there were more—held no thoughts but Adonai's thoughts. No will, beyond satisfying his Master. This determination lives in an ever-occurring momentum. That's what each angel wants. They exist directly connected to their enthroned Supreme Commander. All of them live with a sole purpose: purity of heart and mind, in which their obedience never wavers."

Chapter 26
Another World

Mary asked for a break and drank a small cup of wine. For a short time, she tried to be alone and regroup her thoughts. *What's important, valuable, or best kept private?* She politely shooed away her relatives. She prayed for wisdom. Then after a time, she motioned for Peter to end the intermission. He whistled. All sat down.

"Then the voice of the angel altered in pitch when I made note of the future marriage and consummation—in eight months and possibly nine months for the birth of the promised child. Close to eighteen in all. His tone emphasized timing much sooner. Well, Joseph and I could move up our wedding date, with some complications—nothing we couldn't overcome." Mary stood again and paced side-to-side, head down. She bit her lower lip. "But then, the angel somehow knew my thoughts. I'd never borne a child, never been intimate with a man. I was getting confused. If Joseph, my betrothed, wasn't to sire this child, I'd marry someone instead of Joseph—and probably soon. I only wanted Joseph—always. And why quickly? Even if Joseph and I wed the next day I'd probably be pregnant in less than a year. Excitement about his prediction filled me.

"Again, Gabriel saw my thoughts and read my face. His head shook a little." Mary's audience was spellbound. "No." He said carefully, "The Holy Spirit will envelop and overshadow you." My mouth dropped open and I went limp. 'What? No.' I thought, *This can't be.* Fright shot through me. No, no, this must be wrong.

"I leaned against the wall. The obedient and disciplined side of me rose, swallowing my feelings of isolation and entrapment. My lips said, 'Yes.' Then I assumed that a brief otherworldly visit of some sort would occur—perhaps while I slept—after that a child would begin to grow within me. I cringed, my eyes pleading for correction—tonight? No answer. I was young, so very young in the flowering of womanhood. Like my girlfriends, we found ourselves adjusting to the times of clean and unclean, the monthly rhythm of issuing, common to all females—interrupted only by pregnancy."

Mary raised a finger. "Adonai fathered the Messiah, not an angel, nor a man. Gabriel said, 'Nothing is impossible with Adonai'—a wrinkled elderly woman or a young virgin.' I crumbled, stunned, shocked, wobbly, amazed and…and so scared in different ways. When I awoke the next morning I knew…I just knew. Within my womb, I carried my first fruit."

A sea of wavering emotions roused the crowd. Everyone started to loosen and go inward yet those standing spread their steps aimlessly. Vibration filled the air. A few men from Galilee debated how they knew Jesus' father, Joseph the carpenter. One said that he'd "Watched Jesus growing up doing carpentry. He took right to it even as a little boy." Another said, "Jesus was my friend; we played together in the fields, us against the Romans." He emphasized, "We always won."

Jesus worked with his father and the occasional younger brothers until his late teens when Joseph died. Joseph, the most influential man in Jesus' life, had died in a way people just didn't talk about. Now his secret role as step-father emerged.

Peter stood. He had to. Not quite himself, not steady with this additional divine news. "Jesus became my respected friend and evolving authority figure." He bent, took a deep breath, started to whistle, and straightened, finishing with his back arched and whistling louder and longer than any time in his life. Then, with outstretched arms, and level hands held high, he motioned—imploring—for all to settle back down and quiet themselves. He appeared larger than ever, and in control.

Chapter 27
Debate or Learn

Next, Nicodemus rose. He motioned for complete quiet and total attention. Perspiration ran down his reddened face. He tugged at his beard. The perplexed audience waited. "I will not take the time now to present a detailed study of pertinent Scripture. However, I assure you that centuries ago the Prophet Isaiah wrote of a unique sign, an 'unmarried virgin shall conceive and bear a son.'" Nicodemus, proficient in instruction, spoke in a firm and captivating tone. His superior robes and elegant turban helped his conviction. "Bear in mind, this sign was no sign a woman could prove. A woman is pregnant only by man." He wagged a finger. "Nothing else!" Heads nodded. "Then a sign, a miracle, this would be—but hidden. For any woman to say that God somehow had relations with her is blasphemous. In pagan religions with various male and female gods and goddesses, a male god occasionally comes in human form and lies with a virgin, sometimes resulting in a pregnancy. One such child is the mythical hero Hercules.

"I'd say Mary has prudently waited to tell her life-changing—nay, history-changing secret. Only after her son performed miracles, raised the dead, taught keenly from Scripture, promoted holiness, and pointed at corruption in the priesthood..." Nicodemus stopped, gazing with compassion at Mary. "Died by a most terrible manner, and then did as he foretold, entering back into life three days later. And I might, dare say returned to heaven, as some here witnessed. Only now could his mother tell strangers—you and me—and speak it with warm, yet defiant confidence. She is safe and insulated against reprisals. There is too much to say otherwise. I believe her account fully. Jesus was a walking miracle and at times extremely difficult to accept," Nicodemus pounded his chest by the heart and looked upward, "Her holy son still beckons."

The teacher's expression changed as he faced Mary. "Not much for Joseph, to whom you were engaged, to go on and trust your word. My, my, how you convinced him is another story. But, what a righteous, unique, and wonderful person he must've been, picked to be the father and to raise Jesus. Your husband adopted him secretly. Joseph took blame and shame for the early pregnancy, no doubt. I am seeing circumstances that I never would've considered possible. That carpenter surely more godly man than me or any man here." He spread his arms again and looked at the enthralled faces. Shouting, he repeated, "Godlier than any here!" Exhaling a deep breath, Nicodemus extended a hand to Mary in a complementary manner and asked her to continue. He made a slight bow and settled back on the floor.

Mary spoke from a place deep in her heart. "Yes, Joseph was a loyal, smart and unique man; I miss both of my special men."

However, Barsabas, who had lost the casting of the lots, stood. He flung an open hand in her direction and turned to the audience. Pleading, he spoke what many wondered. "Do you ask us to believe that you remained a virgin while you and

Joseph lived together as husband and wife? And that when you gave birth you still had your virginity?"

With a frown, Nicodemus commented. "Yes. Yes. Good questions. True. But, why didn't we, and why didn't Jerusalem believe his words?" He turned to the seated Mary. "Your Joseph, he went along with this? This angel must have visited him too?" He glanced at her.

Mary said, "No. Oh, no. Only in a dream!" Her face shone a deeply rooted smile and said, "Thank you. As I said, I believed the angel. While newly pregnant, but not showing, I traveled to Hebron to visit our cousin Elizabeth, already six months along. We had precious days in our pregnancies, so close to each other. We knew that one day our children's lives would entwine." She paused and blushed, lowering her voice. "These are hard words to share, private and personal. I want to finish telling you about the angel. Let's go back to my parents' home. Gabriel and I locked eyes and I nodded. I agreed to the plan Adonai had ordered him to tell. Now he could leave. His great wings spread wider than the kitchen area, the wingtips passing through our walls. I gasped. He crouched, flexed vigorously and then, with a push off of our earthen floor, Gabriel rose. Wind passed within our home, drawing upward to the flat, plain ceiling. His massive body flew, dissolving into tiny pieces of brilliant color, and...and, I was alone. A living jewel left our home. After he vanished, I found I'd risen onto my toes, my body straining to follow higher and higher too." She paused and swallowed. "I felt different, more than I thought I could ever feel. Filled, yet somehow longing, strong with life, but unable to take a single step."

Mary dropped her voice. "He touched the depth of me. After he left I felt that I'd moved on to a higher level of responsibility and a deeper sense of life."

Then Mary looked at her companions with searching eyes—eyes which had seen an angel, a creature not born of this world. "I pondered—that I do remember. Would the messenger, this citizen of Heaven, go now and report his meeting with me to the Creator and Maker of the Universe? The Almighty listening to what I had said. Could I so important?" Mary sipped at her cup. Tears flowed down her cheeks. Thoughtfully, she expressed her remarkable awareness. "I was known in Heaven, I'd been watched for some time...days, months...years maybe. I hadn't thought to ask. It didn't matter, did it? I pleased Him. Pleased Him greatly. I never thought of myself as someone special or deserving of notice."

As she wiped her face dry, an excited smile returned. "They're not humans with wings. They are so beyond us. So rich, so praiseworthy! I wanted to worship Gabriel, but then thought not." She sipped again, collecting her thoughts. "I will never look at birds the way I used to, because they remind me of the flying-man from Heaven. How far away is Heaven? How long did Gabriel's flight take to the throne of Him who makes everything?" She paused. "They're above us right now, looking down. We just don't—can't—see them. They exist in splendor, beauty and, and—"

At this point, Mary's children and grandchildren swarmed around her. Hugs pressed them closer and closer. Mary swooned at the center of the bouquet of lives important to her.

In time the hugs loosened, she asked her family to sit down and she continued.

"I've one more addition to the story, at least for tonight. When I stayed in Hebron with Zechariah and Elizabeth, we exchanged our angel stories. More than six months had passed between Gabriel's visit with Cousin Zechariah and his visit with me. Also, why the connection of these future cousins and concurrent pregnancies? A double miracle."

Mary lifted a hand. "Oh! I also recall one other important discussion we had. Mary changed her voice in her storytelling to act out the two characters. Mary did character voice changes when she told stories to her grandchildren—they enjoyed this. "Elizabeth commented in her dear, older women voice. 'Gabriel found faith in Daniel, too.' This caught my attention. 'Who? What?'

"Elizabeth answered, 'Mary, when he visited the Prophet Daniel.'

"'What do you mean?' I asked.

"'Mary, come now. You know your history. The angel Gabriel visited the important Prophet Daniel in Babylon. Remember, the king put him in the lions' den to be eaten.'

"I perked up and said, 'I know that story! Everyone knows that story—it's a good one.'

"My cousin continued, 'Well yes, I thought you would. So, during that long night among hungry lions, might Gabriel have been the unknown protector keeping Daniel from the jaws of death?' Elizabeth showed a contented smile.

"I replied, 'But, but, but t-that's, that was, that, ahh … *oh!*' My forehead creased a lot. 'How long ago?'

Elizabeth answered, "'Around 500 years ago, Mary.'"

My jaw dropped. Mary raised one finger high. "Shocked. I said, 'I've talked with someone who is 500 years old! On top of everything else, I found this too hard to believe, too, too, much for me. And to whom can I even tell such a story? Not my friends or family. I'm just overwhelmed, cousins, completely overwhelmed.' My mind spun.

"Then Elizabeth added—remember, her husband Zechariah could not speak … or, or did I forget that part? You see, the angel punished him for his unbelief about his elderly wife having a baby. Imagine being alone in the great Temple and not believing the words of an angel! Unbelievable. Zechariah's voice would return at the birth of his promised son John, nine months later. The high priest had to relieve him of his priestly duties because God had punished him. Also, because he'd worked longer than the rules allowed for priests to serve; his time was up.

"So, as I was saying, Elizabeth added, 'Mary, Gabriel is much older than that. More years than the human mind can comprehend.

"I gulped and said to Zechariah, 'So unforgettable?'" The dear old man grinned and nodded vigorously."

This ended Mary's talk. Her grandchildren surrounded her with curious questions about angels. They asked, "What else did the angel Gabriel do during those six months between announcements? Does he only fly around telling couples they are going to have babies? Is there a different angel who speaks to future parents of girl babies?" Mary and those nearby chuckled at their eager imaginative wonderings.

* * *

When she could get away from questioners and praisers, she went alone on a long walk. She thought, *After all these years, the truth, my truth, his truth, is out. It feels good.*

Chapter 28
A Surprise Visitor

The next day a traveler named Ami, a middle-aged woman, walked through Jerusalem looking for Agas Street—Pear Street. She sought the house of Jashen, a large two-story home. On his wooden door she knew she'd find a lightly scratched, one handbreadth tall, faint symbol of the Hebrew letter *dalet*, the fourth letter in the alphabet. That symbol meant "door" or "way." The disciples decided to use the dalet as a secret code indicating safety.

Ami cautiously approached one house and looked at its height. She listened but could hear no one. Suddenly, a man from the street stood beside her.

"Shalom! If you are here for the meeting, you are early, but just as welcome now as later. Anytime upstairs is the right time." Smiling, he said, "My name is Thomas. May I ask yours?"

"Yes, yes, of course…Thomas. I'm Ami." Her eyes looked away.

"Ahh, you've got a strong Galilean accent, like most of us here!"

Her eyes drifted to his feet and tried to remain there. She glanced little more than a flutter or two at his face. Ami said, "And is 'here' the home of Jashen? I barely know my way around the capital—it is so huge. I'm from the village of Chorazim, at the north end of the lake, you know, in the countryside."

Thomas nodded and pushed the door open. He motioned for her to enter.

She hesitated. "I'll do that soon if I can. Is that allowed—I mean to stand outside here? I need to think this through first." Ami caught the stranger's pleased look. He entered, and the door closed behind him. Ami took a deep breath and let it out. For over a decade she hadn't talked with men; not even a simple conversation like that. She hadn't made friends or acquaintances for twelve years. Physicians or those who called themselves so, passed as the only occasional men in her awkward, shamed, lonely life. Those men came and went with her money and her family's money too, and her health never improved.

Her relatives and close family helped support her. "Unclean" and "outcast" meant restrictions: no synagogue, no Temple, and keeping a fair distance from others. As best as she could, Ami did odd chores for money and food, in the Upper Galilee region. Some presumed that her affliction came straight from God as due punishment for unknown sins.

Fourteen years ago, she had married. Her husband left two years after the bleeding started. Her menstrual cycle stopped. She hemorrhaged and then bled daily. Since the marriage would not produce children, her husband divorced her. Religious law allowed this. Those who knew her condition considered his decision sad, but reasonable. He remarried and is raising a family—a pain that caused Ami many tears. He avoided her, and they never talked again.

But that was past. She'd had an encounter with the Messiah six months ago, and she now enjoyed good health. Her story would encourage those in the Upper Room, and she hoped to share it that night.

She eyed the door again and considered enjoying the company of others—normal people. Then she noticed the mezuzah—doorpost—and the small animal skin parchments on either side of the entry door. Each measured about the size of a man's hand, tacked down because of wind, and placed out of direct sunlight for durability. Ami knew their significance and centuries of tradition—they identified a Jewish home.

These small portions of written proclamation reminded Ami of Pentecost and the giving of the Laws and of the Exodus. Ami recalled, *And as you walk in the way...* she read the tiny signs, which a sofer—scribe—had written. All soferim were capable of drawing wonderful, tiny letters. Ami quietly read what she already knew by heart—but as the custom, people read out loud. "Hear, O Israel, Adonai is our God, Adonai is One. You shall love Adonai your God, with all your heart, with all your soul, and with all your might. And these words which I command you this day shall be upon your heart. And you shall teach them to your children. And speak of them when you sit in your home, when you walk, when you lie down and when you rise. Write them on your doorposts and gates. Tie them to your hands as a reminder, and wear them on your forehead, they shall be an ornament between your eyes."

Just then the door opened. An older woman glanced at Ami. A sweet smile filled her cheeks. "I'm Mary; are you joining us? I can take you upstairs," she said motioning with one hand, "and get you settled, er...?"

"Oh. Oh, yes. My name is Ami. I do want in. Thank you very much, how hospitable of you... Mary. But, but, I want to do it my way. This is the entry point of my life merging with others, other disciples."

Mary's eyes shifted and looked Ami up and down. She made a swish with one arm and chuckled. "I think you look safe enough! Do it your way."

Ami beamed. She breathed deep, let it out, and ran up the flight of stone steps laughing, leaping full of life. She didn't see Mary's growing happy expression. However, Ami might've heard a loud whoop from Mary, who, feeling light of feet, soon ran behind her inspired.

* * *

Later, a small group listened to Ami, and the crowd grew the more she spoke. She had already explained her past illness. "So many people, hundreds, thousands gathered on the west side of the lake. They swarmed around one man who I'd heard cured the sick and didn't charge any money. Everyone sick, lame or blind, each made healthy, healthy for free! I thought, *A dream, I'm dreaming.*

"I pushed into the noisy crowd, closer and closer, and figured where he might pass. A frenzy is the only way to describe the scene. I barely overheard a man named Jairus, a leader at a local synagogue tell Jesus of his deathly ill twelve-year-old daughter." Ami looked at the faces of her audience. Her expression changed from serious to somber. "Twelve years. I've been living this horrible life for twelve years, the entire life of this girl. Something rose in me. I believed, yes, I believed without a doubt that this physician rabbi would want to cure me. I took the number twelve not as coincidence, but as a sign to motivate me. Maybe I gave into superstition.

"So, with more determination, I struggled and even shoved to get to Jesus. I didn't know how he did his healing. If he just touched you—that seemed like magic. If indeed, he served as a prophet, where in Scripture did one ever heal multitudes? Our people never surrounded Moses like this. He didn't touch people, did he?" Ami spread her hands and scanned the quiet listeners. No one answered.

"Then I froze. Touching Jesus meant that I'd make him unclean too. I decided to sneak close to him and touch only his clothing. If he didn't know—then he wouldn't be unclean, right? When I could, my fingers lightly pinched the tzitzit fringes of his prayer shawl. That tallit of his had handprints everywhere and smudges. Anyway, power entered me, his power. I almost lost my balance. With that, came truth, and understanding. My ailment stopped. I became light, happy and clean. Me! Then I backed away, pushing against the crowd. But something terrible, but wonderful happened next.

"This strange popular rabbi stopped his activities. He looked at the multitude with searching eyes and asked the last question I wanted to hear, 'Who touched me?' I knew I'd done wrong and made him unclean, and somehow he knew it. In such a crowd, who could tell who touched whom? Then a terrible thing happened. Nobody admitted touching him. The scene quieted, so everyone realized this event carried importance for him, though we didn't know why."

Ami pointed to Peter and other apostles present. "You were there. I remember your perplexed faces. How could he ask such a question? Peter, is it? You tried to talk some sense to the rabbi. Hundreds sought to touch him and most did. Yet, the rabbi showed only patience and curiosity. He waited. He waited some more. 'Who?' he said, 'Who?' Well, my joy dropped to nothing, and guilt overtook me. Trembling, I turned and squeezed in close once more. I fell to my knees ready for my punishment and said, "It was me." Gritting my teeth, I told—with the crowd listening— my misery and the private facts about my body. Also, when I touched the littlest strands of string of his prayer shawl, my bout with the bleeding ended *won by him!*

"He listened and smiled. To my shock the man lifted me with his hands— unclean no more. He said with great sincerity, 'Daughter, be comforted. Your faith in me and in Him who sent me has worked rightly. You are whole! Go in peace and health. Live your new life.'"

"I thought, *No more medicine? No more embarrassment? A normal life? This nightmare is over!* I almost fainted, but some of you men here helped steady me. You touched me—this amazed me—men holding; not afraid."

Peter burst out, "Now I remember you! I thought you looked familiar when you skipped up those stairs. But you were so sickly and quivering in Galilee, and now a bright smile adorns your features."

Several others made similar remarks. "That was you! So frightened. Now you are doing wonderfully! Adonai smiled on you. I'm sure that there are those still talking about the miracle hand of God that day. You were special—are special to Him!"

Ami cried.

They hugged her.

She stayed with them for Pentecost and what followed.

Chapter 29
Chat Room

In the Upper Room, discussions stirred constantly about the last three years. People having answers to prayers, and needs met, seemed a thread in every topic. Musicians brought instruments and played familiar psalms. Other times a worshipper sung as if singing in a vacant room. Yet, the singer knew better and sensed no embarrassment.

Each considered how Jesus gave them what they had wanted; he even filled thousands of empty stomachs more than once. Savior, Counselor, Encourager, Healer, Prison Demolisher, Doorway, Burden Taker, Peace Giver—Death met him and sought for an exit.

The list of otherworldly activities started with the very best of wines at a small country wedding in Cana of Galilee. There, not even the wedding party asked for anything. Over three years later, at the completion of his list of godly chores, at the end of his public miracles, Jesus had one more surprise for the people of earth. In an olive garden in the torchlit dark of night, while being arrested, he restored what one stranger wanted most and didn't even ask for—an ear, one perfectly good ear. Severed by a protective and spontaneous Peter, the bloody, useless flesh had fallen onto the dirt. Jesus, saw this stranger standing with the mob of his enemies. Yet, due to kindness, Jesus bent, picked up the ear and reattached it to the man's head. Who would do that but Jesus?

Matthew mumbled to himself, "The arrest of Jesus...ah yes." Those who were close, gestured for him to say what was on his mind. "Late at night, after the Seder, we went to the Garden of the Oil Press, Gethsemane. While the Master prayed, we slept. Out of the darkness, at least 200 or perhaps as many as 600 men, some with clubs, swords or torches found us out—due to Judas. In the flickering light I couldn't accurately see how many. Jesus boldly asked whom they came for. We knew who they wanted. One leader said, 'Jesus of Nazareth.'" Matthew paused and went somber. He slowly eyed his listeners. "The Master stated, 'I am he!' We stood near him, yet we didn't see how this miracle happened. After the proclamation, an invisible wave—not wind—knocked down all of our opponents, even our betrayer. The hundreds of men lay flat on the ground disoriented. We Eleven, cheered and some slapped Jesus on his shoulders. In joy, in victory, we finally saw what we'd yearned to see: our Master take charge and let loose his heavenly might. We found he *would* fight."

Mary shook her head and wailed, "I never knew about these acts, his real power. Making wine from water, how would that chase the Romans from our...Adonai's Land." Onlookers marveled at her and the overwhelming facts taking root.

Men exclaimed to each other, "What's this about wine?"

Matthew continued. "The unwanted, wobbly mob found their footing. As men awakening from a dream, they regained their purpose in that place. Sadly, and strangely, his show of force ended. No momentum followed. He made his point of who was in control, and without resistance. Jesus allowed them to arrest and mistreat him. In these confusing moments, we Eleven ran for our lives."

Silence blanketed the room. All pondered the scene in their imaginations.

*   *   *

Matthew said with eagerness in his voice, "I'll always remember him standing with one hand holding the sail rigging and flashes of lightning revealing Jesus, like an ordinary fool, challenging the unbending forces of nature—and no fear of falling overboard. But he took control of the raging wind, the endless merciless waves, and the drenching sheets of rain. And then the fury stopped abruptly.

"Jesus showed annoyance with us for not telling the storm to cease on our own. He had that look in his eye, the same as when he came down that bright mountain. There, nine of us were left below to keep camp. A father wanted us to remove the demons from his son, but we couldn't. That annoyed the Master, that was clear. He freed the boy with little effort, pulled us aside and gave us a good talking to."

An older woman interrupted. "I've lived my whole life on the lake shore near Capernaum. Dozens of storms have whipped and churned the lake in my time. I recall one storm in particular. Our goat nibbled in its pen next to the back door. Thunder spooked the creature. His tether broke. I went out to find the animal in the midst of one of the worst storms ever. My clothes dripped; I wiped rain from my face." She spread her arms wide and looked to the ceiling. "In one moment in the time it takes to close a gate and lock it, the entire storm ended. I could see stars and the quarter-moon. No wind, no thunder, gone all gone. I shook my head and didn't know what to think. That was that. Now I know; the Master stopped the raging storm. How amazing!"

*   *   *

What could Jesus not do? Only the lack of faith restricted what benefits the House of Israel most wanted or needed. For instance, in Nazareth, he could heal only a few sick folk. The community didn't honor him or believe his claims—which mysteriously shut down his power.

The disciples swapped stories. A few themes kept coming into the talk. People shouted to Jesus to do things for them, some were just, some just self-centered.

Tzabi from Acco recalled, "One man yelled out of the multitude to him, 'Teacher, tell my brother to divide the family inheritance with me.' Jesus replied, 'Friend, who made me a judge or a divider over you to decide such things as that?'"

A man said, "Odd word pictures, scripture, short stories, and parables whose meanings few could readily grasp, proved his favorite ways of communicating. Asking him a question and getting an answer could get a person twisted up for days. But his interaction with the public set in motion an amazing amount of good deeds and obeying the commandments."

A woman added, "The Galilean could heal, making anyone normal again, even tormented people, sane once more, and shock of shocks—like the ancient tales of Elijah and Elisha—the dead back to life, healthy and strong for new years ahead."

Another man ventured, "Like a carpenter and stone cutter, I've heard it said, 'he can build people into what they weren't, construct something useful out of their raw human nature with help from the Holy Spirit above.' Or, yet still like a carpenter, he will fix what's broken and fix it well."

A previously timid woman stood and boldly proclaimed, "This man, he looked like you and me, but he could see into your heart, read it like a parchment scroll—the good and the bad. Your wrongs and hidden sins brought into the sunlight in a way that may cause disgust at first, but sorrow soon followed, and repentance will surely engage you. Yet, Jesus looked at such a collection of failings like he'd take them off your hands. And why? And for what, I ask you? In return to let you start with a fresh, crisp attitude growing inside your heart. It's amazing. What a blessing."

Yet another woman said, "Do not be surprised if you hear that the worst people in a town wanted to be in his company, be his friend. The worst he wanted for friends! All people need changing. You and I are not above such company."

Phillip added, "Those crowds, so many shouting this and that. One husband and wife expected him to foretell their future and how many children they'd have. Another person questioned him on whether he should proceed in a certain business deal. Others begged him to pronounce curses on a troublesome neighbor. Someone else wanted Jesus to put his hands on all eight children, pray blessings and long life on them. Too many had Jesus downright wrong."

Chapter 30

Zacchaeus

During these ten days between the ascension and Pentecost, a letter arrived by messenger from Jericho, two miles to the east. Peter accepted the small papyrus scroll. He read it out loud.

He chuckled when he saw who sent it. "Listen up, everyone! Remember that greedy little man who made himself ungodly rich by his tax collection in Jericho?"

Matthew raised his hand and in a loud singsong voice said, "Zac-chae-us!" For years, Matthew worked as a tax collector in Galilee, before Jesus offered him something better.

Peter continued, "Yes. Our short friend. Our…very…short…friend."

Those who knew the tale shook their heads and laughed.

"Zacchaeus is asking if he's welcome to join us here at Jashen's. He'll be in the city for Pentecost. That man has come a long way from his perch in the sycamore. I remember after Jesus pointed him out, watching Zacchaeus shimmy down that tree right quick." Peter raised his eyebrows. "And how *did* Jesus know his name—anybody ever figure that one out? Anyway, we had dinner at his home, which caused a ruckus with the villagers."

Lazarus looked at the ceiling and rolled his eyes. "That filthy, dirty runt of a rich man. Stealing much and acquiring good people as enemies. What a profession. Now he's humbled and most everyone in Jericho accepts him—"

Lazarus' older sister Martha chimed in, "Because he sold half of his properties and gave the money to the poor—"

Her sister, Mary, added, "And then paid back four times the amount to everyone he'd cheated over the years. Most have forgiven him, but some never will."

Peter smiled. "Anybody want to take a walk to Jericho and tell him, yes, he's welcome? Oh, and ask him if he wants to ride here on somebody's shoulders!"

People laughed.

A tall, strong man named Mikhah, clearly liking the jest, volunteered, and left.

Chapter 31
Peter Talks

Peter stood and waved for silence. When the room went quiet he said, "There are more stories than that! Believing them here and now is a mere shadow, a rustling of the wind. Not like having been there." He sat down and told a tale. "The day we heard of the beheading of John, Jesus wanted to go somewhere and be alone. He took the news like a sudden punch to the stomach. Remember, John also was family, a cousin to Jesus. The twelve of us were more than depressed, we were scared. If such a powerful and holy figure such as John could be arrested, kept in prison, and murdered—so could we. He had inspired so many to repent and expect the arrival of God's servant. He went so far as to challenge the corrupt Temple authorities when they visited him in person." Peter rubbed his chin. "We were sickened when we heard of the cause of his death—a dancing girl's wish at a birthday party for one of Herod's ruling sons." Peter hung his head and wiped at tears. "John was such a good man…better than any of us here…a true prophet in the spirit of Elijah." He looked at the audience again. "Jesus needed to get away from people. He wanted to weep, pray, and mourn and to hear from His Father about this tragedy.

"We crossed the lake in hopes of finding solitude in the eastern hills, but the previous crowds and many new people from other villages saw our direction and followed us there on foot and boat. People walked for miles. During the voyage, Jesus sat wordless, eyes closed or staring at the bottom of the vessel. Therefore, he hadn't noticed the crowds waiting for us and that the multitude grew by the minute. As we neared the shore men swam out and we tossed them our ropes. Other men waded and they all hauled our boat high onto the beach.

"Roused by the crowd calling his name, the stone face of despair on Jesus dissolved. He had what people wanted   needed. The twelve of us left the vessel as sailors and turned to our other jobs—bodyguards. Without us he would've suffocated.

"Overcome by compassion, Jesus served the people's needs with a new vigor. What a long day on the lake's eastern shore. We estimated over 5,000 men, not counting women and children swarmed us—close to 20,000 people."

Considering such abundance, the room buzzed like a crowd gone wild at a Roman chariot race. Peter's chest swelled and he let out a guttural howl and raised a fist in triumph. Others in the room had their mouths full of praiseful heightened hope and success.

When those in the Upper Room, though delirious, did quiet down, Peter spoke. "After the hours passed, the people were hungry. In one of those peculiar moments, which we had with the Master, we tried to do whatever he instructed. Jesus asked for any food at hand. Anyone here remember what we found—one lunch of bread and dried fish. Jesus then prayed over these and broke them into pieces. He kept breaking them into pieces and placing them into baskets borrowed from women nearby. We Twelve distributed and distributed and distributed the food until everyone had a full stomach. Somehow, God multiplied two fish and five small loaves into thousands!" Peter raised a finger and said, "What a haul of fish that would've been—probably every fish in the lake."

A man called out, "Like the Prophet Elijah and the multiplying the widow's cup of oil!"

Another said, "Manna from the sky!"

James nodded. "Yes, but much, much, more so. We had twelve large baskets of leftovers." He added. "What of Jesus stilling the violent, deadly storm on the lake?"

Peter added, "After the meal, we and Jesus shooed everyone away, sending them home. He had to be stern with some people. Then as a surprise to us, he told us to sail across back to the west side of the lake without him and he'd catch up with us the next day. He told us that he needed a break from everybody and everything— well, not those words exactly, but we knew the look and tone of voice. Late into the evening he finally found himself alone and hiked into the hills.

"We rowed and sailed 3 or 4 miles against rising rough waters; wind and wave tossed. It's about 7 miles to cross. Trouble surrounded our boat. All smiles were lost. Worry set in. Darkness compounded navigation. We strained at the oars for over six hours, battling for our lives. The fear and dread of drowning replaced thoughts over John's gruesome death. Meanwhile, as the faintest purplish-blue showed behind the eastern hills a strange thing happened." Peter gulped.

Someone quoted from Psalm 107, "They cried out to the Lord in their distress, and He brought them out of their calamity. He transformed the storm into stillness and the waves were quieted."

Peter continued, "Jesus had a way to do the impossible, time and time again, day in and day out. He defined miracle here, miraculous there, and not quite of this world such as walking across a lake instead of following the sandy beach or taking a boat. He found us in the dark and climbed into our boat and held onto to the mast. We beheld him when the lightning flashed. His determined expression caused us to forget the travail around our craft. Defiant, Jesus said into the night, 'Quiet! Be muzzled and still.' The storm obeyed. Within moments, somehow our craft came to the peaceful shore like side-miracle. I'd say."

Chapter 32
News of Thomas

Coming down the street, Leah greeted her father and older brother, bubbling over with joy. Leah shouted, "Shalom, Abba. Shalom Giddel! They were coming home from work. Both masons on one of the many construction projects on the Temple Mount, several miles away. The two tired men entered the house. The girl continued, "There's a surprise and it's good news, really good news! Thomas is in Jerusalem! The holy man he follows or did follow, who died … and well, you know what he says … recently told his followers to stay in the capital. So, Thomas is going to celebrate Pentecost and stay longer, maybe a lot longer. We'll see Thomas, I just know it. Isn't that exciting? I miss him so much. Think of the stories he'll tell. I hope he'll stay with us, too, don't you?"

Yishai's ready smile dropped from his face and he dropped his heavy tool sack on the floor of his home. A puff of dust arose. Weary from the walk, the sudden news sent his heart laboring. Overwhelmed by crossing emotions, Yishai scarcely saw his daughter's beaming face. A needy expression overtook him. Shoulders and head slumped as weakness spread throughout his body. He looked for his wife's face. Yishai's pain filled eyes, and quavering outspread hands gestured for her in hopes to guide him to a better state of mind. Aliyah saw the look and took his hands and clasped it in hers. She winced. Her eyes welled, but she didn't speak. A single tear fell.

In the moments after the daughter's flurry of excitement, stillness lay on the home. But little Leah hadn't noticed. When her father didn't respond she added, "Dinner is ready to eat! I made the meal with Momma's help. I hope you're both hungry?"

With quiet movements and slow effort of a much older man, Yishai turned to his youngest child, Leah. Carefully he took her chin tilted her head up and searched her eyes. She stood smiling, not seeing the sadness and heavy expression her father bore.

In the morning, a neighbor arrived with the unexpected news, then controversy overtook Aliyah. She lived with this bittersweet news of her son Thomas, for hours. The possibility of seeing his face always caused hope to stir and fluttering throughout her soul. But now what would happen, merely another visit, or his final return?

After the neighbor had left, little Leah realized her Momma didn't talk much. She quizzically asked, "Don't you want to see Thomas, Momma? I know Abba and Giddel will be so excited, what a surprise! You must miss Thomas terribly? It's been so long."

The troubled mother, confused with emotions and tangled thoughts pacified her girl with a faint grin. "Yes, it has been a long time. A long time. Of course, I love and miss your brother, more than you know."

Aliyah's motherly supervision of the evening meal turned into a sluggish, tedious task. As the day wore on she did her best to hide the tears and keep up a good pride-filled appearance for young Leah's diligent efforts. But the heave of swaying emotions bent her spirit, and she stopped looking forward to the men's return.

Now, as the parents' eyes met and they held hands, all words failed. Each knew what the other felt. They had discussed this possibility many times—too many times. Both wanted to see their son, they wanted him back home—back for good. They needed their children to provide for their old age. Would Giddel, the responsible one, be solely burdened with that concern? Or, could their daughters' future husband provide? These were concerns of his parents.

At the doorway, Giddel cringed when he heard the news. He put an arm around his abba, but Yishai never felt the loving touch. Giddel attempted to stop the invading, life draining silence. Adding a lively pitch to his voice and standing on his toes, he forced out a cheerful, "Well, I'm certainly hungry and believe me Leah, Abba is too. He's been looking forward to your splendid cooking all the way home. But Leah, I think he worked extra hard today and first needs a cup of water to refresh him." Giddel looked over to his downcast abba and ventured a change of tactics. "Abba even talked you up to some of the workers, telling them to get their fine sons in line for marriage!" Leah grinned and blushed.

Yishai rose out of rummaging in deep thoughts. Mustering his best sense, he received the cup of water from the anxious little princess and drank. Feeling refreshed, he spoke with a spark in his voice, "Then let's eat!" A smile grew on his face, rising from the depths of fatherhood for the children at home and the missing child not at his table. Leah returned the smile and pulled her father's hand to where he always sat.

Living a normal life, that's what parents wanted for all their children. This they made clear during every homecoming of Thomas. And so, a visit with his parents meant incurring these controversial stabs, made by two pairs of loving hands and divisive tongues. "Why can't you be more like your brother Giddel? He's stable, betrothed, working, and here for us." This pain lay stranded on their pronounced expressions.

"It's like he's been bitten by a bug! Who raised him this way? So religious now— why? Tell me who did this to him?" Yet neither could blame the other.

Sorrow lodged in Aliyah's mother's heart and gripped it tight. Ruffled with bitter wailing, her mind spun to the point of harsh anger. "Our sons, identical look-a-likes, —yet they are as different as the rising sun and setting moon. Both—born to be the light of our days, yet one has dimmed so much." The parents shuffled around the house, vacillating between brief smiles and head shaking and frowns. Bitter anger and warm, loving desires wove lengthy knots of mixed emotions.

Over the last three years, Giddel soaked in their pained remarks, "Our son, he had followed that magical rabbi—now crucified. Crucified do you hear what I say! Now what he needs to do is come home and get back to work." Thomas' mother would also say this to any who asked about him. His father would nod, adding, "And sooner the better!" Stretching his arms wide, Yishai said, "I've heard that that crazed rabbi told a whole crowd that they needed to eat his body and drink his blood! Did we raise a foolish son who continued to follow such a one as this?"

With resentment, Aliyah smirked. "My son wants to eat a man for dinner and wash him down with the blood—like my cooking all these years isn't good enough?"

Yishai would add, if only for his own ears, "Thomas called this teacher, 'Master.' He traveled with other men, a dozen or so, and women too. They are said to be good, moral women, helping to support and feed the disciples. But at least one of them, I heard used to be a whore, and not so long ago, mind you. Maybe my son will marry one of these do-gooders. And—" he raised a finger, "one man close to this teacher was a tax collector—may God forgive his many sins, the traitor. What has my son got himself into?" He sneered, "I've heard one story about this miracle-man, if indeed a miracle man he be. Thomas said his rabbi turned water into wine! Gallons and gallons of quality drink. I don't know." He emphasized with a wink, "Now if this rabbi did make water become wine, that's my kind of prophet to follow. There's a real man. May he fill up the Sea of Tiberius, so the Jordan River runs the color of grapes all the way through Judea right to me! Then, I'll be number 13 in that collection of disciples."

Yishai and Aliyah had never met or talked with this self-taught Galilean rabbi, Jesus. And honestly, they had no desire to. They discussed such contact, of course. Thomas mentioned the possibility. However, his parents reasoned that meeting such a busy, political, and religious man with an out-of-the-ordinary lifestyle would be awkward. "What would we talk about?"

Also, they'd heard more than once, the holy man spurned his own widowed mother and close kin when they came to visit him. "This teacher can be kind and respectful when he wants to everyone—except his family. Thomas said there was a house full of people. But did this Torah teaching, Jesus, go out to his family or make room for them to come in? No." Tightening a fist, he stammered, "I tell you that's a sin to do such a thing, a sin!"

In a dejected tone Aliyah pointed out, "Concerned for her son's well-being, like a family should, they desired this Jesus slow down his whirling zeal and get together with sensible rabbis. Then he could discuss his outspoken ideas. But no! He and he alone, knew Adonai's will—even referring to God as his own father. Bah!" She bit down on her lip, shaking her head. "All it got him? Nailed to a cross."

Yishai and Aliyah commiserated, "Who can talk to such a one? A-know-it-all! And my, my, abrupt too. Why bother? No thank you." Throwing their hands up in turn, they continued exchanging criticisms. "What would this man's own abba say to such arrogance coming from his child? A carpenter calls himself a rabbi! Maybe one day a mason will become high priest, too!" With eyes toward heaven, the worried parents pronounced, "May he not turn our son against us!"

Giddel respected his brother's unusual decision. At present he wove his own misgivings about the so-called back-from-the-dead rabbi. He didn't like the uncertainty of his brother's future. Where would Thomas be in 5 or 10 years? Most important of all, was he safe?

After dinner, Giddel carefully added his own input. Trying not to plead, he interjected, "But Momma, even your sister's daughter Mei-Zahav in Tzippori, went to a Jesus gathering. Remember she fell out of a tree years ago. That girl's twisted leg and her limp, were healed when she asked him to pray. Her leg became straight as anyone's. She jumped and ran happy as can be and still does. Mei-Zahav and her parents now tell everyone about Adonai's miracle."

The parents grunted, dismissing the unwanted evidence. Getting an apology from them rarely happened.

Chapter 33
Mary Speaks to Women

People constantly wanted to speak with Mary and that drained her energy. Synagogue women, neighbors, and even strangers dogged her. The pressure of popularity strained the already busy mother and grandmother. People wanted to bond with Mary. In the Upper Room, she found herself encircled by mothers and girls. Cradling a baby, patting a toddler's head, or accepting the fixed gaze of a smiling stranger, she tried to fit her role. At times her eyes penetrated the depths of hungering feminine souls. From the wellspring of her maturity and ever-broadening love, she instructed them or just listened.

In such circumstances she said, "I may be thanked for my submission to the special role Adonai chose for me, but please, do not venerate or adore; little honor is due me. Instead, exalt our Messiah, who I birthed. Was I a good mother? Yes, and Joseph a good father, that much is true. However, I have known times of overwhelming emotional torrents—that seems the only word to use, 'torrents'— either ripping my heart apart or bringing it back together.

"Listen. Before I showed in my pregnancy, I immediately left home to visit relatives in Hebron. When I returned after three months, everyone could see the truth. Long before the physical consummation of our marriage, my husband-to-be, Joseph, and both sets of parents believed I'd been unfaithful. That crushed me so hard. I had no friend, not even one, to support me at home.

However, God convinced my Joseph, that I'd been faithful and to marry— sooner than the date set. The villagers gossiped that I'd been an adulterous corrupt woman, unworthy of him. He gained no honor in continuing our marriage plans. "Why marry one with another man's child in her belly?

"But do you remember thirty-four years ago, the Romans required men to return to their ancestral towns in order to count them in their empire census. With my first baby almost due, I rode a donkey many miles from Nazareth to Bethlehem. Joseph walked beside me the whole way. I wanted to be with my man who came to accept God's secretive plan. Yes, a sacrifice and not supported by anyone to travel so great with child. I would likely give birth away from home without able help. Though Bethlehem overflowed with travelers, Jesus' birth found us lonely—no family or midwives.

"Then shortly after Jesus' birth, total strangers, holy in their beliefs, blessed my promised infant, including my husband, and me at the Temple. They foretold both good and hard themes in our lives, all pivoting around our unique baby. One prophesied that a sword would pierce my heart. I lived many long years waiting, watching, wondering what that meant and fearing that cold shaft of steel.

"Years later, I watched my beloved, faithful, husband die. Then I watched my firstborn suffer a terrifying death. And for three long days that sword pierced me and stayed rigid in my ripped open heart. Think of the drenching torrents of bottomless grief, and then, praise God, to see Jesus alive, healthy and strong, three days later—grief turned to a flood of amazing gratitude."

Chapter 34
First Time Parents

"But to backup in my story. Joseph and I needed to stay near the Temple for forty days and submit to the purification rituals of birth. During those weeks in Bethlehem, my husband found work. God blessed him and gave Joseph favor. We made a very hard decision and remained there until we perceived Adonai's next will for us. No doubt back home, neighbors and others would judge and criticize the circumstances of my pregnancy and early wedding.

"A happy toddler, Jesus' first baby steps were in Bethlehem. We made friends, I babysat with other young mothers, and we were accepted. Our situation remained secret. One night, three travelers, learned men from the east, sought us out to"— Mary choked, her word picture so deeply entrenched. Wiping tears, she cleared her throat. Hesitantly, looking around at the listeners, she said, "to worship my child and present valuable gifts. God drew these wonderful, yet odd men, right to us."

Many listeners Oo'd and Ah'd. "But then, during the night, how so very strange, Joseph and the three visitors all had the same dream. They woke up in dread fright and discussed this bizarre event. The dream warned us all to pack up and escape for our lives immediately." Mary choked up and wiped at new tears.

The audience murmured. Someone Mary didn't spot called out, "Four men had the same dream at the same time?" She nodded her reddened face with a smile. Another person muttered, "Remarkable. Only God can do that."

Mary collected her thoughts. "The next day, King Herod, enslaved by mad, raging jealousy, sent soldiers into the area to kill every little boy they found. His vicious goal was to murder our son." She dried her face and added, "We didn't learn of the slaughter of the eleven littlest boys until our return from Egypt two years later. Several of those families had become our close friends. Imagine the guilt we felt disappearing to safety, not knowing the murders of the coming day. Those innocent grieving parents in Bethlehem and the nearby region never knew why their children suffered, torn from their arms and killed. I doubt that the soldiers did either."

Realization struck. No one in the audience had known that this thirty-three-year-old tragic story of Herod's evil reign centered around Jesus' childhood. And no lack of horrendous evil caused by the long deceased king.

A woman of Mary's age waved her hand. In a pained voice she said, "My sister and her family lived in Bethlehem during those years. My nephew, Ezra, just a little boy learning to walk, didn't survive due to Herod's murdering men." She broke down in tears.

Getting up without thinking, Mary found herself on her knees embracing the woman. They both cried and time stood still.

After quiet moments, Mary composed herself and returned to her seat to start again. "Oh! And when Jesus was twelve years old, he disappeared from our Passover caravan leaving Jerusalem, heading home to Nazareth. We lost him for three days. And each moment we feared God's judgment on our failure to be responsible parents. Then we found our lost foal grazing, enjoying himself on the Temple Mount—with the Torah teachers and scholars. No guilt or apology, he simply expected us to have gone straight to the Mount on the first day. We never really understood his thinking. However, he assumed that his love of Adonai would've been obvious to us and that he wasn't ready to go back home. In his youth, we witnessed his amazing grasp of Scriptures. He studied far beyond his years at twelve years old."

*　*　*

Mary liked to wander in the Upper Room and see the faces of her listeners close up. "Do you think Adonai chose me to carry His child, the Messiah, because I had no sin? Ridiculous! Yes, I've sinned. Do not think I am different from you. Please do not set me above yourselves. If Adonai needed to find a sinless woman, He'd still be looking." Heads nodded, a few grinned. "Like many of you, I submitted to John's immersion for repentance at the Jordan. We didn't recognize each other at first. We'd aged in the years since our families last visited. Now he was tall, hairy and had a wooly beard, a fully grown man. But, my, my, when our eyes looked deep into the others, John remembered m. With that realization he let out laughter rooted in a truly righteous heart. 'Mary!'"

Subdued, she quietly closed her talking time with, "I always think of John that way—waist deep in water, happy and brimming with enthusiasm."

*　*　*

During her days in the Upper Room, this Galilean peasant woman of prominence, drank in the esteem of the bevy of females, young girls, married women, and widows who sat at her feet or who walked by her side. She had a mother's heart and a grandmother's soul. A sisterhood. "Do not seek, nor aspire, acknowledgement from me or aspire to be my daughter-by-heart. No. We desire, I desire, Adonai to reckon me as His daughter-by-heart; you do the same." A warm glow emanated from her beautiful eyes, cheeks and smiling lips.

"The saints we revere in Scripture were fallen humans also. Yet, Adonai used them. Did Moses' mother have no sin?" She paused to allow that point to clink into place. "Know that my mother gave birth to a baby girl born to fail in keeping the God-given laws of the Torah, laws that represent Adonai's heart. My heart desired and still desires to please Him and fulfill all that apply to women."

Focusing on the eyes of a young girl, she knelt before the child. "Men daily thank God that they weren't born females. We have fewer laws to obey than men do. They pride themselves in having more to glorify our Creator. Of course, some women get jealous. This isn't because there is a difference in the level of sacredness between men and women. Men are showing gratefulness for having more opportunity to serve God. Some men feel fortunate and privileged to have more obligations." Mary ran an affectionate hand over the girl's hair, stood and went back to her seat.

"We aren't less privileged, do not be mistaken. A woman's obligations and responsibilities are different from a man's, but no less important. The more commandments one is obliged to observe, the more privileged one is. Because women are not obligated to perform as many commandments as men, they often regard women as less privileged. Women are inherently more spiritual; intuition is a talent within us. Men need more tools to learn spiritual skills—laws, guidelines, study, repetition—to stay close to God."

Mary recalled valuing the teaching and mentoring times with her cousin, Elizabeth, during the three months the newly pregnant Mary stayed at their home. She thought, *Now I sound just like her, mentoring friends and strangers!* A chill raced in her spine. *My life sure has changed.*

Her audience sat patiently.

"Rather, these exemptions allow a woman to be more devoted to her family without the constraints of having to fulfill certain laws at the correct time. Women's obligation of prayer is only superseded by her role as the pillar of the family. Throughout the ages, Jewish women have instilled spirituality into the home. Jewish women, we have long been praised for our ability to speak from the heart and pour our emotions out to God. Remember, a woman's choice of dress and behavior should be reflective of her natural dignity." Her eyes roamed eyeing the females. "My given name is that of Moses' older sister, such as many of you, too. A woman of authority. A prophetess with discernment, and a song maker."

Mary's precious teaching and revealing of heart ended. She closed the session with prayer. "May we make our households complete, crowning our homes with Your Presence dwelling among us. Make us worthy to raise learned children and grandchildren who are wise and understanding, who love and fear God—people of truth, holy and attached to God, who will dazzle the world with Torah and goodness and service to God. Please hear our prayers in the merit of our matriarchs Sarah, Rebecca, Rachel and Leah, and ensure that the light of our lives will never be dimmed. Show us the glow of Your face and we will be saved. Amen."

Chapter 35
Mary's Dream

In the early morning light, Mary wanted to find Peter. She shook and roused him from sleep. Mary knelt beside him, a far-off look in her eyes. "Wake up! I must speak with you."

On hearing her whispery voice, he sat up. Before sleep left him and his mind cleared, he stared at Mary, seeing a pressing need.

Peter motioned for Mary to meet him in one of the corners of the Upper Room. Yawning, he asked, "What is it? What is so troubling you?"

She said, "Yesterday I spoke to the women and girls about serving Adonai."

Peter nodded. "Yes, I recall the sincere and dedicated instructions you gave."

She responded in a whisper, while her hands wrestled against each other, "Yes, true. But during the night I had a most horrible dream which weighs heavy on my heart—crushing me. I need to tell somebody—now."

Solemn and firm, with a wave of his hand he whispered, "Go on."

"I dreamt that after I died, certain female disciples followed in the idolatrous ways of our ancestors. Their sins reminded me of the stories of judgment in Joshua, Jeremiah and the other prophets concerning the pagan goddess Ishtar or Asherah—Baal's wife—but they worshipped me. Me! They broke God's commandment given at Pentecost from Mount Sinai, to not have any other gods before Him!"

The growing plea in her voice awakened James, John, and Nicodemus. Now they stood close, heads inclined. Nicodemus, the most educated of them, interrupted Mary. "Yes, Ishtar is revered as the Queen of Heaven, goddess of motherhood and fertility, Moon-goddess, and she represented the evening and morning stars. In ancient times our people built temples to worship her. These contained graven images of Ishtar made of wood. Male and female priests led Israel astray with many a sinful king's help. Such immoral reverence even corrupted the heart of wise King Solomon. Due to disobedience, we Jews have a terrible history of dreadful evil rituals. Recall that Jezebel hired 400 prophets of this goddess and brought them to our land. The Prophet Elijah dealt death to them all." He paused and gave Mary a curious look. "Why do thoughts of this imaginary goddess trouble you now?"

Fidgeting, Mary lowered her eyes. She explained her dream just above a whisper. "Years after I died, my son's ... well, by the Messiah's disciples worshipped me. I know our people do not worship idols anymore—we've learned our lesson. But I saw in the future, Jews prayed to me in order to have me influence my son for their benefit. They had vain admiration, adoration, and false ideas of me well beyond my personality and human duties. They believed I had otherworldly powers like I was God's favorite woman, or but not human anymore. Now, I remember 34 years ago, while pregnant in Hebron. Zechariah and dear Elizabeth warned me of such possibilities for Joseph and me." Mary's voice quivered as her eyes searched the listeners' faces. "In my dream, they laid tributes at my statues—I saw hundreds—thousands, of identical graven images. There were little me's, little Marys and life-size ones too. Many disciples spoke to the statues, lit candles, even put a crown on my—its—head. I existed without voice, silent, and couldn't make them stop their heathen practices. Jewish women were devoted to me!" Mary put her arms around her waist, squeezed hard and moaned. "Tell me this is not true. Tell me my nightmare was just that, and never will come to pass."

In a fatherly manner, Nicodemus gripped Mary's shoulders. He let out a light chuckle. "Yes, daughter, that was only a dream. However, do not fear either the wrath of Adonai or the men and women committing these wicked deeds you witnessed. You do not seek such tributes and shameful attention. Of that, we here who have come to know you have no worries." She nodded, but her features lay troubled. Mary wandered off shaken and distraught. When any of the females approached her that day, she acted curt and unavailable.

Chapter 36
Jashen and His Baker of Bread

Jashen considered his crowd upstairs, their resources, personal sacrifices, and desire to serve the risen Master and follow the Torah. What will the future be? Early in the morning he realized that the men needed the required two loaves of bread which they would take to the Temple in 48 hours. Bread vendors, and any homes which had the means, would be selling loaves until sunset tomorrow. Pentecost, a Sabbath holiday, meant all businesses closed, no financial transactions took place or ordinary work done.

He went upstairs and took a head count. Then he asked questions about who wasn't present, and any plans made for the holiday. Jashen announced that he'd provide all of the loaves for his guests. Of course, the loaves were a significant concern. They thanked him repeatedly. Generosity made him the man people knew, part of his lifestyle, but praise made him fidgety and awkward.

That morning, he left immediately to go to a favorite baker named Nahbi. The generous man decided on seventy-five sets of loaves. Every baker lived for Pentecost and the surge of profit. As he walked, he berated himself for not planning for the bread sooner—Nahbi could bake only so many loaves in one day. These were rectangular in shape, measuring seven handbreadths long and four wide. The loaves were fashioned so that there would be a hornlike protrusion on each of the four corners. The priests would carry the two loaves and the other offerings up to the altar accompanied by Levites blasting trumpets and playing flutes. Before leaving the Temple Courtyard, each pilgrim would prostrate himself before God.

Happy to see Jashen walk in, the squat, broad shouldered baker smiled and lifted both hands. That is, until Jashen apologetically placed the order. Using a rag, Nahbi wiped his bald head dripping sweat down his brown skin. The customer spoke and then the baker erupted. "How many loaves? You want seventy-five pairs of loaves! Not by me, my friend, no!" Nahbi put his hands on the front counter and pressed down in hopes to loom over his customer. After a hard stare, one hand flew up. "Tell me where were you yesterday or the day before that? Now, I bake you 60 loaves, that is all."

A hefty sigh came from Jashen. He glanced sideways and back to the unpleasant face of Nahbi. "One hundred and fifty."

The baker rocked his head, and from his weary tongue he said, "Ninety…no more!"

Stymied, the generous man flapped his arms in useless gestures of disappointment, He dug out his leather purse and spilled shekels onto the front counter and took a step back.

The wife of Nahbi came and stood by her exasperated husband. She whispered in his ear, then said to the customer, "Yes. That's plenty for such a rush order." That remark started the two of them bickering. The fray ended when she stared him down and he bared his teeth, and took a fake swing at her.

The baker turned to face Jashen dead in the eyes. Red-faced with a finger pointing up, he said, "Not by dawn, my friend, not by noon—but certainly by sundown." The baker made a sweep of his hands toward the surplus of wood for the oven, grain and oil. One hand gestured over his shoulder with his thumb stuck backward. Evidently, his children of various ages and an array of relatives cluttered the work area. "Look!"

Then he pointed at his customer. "Only you! Only for you will I do this—"and in a sarcastic grumbling tone added, "and because of that wife of mine, my ever-so-unique, special gift from God. One of a kind she is…I hope so. But tell me, Jashen, why so many loaves; are you selling them in competition to the priests at the Temple?" The baker smiled and didn't wait for an answer. "Be on your way. Oh! You will be sending a cart to take the bread. Correct?" He leaned in, smirked, and shook his head. "Correct?"

Jashen nodded vigorously, managed a smile through a guilty conscience. He added a few coins to bless the baker and went home.

"Fine, I'll send a boy to your house when the order is almost done." He shouted over his shoulder to the busy crew, "Everyone! New order, folks. One hundred and fifty more loaves for tomorrow."

A collective groan came from behind him.

Chronicle Five
Pentecost Morning

Chapter 37
Holy Spirit Descends

When seven Sabbaths were fulfilled, from Passover to Pentecost, the disciples gathered and they were all of one heart. Holidays started at sundown, the beginning of the new day.

Joseph of Arimathea made it his duty, along with Jashen, to make sure that none went hungry, had need, or felt discomforted.

After the Resurrection, certain priests and Torah teachers came forward as believers. Their presence at Jashen's encouraged many.

Prayers, praises, and confessions blanketed the room. Scripture long known from childhood rose to the forefront of minds and hearts in fresh and startling ways. A few quiet conversations took place in these intense episodes of seeking Adonai. Songs poured out as if the worshippers sang in a vacant room, before the throne of God. The singers had no embarrassment.

Within many ardent worshippers they received what they wanted, in prayer, as God taught fresh, in-depth teaching, and personal counsel. In the room, private memories and troubles swirled, unseen, except for the outward clues. Due to forgiveness and desires for reconciliation, cheeks went red, throats choked, and yet, smiles and tears were the mere surface of intense gratitude. Eyes distributed rivulets of tears ending in drops falling to the holy floor. Family members hugged friends and friendly strangers, too. Words spouted to heaven—leaving no doubt that thanks filled God's hearing.

*   *   *

In this spiritual climate something happened. A powerful, unseen cyclone hit the roof of the Upper Room. It was the breath of God. Those in the street marveled at the sudden and extremely loud noise of gusting wind. A violent whirlwind or sandstorm surely must be the reason. But no dust flew in the sky? People in nearby streets of this epicenter found that they had to shout to communicate. Some spoke of a pillar of cloud reaching to the heavens. Others said a rapidly descending golden cloud entered through the roof of a building. One said that a dazzling, white funnel cloud appeared out of nowhere. Someone said, "Then why didn't we see it too?" The swirling sound of velocity left most curiosity seekers speechless.

Indoors, everyone looked at the ceiling, with an inquisitive face. Shoulders shrugged. Arms spread; hands opened in wonder. Praying stopped. Those with musical instruments to aid in singing psalms let their arms hang loose. The captivated, startled worshippers tried to talk. No one could hear the other. Though some shouted "sandstorm," or "whirlwind" or "thunder," fear found no foothold in the congregation. Dozens went to look at the sky from the surrounding windows. A calming blue color with white puffy clouds met their eyes. A few looked down and saw the street filling with curious spectators. A few worshippers wanted to make their way down to the street and look around—get an answer to the mysterious noise. They had no idea why a crowd gathered at the building they were in. Jostling people of all types, in every neighborhood pointed toward the center of the thunder. This web-work stretched and drew thousands.

Out on the streets people headed to the noisy location in Jerusalem. Tracing the sound, more arrived in the neighborhood and surrounded the building. They looked past the roof expecting thunder. Whatever made the sound of howling wind remained invisible. Their bewilderment matched those upstairs; curiosity prevailed. The sound of a funnel cloud intensified. The 120 couldn't hear what anyone shouted—they could not even hear themselves.

In the next seconds, each worshipper identified the strange occurrence in an unexplainable heavenly way, but didn't understand why it linked to them personally. No one had answers.

If viewers could see into the spiritual dimension in a cutaway perspective, here's what they would see. A dazzling white whirlwind flecked with gold, its top stretching to the corners of the sky. It narrowed miles below, tapering into a flaming arm and fist, whose force fed into a single extended finger. The tip of that finger blazed with fire and made a sudden hearth at one spot in the city. There at the bottom of this fast-moving spinning funnel, bright sparks of an unknown hue spun into kindling on the roof. The street viewers could see the stone brick building with limestone steps leading into the two-storied home. Once inside, the steps turned and hugged the wall to the floor above. At the top of this passageway the entire second floor of people gazed at the ceiling. They appeared in awe by a presence, as if snug under a warm huge blanket on a chilly evening. Clearly, an inviting pleasurable pressure settled within everyone. Outside, a growing crowd pointed at an empty yet noisy sky. They stood shrugging shoulders, and few had guesses on their tongues. Shouting, protesting questions went one to the other. There was no answer; not yet.

Then around the room, a slow hum evolved into a roar of mingled words. On the ceiling, in the center, a flame of fire emerged. Holy fuel fired the oddity. Everyone took a step backward. Parents reached for their children. Dozens pointed. Eyes went wide. Perplexed, open handed, people turned to one another. They said, "Is the roof on fire due to the windstorm? But the color of this blaze is wrong. Not yellow, orange, green or blue." Their eyes beheld a brilliant color from another world; no hue on earth came close.

Later, trying to describe the vivid color to outsiders proved impossible. More fire came through the ceiling, yet nothing burned. Then the fire split apart. Everyone watched as the single flame quickly spread and fanned out. This stumped the worshippers. Within several heartbeats everyone understood that this uncommon sight went beyond their common understanding. The temperature in the room remained comfortable and no smoke could be seen. Nothing caught on fire—nothing would.

Then one by one, all realized this intruder held certain intelligence and had orders to fulfill. No random event, no, for the fire quickly separated into individual flames aiming and settling only on heads—every human head present—targeted. The flames had will and destinations, but what purpose? A refreshing brilliance lit up faces like the sun showing itself after being hidden in dark clouds. Finally, not a spark remained on the ceiling.

People pointed at each other. No smell of burning hair, no scorched skin. Curious hands ventured to their heads to feel the fire. Some touched the flame on the person next to them. No pain. Momentarily hot, this sensation raced through each head and out their feet. Supernatural beauty crowned every head. A few recalled the ancient story of Moses and the Burning Bush—really, the bush that would not burn. Soon, all those who came to that conclusion wondered, *Are we in such a story?*

The sound of storm winds continued. Some plugged their ears. Families had huddled closer. But now, the few children stopped clinging to a parent's hands or legs. Breastfeeding infants remained at peace.

Then, scattered laughter, pure laughter, and giggling meandered through the 120. Some wobbled, quaked or shook under the powerful anointing. This serious event had a fun and special edge. They felt good. Young children swiveled around to see the strange, yet harmless actions of the grownups and found they were soon acting just like them. Some even saw visions or went into a trance. No one was in charge, and no one aspired to such a role.

Chapter 38
Spirit and Response

As the wind slowed, remarks and short conversations started. Though comfortably startled; people considered various otherworldly miracles. "What of Jesus sending out a few dried fish and loaves which fed over 5,000 men, plus women and children—more than once? And, what of that fig tree which displeased him? Withered during the night—only one night." From the back, a man remarked, "The dead whom he called back to life. What of his own death, his own life, his own flying toward heaven without wings. Were these his flames what he said to wait for? Immersion in fire and the Holy Spirit."

Someone happily shouted, "We've all just been filled with the Holy Spirit! That's what I think."

This fuel from heaven made each praise of Adonai a flexible adventure. Their hearts found a new source of intensity. Smiles spread. Joy filled each one. All were in love with the same Person and swooned in His love for them. Then while they still could not even hear much of their own voices—something happened. Their words muddled. In their mouths words came out which were not what they had intended. Internally, they noticed new thoughts and concepts—with words to match. Around the busy room, worshippers were choosing these other praise syllables and words which were not of their minds' design. New words, but eternal truths. "Is this a language spoken in another land? Why am I doing this? What is the benefit—if any? I do not understand, but I like it!"

Indeed, no one appeared stressed, reserved, or kept their lips closed. Some did weep under the weight of insight and revelation, bridging from unholiness to holiness to the inconceivable. Grieving and repentance filled up a few, but this passed. Some made gestures as if they were unloading, washing arms and hands, or standing straight at attention before a leader. Little children pointed and laughed at their parent's heads. No one judged anyone's actions or behavior.

The soul of each person fell before the Holy Spirit. Unpleasant emotions, grudges, memories, and hurts submitted to the lovely, overwhelming presence of God. Later, in discussion, some likened the change in their thoughts and words to the Holy Spirit judging, or a referee deciding moral conflicts. Some said they could question or debate and talk back and forth with the unseen Lord. Others spoke in lively and dear ways of how love, joy, peace, kindness, patience, gentleness, goodness, and self-control welled up or beckoned them to take and call the quality their own. Gladly, many reached and took as if they picked ripened fruit in an orchard. One person said, "God does own an orchard, He really does! Remember, He started with a garden in Eden. He grows things, He grows people."

Each person had a nudging to venture. Fresh phrases, sentences, and words agreed. Independently, truths in foreign words filled their mouths, filling the room.

Each had a greater desire and reason to praise. They worked at sorting out this new additional and optional language. Each could choose which—most preferred trying the new words—soon all did. Though they could speak praises in Hebrew, a tug to use the other syllables which vied for life and volume. Each of the 120 dealt with this unknown oddity. As experimenting continued, more worshippers choose the strange syllables which then made sentences, which then became a language. They didn't and couldn't choose the words, but their spirits understood the words and divine messages. Without acknowledging, everyone knew.

Later, one person described the new language as how a hinge swivels. A hinge permits moving a door one direction or another. As each person experienced a filling sensation of the Spirit of God, they recognized the difference. The average person there spoke Hebrew, Aramaic, and Greek. An inspired fourth alternative presented itself. Some prayed, while others spoke using their new tongue.

They knew why Scripture portrays that odd variety of heavenly beings continually praising their Creator. Here, the Holy Spirit flooded their beings like never before. Roving amongst the faithful and committed in the Upper Room, the Heart-Searcher, the Heart-Knower strengthened, comforted, and exhorted.

As this agreement of souls progressed, the flames and rushing wind died down and then were gone, but never forgotten.

What each one said rang true, and as they spoke, more words and phrases formed. Everyone, including children, had a desire to speak forth and speak out. In the noisy crowd each one felt joyously alone, independent, and filled with purpose. These youngsters, though close to family members, found their hearts were pleasantly distant from them.

No one concerned themselves with others in the room. Obviously the surge of holiness entered when the flames changed or fulfilled each one's heart, mind, and soul. Moses would have smiled at the little fires, like separate bushes, which lit up the room. The morning sunlight filling the windows was outdone. Some clapped, some shouted and whooped, many raised their hands, and others knelt. Twirling in delight, eyes closed, smiles, and other simple actions of worship accented the secluded crowd. A few lay on the floor prostrate, face down, and others face up. Sounds of crying by men and women rippled through the room. Some stood at attention. Others declared, "Yes! Yes!"

The unusual presence passed through each personality's individual unique self. Everyone talked, a few made melodies. Each could turn the praise words on or off. They enjoyed what their lips produced.

Each sensed a layer added to their lives, a renewal, an empowerment. Enlightenment filled worshippers moving from the outside to within. Holiness resided in everyone's minds, thoughts, and attitudes. A purifying energy, a cleansing fire of the heart worked in each one. An immediate acceptance, lightened by love, enhanced the recognition when one person saw another.

Those who loved Adonai loved him for more reasons. Those who had loved Him less now loved Him more.

Everyone's tongue could interchange with the new and foreign one. Then at the same moment in time, each flame subsided. The last little flames burned out. The heaven-lit fire remained inside each one. At that realization, for a short time no one talked. 120 people looked around in wonder. No one felt the same as when they had walked into the room earlier. "What's next? What do we do now?"

* * *

Barsabas ventured a curious idea. "Remember the evil pagan prophet Balaam on his way to curse the tribes in the Wilderness? Adonai opened the mouth of Balaam's donkey in order for the animal to speak the wisdom of its mind. The beast knew better than its owner, for it beheld the angel ready to strike his rider! However, I say to you, beloved, who taught the beast the language which it spoke? With what vocabulary did it use—perhaps while pondering life as it chewed grass? Did not Adonai make the beast aware and able to discern a human tongue? If so, are we belittled by a room full of languages not our own? Are we not to speak like the Master did, and draw together hearers?"

Several in the room, who had traveled to many lands, identified certain languages. They marveled at the fellow Galileans' immediate accuracy, without need of learning or interpreting.

Joseph of Arimathea cleared his throat. His voice drew solemn attention. He held up a hand with one finger pointed in a sweeping motion. "Recall with me when our people were about to enter the Promised Land. Do not forget that Adonai worked a wonder by a sorcerer's tongue. The enemy, King Balak of the Moabites, and his princes, paid a sizable amount of money for Balaam to curse our ancestors. But the Spirit of Adonai came upon Balaam. Three separate times when Balaam tried to speak misfortune, yet only blessings were uttered!" Joseph held high three fingers and continued, "An enchanter and diviner, whose reputation of pronouncing curses—his words held power and forced nature. But here he tells his wealthy and frightened royal employer that he can 'only speak the words Adonai puts in his mouth, only do what He commands. What Adonai says I must speak.'"

Head down and one fist under his chin, Joseph appeared deep in thought. "I too have many servants, and I too tell them what to say and to whom. However, I am no master of their tongues. They may say as they please or according to my will, which I've charged them with."

Peter's wife, Naimah, a contented woman, had been known to have a smarter edge than her husband. Though typically overshadowed by her husband's loud and spontaneous personality, Naimah spoke her thoughts. "And remember Mount Sinai! The top of the mountain in flames as Moses met with Adonai to receive the Torah. After all, that's why Jerusalem is overwhelmed with our people from the wide world to celebrate the giving of the Law. Now, Jesus knew we'd be here for the holiday. I believe he meant for us to receive the Promise of the Holy Spirit on Pentecost—he just didn't want to tell us the exact day. But his will came to pass."

Nicodemus added, "Correct, woman! Adonai visited our forefathers in flaming fire on Mount Sinai. Thunder, lightning, and smoke, and remember the loud shofar blast which increased in volume. Then Moses, that mighty courageous man, spoke to Adonai. It is written that Adonai answered him with thunder. Our thunderous sound of wind reminds us of that ancient day of the giving of the Law. That is, of course, why we and all of Jerusalem are here for the holiday of Pentecost. We celebrate Adonai's giving to our nation wise tools and rules to live by. And of course, the bountiful harvest of fields and orchards."

John added, "Yes and the giving of the firstfruits to the mighty hand which delivers our rain and sun." He put his hand to his chin. "I just remembered something which goes with our mysteries! Adonai spoke to Job from out of the whirlwind. And we've lived through our own private storm. Now I believe he wants us to speak his revelations to each other and those below whom we do not know."

One man named Yishai spoke up. "I arrived in Jerusalem yesterday. On the journey from Arabia, my horse had thrown me, causing one leg much pain. Now, after the coming and settling of the Holy Spirit, the pain is gone." Much praise rumbled at this.

Tzabi, a follower from the port of Acco, added, "Me, too. I've had pains in my lower back for months. Now I am free. It must be due to the Promise. God is in this place! What other good can we anticipate?"

Quietly, Mary said, "Three miracles: the sound, the fire, and the untaught languages. What's next?"

A girl innocently said, "The sound reminded me of the roar of the sea and of waterfalls."

Waving both hands high, Thomas motioned for attention. All looked toward him. First, he eyed the other apostles. Then he said with curiosity in his tone, "In this room, this very room. Jesus visited us core followers." Pointing, he emphasized, "He walked through that wall right there. As you know, there's only air on the other side. This amazed us. He spoke a variety of truths to us. We finally, and with firmness, understood much better those many discourses of his during the past three years. But, remember with me after the Passover Seder ended, he did a peculiar action. Looking into our eyes, Jesus took an unusually deep breath. He then let it out in a whoosh blowing on to each of our faces. That got our attention. He followed this by saying, 'Each of you, receive the Holy Spirit.'"

Phillip said, "Yes, and perhaps now we have fully."

Chapter 39
King Saul

Matthias stood and shouted, "I have something to say." People came near. Then he sat back down, placing his young son on his lap. "Listen. Friends, we're all excited about what just happened, but please hear me out. I think this story will have a bearing on our experience today. I want to tell you about one of King Saul's bad times. An episode when he chased young David, the future king—for no good reason, with only fear-driven, self-centered, evil motives. The king hunted David, thirsting for his blood."

The little boy looked up and said, "Abba, I thought everybody loved David."

A young woman nodded, saying, "I know about those stories but don't remember much. Why did he hunt David?"

"Good question." Matthias answered, "Jealousy and failure were in the heart of the king. He knew Adonai wanted David to replace him. Remember Samuel? One of our most important prophets? For a time he protected David, hiding him close to his own abode, a place called the Prophet's Village in the area of Ramah. The Holy Spirit must have continually hovered there due to the constant study of Scripture, worship, intercession, music, and dance. The inhabitants desired to live righteously before Adonai. Because of these sacred practices, special divine protection rested there."

Mary looked up at Matthias and said, "Sounds like a town I'd be happy to visit." Others nodded. A few children added, "Me, too!

Amused, Matthias clapped and rubbed his hands. "Now, three separate times, a different company of soldiers sought to find, arrest, and bring David to their vengeful king. However, when approaching the privileged residence of the prophets, each military contingent collapsed overwhelmed—internally overwhelmed. They forgot about King Saul, their orders concerning David, and—hard to understand—even forgot themselves. They laid down their weapons and removed their armor; their priorities vanished, forgotten, replaced by ecstasy of our amazing Adonai. The Holy Spirit eased them out of their military identity and they yielded control of themselves—happily."

A grinning Peter interjected, "Intoxication by Adonai. The best wine there is. And no sorrows fill the head come morning!" Chuckles affirmed this statement.

Matthias continued. "Yes! Unable to resist, impulsively, with delight in their hearts, they worshiped, joining the ranks of the prophets and families. Each spoke Heavenly truths and sang praises to Adonai. The uplifting holy nature settled on the soldiers for two nights, and nothing else mattered. As I said, this happened on three occasions, with well over a dozen new soldiers each time!

"So, after these peculiar and decisive failures, King Saul decided to take hand-picked soldiers and go arrest David himself. On their way to Ramah—not even there yet—Adonai touched the king and the fourth military escort. When he arrived, the Spirit eased and surrounded him. Did Adonai take complete control of him due to his evil intentions? Saul even stripped off his royal clothing and lay in the dirt humbled, naked, all day and night, prophesying and praising the King of Heaven. Saul lay drunk by the wonders of his Creator. His life, so fueled by vain hatred, entered into a cleansing, washed clean, made fresh and new."

James quietly said, "Those soldiers had themselves a good time. They were all immersed—soaked. And we too, though not soldiers, nearly had the same because our hearts follow a different commander and his instructions."

A woman observed, "The soldiers could not, or like us, didn't want to resist. All gave control over to the Almighty." She paused and looked around. "None of us are captives or slaves by force." Listeners agreed by words and nods.

Nicodemus said, "This story reminds me of an incident at the Temple Mount. The chief priests sent Levitical officers with guards to arrest Jesus. When the guards arrived and heard him—they listened. Those of us who noticed their strange behavior grinned.

"Later, I followed the guards back to the baffled and angry authorities who asked, 'Why didn't you bring him in?' The captain spoke in a strong clear voice while his eyes gazed far away, 'Never has anyone spoken like this man does!' The expression on the captain's face meant one of contented surrender."

Matthias set his son aside and stood. Arms outstretched, he added, "The storm that has been above us, the sound of the four winds, has reminded me of another story in Scripture. You recall the Prophet Ezekiel and the Valley of Dry Bones—our ancestors. 'The Holy Spirit said to Ezekiel, prophesy to these bones and say to them, 'Dry bones, hear the word of the LORD! Prophesy to the wind, prophesy, son of man, and say to the wind. Come four winds, O breath, and breathe on these slain, that they may live.'" Matthias concluded, "A new Spirit and new heart of flesh."

Others spoke to those seated nearby. "Are we then…or were we also like the dry bones?"

A young girl brushed her hair aside and asked, "Has the wind entered into us, raised us up, cleansing with holy fire? Are we to be an army as did rise up that day?"

A teenager with a keen mind questioned, "Is that what Jesus meant when he said that I must be born again? I feel wonderful. God's kindness has visited me. I've been turned inside out; goodness churns—I want to serve God and please Him."

Chronicle Six
Surge to Go Outside

Chapter 40
Holy Feet Tread

At this time, they were overwhelmed by purpose. Their holy feet tread pursuing more awe. Dumbfounded, many experienced a pleasant refining energy. For a moment, that seemed more like minutes, silence ruled. No one said anything—all words remained as thoughts. People looked around with expressions of asking, beckoning, of what to do next. Passion like the mystical fires touched, motivated, or consumed everyone. A compelling boldness stirred. Everyone found this appealing and made a personal surrender. They and the Spirit blended.

Independent yet unified, they had found a way to express praise, thanksgiving, honor, and awe beyond their own personal knowledge. And they liked it. An otherworldly source flowed into them. It felt right and curious. As they spoke, they knew all who surrounded them were experiencing the same marvelousity. No one needed to be in charge. Every person enjoyed personal, private, and intimate with a heavenly Person. They felt the presence of God around them and Him filling them up with His Spirit. He opened their understanding.

People saw glimpses of stories from Scripture as if they were watching the ancient scene in person. This intrigued them and gave them much to ponder. Was this day, Pentecost, a smaller version of the first, at Mount Sinai?

One of the teachers boldly laid out a question for the group. "I recall what the Prophet Jeremiah foretold, are we living that out, right now?" He quoted, "This is the new covenant I will make with the people of Israel," declares the Lord, "I will put My Torah, My laws and instructions in their minds and write My teachings on their hearts. I will be their God, and they will be my people." This proclamation made sense. Heads nodded. Many intensified their worship with song or raised arms. Others placed a hand on their hearts and bowed.

In waves, wooziness passed through the room. Certain people appeared more affected. Their bodies made repetitious shaking or quaking movements; a few fell over backwards and were unharmed. On the floor several men and women lay on their backs, sides or bellies with laughter, pure laughter, and wonders in their mouths. Others lay motionless, in a cocoon of God's love. A couple of small children investigated and watched. One child asked someone lying on the floor, "Is it like God is tickling you?"

A man answered by nodding his reddened face.

Another child commented, "This is fun."

Eventually, the curious looked for Peter, James, and John to lead. Yet, those three each knew what the entire 120 really wished for—they wanted Jesus to appear and tell them what to do—but he was gone. Ten days since they last saw him, fifty since his death—well, temporary death—and forty-seven since he returned to life as the new, glorified Jesus, his feet of flesh rarely touched the raw dirt of Earth. Until when? No one knew. But Jesus foreknew these promised signs.

The three of them agreed that this manifestation of three signs and wonders, and the renewal and refreshment surging within them must be the "Promise from the Father." The immersion in the Holy Spirit had indeed come with fire. They held a bold secret which must be boldly told.

In the past, at least once, Jesus commissioned the 12 core followers (two to a team) and then later, another 70 (35 teams) to venture throughout towns and villages of Israel. They taught, prayed for the sick, took authority over demons and oversaw the immersing of the repentant. For those now present in the Upper Room, they'd be up for the challenge to speak and promote the Master's message.

A whoosh of ballooning intensive love prompted the 120 men plus women and the few children. Each had a quickened common sense, moral courage, and spiritual insight. In unison, by the irresistible guidance of the Spirit, they wanted to pursue an audience of strangers. Once verbalized, everyone agreed. Some shouted, "Yes! Go to the Temple! On our way we shall be a parade of worshippers."

In minutes the room would be vacant. The discussions of analyzing the wonders didn't seem to take any time at all.

Using a plain-spoken manner, Joseph said "We here only speak God's praises and His glory. Our messages honor as we obey this infilling of languages new to us because the Holy Spirit resides in us. Though the winds and flames have subsided, one proof remains—this odd ability. We are indeed blessed," Joseph clearly thought on this for a moment, then he added, "Now let us bless others who are in need of hearing the truth and that truth upon exceptional truth!" He raised a fist in the air. "Come!"

A voice shouted over the funneling group. "Pray that they hearken to the truth expressed in our praise."

Someone else questioned, "And after that, when they believe?"

The first voice answered back, "Whoever hungers for more clarity of the words of life should reveal a repentant heart and be immersed in water as a sign to God, in Jesus' name—as his disciple. Since many of us daily worship at the appointed times, tell them to meet us at the Temple portico for more discussion. God knows what will come next."

Peter turned and shouted, "Let's not daydream about such things. Our direction is to the Temple for the Pentecost offering. That's our first goal. Later, those in the street, travelers, and Torah teachers shall have our ears."

But Thomas called out, "Look out the windows! The streets are full of people; they're all looking up here for some reason."

Peter looked for the first time; it took his breath away. He made a curious expression and muttered to his wife, "Maybe we've got work to do down there first."

Close to the exit, Jashen's servants placed 150 loaves of fresh bread stacked on three large tables. They had shopped at the shuk to purchase the seven prescribed fruits. Dozens of Firstfruits straw baskets with properly arranged items, rested on the floor. Those who had need for the sacrifices smiled and took two loaves and a basket. As Peter headed toward the stairs, he stopped and looked at the unexpected bounty. His wife whispered, "Jashen's daughter and several of her girlfriends have been weaving these baskets the last few days. Wonderful." Then he shouted, "Grab your loaves and fruit offerings to take to the Temple." He hadn't noticed that his wife held their loaves and basket.

Chapter 41
DOWN

The Torah required that for Pentecost, each household bring two loaves of bread and other sacrifices and offerings to the place God would choose for His dwelling. The most important place on earth? Jerusalem. When the 120 people passed through the street door, they expected to see hundreds of men, women and children clutching loaves of bread, baskets of fruits on men's heads or shoulders, perhaps a lamb, goat, oxen, caged doves, and wine. They would be on their way to the Temple, hoping to get there earlier than most. The line would be long all day.

*   *   *

Naturally, Peter was the first to go. The bustling, excited crowd backed him up. He walked down the stairs, not knowing what to expect. When his feet touched every stair step a maturity made small leaps in the man. All that he'd done wrong, small to large—even denying he knew Jesus three times—fell off. Those whose feet followed his, stepped into Peter's wake of maturity, personal strength, and freedom.

The bright sunlight pained Peter's eyes. He gasped at the crowd staring at him and felt self-conscious. His wife whispered in one ear, "Be the big man that you are, and catch fish." He nodded. When he reached the last steps, an empowerment rested on him tingling from his head to his sandals. His mind cleared. In a moment's time his intellect and God's Spirit connected deeper than before. Peter knew he thought beyond his own reasoning. He did have a 'big' job to do.

Everywhere, people focused on Peter and what explanation he'd give. Silence took over the large crowd. Then they heard the noise of robust voices. The stairwell turned into a funnel and exiting the narrow passageway came a parade of languages.

Someone placed a shofar in Peter's hand. He didn't even look to see who. He didn't need to look at the horn; he knew the feel from the fishing vessels at the lake. His wife stayed one step up from him and put her arms on his shoulders. Peace settled. He took a deep breath and blew hard. Everything stopped.

The 120 spread further away down the intersection in front of Jashen's home and beyond. They did so to cause less confusion to foreigners who were trying to hear the speeches. Because of the press of the curious, many had to fan out. This created clusters encircled by the curious, the cautious, and the condemning. Everyone who joined the wide crowd heard somebody speaking in his native tongue. What they heard about Adonai created wide-open astonishment. Wonder grew. The strong linguistic powers made listeners perplexed, puzzled, and amazed.

People in the street crowded to hear familiar words in their own languages and searched out the voices. In a matter of minutes, the thousands of international travelers migrated to hear these boisterous, happy, odd Galileans.

Listeners meandered in the ever-increasing crowd filling the intersection to listen and discern the number of languages. Merchants and sailors of the Mediterranean Sea knew several languages. As if drawn by a magnetic force, members of the bewildered found each other near strangers speaking praises which they understood. Though no one could hear and understand all the languages spoken at the same time, an amazing miracle pieced them together— yet, who could grasp the depth or span?

The street crowd didn't question the upstairs crowd about the powerful windstorm, which had raised no dust and shook no palm leaves. What could those who'd been indoors know of what happened in the sky above? Yet, people wondered if there was a connection. If so, what might that be?

Most Jews from upstairs and on the street spoke Hebrew, Aramaic, and Greek. Yet, Adonai wanted to make His enticement, His loving hook, personal. He used their regional home languages—over 17 different tongues. They recognized the indigenous languages of their native lands. Yet, the Galilean accents were easily recognizable too, and this confused some of the audience.

For the holiday, there were faithful Jews, God-fearing Greeks and pagan converts to Judaism staying in Jerusalem from every Mediterranean nation and beyond. Streams of Jews came closer together in puzzlement because each one heard their own language. Utterly amazed, they asked: "Aren't all these who are speaking Galileans? You can tell by the strong accents. Then how is it that they speak in our native languages? This sound is a collection of languages. Why is it that they are declaring the wonders of God in our tongues? This isn't a synagogue or the Temple or holiday parade! Why this spontaneity on a residential street?" Indeed, there were Parthians, Medes, and Elamites; residents of Mesopotamia, Cappadocia, Pontus, and Asia; Phrygia and Pamphylia; Egypt and the parts of Libya near Cyrene; visitors from Rome; Cretans and Arabs—at least twenty language groups.

International visitors and local bystanders asked one another, "What does this mean? Why this boisterous, sudden praise? And, what of that rushing wind sound in the sky, yet nothing stirred?"

Some, however, made fun, only hearing a circus of voices and animated people. "Some are barely able to stand—leaning against one another. Apparently they've had too much wine. A rabble of early morning drunkards, quite entertaining though."

"A party is it? An early morning one at that! Or, one that's gone on through the night."

"What's this all about? They make sport of God with garbled words and laughter—must be wine."

Someone else shrugged and said, "Drunks always think that whatever they have to say is special and we must listen to every word. They get careless with their tongues and jabber. Look, some can barely stand up."

As the defiling rumors spread, Adonai firmly put into the minds of the 120 that this is His empowering joy running through them in the privacy of the upstairs and now on public display. Scriptures stood out in their hearts. Yes, He gifted joy for the faithful in life. It usually manifested by something tangible. However here, the mostly Galilean speakers had neither skins which held alcohol, nor a jest or antic to cause this strange scene.

Another bystander kicked at the ground. "Drunkards find ears. They're tanked up on new wine, that's obvious. Ahh, that one-year-old sweet wine gets you every time."

An old woman put her nose up in the air, waddling her head in rebuke and ridicule, she spouted, "Fools drowned in alcohol gushing with wisdom—what next?"

"What babbling nonsense is this? Tall tales to tell? Drinkers waste the time of the sober." Men and women jeered at this tiresome truth. One woman pointed at a giggling, broad-smiling man who could barely stand. "Whatever this is I'd rather be like him, overflowing with joy and in his own world, than my set of problems."

The Greeks used the term 'barbarian' for all non-Greek-speaking peoples. Here accusation of "barbarians" came forth from more than one confused heckler.

But Ami, leaning against Mary for support, shouted, "It's the joy of Adonai, He is our strength!" and because the words came out in Aramaic, almost everyone understood.

James cupped his hands and added, "Shout aloud and sing for joy, people of Zion, for great is the Holy One of Israel among you." He didn't know which language he had, but those nearby nodded with understanding.

In the midst of this conflict, Adonai sent a spirit of curiosity over the pedestrians. The desire to listen started to overtake the verbal jousting and general chattering. Those who balked now listened with earnest, open ears.

The 120 praised and continued to draw attention. "For the kingdom of God is not a matter of eating and drinking, but of righteousness, peace and joy in the Holy Spirit. This is the day that Adonai has made; let us rejoice and be glad in it. Adonai is my strength and my shield; in him my heart trusts. Joy comes to a man by the answer of his mouth, and a word spoken in due season, how good it is!"

Some praisers considered it a parallel with an ancient story. At the ever-rising tower of Babel, and at the height of the tower builders' sin, Adonai had said, "No more." He removed each one's knowledge of the one known language. In place, new languages settled into rebellious minds. Each one's realized thoughts exited their mouths in languages they instinctively knew without learning. Was it magic? No, it was God.

At the Tower of Babel, disorganization immediately stopped the construction. Humanity spread in all directions. Helpless, those workers with the same new tongue paired up and traveled off to other lands. They had the task of teaching their wives and children, Daddy's new language—God prevented their minds from making their tongues speak the common language.

Now, at Pentecost, in Jerusalem, a keen reversal reigned. Adonai drew those from distant lands of the Diaspora, from the far corners of the civilized world. In a fresh way, He wanted them to hear in their own local, native language His holy truths challenging men to come closer to Him in their hearts.

Peter went up a few steps toward the Upper Room and planted himself. The varied ridicule, hooting and heckling quieted down as Peter waved his arms and shouted in a sober tone "Listen!" By then most of the crowd had entered a quandary with honest curiosity. People shushed those around them. "Let's listen to the big fellow. He's got something on his mind, seems sincere enough. One of 'ums not had too much to drink." The crowd, more than 1,000 strong and gaining, quieted; all wanted to hear. Then Peter put two fingers to his lips and made a long, loud whistle. Then for a laugh he gave the shofar a hearty blast too. He had everyone's attention.

Chapter 42
Peter's Street Speech

Peter entered the silence. "Listen, men of Judea, and all who dwell in Jerusalem, and those staying here for Pentecost. What you see this moment, the Prophet Joel predicted centuries ago. Adonai said, 'I will pour out my Spirit on all people. Your sons and daughters will prophecy, your young men will see visions, your old men will dream dreams. I will cause wonders in the heavens above, and signs in the earth below, blood and fire and thick smoke. The sun will be turned into darkness and the moon will turn blood red and before the coming of the great and awesome, fearful day of the Lord. And anyone who calls on the name of the Lord will be saved.

"People of Israel, Jews from afar, listen! Hear these words. God publicly endorsed Jesus of Nazareth, by the powerful works, miracles, and signs He performed through him in your midst, as you well know. Though unjustly arrested in accordance with God's predetermined will, you followed this prearranged plan, without the foreknowledge of God. You, with the help of lawless gentiles, forced pagan hands to crucify and murder him on a Roman cross. You put an innocent man to death. Not an accident or coincidence.

Peter fought not to let the facial expressions of closed-minded skeptics and scorners get to his momentum. "This prophet, Jesus, God raised up from the grave three days later—even as Jesus told us he would. His tomb is empty—but angels waited there to greet some who came to tend to his body after the Sabbath. A dozen of us here watched Jesus rise into the sky, engulfed by a glorious cloud. Then two angels appeared and spoke to us. We, here, are all witnesses that he now sits on the throne of highest honor in heaven at God's right hand. At the start of his ministry, he received the Holy Spirit from the Father. After his Resurrection, Jesus promised, and has poured out the Holy Spirit as a gift on us, just as you see and hear today.

"Therefore, let the whole house of Israel know beyond doubt that he whom you crucified, God has made him both Lord and Messiah. You are well aware of it, you know this by the powerful works, miracles, and signs that God performed through him in your presence!

"King David, a prophet, knew God had promised, even sworn with an oath, that one of his own descendants would sit on David's throne as Messiah. He will return one day on an earthly throne. This prophecy spoke of Jesus whom God raised from the dead. David also wrote, 'I know the Lord is always with me. I will not be shaken, for He is right beside me. No wonder my heart is filled with joy, and my mouth shouts His praises!' And so, we too are as David was when he penned those words."

Now when they heard this, they were cut to the heart. Peter's words convicted them deeply—stunned by his indictment that they had killed their Messiah. A few were even ones who had grasped rocks to stone him, or mocked Jesus while on the cross. The crowd cried out, and said to Peter, the other apostles, and any of the 120,

"What shall we do?"

Peter replied with urgency, "Each of you must turn from your sins and turn to God and be immersed on the name and authority of Jesus the Messiah for the forgiveness of your sins. Then you will receive the gift of the Holy Spirit. This promise is to you and to your children, and for those faraway—even to the Gentiles—as many as our God may call. Save yourselves from this generation that has gone astray!" Peter continued preaching for a long time, strongly insisting all listeners to submit. He pressed his case with many other arguments and kept pleading with them. "The Prophet Joel declared that 'Whoever calls upon the name of Adonai shall be saved. Take action to change your sinful course!"

As the hours passed, more people sought out the proper repentance and required immersion in water. Listeners came and went. Some walked to the Temple, worshipped, brought their Pentecost offerings, and returned to hear more. But in one of the side areas at the large Temple grounds, groups of some of the 120 had attracted those from the street event, along with new, curious observers. These disciples exhorted and testified from Scripture and personal accounts of the last three years. Those who believed joined with the others and devoted themselves to the apostles' teaching and fellowship. They continued faithfully and with a single purpose. The Holy Spirit filled the new believers. Manifestations of emotional and physical healings took place. Demons departed. Visions of Adonai's realm, including busy angels, and sights unimaginable set people into exciting declarations. Spontaneous worship, words of prophetic flair and importance, and unlearned languages spoken in praise, spread throughout the crowded city.

Countless bystanders exclaimed, "What a mystery! A terrible mystery and one with beauty." Cheeks ran with tears. Faces blossomed with smiles.

At different locations around Jerusalem and especially the foot of the Temple Mount, were many street-level enclosed mikvot or small pools, male and female bath houses, for use in the nude, for spiritual purity. Outdoor fountains or pools were used with outer clothes removed, tunics on. After hearing much, many sought out such a mikveh for the symbolic cleansing of the soul. Others followed their repentance to the 120 leaders and desired the Holy Spirit. After taking off garments, each new believer brushed aside the temptation to race through the self-immersion procedure. Instead, they slowed down, knowing they were not alone in this searching of the heart. They sought assurance from Adonai in a short but heartfelt kavanah—meditation, desiring rest and trust in Him. Each walked into a pool, stood toward the water source, held their breath, and went under the waist-deep water to a brief bow and crouch. A veteran believer escorted the new converts in prayer if needed. An escort helped those emotionally undone and in need of assurance. Prayers answered, peace cut loose their bags of tension. Still dripping, they put on their garments and met outside minutes later.

Outpouring from above continued. Faith filled anyone. A part, a door, within them opened. Next to this entry stood a welcoming presence. In the exuberance of release from sin and judgment, all spoke thanks to the unseen, but noticeable God, Adonai. Minds, hearts, and spirits understood—but this sign, this wonder pleasantly rearranged people's relationship and future with God. His distance gone. The Jews knew that He had come to make a way for them to follow His commandments and know Him personally as He strengthened their righteous desires.

Chapter 43
Later That Night

"What a day!" Peter said as he trudged up the stairs. His wife, Naimah, held his drooping, yet strong arm. She smiled at her husband; pride stretched the corners of her grin. In her heart, she felt gratitude for his leadership.

As they reached the second floor, dozens came up behind them. Naimah said, "You were a proud man today, and I am proud of you Peter. I've never seen this side of you before. You cared about everyone. Standing beside you... I, I had feelings I didn't know I could have." She looked up at him. "Your voice is so hoarse from talking and shouting the whole day."

He looked for the pitcher of water, a cup, and a soft place to sit down. Half addressing his wife and half-trying to manage exhaustion, he replied, "Huh? Oh, yes. Today... a very long day it was. The throat is sore, you're right. I posed so many questions and answered so many questions."

Naimah helped him get water and find a seat. After he swallowed several cupfuls, Peter looked at her and yet through her. He rubbed his jaw and stretched it sideways.

She somehow understood his stare. "Peter, today I saw pictures, vivid images, whether in my imagination or spirit, I do not know. I did see with my eyes, too." Her husband grunted and let out a long breath. She hesitated, "An angel stood next to you—an angel similar to Mary's description. I saw it with my eyes, these eyes." Two of her fingers of one hand pointed at her face. "He drew his sword to protect you."

Peter nodded. "I didn't see him, but I knew someone good and strong...," He tilted his empty cup left and right a few times, went quiet and closed his eyes.

Due to his years as a tax collector, Matthew could count large numbers. He said what many had on their minds. "I tried to estimate the number of listeners today. People came and went. I counted about 3,000 apparently sincere—"

In mid-sentence Naimah interjected with a laugh, "Ah oh! My husband makes himself a friend of everyone he sees at the lake. Now, he just added 3,000 new friends in Jerusalem!"

People chuckled. As that died down, young John wept. In his sobs, he voiced what others had on their hearts, "3,000 firstfruits, quite a harvest, that's good. But, I miss one. I miss the Master. I miss Jesus. He would, he is, I'm sure, proud of us!" The room went silent.

James overheard the conversation. He sat and pressed his back against the wall, cup in hand. He wept at that remark. Others joined.

Someone said, "Jeremiah wrote, 'Is not my word like fire, and like a hammer that breaks a rock in pieces?' Today, He broke through the language barriers. He used an attention-getter, and He got the attention of many."

Matthew interjected, "Certainly ours."

Peter perked up. "None of us left this building the same, and any who return here will not be either. From what I understand, the Promise of the Father, the Holy Spirit, immersed us. Did I squeeze my head up through a hole in the sky and saw into heaven? Then in mere moments I understood the whole world and how God makes everything work!"

Normally, Naimah would have rolled her eyes at one of Peter's boasting sessions, but she knew he spoke a strange truth.

Peter, with a light fist pounded on his thigh as he spoke. "I mean, I especially understood all the Scriptures which Jesus tried to teach us, which he claimed pointed at him. I had the whole net of fish on my boat. I just wanted to get to the shore with the catch." Peter checked Naimah's expression and continued. "My yelling or preaching to that crowd down below on the streets reminded me of when Jesus sent us out, the 12 and the 70, two by two. I think, after today's windy noise and the flames, an appealing compulsion of love blended our bodies with a breeze sent from God. Wind blew away the unnecessary parts of me and God's love filled in those places. This required my personal surrender. After that, a boldness rose in me; a newness, or a new me, at the same time. His love for people consumed me and I wanted to partake of His love. When I did, I identified His qualities…or some of them."

John crouched down, and then in exhaustion he lay down and propped his head up. "I know Peter, I know." He sipped from a cup and added, "Our fallen human nature wrestles with His commandments because they are rooted in God, who is Spirit, but we are flesh and bones."

Peter remarked, "My mouth is tired from talking. Yet I wonder what those, did you say 3,000? I wonder what they are thinking and doing now." He dug into his beard and rubbed his jaw.

The Upper Room filled up with old and new faces.

Nicodemus said, "Before I go home for the night, I thought I'd stop by and see how you are doing here. Peter, you were amazing today. I agreed with everything you said. You used the right Scriptures. I could not have done better. Your boldness convinced me all over again. God is glorified when He is accurately represented."

John spoke up, "We are trying to sort out what happened in the past and what happened today. What I mean is, two years ago, as you said Peter, Jesus sent us 12 out, two by two, to many villages—later he did the same with 70 of us. We were to teach about the Kingdom of God, and pray for the sick and recently dead, and those with demons. God gave us power to do so for a limited time. Besides the miracles, we sensed a better version of ourselves. We loved people in ways that Jesus or God must love. We also thought differently too—better. Now, today we feel that again. Will those feelings go away like before? Or, or, what?"

After moments of thought, Nicodemus answered, "So, whoever is devoted to the Messiah, certain personality traits pass away; new or improved ones come; is that it? Anyone who belongs to the Messiah can be a new person inside. Is 'new creation' too strong a term?" Seriousness and Nicodemus were one; he looked at the listeners.

Mary came up the stairs, her eyes drooped and shoulders sagged. She dragged herself into the small group but remained quiet for some time. She looked like she could barely stay awake another minute and leaned against the wall. But Mary managed to volunteer, "I think it's too soon for such deep decisions. We shall see how this all plays out in time. We are all bold and inspired to do God's will. His Spirit has blended with us and those on the streets and Temple today. Perhaps, what the prophets of old experienced in their episodes of miracles, teaching and writing was temporary…is anointing the word—the prophets had a holy anointing? Maybe now…." She drifted off and seemed to have fallen asleep standing up. Her sons led her to her bedroll.

Soon, everyone else lay down too. Each one pondered the eventful day. Something new swelled in the city, and God had started it. Many considered their conduct under pressure in the unusual setting: love, joy, gladness, peace, patience, kindness, generosity, humility, goodness, faithfulness, benevolence, gentleness, and self-control. They lived these out—empowered in the Holy Spirit as needed. They wondered if, indeed, the Holy Spirit dwelled in them…just a little and increasingly so. Such ideas dared their identity, but they served and knew a daring God. He'd spoken within them, to them; guided them, made them more intelligent, and more loving. God's life lived in them.

Those who returned reflected on the busy day: strangers eager to hear, hundreds and hundreds; many from foreign lands; so many wanted what God had for them; dozens seemed to want personal prayer by those of the Upper Room— they believed them to have a special connection to God—one not to pass up. Scores of people wanted the life-changing Holy Spirit inside them, and water immersion to symbolize repentance and discipleship. As they drifted off to sleep those in the Upper Room spoke the Shema, "Hear O Israel, the Lord our God, the Lord is One." The days of Counting the Omer were over.

Chronicle Seven
The Next Day

Chapter 44
To Believe or Not to Believe

In the morning, strangers entered the room and the regulars acted hospitably toward them. Many of the 120 had stayed the night elsewhere. Now, the Torah teachers and several priests stood still, not knowing what to do. They brought papyrus scrolls of Scripture. The bearded men wore clothes of distinction. Soon Nicodemus showed up. He explained they'd stayed up most of the night at his home discussing Scriptures and the claims of Jesus. "The discussion will continue here."

They sat on the floor. Peter and many others respectably sat in a semi-circle to listen.

Lozon, the eldest of the visitors, sat straight and by his tone seemed to be in charge. "Nicodemus here, dared us to come and hear more tales of the Galilean rabbi. We arrived early in the morning yesterday in front of this house, dumbfounded and curious about the violent windstorm without wind. In the street, we caught opinions from others. After a time, just when we decided to knock, the door opened. Out came a hundred or more excited people of all ages. Their mouths, filled with praise of Adonai, seemed quite out of place. Then you spread into the crowded streets. I and those with me here walked along to investigate. Most of your congregation are Galileans, made plain by your strong accents. Yet, we counted close to twenty languages, presumably, uttering the same exuberant praise. Of course, in our lives we've done our share of traveling and not all of us are from Jerusalem. And so, we recognized the languages."

One of the priests started to say something, but Lozon lifted one hand, and continued. "Peter, as Nicodemus identified you, taught from Scripture to the growing crowd. What you said made some sense to us, but we had no foundation of belief, or should I say, we never knew this Jesus of yours. There were wild rumors, of course. We expressed that during the night. Nicodemus had tried to explain this required 'born again' transition or shift."

Then the priest Melatiah made a nod and Lozon motioned for him to talk. "The main teacher," he motioned to Peter, "his mannerisms and conviction hooked our curiosity. We understand that he knows how to fish, being from the lake. Yet, now it seems, he's fishing for men. His hook is Scripture, and his bait is the manifold words and works, death and Resurrection of the Galilean Rabbi Jesus. Holy, just, and good? Not sure. But, amazing tales, yes. We question certain of Jesus' motives."

Peter replied. "Spirit empowered activity startled us, and the crowds. As I preached the truth to the wide variety of people, those with prepared hearts...took the holy bait—as you coined it—and are hooked, wonderfully owned by God. My instruction became more and more effective."

Matthias volunteered, "Three years ago when Jesus started as Adonai's servant to the House of Israel, he first spoke at synagogues near his home in Galilee. Among the men present for Sabbath morning, he'd always be one to volunteer to come forward. He'd make aliyah to the bimah and read a portion of Scripture. He often chose the scroll of Isaiah. I recall that in Nazareth, Jesus read one of the sacred prophecies. But then he applied the revelation to himself.

Lozon interjected, "You mean Isaiah wrote about Jesus over 600 years ago, bah!"

Heads shook in disbelief.

Chapter 45
Claims

Matthias motioned with outstretched arms beckoning silence.

With a lifeless wave of a hand, Lozon rolled his eyes. "Yes, yes, go on."

"Jesus unrolled the scroll to a favorite passage. Before he read, he looked at those sitting on the floor and tried to make eye-contract with each person. Then Jesus smiled, and declared, "The Spirit of Adonai is upon me in order to anoint me to bring news to the poor and humble. He has sent me to care for and heal the brokenhearted, to proclaim freedom for captives, those imprisoned and exiled; to recover sight to the blind and heal the lame; to release those who have been crushed, to send the oppressed away free; to proclaim the acceptable year of Adonai." Jesus carefully rolled up the parchment scroll, gave it to a helper, and sat down to teach the congregation. "Then he startled them with this, 'Today, this Scripture is fulfilled in your hearing.'"

Lozon said, "Then Jesus clearly claimed to do what only the Messiah would be capable of! What lofty assertions to make in his hometown. My, my." Lozon grunted. "And from a carpenter…what next, a fig picker becomes a priest!" Putting his hands on his knees, Lozon leaned back, air whistled between his teeth.

One of the visiting teachers named Shimrith, sided closely with Lozon. He said, "Between Peter's words and wrestling with Nicodemus throughout the night… whether this Jesus was or is *now* our Messiah, he's not the Messiah we wanted or expected. Yet, we have submitted ourselves to the possibility of his divine origins. He mastered supernatural deeds, we agree. I understand that this has been a stone of stumbling for many across Israel, too. During Jesus' ministry he'd say bizarre and outrageous expressions, such as needing to 'drink his blood and eat his flesh.'" The huddled priests and teachers looked as if they'd walked by a pile of warm camel dung on a hot day.

With arms spread wide, Melatiah continued, "Israel hoped for a conquering, military- minded Messiah, one who'd vanquish the Romans, and then recapture our much larger, original God-given lands noted by Moses in Exodus. Then we expected the Messiah to set up a Jewish world-empire from the four corners of the earth in Jerusalem, making it the capital. Persecution, exiles, and slavery of Jews would cease. Paganism and idol worship end. Lastly, the long-awaited Messiah would reign where nature itself reverts to the peace that the Garden of Eden enjoyed—the lamb and the lion resting together, safe snakes, and so forth." All nodded. He added, "Perhaps just one more of the many false messiahs that have arisen and then met a similar fate? They leave disappointed, infatuated, fanatical followers with nothing but sand falling through their upraised, squeezed fists."

Matthew had sat down, and clearly he wanted to participate. He explained, "When we had the last opportunity to speak face to face with the Master…to Jesus, we brought up this topic. Our curiosity brimmed over. We too wanted the fierce Lion of Judah. To our disappointment, he didn't want to discuss these matters. Instead, he emphasized to 'Stay in Jerusalem a few more days and wait until the Father sends the Holy Spirit.'"

Phillip interjected, "He said, 'John immersed with water, but you'll be immersed with the Holy Spirit and fire.' That happened yesterday at Pentecost. I think those who submitted to the message are, like the First Fruits of Pentecost's holiday harvest, except it is a spiritual harvest of souls."

Nicodemus stroked his beard. All could tell he went deep into his soul. Eyes ran with tears. "God's First Fruits are people, and they belong to Him. Yes." The men went silent evidently considering this profound concept.

However Shimrith spat. He said in his lofty style, "Souls, now is it! We all know that Jesus made trouble for himself by whipping the money-changers and animal merchants in the Court of the Gentiles. As I'm sure you know we let the Romans take their cut from the profits. Your friend wanted to stop that stable supply line— for good. He did this prank twice and it got him on the Romans list of unnecessary Jews. Do you recall several years ago another zealous one? For his idea of purity, he tried the same tactic. A 'Thief of the Empire' is what the sign said on his cross. Please don't pollute the waters with a rabbi of magic who couldn't resist letting monetary things be! No way to make friends of strangers. How arrogant. Just what we don't need another self-proclaimed prophet."

A rumbling of upset disciples who loved this 'polluter' filled the suddenly, stuffy room.

Lozon spoke again. A fiendish grin, which later reminded some of Judas, strained the wrinkles on his face. "Clearly a case of spiritual snobbery, hmm. But, let's move on shall we? From our personal libraries we brought scrolls of the prophets. Yesterday, Peter, in your street teaching you quoted from Exodus, Isaiah, Ezekiel, Jeremiah, Joel, Zechariah and Psalms." With a bemused expression he opened a hand to Peter and said, "For a fisherman you have remarkable insights into Scripture. Your carpenter-turned-rabbi never attended a yeshiva for training in Scripture, and he too had remarkable insights." Lozon leaned back, while a wisp of haughtiness hung in the air. "God coined us a 'peculiar people' but this is too much."

Phillip added, "Insights yes, even when Jesus' childhood, we are told by his mother here."

The men followed Phillip's outstretched arm to a graying woman asleep in a corner. Their heads bobbed in recognition.

One of the apostles retold the story Jesus raising Lazarus from the dead. This caused much chattering among the visitors. A teacher said, "As you know many believe that the spirit of a man remains at the corpse for 3 days after death, in case the body revives. Then the spirit travels on. However, certain leaders teach that the Messiah will raise the dead no matter how long the person has been laid to rest. Your tale of Jesus purposely arriving to Lazarus' tomb 4 days after his death is quite fitting. The act confirms a sign of the Kingdom of God. No wonder that after this proof, certain members of the Sanhedrin eagerly sought the death of Jesus and this Lazarus." The room went silent as this deep truth pervaded all minds.

Nicodemus solemnly added, "Do not fear. Do not run from what your mind does not understand. Consider these claims prayerfully, and there, rest is to be found. Fire on Mount Sinai, and now tongues of fire at Jerusalem. In some way the heartbeat of Mt. Sinai included the heartbeat in Jesus. Many centuries of traditions have clouded the instructions at Sinai. I do wholeheartedly believe that Moses would've approved of this man…this unique man. Jesus balked at certain traditions of men, which have been placed as divine explanations. And I agree with his desire to trim back Judaism to the essentials; complications which obstruct seeing the face of God. We've loaded too much on the backs of the common Jew. Jesus despised that."

Then Lozon gave a daring stare. "And do you, as Nicodemus and other learned men, believe your teacher lived without sinning, and able to actually able to forgive men's sins? You defend the audacious and impossible? That this 'Master' did not once transgress across the heart of Adonai?" Lozon huffed and flexed his arms wide. He glared. "Hmm? How can you authenticate such an outrageous pronouncement?"

Peter uncrossed his legs and stretched. "An astute point, Lozon. Only God sees a man's heart from dawn to dusk and from birth to death. As you've heard from others, Jesus wasn't merely a man such as we are. No. He had no earthly, fallen father. Even as with the First Man, Adam; Heaven played the part of fathering. Unlike Adam, Jesus remained in love and amazement of such a relationship his entire life."

Shimrith spoke in a condescending tone with a flair of glee, "And that life of his didn't last too long once he started to invent a new life for himself!"

Glum, and after poking his tongue in one cheek, Peter continued. "Nothing, no forces, seen or unseen, could lure him away from a righteous life. Make no mistake, Satan tempted him in every way which is under the sun. A man free of sin? Every temptation sought him out. He had enemies always at work to make him fail. We could tell you in detail. Women tried to entrap him in lust for years. Greed, power, pride, wealth and even an army, could have easily been his. Nevertheless, I tell you, nothing could stop him—not even a storm at sea. His righteousness served God, and God empowered him to do His will. Jesus became the holy sacrifice for our sins, as a lamb without spot or blemish. We know that our names are written in the Book of Life. We are purified by his holy blood sacrifice and then immersion in his name. He has been our rabbi, but that's just the beginning.

"As preposterous as it seems, concerning Jesus, we do not speak blasphemy or heresy. Nor one of endless human sacrifices to appease a god or goddess. The Roman cross is no holy altar tended to by Jewish Temple priests. That is because, though beyond our comprehension, Jesus lived fully as a man," Peter hesitated and peered into the faces of the visiting men, "yet he was and is part of God, who came to earth as Adonai's Son. Such information and his atonement is still beyond our grasp. But, truthfully, there is no other way to explain the Master. We know that there is only One God, and God is One. Though Jesus claimed his identity as God's only Son, that hasn't changed the truth passed down by our forefathers. There are not two Gods."

One of the priests shook his head and said, "This is confusing!"

Another priest fingered his beard and thoughtfully questioned, "If we only obey what we understand, are we then worshipping our knowledge?"

Phillip said, "An interesting point, and one to consider. However let me educate you some more about the man Jesus. He never sought worship of himself. He told people to stop if that happened. Worship God alone, is what Jesus declared." Phillip wrinkled his nose, paused, obviously choosing his next words. He choked out, "After his suffering... his horrible death, and came back to life in a... well, heavenly body, and he allowed worship." He wiped his runny nose with a sleeve. "What has happened blended into accordance with Adonai's predetermined plan and foreknowledge. Not an accident, nor a miscalculation of his dire enemies. Shocking as it sounds, he chose crucifixion as his goal. Resurrection followed, which he instructed us months before his arrest." Phillip looked at the ceiling and quietly said, "The smartest man I've ever known."

Chapter 46
Accept the Outrageous

Nicodemus wrung his hands while eyeing his companions. When he spoke, his hands opened wide. "The Messiah, or Teacher, conveyed new truths in ways that emphasized their connection with old truths." He held up one finger while obviously deep in thought. "We all know the game or competition, called tug of war. Two sides of equal strength grasp a length of rope. A central point is marked on the ground. Both sides pull. The taut rope connects the teams, yet it is neutral. However, here, gentlemen, let's say the rope represents a truth—can one side win and so, own the truth? Listen, if both teams are of equal strength and footing, after a sufficient time, the game must be called a draw. No team lost, however, or lacked dignity nor muscle as absolute winner. Correct?" Nicodemus exhaled a deep breath. "God is on His side and we, the Jews, are en masse the other. We exert faith to reach His truths, but some are beyond are comprehension … or, we'd be like God Himself."

Lozon broke in with a sneer. "Games, riddles and sweaty exercises, get to your next point, O learned friend."

"Yes, yes." Nicodemus now had everyone's attention. "Ah hem, the length of rope in the middle remains there, stable by tension, belonging to neither side. That represents unusual knowledge gripped by faith. In the Torah there are commands that we do not understand why we are to obey them. God doesn't explain why, and so, without a reason or beyond reason—they seem unreasonable. These few instructions are sensible only to God."

Lozon shirked and remarked, "You mean the verses we refer to as chukim."

"Yes. Even King Solomon himself, with all his wisdom, didn't understand them, the hidden gem in the core. Certain of the claims of Jesus and what happened in this very room … are similar to chukim. But other teachings of Jesus are simply held in place by tension and will be so until the Last Day. The two teams have the Messiah from Galilee—"

"—in the middle." Lozon smiled in a sickening way. "A test of faith I'd say. Just accept his teachings and obey; do you mock us, O friend? I ask you to recall what the Prophet Isaiah wrote, 'Thus says Adonai, the King of Israel, the Lord of hosts and Redeemer, I am the Lord, and there is no other beside me, there is no Savior, no god.'" Lozon hunched his shoulders, no life set in his eyes. "No wonder I picked up a stone to hurl at him at the Temple, when Jesus said, 'I and the Father are One.' Bah!" He smirked adding, "Though King Herod has been dead for three decades, his extensive plans for further construction on the Temple Mount will continue for many years to come. In the meantime, there's plenty of scrap masonry suitable for stoning the deserving."

Joseph of Arimathea had arrived and sat down. He carefully listened to the discussion and then interjected, "Learned men, Isaiah also wrote, 'For out of Zion shall come forth the Torah, and the Word of Adonai from Jerusalem.' My friends, do you recall Moses' prayer during the Exodus, that 'Adonai would put His Spirit on all of His people.' Up here, yesterday, we felt drawn in to enjoy life—His way. We didn't resist, wonderful is the word. The situation intrigued us. Some saw visions in their imaginations of God's goodness and nature. Little children hopped and clapped and loudly praised. Because of the the open windows people below heard our noisy worship. They stopped and listened.

"And what of the miracle, or at least the unusual ability of praising in various languages accomplished by who else than the Holy Spirit? I must consider that overwhelming activity amounts to a reversal of Babel's great sin. There, God confounded language to strike a wedge of dis-unity. However, here, He enabled people whose different languages separated them to understand others praising God, and isn't that the best use of unity?"

Lozon remarked, "Bah!" He smirked and countered, "What a ridiculous— miracle—is that what you called it? Remember, friends, that false prophet and sorcerer Balaam. He owned a donkey which spoke too! Now if outside on the street yesterday there were a herd of donkeys braying or chatting in different languages, I'd call that a miracle. Only a fool wouldn't."

Peter let out a "Grr" and slumped to one side.

Shimrith smiled, clapped his hands once and then rubbed them. "So, you say that the remarkable activities yesterday—what went on in this room and the gibberish out in the streets was planned and somehow caused by this Jesus friend of yours? If I understand this right, he's in Heaven making people behave as his puppets. And tell me, just when did God install a second throne next to His, hmm?"

*　　*　　*

Mary awoke and overheard the discussion. She arranged her two long braids into buns on either side of her head and wrapped a veil next. After straightening clothes, and rinsing her face, she approached the semi-circle of men, but didn't sit. She wrinkled her brow and sternly interjected, "Men, I place before you more of the impossible. I became pregnant not knowing any man, and I remained a virgin for those 9 months. Simply put, I had a virgin conception and a normal birth. Dare I say without fear and trembling, no man fathered my son. I am no liar. Learned men, this is no pagan myth."

In a somber tone, one of the priests wrung his hands, and without looking up said, "The pure Passover Lamb for our people. Jesus, a sacrifice to God on a Roman cross? Why not be slaughtered on the altar at the Temple—would've made more sense to me. Another martyr for what chimes in their heart."

James nodded. "I'm sure Nicodemus has taught well from the Prophets. However, let us here, who knew him for over three years, and some longer, tell you about the man." Many heads nodded. "Someday we might write down certain stories, his teachings, and final suffering," smiling, James threw up his hands, "and rebirth from death!"

Mark turned to Peter and said, "I've been writing notes and even copying stories from a variety of people. I like to write. There's a list of what miracles took place where. Also, I have teachings which he gave to crowds and privately to us." Mark got up and went to his belongings. He returned with a leather bag and carefully emptied his collection of narrow scrolls. "Peter, one day we need to discuss your favorite memories, so that I can record them too."

Peter rubbed his beard and stared at the scrolls. He shook his head. In a somber tone, he told Mark, "What a good project, a wonderful deed. But that will take more than a single day." Peter muttered to himself, "How many scrolls would the last three years take?" Then he added an important point. "Concerning the miraculous, Jesus never bragged, nor boasted, never a show-off. I think this made him approachable, apprehensive. Understand that during his three-year prophetic ministry, Jesus never did one sign or wonder just to fascinate the crowds."

Matthias sat down and offered this. "He is no replacement for the Torah, yet he instructed us in deeper meanings of the Laws and of God's personality. Jesus referred to God as his Father. When he spoke of being older than our father Abraham...we learned to accept this as truth. Jesus could teach on anything in this world. There were many instructions Jesus said to us that we only now comprehend, we are still navigating within and without. We yearn to comprehend and have no doubts as to their fulfillment."

Lozon interjected, "Then he must not have been much of a teacher to cause this inability. Humph! We are here to consult together and compare opinions. But, we do have our limits of decency."

Matthias ground his teeth, and stared at this unpleasant man, but he let that ill comment pass. "Listen, we here, accept that we haven't understood enough to satisfy ourselves," he looked glum and turned aside, and added, "Though the closest and most dedicated, we weren't the best pupils." Matthias spread his arms indicating all of the disciples. "Three years and we understood little. But what he taught and the Scriptures he dug into are coming alive now."

Phillip spread his hands and quietly stated, "Learned men, your scoffing is understandable, really it is. We lost our faith in this man from Galilee when they arrested him, and then tortured by whipping and other abuse. Confusion and a dreadfully rotten feeling overcame us. His death? We were undone and scared. Did our time and investment of our lives equal failure? However, we've decided that when you welcome, no, yearn, to seek...perhaps trust is the word, Jesus as Messiah, the Holy Spirit takes up residence inside of you. The Spirit actually fuses Himself together with your spirit. That's what happened yesterday, and will continue to as faith is fed. Any person can become a child of God, be a partaker of His nature! His child, in a loving and yet formal relationship! Less manmade rituals and more of the spirit of Scripture. You'll have some of His divine nature inside of you. You are a new creation, with new desires and a new or born-again life. A person's core identity is transformed in Adonai's eyes. The Messiah's sinless nature and identity forms and matures your spirit, and a glorious transformation is at work! This faith is active, making a defiled human holy, righteous and clean in spirit!"

Mary looked at the faces of the strangers. "I, too, have made a pact with Adonai to forgive my sins through the sacrifice of my beloved, innocent son. And that is our message; the Holy Spirit will enable us to obey the Laws of God better setting sin aside. This is His help, His New Covenant to live out the Laws set down in ancient times. They will be in our hearts. The Holy Spirit will guide us in personal ways to please Adonai and fulfill His desires. We have His help within us; we all need His help. We are created in His image and yet every human has lost much of that quality. If you and I can rebuild and live a more pleasing godly life, we believe His means is His Spirit aiding our thoughts and judging our motives—a living righteous judge and leader."

James added, "And as you witnessed yesterday, the Holy Spirit can fill men and women with courage and strength to do His will in testifying of the Messiah's impossible plan. Immersion in water is an outward sign of an inward cleansing."

Chapter 47
More Voices

The visitors leaned back and eyed one another and then momentarily fixed their view on the ceiling. One disciple stated, "Right there the wind entered, and a ferocious fire...but you see no damage or burn marks. Are you implying that at Sinai, Adonai gave the Torah externally to the congregation as a whole, while here, even in this upper room, the Laws were put within individuals—by a storm of wind and flames."

One of the teachers quickly added, "Yes, and what of the Temple, the Laws of Moses and lives of our forefathers? Will you continue to observe the animal sacrifices for sin and offerings? This is no Mt. Sinai, yet you dare to compare the two as equal events."

Matthew answered. "We are far from replacing, canceling, or contradicting the Laws of God given to Moses. As you know, blood sacrifices or offerings, wipe away our transgressions and erase our sins in God's eyes—by faith. Such acts restore us to Temple or community life, and we start over again. Righteousness has only ever been achieved by faith. Extra emphasis on rituals and tedious traditions do not necessarily change a man's heart. To answer your point, we now see that all previous and future animal sacrifices point to the one sacrifice which could and did provide a way to God— Jesus.' Yes, it does seem like the Almighty desired a human sacrifice— of course. The difference is that he lived fully human, sinless, and in a way—in many ways, Adonai in person. Your head will ache when you try to piece that together. Listen, in the era to come, of which the Prophet Ezekiel wrote, a new Temple on earth will be built by the Messiah. You know from Scripture that animal sacrifices will continue. However, these will still point backwards to the altar of the wooden Roman cross and especially the Temple's priestly altars. What happened yesterday, during Pentecost? The further birthing of the Messianic community. Confused, overwhelmed, and amazed? Yes!" Matthew hung his head, lowered his voice, "If only you had met him."

Shrugging his shoulders, Lozon again made his point. "I picked up a stone, a good stone too, one to do damage your friend. But this man-god of yours eluded us. I hear nothing new which would make me drop that stone. Dare I say that this Jesus of Nazareth was a mere, unnecessary, so-called human sacrifice and you are mistaken? I pity you and your pagan storytelling. Next you'll say he walked on water, hmm? Nicodemus tried that one on us—I'm not buying what you're selling. If you had some fish, that'd be different."

Andrew, Peter's brother said, "Jesus quite firmly exhibited loyalty about our heritage. More than once he told the crowds 'Do not imagine that I have come to violate the Torah or the words of the Prophets. I have not come to violate but to fulfill. Solemnly I tell you, until heaven and earth pass away, not even one tiny pen stroke, not one jot, tittle, or iota, shall pass from the Torah, until all has been accomplished and established. Therefore, the man who breaks or annuls even one small law and teaches to do like him, will be called small and least in the Kingdom of Heaven. But whoever practices and teaches them will be called great in the Kingdom.'"

Peter patted his brother's shoulder, grinned, and said, "I knew you'd find your voice brother!"

Emboldened, Andrew continued. "The Prophet Zechariah wrote at the end of God's revelation to him, 'On that day His feet will stand on the Mount of Olives east of Jerusalem, and the Mount will be split in half from east to west, leaving a great valley. Then the survivors from all the nations that have attacked Jerusalem will go up year after year to worship the King, the Lord Almighty, and to celebrate the Festival of Tabernacles. If any of the peoples of the earth do not go up to Jerusalem to worship the King, the Lord Almighty, they will have no rain. Adonai will be king over all the earth at that time. There will be one Lord.'

"Recently, after his torment and Resurrection, he appeared in person in Galilee to us and around 500 people there. I and other men here stood on the Mount of Olives, some ten days ago with Jesus. We watched him rise up from the ground as if he weighed a mere feather. A glorious cloud moved lower and took him beyond our sight. Two angels appeared and said that Jesus would return from Heaven to the same spot, at the right time."

A priest commented, "And yet we see no proof that this Messiah of yours did anything of lasting importance. You expect me to believe this Roman torture, whipping and shameful, horrible death was voluntary—was planned? Plus, Jesus suffered unjust insults … for me, took my place to take upon himself my own sin— all of our sins? Isn't that too much to ask us, or anyone to believe?"

Confident, Mary smiled, put her hands on her hips and agreed, "Difficult? Yes. Miracles are the impossible!" At peace, she looked at the men and hospitably proposed that they needed food and drink. "I think you men will be here a while." Amused, they opened their hands in appreciation. She grinned, turned away, looked to heaven, shook her head lightly and rolled her eyes.

Epilogue

In the days following, those who believed met together constantly. They did something unique, something perhaps which Jesus had instructed in his post-Resurrection visits. The growing multitude of believers had all things in common and sold some of their possessions and goods, sharing the proceeds, as anyone had need. Jashen smiled. Nicodemus grinned. The Apostles became a true brotherhood. A movement stabilized while gaining new faces.

Those travelers from near or great distances partook of the Gospel. They deposited the teachings to their families, synagogues and strangers in other cities and lands. There, the Holy Spirit produced signs and wonders too.

Fear came upon those in Jerusalem. A deep sense of awe came over all citizens, and many miraculous signs and wonders were done through the apostles. So, continuing daily with one accord in the Temple for prayer and worship, breaking bread from house to house, they shared their meals with generosity, gladness, and simplicity of heart. They praised God and had favor, respect, and goodwill of most people. And the Lord added to the Messianic community newcomers who desired salvation.

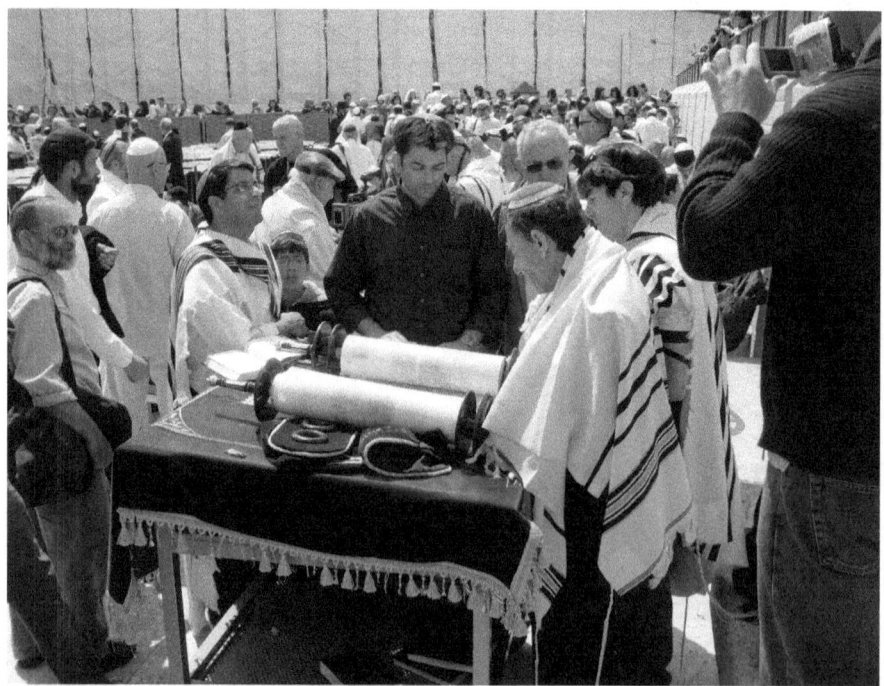

Jewish Men at the Western Wall (Kotel) plaza, Jerusalem, Israel.

Notes and Weighty Matters

Where's the bibliography? Normally, books of fiction do not provide one. Therefore, footnotes are absent too. My sources are a scattered and smattered affair, which include ancient books on early church history, ancient rabbinical writings, ancient history, and Jewish culture. These studies took me down a multitude of rabbit trails. As I sought accuracy and details of interest, interviewing and debating with scholars, rabbis and pastors; plus endless Internet searches, scouring websites such as the Temple Institute, Torah Resource, Chabad, Bible Hub, Judaism 101, First Fruits of Zion, plus light and deep research using Bible commentaries; various Bible translations, Chumash, Talmud, Siddurs, and the mix of attending synagogues and churches, prayer, pondering, meditation, brainstorming, and imagining myself being there, in the First Century—all merged into this book. Prayerful, quality insights happened while writing!

Scripture in this book is paraphrased from many translations. I've tried to convey the essence of each.

The word "god" is used without a capital "G" in certain contexts for those who did not believe or understand that there was only One God. It's not meant to diminish God in the broad truth as the Supreme Being. Concerning the multitude of Egypt's gods and goddesses, through the centuries certain attributes and characteristics transferred or overlapped and names changed, and many gods served multiple roles—very confusing.

Adonai is a Hebrew word for Lord, or my Master. It is used interchangeably for God. The name Adonai wasn't strictly used for divine titles. Lord could mean a man of authority.

Bible teachers disagree as to where the promised coming of the Holy Spirit occurred, either the spacious, busy Temple Mount courtyards or (my choice), the Upper Room. The Temple complex had over 40 rooms of different uses, a basement, and much outside empty space. The Mount didn't only have a Temple.

Chapter Seventy-Five "Up the Mountain" is based on Exodus 24:9

Torah. What's a Torah? The instructions/laws of God as revealed to Moses and recorded in the first five books (scrolls) of the Hebrew Scriptures: Genesis (*Bereshit-In the beginning...*), Exodus (*Shemot-Departure, Going out...*), Leviticus (*Vayikrah-And He called...*), Numbers (*Bamidbar-In the wilderness...*) and Deuteronomy (*Devarim-The words...*). The titles are the first words of the book. Torah can also mean all of the writings in the Hebrew Bible. The root word of Torah, yarah, means "to shoot" (such as a target). So, the root meaning is "correct direction." The teachings are to point us in the right way. The Torah is the backbone and the showpiece of God having chosen the Hebrews. It's the only jewel in Judaism. The collection of writings by the Prophets are significantly less important. Usually, the single Torah scroll is 24"tall and perhaps up to 148' maximum length, weighing approximately 25 pounds and 304,805 words. Even today they are handwritten by scribes and never printed as a scroll.

Descriptions of angels are a mix of what little Scripture reveals and collected stories from contemporary people who I believe have seen angels. One of my sons, and wife, are part of that unique group. Only in the book of Daniel 10:12-14 do the Old Testament Scriptures describe a battle of angels. The concept of spiritual warfare, enemies and defense dealt with in the New Testament.

Tales Untold. Centuries old Judaic literature such as the Talmud, contain extensive rabbinical commentaries by a multitude of learned men. Certain interesting teachings might be considered fables by some and holy by others. I've dabbed a little into my book.

Sea of Galilee, Sea of Tiberius, Lake of Gennesaret, or Lake Kinneret? Today, Israelis call the body of fresh water, fed by the Jordan River, Lake Kinneret (spellings differ). Interestingly, the bottom of the lake has saltwater springs. There's a pipe system which pumps that to the extremely salty and evaporating Dead Sea far to the south.

Anti-Semitism. The pharaohs after Joseph feared the growing number of Hebrews. They thought that if the country was attacked that they might turn against the Egyptians. What followed was a systematic discrimination and eventual murdering of Jews. Pharoah instituted slavery and drowning male babies in the Nile River. So, pharaoh's fear-driven, treacherous solution to his Jewish problem became the first acts of anti-Semitism (anti-Jewish) in history. The acts of hostility, unjust laws, hard labor, racism, and extermination were repeated by others in power through the centuries across the globe.

Anti-Semitism is the belief or behavior hostile toward Jews just because they are Jewish. This may take the form of religious teachings that proclaim the inferiority of Jews, or political efforts to isolate, oppress, or otherwise injure Jewish people. This may also include prejudiced or stereotyped views about Jews.

Salvation by works? It's an erroneous concept that ancient Jews had to live out the 613 commandments, statutes, and ordinances of the Law, in order to earn salvation. No one person could obey them—not even Jesus! Why? Many laws explained the details of a functioning priesthood and procedures for Temple sacrifices. Certain other laws concerned females and their menstrual cycles and birthing children. Other requirements were inclusive only in the Promised Land, especially concerning holidays. Laws if you owned slaves. Punishments for criminal acts were judged and carried out by the Sanhedrin, not by common citizens. You would need children. You would need to be king. There are some 30 categories! Obedience to laws dealing with morality could never be 100% observed (except by Jesus), because humans make mistakes.

Mary's personage is a controversial and debated subject. Were Mary and Joseph a normal married people? Did Mary and Joseph have children of their own after Jesus? Certain styles of Christianity emphatically teach, 'No.' These branches teach that Jesus' mother is now the Queen of Heaven, the Mother of God, mediator between humans and her son Jesus, and is essential to the workings and operating of Heaven. Anything less fails to comprehend God's plans. Mary's Hebrew name is Miriam or Miryam. The English form of the name is Mary. No one never called her Mary during her life.

On Earth, could Mary worshippers revere a mythological personality far removed from the slight record of Holy Scripture? Could this veneration of her be disproportionate, pagan, and cross the line of blasphemy? If so, at its worst, she's likened to the fourth member of the Godhead, the fourth member of the Trinity.

No Last Supper? The last meal Jesus shared with His Apostles was a traditional Jewish Passover Seder or ceremony. A tradition commanded by God to be observed throughout all the generations of Hebrews. This holiday is still celebrated annually around the world. The gentile led church, far from its Jewish roots, took the obvious title and replaced it. The term "Last Supper" does not appear in New Testament writings—and not in Western language until the 12th century. Seder in Hebrew means order.

Twin brothers? The Apostle Thomas is listed in one gospel as The Twin. His name means Twin. He would have been the second born to have such a title. If he had a twin sister, whether first or second, he most likely would have been given a more suitable name.

Drunk in the Spirit? Hype or holy? Certain spectators deemed the behavior of the 120 people baptized (immersed) in the Holy Spirit to be intoxicated by alcohol. Years after that particular Pentecost, the Apostle Paul, a rabbi, wrote in Ephesians 5:18, "Do not get drunk with wine… instead be filled with the Spirit." Life displays that there are happy drunks and there are mean drunks. Good-hearted intoxicated persons can have positive and even envious behavior. Paul's direction is to replace substance use or abuse, with energized joy of purity. Perhaps his own experience drew this strange comparison. In Paul's letter to the Galatians, one of the Fruits of the Holy Spirit is joy. In essence, the feelings one may enjoy by drink, can be superseded by devotion to an ongoing relationship with God. Laughter is an expression of joy. Love can be rooted or companioned in joy. Loud speech, shouting, singing, giggling, and dancing can be expressions of joy. The Holy Spirit can reduce an alcoholic to a state of purity that resembles alcohol induced drunkenness, but with no hangovers and selfish behavior.

I believe this is what happened with King Saul and his troops. Recall that none of the men were on a mission which pleased God.

Aside from fine furniture and hearty oatmeal, consider this. Founded in the 18th century in England, the Shakers and Quakers were Charismatic. Their services included much prophesying and speaking in tongues. They also danced and shook. Anyone could preach or prophesy. Music was especially important in Shaker worship, and revelations could take the form of new songs and ecstatic dancing and spontaneous speaking in tongues.

I've been in many meetings where Christians appear drunk, and they had a wonderful, pure time. This has occurred before, during and after worship. Sometimes a person in such a state simply touches or stumbles into another person, and that one is instantly changed into such a state and is thoroughly happy. (I'd call that a miracle.) Think of it as God tickling someone. My wife, both sons, and several grandchildren have had this joyful fruit of the Spirit—even in their homes!

Finally, in the Gospels, "signs and wonders" were promised to believers. This silliness is such to me.

I think possible signs and wonders are confusing for a majority of churches. Modern reasoning is splintered on the means and methods of those people with gifting to create Biblical supernatural or paranormal phenomena. Bear in mind, outside of the Christian church someone can be a witch, another person a psychic, someone else a priest, shaman, a prophet and perhaps a thing which isn't from this planet at all. After all, we are only human. Ancient and modern sorcery attempts to control nature through the powers of impurity and thus to deny God's creative mastery.

This goes back to my Foreword. Church staffs want order and agendas carried out like a practiced performance. If God chooses differently, that could be and certainly has been rejected.

Church, Jewish Church, or Christian Synagogue? Bear in mind, the Early Church had a strictly Jewish infrastructure. Years went by before God convinced Peter that Gentiles, such as Cornelius, were of the same interest to God as Peter's own people (Acts 10). Also, that when Acts or the Epistles mentioned a church, this implies a Messianic Community, led by Jews and converts to Judaism. But don't image a small steeple church. No, actually, meetings took place in people's homes. So, the church in Corinth might've meant 12 Messianic home groups.

Christians are quick to point out only part of the passage in John 1:11-13 and leave out the end. "He came unto his own, and his own received him not. *But as many as received him, to them gave He power to become the children of God.*" True, as a national proposition, Jesus was rejected. However, thousands of Jews believed on Pentecost, the Apostles were Jews, all of the New Testament writers were Jews. From Acts 21:20 "When they heard this, they praised God. Then they said to Paul: "You see, brother, how many tens of thousands of Jews have believed, and all of them are zealous for the Law (Torah)."

An interesting question: is Jesus still Jewish? Is God Jewish? John writes in the Book of Revelations Chapter 21, of the "New Jerusalem, the holy city, coming down from Heaven to earth, where God will dwell with mankind." In Chapter 11:19, there is God's Temple in Heaven where there's an Ark of the Covenant.

I propose that if Jesus' glorified body has the scars of crucifixion on his hands and feet, then he is still circumcised as well.

In Zechariah chapter 14, he prophesies that (apparently after the Second Coming and in the 1,000 year reign) God commands for all nations to come to Jerusalem to celebrate the ancient Jewish holiday of Tabernacles/Shelters. Which commemorates the 40 years of wandering in the Wilderness. Wow!

Jewish Baptism? In ancient and modern times this ritual might be the least known or understood by Christians, yet it is an important Jewish ritual. Immersion in an outdoor source of water or manmade pool (mikveh) started at the time of Moses and the Wilderness Wanderings. A mikveh (gathering of waters), can be a sanctified bath house or small pool-like structure done for taharah—ritual purity. Never used for hygienic purposes. This sacrament was a method of spiritual purification instituted in the Torah by Moses and found in Numbers 19, Leviticus 15 and elsewhere. That was 1,400 years before John the Baptist. John the Immerser would be a more accurate interpretation.

The act of baptism in Church history is a sad affair. Christians have been sternly divided on the godly procedure. The Quaker denomination doesn't teach water baptism.

A rabbi, scribe, teacher or congregational leader at a Torah school or synagogue, had required immersion at 30, when such vocations started. And so, Jesus began his vocation at age 30. He chose (public) immersion by John (a priest's son), for the beginning of his mission. His action wasn't immersion to cleanse himself from his sin—t'shuvah. Jesus hadn't any sin to repent and be cleansed of. The average Jew in the crowd approached John due to the call for repentance. Christians have been confused by this story of Jesus ordering John (his forerunner) to immerse him, as perhaps, an empty gesture for the witnesses' sakes—feigned obedience. His unique reason, different from those waiting on the river's banks, was only to officiate the start of his own ministry. Indeed, he was the only person there who didn't need cleansing from sin. John *did* need it, and most assuredly immersed *each day* as an aid for heart-cleansing (tevilah for t'shuvah) before engaging his daily audiences.

This common ritual didn't require the physical aid of an attendant or priest. A person can accomplish the cleansing rite in total isolation and privacy. While standing in at least waist-high water, the person bent, then crouched, held their breath, and submerged, before standing back up. In flowing water, such as a river, the person faced upstream, toward the source.

When we read in the New Testament of a disciple baptizing someone, understand that the disciple most likely officiated the procedure. When the Gospel accounts report that the disciples of John or Jesus "baptized," they didn't lay a person backwards under the water, and then muscle him back up. This posture for immersion started centuries after Jesus' Resurrection. It symbolized death to sin and a new, born-again life via Jesus. This posture developed over the centuries as Jewish Christian authorities declined and gentile Christians saturated the church with pagan influence.

Jews immersed for various heartfelt purposes, such as landmark events in one's life; on the morning of one's wedding day; preferably the couple separately used a different water source or mikveh. Also, the morning of a boy's Bar Mitzvah ceremony (age of responsibility) at 13. And, entering into the military at age 20; repentance from sin and rededication to Adonai, or a person or married couple had an anniversary. Even a serious or deadly disease of which a person fully recovered (leprosy perhaps), an immersion took place. And yes, babies dedicated to Adonai could be immersed. A male proselyte underwent circumcision and immersion and then called a newborn. Female proselytes also immersed. Scholars have held that immersion cleansed a convert from the spiritual pagan uncleanness in which they had lived.

Women used mikvehs for post-menstrual purposes, one day each month—seven days after the blood-flow stopped—never for hygiene. Immersion once again, 40 days after the birth of a male child and 80 days for a female. Immersion causes a woman to become ritually clean again, as mentioned in Luke 2:22. Joseph and Mary needed to "purify themselves."

Men immersed while entering the priesthood. On the Temple Mount, the priests used secluded, priests-only mikvehs each morning. Interestingly, on the Mount, there were over two dozen cisterns collecting rainwater, or melting snow or ice. The high priest had a private mikveh which he filled and used only one day a year for Yom Kippur. The day before Yom Kippur— the Day of Atonement—everyone sought to purify (taharah) themselves by immersion. No doubt people waited in long lines at mikvehs. (Plural, mikvot.) Regular people conducted self-immersion before walking up the Temple Mount.

See my website www.markleegoldenwriter.com for more information and color photos of ancient and modern mikvehs. Locate the article *Baptism for the Dead.*

Did You Know?

Pentecost is referred to by some Christian denominations as the birthday of the Church? Meaning, the early Messianic Community of Jewish disciples, were a new sect or branch of Judaism. In contrast, in Jesus' day, the ancient holiday of Passover was Israel's national birthday, because it marked the House of Israel's liberation from Egypt. This commemoration continues today.

Why? The enthused 120 felt compelled to leave the haven of close fellowship and go willingly to the crowded streets to tell of God's mighty deeds. These proclamations pivoted around the ministry of the Messiah during the past three unforgettable years—and Resurrection.

Today, disciples of Jesus have never stopped doing so. The nutshell of the Gospel is spoken in many languages known to man…if not all, it will be soon.

On To Jerusalem. Why?

In ancient times, one month before Passover, everywhere across the country of Israel, preparations took place, such as repairing roads and bridges. Also, sepulchers received a fresh coat of whitewashing, making the graves more noticeable, which caused travelers to avoid defilement by stepping on or passing too close.

For Passover and Pentecost, sometimes, a whole family made the journey to Jerusalem, the capital. But each home had its own complications of pregnancies, newborns, illnesses, care of the elderly or unforeseen circumstances. Those who couldn't come and worship would try to attend a central synagogue in their district to worship, fast and pray. Levite towns dotted the landscape and so a priestly Levite could officiate at these meetings. Also, from Deuteronomy 14:24-27, "Now the place the Lord chooses for His Name to be honored might be a long way from your home. If so, you may sell the tithe portion of your crops and herds and take the money to buy anything you want—an ox, a sheep, some wine or beer. Then feast there in the presence of the Adonai and celebrate with your household. And do not forget Levites in your community, for they have no inheritance as you do."

For example, men from the village of Nazareth formed together for the journey to Jerusalem. Then they joined others from around the region of Galilee on paths and roads funneling to Jerusalem. Every highway in the country grew crowded with throngs of joyous pilgrims heading toward the Holy City. They sang specific pilgrim psalms. Every town and city along the way celebrated with music and parades.

In the territory of Galilee, with non-Hebrews so common in number, the religious peer pressure to observe the holidays fell short. In times past, not all Jews lived as they should, just as now. Many in Nazareth never attended a gathering at the synagogue unless a wedding or circumcision drew them. Wine and food always helped to make that decision easy.

On the eastern shore of Lake Kinneret, in the territory of the tribe of Gad, certain Jews raised pigs. Eating pork was forbidden, not being kosher animals (a chuk commandment). On one trip, Jesus sailed there, on landing, two extremely demon-possessed men accosted him. The demons knew they had to exit their victims, and asked Jesus to send them into a nearby herd of 2,000 pigs. Crazy with invasive, evil, foreign beings, the pigs ran in a wild stampede over a hillside into the lake and drowned—probably unexpected by the demons. The compromised Gadarene community had known better.

Concerning the trips to Jerusalem, Joseph probably brought along the young Jesus when he grew more independent, before he turned 13, one or two times a year. Otherwise, Joseph left him home. At 13, Jesus, then a Son of the Commandment, might've traveled every holiday. Eighty miles of traveling made for little fun with small children. However, the festive trips took a person where God wanted them to be. Weather, scenery, and even the different air brought new life and adventure in a pleasant disorientation of travel. The spirit of obedience rested on them. Moving with their gear, food, clothing, and essentials, they enjoyed getting away from life's daily routine. Though not that far, staying at a different home, not seeing the everyday faces of Nazareth, and time away from labor, would refresh Joseph, Mary, and their children. The slow journey, for the pilgrimage was to be a joy and privilege, not a rush of toil or weariness.

In the spiritual darkness of the land, off in the distance, set on a hill, shone a brightly-lit city, and it was all anyone needed. The lights drew travelers and wanderers from many nations. Jerusalem sat as the seat of the world and the apple of Adonai's eyes. And when the carpenter's feet walked on the Earth, God's footstool, Adonai peeked between His own holy heels and His mind dwelt upon Jerusalem. One day, in stepped Jesus—and God noticed.

A Deeper Level of Interest in First Century Pentecost
Counting the Omer and How Hebrews Celebrated

Pentecost has two themes: the revelation of God's laws and the harvest season. It recalls the day that the whole mobile, Jewish nation stood at Mount Sinai to receive the Torah, and as such required three days of preparation.

Manna had started to fall from heaven daily, and with it came certain simple divine do's and don'ts, decrees to discipline the freed Jews toward a new society. Many instructions applied to the traveling sanctuary and future activities in the Promised Land.

Pente in Greek is the number five; Pentecost in Greek means count fifty or fiftieth. In Hebrew, Chag ha-Shavuot (known in English as Festival of Weeks, Festival of Reaping, First Fruits, or Festival of the Harvest) is one of the 3 great annual festivals. It's believed that every Jewish male, 12 or certainly 20 years old, living within 20 miles of Jerusalem was legally bound to come.

Pentecost meant a festival day, celebrated with singing and dancing and rest from work; it was a holiday for all—a Sabbath—though not necessarily on a Saturday. The Temple resounded as a place for music. A 300-strong Levitical choir, and 120 musicians played trumpets, harps, lyres, and cymbals. Such were particularly impressive during the great pilgrim festivals. Pageantry flourished. Worshippers sang along. (The musicians and choir were routine throughout the year.). The priests would focus their minds on the higher spiritual spheres, according to mysterious traditions.

That explains why they had the Levites singing and the musicians playing. After all, it amounted to a grand barbecue, with inspirational music. And yet, deep spiritual experience for all involved. You went away truly elevated.

Pentecost is also a significant spring agricultural festival of harvested grain: two parts. On the second day after Passover, worshippers brought an Omer of freshly cut barley to the Temple as an offering; about a quart or four pounds, and olive oil. An Omer is a unit of measure, literally, a sheaf. Typically, men brought the first sheaf of barley reaped that season— barley was the first grain to ripen of those sown in the winter months. These firstfruits could be brought only by the farmer, not by his tenants or employees. Originally, the size of the daily ration of manna per person was an Omer.

Counting the Omer, also known as Sefirat HaOmer, was an important process for each of the fifty days (seven complete Sabbaths or weeks) between Passover and Pentecost as stated in the Bible, Leviticus 23:15–16. These fifty days are counted off aloud (reading silently wasn't practiced in the Hebrew culture). By this ritual, Jews symbolically connected liberation from slavery with the idea of the giving, and purposes in the Torah. The Israelites' weeks of counting is connected to the harvest holiday when the 'firstfruits' of the harvest would be brought to the Temple.

From the Torah: "You shall count for yourselves seven weeks from when the sickle is first put to the standing crop. Then you will observe the Festival of Pentecost for the Lord, your God. From the day after the Sabbath, from the day when you bring the Omer of the waving—seven Sabbaths, you shall complete. Until the day after the seventh Sabbath you shall count, fifty days. So, Pentecost is a holiday for all, no work is to be done—it is a Sabbath." See Leviticus 23, Numbers 28 and Deuteronomy 16.

Pentecost was designated as a time of thanksgiving for the early harvest. An early wheat harvest increased hopefulness for an abundant fall harvest—the Festival of Shelters (Sukkot) also called the Festival of the Clouds—specifically, the Festival of the Cloud of Glory. In other words, the counting of the Omer was the time lapse between Passover and Pentecost (Shavuot). Grain ripened 50 days later. When the first fruit of each crop began to ripen, the farmer would tie a reed-grass ribbon around the branch to designate it as first fruits. This signified that the fruit was to be used for the first fruit offering (Bikkurim) when picked.

Counting of the Omer is forty-nine days between the holiday of Passover and the holiday of Pentecost. For 50 days, starting from the second day of Passover, Jews scattered in the known world counted the Omer. The Jews recited the appropriate blessing every evening, "Blessed are You, God, King of the Universe, Who made us holy with His commandments, and commanded us to count the Omer." Every night, from the second night of

Passover to the night of Pentecost, Jews recited the blessing and stated the count of the Omer in both weeks and days. For example, on the 16th day, they would say, "Today is sixteen days, which is two weeks and two days of the Omer." Jewish days start in the evening, so one would not perform the two rituals until after sundown.

The count culminates with the holiday of Pentecost. Remember, ancient Jews didn't have the convenience of printed paper or digital calendars like we do. All spoke the calendar count of the Omer and recited the blessing. For instance, on the evening after Jesus ascended to heaven from the Mount of Olives, Peter, James, John, and the rest would have said, "Today is 40 days, which is five weeks and five days of the Omer." The Resurrection did not nullify religious Jewish life or godly rituals.

The Second Temple (Herod's Temple) in AD 70, roughly 35 years after Jesus' Resurrection, the Romans destroyed it. Gone were centuries of sacrifices of honor, offerings, thanksgivings, priestly and common blessings—and the Temple-centric annual festivals in Jerusalem. Then the Romans abolished all Temple-related activities in Jerusalem. After the destruction of the Temple in 70 CE, the commanded food offerings and sacrifices ceased. So, the rabbis switched emphasis to the Revelation at Mt. Sinai.

In the ancient world, people regarded an altar as a touch point between heaven and earth. Think of it as God's table.

How Jews Celebrate Pentecost Today

The Christian observance of Pentecost has no resemblance or significance to the Jewish observance from which it derives its name. Jewish people do not observe the Christian Pentecost. Jews still observe Shavuot as commanded by God in Torah.

Pentecost is a Greek word transliterated into English for the Hebrew holiday of Shavuot. A theme of Shavuot is revelation, God's revelation of Himself. Jews celebrate the giving of the Torah at Mount Sinai. That day, the Hebrews solidified as God's Chosen People. He formed a bond with Jews that will never be broken. The voluntary acceptance of God's Laws is commemorated.

Synagogue readings for Shavuot might include Exodus 19-20, 34:22, Leviticus 23:15-22, Deuteronomy 16:16, Ezekiel 1-2, and Habakkuk 3. Some communities publicly read the Book of Ruth because it's a story of harvesting. However, it tells of the joining of a foreigner to God's people. Ruth's conversion is thought to reflect the Jews acceptance of the Torah on Shavuot. Tradition is that this was the date of King David's birth and his passing—he was a descendant of Ruth the Moabite (her great-great-grandson). Children may be asked to recite the Ten Commandments and receive a small gift or treats.

Jewish holidays often have food-related component and Shavuot is no different. As on other holidays, special meals are eaten, and no "work" may be performed. According to tradition, Jews should eat dairy foods such as cheese, cheesecake, blintzes, ice cream, and milk. No one knows where this custom comes from. Dairy meals can be a reminder that Israel is the "land of milk and honey." Slices of apples or specially baked bread are dipped in honey and cinnamon. The Word of the Lord is likened to "honey and milk."

In Israel, Shavuot is an agricultural holiday that honors the wheat harvest. The early spring and summer bounty is just about ready to pick in most parts of the country. Visit a pick-your-own farm and enjoy gathering buckets of ripening berries in the warm sun to take home and smother with sweet cream or bake into pies and cobblers.

Women and girls might light special candles to usher in the holiday. Decorating synagogues and homes with roses, plants, and other flowers, even trees or aromatic spices, is a custom based on a teaching that connect the events at Sinai to sweet-smelling spices and roses. The custom widely prevails of displaying greens on the floors.

Many deeply religious Jews commemorate Shavuot by trying to spend the entire night studying Torah at their synagogue or at home. They also study other biblical books and portions of the Talmud. This all-night gathering is known as Tikkun Leyl Shavuot and at dawn participants stop studying and recite shacharit, the morning prayer.

The Bible Versus Us

The book of collected works, the Bible, is confusing at times. Certain scriptures or Bible stories are the most difficult. Not because they are so hard to understand, but because they are so easy to misunderstand. We are literally reading other people's mail. At least forty-four authors were unaware that they were working side-by-side or centuries apart for a future collection. Consider the compilation of 66 chosen writings and note these caution signs. First, the persons who wrote the pages and their readership are long dead. Second, none of it was written directly to you or me. Third, we are thousands of miles from where they lived, with cultures foreign to us. Fourth, chances are you and I can't read or speak the ancient languages used by the authors. Fifth, that crowd of writers and readers wouldn't recognize us if they passed us on the street and we the same. The saints, sinners, peasants, Romans, fishermen, kings, and pharaohs are strangers as we would be to them.

If the Bible was meant to be an instruction book for living, much ranks low on the comprehension scale. Conflicts of understanding—bump, crash, and divide with almost every verse, and within every community. Jewish denominations differ too. The stories which back this up can be found within the pages of Scriptures itself. Corruption started in the beginning and has never stopped. Debates in interpreting, discerning the means, methods and limits have never stopped. These have ended in appeasement, prejudice, torture, and death. The Word of God, though never intended so, has left a corrosive stench in the nostrils of people across the globe. Atheists, heretics, scientists, philosophers, and contrary Christians and Jews have been imprisoned, forced to be baptized, tortured, and burnt alive at the stake for varying beliefs—in the name of God.

Christians especially disagree about the meaning of the New Testament's short four verses in Acts Chapter 2:1-4, and the following. Yet, looking into the older meaning of Pentecost provides clarification for us. The Jewish believers of Acts 2 knew quite a bit more about Pentecost than we do, because they and their ancestors, and of course Jesus, Joseph, Mary, the Apostles and the 120 disciples, celebrated every year, all their lives. Long before the tongues of fire fell in Jerusalem, the fire fell upon Mount Sinai, the first Pentecost, 1,400 years earlier.

The Book of Acts, written by the disciple Luke, has also been labeled the Gospel of the Holy Spirit and the Gospel of the Resurrection. Bear in mind that Luke researched, interviewed eye-witnesses, and gathered similar reports from different points of view. No doubt he kept a travel diary handy during his years of traveling with the Apostle Paul.

Idolatry was a blight of humanity for thousands of years. In a world full of a variety of gods, the idea of a single, Creator God was new. Except for the Persian monotheistic Zoroastrian religion. He introduced Himself to Abraham. Today, Hebrews in the millions, are the descendants of Abraham and Sarah's promised child, Isaac. God chose the Hebrews as His representatives on Earth. They were to reflect His light by His instructions for life. This awareness meant do's and don'ts. As time passed, He also combined a 12-month system of moral rules and religious celebrations.

Now, 3,400 years later, many Jews are continually living out certain of these observances, memorials, and festivals. They do this in over a hundred countries and Israel.

God Fashioned Holidays

In Israel, during Jesus' time, men and families went to the synagogues to hear readings from the Torah after sundown (when Pentecost started). Some men continued and studied all night long. People who owned papyrus scrolls of Scripture might stay home, read and teach members of their household—even servants. On that first Pentecost, 1,400 years earlier at Mt. Sinai, all of the Hebrews "converted" to God's ways for the beginnings of Judaism by accepting the holy laws.

After escaping Egypt by God's strong right arm, the Children of Israel arrived in the desert of Sinai (Exodus 19:1). He descended onto Mount Sinai in a mighty, visual, and vocal display, and gave them the Ten Commandments (Ten Words or Ten Sayings). The festival of Pentecost is the anniversary of the day God spoke these profound Laws at Mount Sinai.

On the first Pentecost, a dense dark cloud covered Mount Sinai, and the mountain trembled. The sound of a loud ram's horn (shofar) filled the air. From atop Mount Sinai all Israel heard His voice. Therefore, Pentecost is celebrated each year as the anniversary of the giving of the Torah. Exodus 19 and 20 recount the story.

Pentecost took place fifty days after the Angel of Death visited Egypt, the last plague that ended Jewish slavery. The Angel of Death "passed-over" or "skipped" the homes of Jews, when they had, in faith, marked their doorposts with the blood of their family sacrificial (Passover) lamb. The angel sought faithless homes with firstborn—men and animals. The commemoration of that final plague is a festival of freedom and celebrated now for over 3,400 years. The Hebrews left the House of Bondage with song, banners, celebration, and free-for-the-taking possessions of any Egyptians. In extreme fear, these surviving Egyptians gave anything which might pacify this ardent, all mighty, God of the slaves. Otherwise, what would He do next?

Pentecost is a biblical holiday filled with a wealth of meaning and symbolism. This is true of both the first one 3,400 years ago and one in particular 1,400 years later. The mountain trembled and the fanfare of a shofar-trumpet heralded the arrival of the Almighty. The voice of God spoke audibly to the entire nation—over one million persons. 600,000 men over age 20 are noted to have left Egypt, along with their wives and children. Some scholars teach that over 2,500,000 people made the Exodus. An unknown number non-Hebrews fled battered Egypt and converted to their Redeemer God.

For as long as the First and Second Temples stood in Jerusalem, approximately 400 years each, the men of Israel followed the commandments to make pilgrimage there and worship. The Lord tells the children of Israel, "Three times in a year, all your males shall appear before the Lord your God in the place which He chooses, on the festivals of Passover, Pentecost and Tabernacles" (Deuteronomy 16:16). "Now then, if you will indeed hear

My voice and keep My covenant, then you shall be My own possession among all the peoples, for all the earth is Mine." (Exodus 19:5).

How did Israel become the Chosen People of God? How did she become the "one flock"? How did she become the bride? She did it by agreeing to the terms of His covenant. By agreeing to hear God's voice. Jesus said, "Out of the overflow of the heart the mouth speaks." Thus, when God broke the cosmic silence and spoke to His creation at Mount Sinai, the words He spoke were the fullness of His heart. Each law, each commandment (mitzvah), no matter how small or seemingly irrelevant, is actually a piece of revelation from God, and an overflowing of His heart.

The same is true in Messiah. When we agree to follow Jesus, placing our faith in Him, He leads us into His flock. It's not as if we merit salvation through our obedience to God's Laws, but certainly obedience results from faith and faith from obedience.

The Epistles speak of breaking of only one law makes the person guilty of breaking them all. This is best seen as the Covenant (Law or Torah) being broken. When a Jew broke the Covenant given at Mt. Sinai, there was an effect against all those seeking to obediently follow which laws applied to themselves. In the epistles, Paul writes the same concept about the Body of Christ. He describes how one part of the body affects all parts of the Body.

Pentecost is one of the "appointed times" designed by God, written into His biblical calendar found in Leviticus 23. The early church, made up of Jewish believers and pagan converts to Judaism, described in the Book of Acts, kept God's festivals, and celebrated His appointed times throughout the Jewish calendar. Today, Pentecost is the only biblical festival that is faintly remembered and (sometimes) observed in some fashion as part of the Church calendar. The others—Passover, Feast of Unleavened Bread, the Feast of Trumpets (Rosh HaShanah, the New Year), the monthly New Moon Festival (Rosh Chodesh), the Day of Atonement (Yom Kippur) and the Festival of Tabernacles (Sukkot), and the Friday/Saturday Sabbath—all long ago vanished from most churches' liturgical year.

Other important holidays are also unobserved, such as Chanukkah, the Festival of Lights, which the adult Jesus celebrated (see John 10:22, 23). Chanukkah commemorates the Jewish people rising up in defense of the Torah and the Temple, against the Syrian-Greeks. Another holiday is Purim, from the Book of Esther. These disappeared only a few generations after Messianic Jewish communities dwindled and the Gentile ex-pagans took hold of the new religion of Christianity. Yet, because of the strength of the presence of the Holy Spirit, Pentecost still occupies a place in Church teachings.

*　　*　　*

In Acts, Chapter 2, the festival of Pentecost already carried extra significance for the believers, because it came some 50 days after Jesus' death, then Resurrection. He had instructed the disciples to wait in Jerusalem for the Promise of the Father, the Immersion in the Holy Spirit. There's no indication that Jesus said to expect this event to come ten days hence, on the upcoming holiday of Pentecost. When Jesus was immersed in the Jordan River, he prayed. The heavens opened, and a (physical) dove descended on him. This was the Holy Spirit. A voice from above said, "This is my Son, whom I love. I am well pleased with you."

As the disciples of the risen Messiah gathered to celebrate Pentecost in Jerusalem, they were gathering also to celebrate the traditional anniversary of the giving of the Torah and the first fruits of the harvest. "All must give as they are able, according to the blessings given to them by God." (Deuteronomy 16:17). Pentecost is also the day when the farmers in Israel were to bring the first fruits of their crops, vineyards and orchards to Jerusalem. It may be reckoned that Jesus was the First-fruit of the Resurrection from the dead. In fact, the disciples and followers of Jesus were themselves the first fruits of Jesus' ministry. On Pentecost, 3,000 Jews added to their number, and the great harvest of souls began. Thousands followed.

He Loves Me, He Loves Me Not
Ancient Marriage and Covenant Customs

Imagine our earth's population with every person knowing God and His specific desires. Consider no conflicts of understanding, no disagreements of what pleases Him. Equality: everyone holds the same divine knowledge, not less, not more. What harmony! What a pleasant lifestyle! Goodness around the globe—what a friendly planet! Indeed, it would be akin to a large family or tribe which only knows peace—all believing that the universe has one God, who brought everything's existence into being, and to accept His claim of benevolent ownership over us. Perhaps God had such a daydream in mind when He chose only one nation in which to devote Himself. Were the twelve tribes of Israel intended to live in a loving, practical accord? Scripture clearly shows God wanting the Promised Land to be such a place. No, not a second Garden of Eden, not without crime, not without sin, but the next best environment—if only the His people held up their end of the bonding marriage to Him.

At Mount Sinai, God officially proposes to Israel, offering to make them His people if only they will obey Him and keep His covenant. It's like a proposal of marriage during that time and culture. In this engagement metaphor God is compared to the suitor and future bridegroom. Israel is the bride. The Torah is the contract (ketubah). Moses, in his role as liaison between God and the people, is sometimes described as the "friend of the bridegroom." In Jewish wedding customs, the friend of the bridegroom is the intermediary. It was the friend's job to present the bride to the groom. Moses fills this role by leading the people to Mount Sinai and conducting the negotiations between God and Israel. When at last the Lord descends on Mount Sinai, Moses leads the people out of the camp and to the foot of the mountain, presenting them to God.

As the friend of the bridegroom, Moses was responsible for negotiating the match. He brings the bridegroom's proposal to the woman. Through Moses, God offers to make Israel His own "possession among all the peoples, a kingdom of priests and a holy nation. You shall be My possession among all the peoples, for all the earth is Mine. Israel is to be My bride. You have seen what I did to the Egyptians, and how I bore you on eagle's wings and brought you to Myself." and "These are the words which you shall speak to the Children of Israel. So, Moses came and called for the elders of the people, and laid before them all these words which Adonai commanded him." (Exodus 19:5-7)

The sages of Israel refer to Exodus 19 as "the Betrothal at Sinai." The picture is a simple one. The people of Israel are the object of God's affection. He asks for her hand in marriage, and she consented. He is to be their God. They are to be His people.

The romance actually began while still in Egypt. There, the Lord had declared to Israel, "I will take you for my people, and will be your God." The expression is close to a legal formula from the sphere of marriage of the Ancient Near East. The groom declared, "You will be my wife and I will be your husband." In a sense, it is as if God has declared His intention to marry the people of Israel.

The marriageable girl says "Yes," and the engagement ring goes on her finger. But in actuality, getting engaged wasn't quite this simple. Betrothal was a formal affair. It entailed written contractual agreements; all the terms and conditions stated. The responsibilities of both parties were spelled out clearly. What will be the bride price? What will be the dowry? What will the responsibilities of the bride entail? What must the groom do? What are his obligations as a husband? What will be the obligations as the wife? When will the wedding occur? All possible contingencies addressed. It is a contract and a covenant, too.

A covenant is an agreement specifying terms and conditions incumbent upon both parties. It's a list of obligations, but it is more than a simple contract. A contract is a business agreement. A covenant is a relationship. It's the definition of a relationship between two parties. In the ancient cultures of the Bible, a covenant's terms and conditions were regarded as being unbreakable.

In Exodus 19, God asks Israel to enter into a covenant relationship with Him, requesting Israel's hand in marriage. Even before hearing the actual voice of God, Israel agrees. The people respond by saying, "All that the Lord has spoken we will do." She has agreed to be his special, intimate people.

At that time, the Children of Israel were a mobile nation wandering through the desert with stop-overs that were perhaps years at a time. After 40 years, they entered and settled in God's Promised Land. There they would become a country with borders like other nations. In those ancient centuries, Hebrew was a race. Yet, pagans from other cultures could convert becoming proselytes, and join the Jews in obedience and worship of their God. He proved God truly cared for His people.

The revelation at Sinai was purposeful and deliberate. When God revealed himself, He gave a legal code, with covenant terms and obligations. He gave laws. Yet they are more than just laws intended to tidy up human society. Each commandment is a small revelation of God, more than just rules for governing human behavior, a reflection of the Lawgiver.

All the people heard the voice of God as He spoke the Ten Commandments recorded in Exodus 20. An unprecedented and unique moment in history. An entire nation literally heard the voice of God speaking. They did not hear God in an ethereal or spiritual sense. They audibly heard.

Why would God choose one people above all others? Why are the Jews the Chosen People? The Bible is very clear on this point. Out of all the peoples on the earth, out of all the nations, God entered into covenant with only one people, only one nation. That nation is Israel. God did not call the Swedes to Mount Sinai. The Irish are not a kingdom of priests. The Italians are not a holy nation. The French are not the People of God. Americans are not the Chosen People. Certain Jewish sages taught that God did visit all the nations around the planet. He asked each one, but only Abraham's seed said "Yes!"

Going a step further, God did not call the Baptists to Mount Sinai. The Catholics are not a kingdom of priests. The Lutherans are not a holy nation. The Presbyterians, Evangelicals, Mormons, Jehovah's Witnesses, or Buddhists are not the Chosen People of God. He hasn't made a covenant with any other race. If non-Jews want to be a part of the People of God, they must spiritually and or physically leave their people and join themselves to a Jewish community or even relocate to Israel. Concerning salvation, any human must believe in the shed blood and Resurrection of the Jewish Messiah. All Christianity pivots on the sinless man from the tribe of Judah.

Through the centuries, Hebrews spread to foreign lands. People were attracted to the Jewish lifestyle, history, and their God. The concept of a Hebrew race altered from only direct descendants of Abraham, Isaac and Jacob to strangers near and far. Are there Chinese Jews, Hispanic Jews or Native American Jews? Yes, and they make up a number of the religious Jews who've never seen the land of Israel. Some might be those who have moved to the modern country of Israel and are of a different race, but have chosen Judaism. They are Jews by conversion, entering into the spiritual commonwealth of Israel. They are Israel.

But there's another side to this coin. Not all current Israelis are of Hebrew background or are interested in Judaism. Arabs, Christians, Moslems, Druze, Baha'i, Hindu, Buddhists, and others live there now. As of this writing, the majority of Jewish Israelis are not religious!

Israel alone, among all the peoples of the earth, had, and still has the potential to enjoy a national relationship with the Creator. How did she become the "one flock"? How does a person enter this covenant? The same way Israel entered the Mosaic Covenant. She entered by agreeing to hear God's voice: "Now then, if you will indeed hear My voice and keep My covenant, then you shall be My own possession among all the peoples, for all the earth is Mine" (Exodus 19:5). The "New" Covenant or Testament, piggy-backs on the earlier one, not annuls it.

Author wearing his great-grandfather's tefillin (Shel Rosh and Shel Yad), his father's kippah (head covering), and his own tallit (prayer shawl) a gift from his parents for his Bar Mitzvah at age 13.

A Glimpse at My Personal Story

I grew up in a home with only half a Bible. Today, I know the Bible—both halves. In 1976, at 20 years of age, I did what no Jew was ever to do. I became a Christian. Though my parents were patriotic to Israel, and cultural Jews, rather than routinely religious ones, I did grow up attending a *shul* or synagogue. I had learned to read Hebrew but not necessarily know what the words meant.

I used to…well, that is, I was raised to think that only one-half of the bigger Bibles should be bothered with—no matter what the other, smaller half contained. I didn't know what was in it but knew enough not to care. One day, I opened a bigger Bible and found these misplaced pages, right next to our holy scriptures (the Tenakh) obviously concocted by non-Jewish publishers, bound into one so-called book: The Bible. What was up with that?

I knew I shouldn't listen to those who read and carried around this kind of Bible. Apparently, they believed mythical stories about a pushy, renegade Jew who crossed too many lines and got what he deserved: crucifixion. By his martyrdom he somehow achieved the title Lord and Savior. Those "saved" types muddled, mismatched and re-fashioned our religion, doing an entire makeover of what they called the "Old Testament." If you catch the drift, "old" implies or requires the need for some kind of replacement, like a "new" testament. Somehow this all made perfect sense to Christians, while they affronted Jewish heritage, traditions, and a boat load of sagely, rabbinical teaching.

Not only were they content with this, but they also wanted us to join their side! How out of touch can you be? We were "we" and Christians were "them." Simple.

While researching this book, I had a family question, so I emailed an older cousin. In discussing our common roots, he told me our mutual grandfather's given name was Abraham. I find this twist so ironic. I had always known him to be Al, short for Albert. He lived 1893-1989. The biblical man, Abraham, is referred to as Avraham Avinu (Abraham Our Father), and the first Hebrew. No doubt my grandfather changed his name in order not to be easily identified as a Jew. My father had done the same with his *last name* (before my birth). Some years into my adulthood, I made a huge decision, and changed my last name, Gaines, back to our family's original name, Golden.

Recently I had a DNA test done to peek into my Hebrew heritage. No surprise, the results showed I am 95% European and East European Jewish. I had known that one of my great-grandparents was a rabbi—an extreme Jew. Three of my grandparents came to America from Ukraine, one further back, from Poland. They loosened up from the lifestyle and rituals of what made Jews a product of the Old World. My relatives trimmed back observing halakhah (Jewish religious and civil laws) and traditions. So, my parents had a watered down Judaism. Then, I and my sibling had something of a take-it-or-leave-it Judaism. My children's generation barely got that.

After my Bar Mitzvah at age 13, like most of my peers, I drifted away from a Jewish religious identity; only heritage and culture remained. Famous movie star, director, writer, and producer Woody Allen (or perhaps it was Mel Brooks) said, "I love being Jewish, but I have nothing to do with the Jewish religion!" This is still true today of over a million American Jews.

At the age of 14, around Christmastime, I remember my father and I watching a highly-respected nightly news program, the Huntley-Brinkley Report. One of the newsman reported a holiday story with a surprising note. Apparently, Jesus Christ was considered a historical figure, and not the long-haired, bearded, sandal-clad, fairy tale character from Christianland. I never knew he really lived!

After age 14, for the next 6 years or so, I investigated what others believed—except Christianity. For five years I used the typical illegal drugs with my peers—and was arrested twice. This was a growing-up time for me and a solo journey too. I shared my self-exploration with friends. I found people chose what currently fancied them: the face on Mars, UFOs, reincarnation, meditation, ESP, ancient treasures waiting for their unearthing, or simply some kind of a cult, eastern religions, or conspiracies and cover-ups. Truth took on a variety of legends, teachers, and books. But Christianity was always a no-no. That was in my blood—practically written in blood. Gentiles were the other team, 'them' so to speak.

Back to 1976. While summer hitchhiking in Oregon, I visited a high school friend from Los Angeles. I noticed a paperback book called *Good News for Modern Man*. This turned out to be a Christian, New Testament book of some sort. In my 20 years I'd never held or flipped through one of these. In a casual, slow-paced setting I went outside, sat down and opened it. The titles, chapters, and names meant little to me and I didn't intend on reading much. I noticed the Gospel of Mark—my name! That made my choice easy. I read all 16 short chapters.

So, at age twenty, I read a little of the New Testament for the first time. Only then did I understand that Christians believed, Jesus Christ was *our* Jewish Messiah! Due to unexpected circumstances, I ended up staying one day and night with a house full of Jesus freaks in Eugene, Oregon. In privacy, I said a required prayer to gain admission into eternal life on God's lap in Heaven.

After that summer I attended college and lived with my parents. They had stopped attending synagogue years earlier. Full of fear and worry, I informed them of my sudden religious decision and commitment. My parents were embarrassed and ashamed. Loud debates and arguments took place. Looking back, I think I didn't know much of what I was talking about, and they knew far less of what they were talking about. Their anger about my decision? I'd been foolishly led by the other side to join the centuries' old enemies of the Jewish people—of which my parents had experienced some prejudice. To them, I, like Elvis, had "left the building." To them, it was as if a child molester had gotten to me in my innocence. For them, they were burdened with shame that they hadn't protected me to prevent such an outrageous crime. They lived with that embarrassment and defeat until they died.

Disappointing my parents reminded me of Jesus' words. "I have come to bring division; father against son, wife against husband." I lived it. I lived it for years. I was the son, and the only kid in the mostly cultural Jewish neighborhood who'd taken that wrong turn.

I do not regret my conversion from hippiedom to a religious lifestyle. I made a serious and unexpected decision which even today causes my continuing evolving attitudes into holiness.

At age 22, after two years of trying to live as an American-style disciple of Christ, I thought God compelled me to attend a particular Christian theology school. This institution was one hour from my parents' house in Los Angeles. I left home and moved near the school. My parents adamantly told me, "We will never visit you. If you have any trouble, we will not help you. If you become a preacher—we will disown you and never speak with you again!" Those unbending declarations did loosen up in time, partly because I was their only child who lived locally, and later, because I never did go into the ministry.

They told their friends, all Jewish, that I moved away because I had taken a job in my trade—partially true. I attended theology school at night.

*　　*　　*

In 2010 at age 54, I stood in Jerusalem for the first time. I traveled there by myself. No guided tour. Once I had arrived in Israel, I said to myself many times over, "I'm in Jerusalem; it really does exist!"

I discovered that the Arabs looked at me and knew I was Hebrew. The Jews knew, too. Something about my race had inherent trace elements I didn't know I'd packed with the luggage—my DNA. Some might call it my spiritual DNA. They looked, reading me in an instant. Back home in America, I was just me, white-skinned, balding brown hair and a reddish beard. I was spooked. Sadly, I learned I shouldn't visit Palestinian-controlled Bethlehem or Jericho without expecting danger. I didn't need danger, and my U.S. passport would not stop a Palestinian bullet.

I went to the Old City, the heartbeat of Jerusalem. I gazed at the broad Kotel (Hebrew for The Wall), also called the Western or Wailing Wall. I knew that over the centuries countless people lived near and walked by this very spot. Yet, this most meaningful and pivotal stretch of ground to the Jewish religion—only 187 feet wide and 62 feet high above ground (43 feet is below ground)—is a landmark where my ancestors started. The Kotel is a surprisingly short section of the original 1,500-foot-wide west-facing wall and one of four ancient, massive walls.

Due to the DNA of my ancestor's past, and forefathers unknown, I had returned home. I wondered how many blood relatives, *like me,* traveled from foreign countries, through the centuries, just to stand where I stood to pray. Who was to follow?

I brought with me a Bar Mitzvah gift from my parents, a fine but yellowing, blue and white, silk prayer shawl—tallit. Also, my father's blue and white skull cap or Kippa in Hebrew. When I packed for this month-long trip, I felt God nudge me to bring my tallit, even though I had misgivings of traveling with this sentimental, 40-year-old item. First, I feared the possibility of theft or loss of luggage. Second, I rarely wore it anyway. Third, I had limited room in my luggage—I carried a large backpack; a day knapsack; and a small, soft bag. This way I could be mobile on my feet.

The silly thing was, where else on earth would be more appropriate and meaningful to put on my prayer shawl and pray than Jerusalem (Yerushalayim)? Only when I stood before that ancient, massive, retaining wall, with its row upon row of huge cut stones and boulders, did I best understand our family's heritage. I pondered my connection to the remaining, mere dust of relatives who'd lived, bred, and died in this foreign country.

*   *   *

Standing in front of that 2,000-year-old, giant, limestone wall in Jerusalem, helped me to get my writer's virtual feet-on-the-ground…centuries after things happened. Penning it for you, as a scribe, is what I've tried to do faithfully. Bear in mind, what you read is speculation, sanctified historical fiction based on biblical truth. May these prove to be pages of quality.

As I put this work into book format, I feel little like an ancient scribe. A scribe of old would have penned this tale with a skillfully severed straw from the watery reed plant or turkey feather. He'd use a hand-blown bottle with pigment and ink of his own mixing. He'd create a paper-like material from gathered wetlands plants called papyrus or would have purchased ready-to-use papyrus scrolls in a marketplace.

Writing from ancient Scripture is literally reading other people's mail, their heartaches, schedules, list of chores, births and deaths. These people lived in countries thousands of miles from America's shores. Their language and cultures are foreign to most readers. Though each person used languages we do not know (aside from Hebrew), we are comfortable with them all speaking modern English in our leather-bound, gilded paged, translations.

Where do I fit in with all of this? I'm just one of the participants in the massive parade of God followers. If Jesus, the Messiah, were walking from Point A to Point B, I picture myself somewhere in the middle. I do not see him with me on his mind. I'd probably have a lot on my mind, or more likely making small talk and joking with those next to me.

My God-given creative abilities have not made me special or kept me special. My failures, mistakes, misunderstandings, and plain old sin are on this author's mind. I've tried to recreate the ancient past with a cast of characters I've never met but believe did exist. The Biblical Jews were not holy, but pockets of holy events did take place. Many feet-on-the-ground writers recorded selections. My own limitations of history, language, intellect, and partially knowing our Creator, bound my feet. Meaning, I've had to carefully hobble to accomplish every paragraph, every page. What I present are unusual and thought-provoking takes on what Scripture provides.

Over forty five years ago, in my early 20s, I attended a para-church meeting, which had Holy Spirit-gift based goals. Spiritual stuff new to me. The guest speaker proved to be a true convert to Christianity. He'd been in the Mafia for years and then met God. After telling his captivating story he personally prayed for attendees. When he prayed for people, things happened. Some were silly looking things, like people falling over backwards, woozy or laughing, shaking or lightly quaking (see John's Gospel 18:4-7, Acts 2:7-13). By contrast, people received physical healings, specific, timely personal encouragement, and intimate guidance with supernatural insight from this total stranger. I wanted in! And, I was curious.

I had joined up with the Jesus thing only a year or two before. Now I stood in line for prayer, how weird. Then, what he said shocked me. "You will find things in the Bible which men who have studied the Scriptures all of their lives have never seen!" A big pronouncement—much too big for little ol' me. Wow! What an exciting concept and how could such discoveries be made—by me? How could passages be missed by decades of reading and countless men? How special and important could such knowledge be? And, why me? Maybe I'd make sense of one of the most debated section of Scripture, the *Book of Revelation*? Whatever, this must be mystical insight which others had somehow missed or misunderstood and not seminary training.

Sadly, that prophetic sound bite has proven true. Back then I hadn't considered there being a downside to this futuristic possibility. Meaning, if learned men missed valuable pieces of Scripture, what affect did that have on their students (the Church)? Also, how many influential men or women have taught Scripture in error? (Too many.)

In recent years, I have researched much for my book *The Ring of Torrents: A Jewish Mary*. In the past three years, I have learned more than over the 35 previous years. I delved into the ancient and modern history of my people, the Hebrews. My life slowly changed. I would say that, in the end, I knew too much. Studying ancient history is endless work and toil in controversy after controversy. Though a Jew, I discovered a vast amount of Biblical Judaism and Jewish history I didn't know.

Then I did know.

I compared the varied teachings of the early Christian church to its strictly Jewish beginnings, and why that changed significantly between AD 135 and 325AD *and worse to come*. Then as I studied, I found conflicting interpretations, agendas in translations, cultural blind spots, and out-and-out unholy representations of God. These all continue to flourish to this day. Much blood has gushed out of the innocent by the misinformed religious or just plain evil Bible teachers. Isn't that how Jesus went to the grave—by evil men? I am fond of the bumper sticker, "Lord, protect me from Your followers."

The term Messianic Jew can mean persons of Jewish heritage or converts, who believe Yeshua ben Yosef, Jesus son of Joseph, is the longed-for Jewish Messiah. They believe Jesus died as a sacrifice for our sins and rose from the dead, and they expect a return of Jesus ruling and reigning on Earth from Jerusalem. Messianic Jews live according to certain interpretations of the writings of Moses (called the Torah), observe ancient holidays, keep Friday night into Saturday as the Sabbath, and

This illustration is a portion of the First Century Temple Mount in Jerusalem.
Illustration courtesy of: Leen Ritmeyer ©

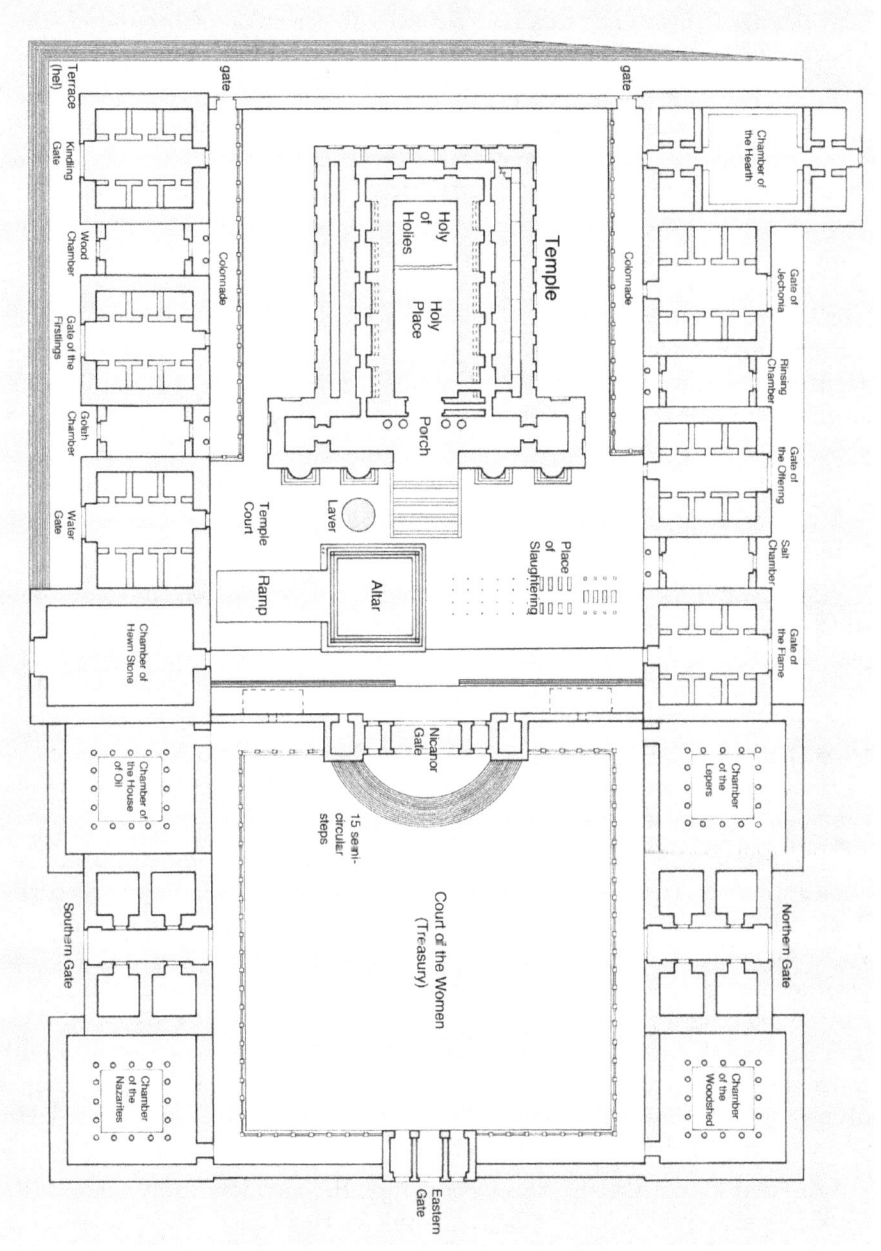

© Leen Ritmeyer

Detailed Floor Plan of the Second Beit HaMikdash or Temple Complex. Surrounding that, is a huge flat area known as The Court of the Gentiles (not shown).

believe the collection of Apostolic Writings (K'tuvei Sh'lichim) popularly called the New Testament. In essence, they keep elements of their cultural background, which Christianity has typically opposed since the Second Century. I do some of that, and it feels right.

My sadness is due to the diluted Jewish-Jesus taught from the Vatican, and the church around the corner. When churches proclaim a Jew-less Jesus, they remake the ancient Jesus into a new image in today's teachings. Many sermons never identify Jesus as a Jewish person or explain what he taught in the historical and cultural context. This erasure perpetuates itself Sunday after Sunday. Christian teachers work on neutralizing or bypassing Jesus' roots and lifestyle as if washing it away will improve the Christian experience. In essence, modern disciples are taught to take the multitude of good promises God made to the Jews—discard the Jews—and apply them to Christians. Oh! Does God care about the Jews, His chosen people anymore? In some churches, though unspoken, they are embarrassed that they have to worship a Jew.

If you've never heard of the term Replacement Theology, I heartily recommend seeking that out on the Internet. Of interest is the shocking essay written by Martin Luther titled, *"The Jews and Their Lies."*

Throughout my studies, the things I found in Scripture became like secrets which the average churchgoer found of little interest. Many Christians part ways with the Old and New Testament, though Jews penned both compilations. Each part amounts to various revelations, the history of a multitude of strangers, along with earthly and heavenly promises. Christians tend to reject the out-of-the-picture Jewish foundation of their religion. Rare is the churchgoer who has investigated— even once—a synagogue for a Sabbath service or holiday. This is a centuries-old condition of separation, and it is a strain on the truth.

The reason I have found things in the Bible which many devoted scholars have missed is because I fell in with Jewish Christians, Charismatic Christians, Messianic Jews, and Orthodox Jews. From them and their resources, I read what Gentile, non-Hebrew theologians or preachers hadn't studied at deeper levels. Certain Christians do know what I know, and they are not Jewish, nor were they seeking any "lost" parts of the Bible—it's not that category. What I've learned interests and at times fascinates me. At times, I feel how Moses felt viewing the masses he had spiritual concern over. He knew this mix of humanity would never conform to childlike obedience—contention would surface again and again. Contention is the birthplace where thousands of differing churches begins.

An interesting final point. Jews are not a race. The current majority of Jews in the world are probably blood descendants of past Jews. However, through the centuries, people from other cultures and countries have converted to Judaism. Chinese Jews? Sure. Eskimo Jews? Not sure.

2010 Me off to the airport for a month in Israel. Traveled light, alone and independently—no tour group.

Jerusalem. Old City. Dome of the Rock. Western (Wailing) Wall..

Me on Temple Mount. Dome of the Rock.

Author at Mediterranean Sea, Caesarea ruins, Israel.

Slow time at the Western Wall (Kotel). Remnant of the 1,500 foot western perimeter retaining wall of the Second Temple.

Free Short Story *ELIJAH MEETS BAAL*
You Can Locate On My Website

If you prefer a Bible story with no romance, but lots of blood and violence, you'd enjoy my short story, *Elijah Meets Baal*. In 42 pages, I retell the dynamic showdown of the Jewish Prophet Elijah against overwhelming and deadly enemies, as described in First Kings 18:1—40. My story is unique because the reader gets into the prophet's mind and heart during the struggle for a nation's soul. You'll see into the world of spirit and the battle fought there.

I wrote this for general readership and it's free to the public. You must download the PDF file from my website www.markleegoldenwriter.com, under the Samples tab. Or, send me a request at markleegolden123@gmail.com.

the
RING OF TORRENTS

A Jewish Mary

Mark Lee Golden

Also by the author
Ring of Torrents: A Jewish Mary

For two years I lived with Mary or Miryam (as she prefers). I watched, listened to, followed, and learned about her in ways no one had before. Mary knew I was there, and that she needed to allow me to report on her and her life.

Yes, in such episodes, I crafted, cared for and composed a Mary of my own making by adding to the Gospels' foundational design. But she understood this. We never talked directly. Yet, our roles were understood. She lived and I learned how she slept, dressed, cooked, ate, worked, made friends, and prayed. Most of all, I learned what Mary thought. Whatever fulfilled her, drove her, and frightened the young woman, I took responsibility to note, for you, the reader. She let me see much of what others had previously missed.

Mary is one of my people, the Jews (maybe an ancient ancestor). My heritage runs back to her sandaled steps, as she walked out the calling on her Jewish core. I watched her growth. This young woman and I had enough in common for me to see her most troubled moods and the truly fragrant lightness of her ancient ways. She spotted me taking notes and was never uneasy—okay, at times she was—you'll read about those. I could tell she took me to be a scribe sent from above. I let that pass. Unspoken, and with a grin, Mary nodded to my purpose to tell others. Though we two remained from distant generations, Mary knew my job trailed past her existence and beyond her imagination. You might say that God had a parking spot reserved for me wherever she was.

I learned to admire that woman beyond the limited print of Scripture.

Why My Mary Book Might Be For You

I wrote the *Chronicles of Two Pentecosts* for regular church or synagogue folk, keeping ancient locations, dates, languages, names, and Scriptures to a minimum. I've been dedicated to broaden and deepen what little we know of persons of the Bible in order to help the curious feel better about their faith.

My similar novel, *The Ring of Torrents: A Jewish Mary* is significantly beyond the description above. Some might label my writing as "amateur scholarship." I'll take that. There are 300 Hebrew words—with a glossary. The novel is a treasury of entertaining facts of ancient history, cultures, names, and places. I sincerely believe that there's not another book like it. Enjoy ancient people to meet and ancient stories to ponder.

Who's my audience? Each book is an effort to entertain while educating. Too many of us know too little about the Scriptures. Each book is carefully drawn from a tremendous amount of research. If you are someone (or know someone) who enjoys a more involved study and understanding, loves history, details, and trivia—then this is also for you. If you are clergy, both are definitely for you. Do you prefer Yosef, Miriam, and Yeshua, to Joseph, Mary, and Jesus—then you'd enjoy my "Mary" book.

Also by the author
The Drop: Secret Delivery

An unknown pursuer chases a woman who bears and protects a cold, darkened heart. Frustrated, she is cornered by something foreign, yet good. The prey? Dr. Lissa Ryons, forensic scientist at the heart of the busy United Nations Headquarters.

Discovered in the Lost and Found, is a formal cloth table napkin. On both sides are intricate writings of an unknown language and perplexing diagrams. Forensics receives the unusual napkin for analysis. Dr. Ryons' senses and sensibilities are set off-kilter and mystified.

One night when she's alone, the cloth comes alive in captivating supernatural ways. When she touches it, she's filled with power and wonderful feelings. The napkin becomes an obsession of hers which also warms her personality. But how could it possibly be an artifact dated to the creation of the Universe? And could its markings prove to be about the origins of the Universe?

Through unusual circumstances this emotionally shutdown woman enters unknown territory where she is valued and finds meaning. Distracted out of her daily routine she maneuvers to search out answers. Veering from her private-self, Lissa questions: My life isn't right, but it isn't wrong—is it?

For the first time she wants to join the human race and live not a normal life, no, a better than normal life. Years of shame and guilt are disassembled by a being from another dimension. Follow the moving experiences which cause her to leave an outdated wooden personality for a real and desirable one. Lissa's pursuer is closer than she thinks. Due to the specimen's uncommon properties her private life is over and made available to the world.

www.ingramcontent.com/pod-product-compliance
Lightning Source LLC
Chambersburg PA
CBHW071837020726
47502CB00004B/1394